BugHouse

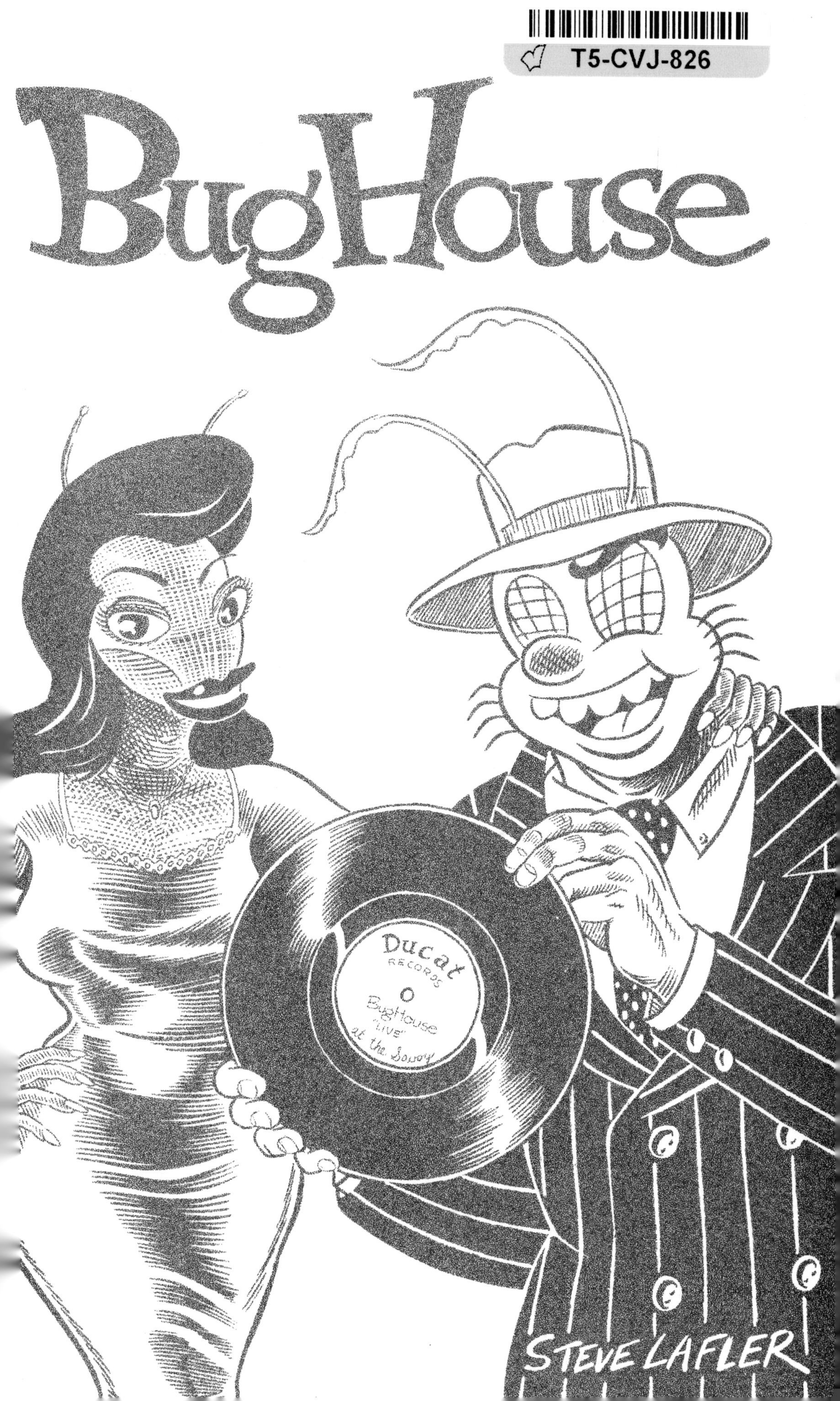
Ducat
RECORDS
BugHouse
"LIVE"
at the Savoy

STEVE LAFLER

BugHouse

ISBN 1-889059-00-5

published by:

Cat-Head Comics

P.O. Box 576
Hudson, MA 01749

Steve Lafler & Stephen Beaupre, publishers
http://world.std.com/~cathead
e mail: cathead@world.std.com

Special thanks to Regent Press. For the purposes of the ISBN number, Cat-Head will be listed as an imprint of Regent Press, 6020-A Adeline St., Oakland CA 94608.

Acknowledgements

Them's what helped me out:

Lloyd Dangle and Hae Yuon Kim for color magic on their cool rig in snappin' downtown Oakland. Mary Fleener for the old plugola, check out her alarming pictographs; Jim Valentino and Dave Sim, the same. I guess that includes young Pat Moriarity too. Thanks to my peers—J.R. Williams, Krystine Kryttre, R.L. Crabb, Dori Seda (Where's the book, Ron?), Roy Tompkins, Wayno, Mario Hernandez, Steve Willis. A tip-o'-the old implement to all the studs & studettes over at Fantagraphics. Donuts & Burgers to Michael Dowers, Maximum Traffic, Mark Weiman, Port Publications. Brendan Smith, noble distribution experiments. Guy Named Tim, cool assignments. Marc Weidenbaum at *Pulse!* All the Musicians. Michael Tower. Dave Cherry. Don Donahue. Bruce & Flower. Fellini, Kate Kane! Denny Eichhorn. Clay Geerdes. Rebecka Wright. Andy Mackler. Zappa. Large appreciation for all the help from Ron Turner & Erick Gilbert over at Gasp, John Davis & Capital City, and Diamond Comics. Terence McKenna and his little plant friends. John F. Lafler. Also Shirley, Don, Nancy, Mary, Judy and her new Doot. Kirby, Crumb, Jimi, Eisner, Kurtzman, Ditko. Caniff for his brushwork (I'll pass on the imperialism.) Rory Root. The retailers who order *BugHouse*. The *Massachusetts Daily Collegian.* Jerry. Nick Nickolds, John Roy. "T" and He-lay. The *Filth* gang. Angela Bocage. All the young artists. Lux & Ivy. Tee-um. Serena Makofsky, comrade in my arms, of course. Michael Perkin and Stephen Beaupre for their amazing feats of strength, good humor and endurance! Love's expression. *Buzzard* comics anthology. The anise and rosemary plants I grab and sniff when I'm out for a run in Oaktown. *The dream, the other.*

for Serena

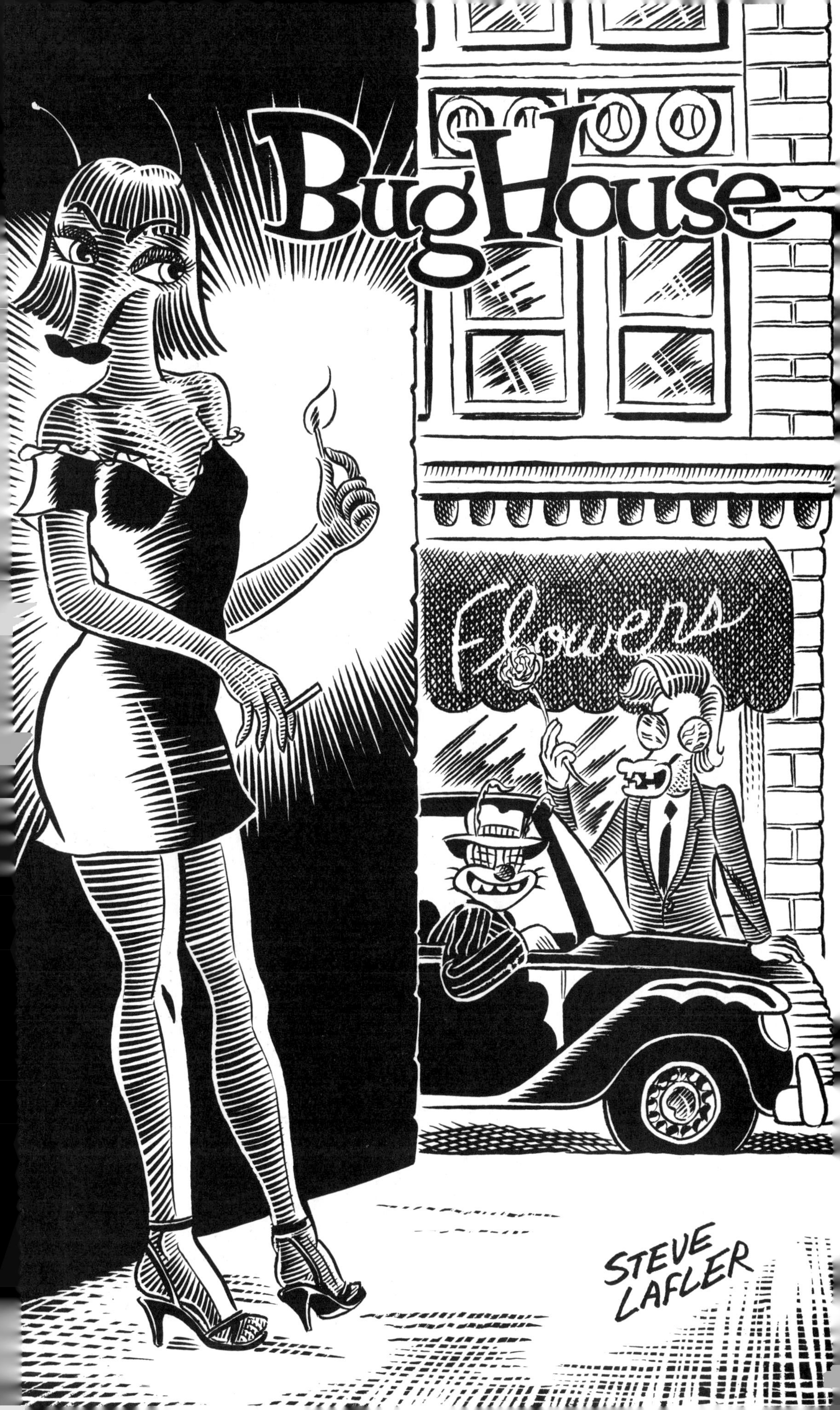

BugHouse
Flowers
STEVE LAFLER

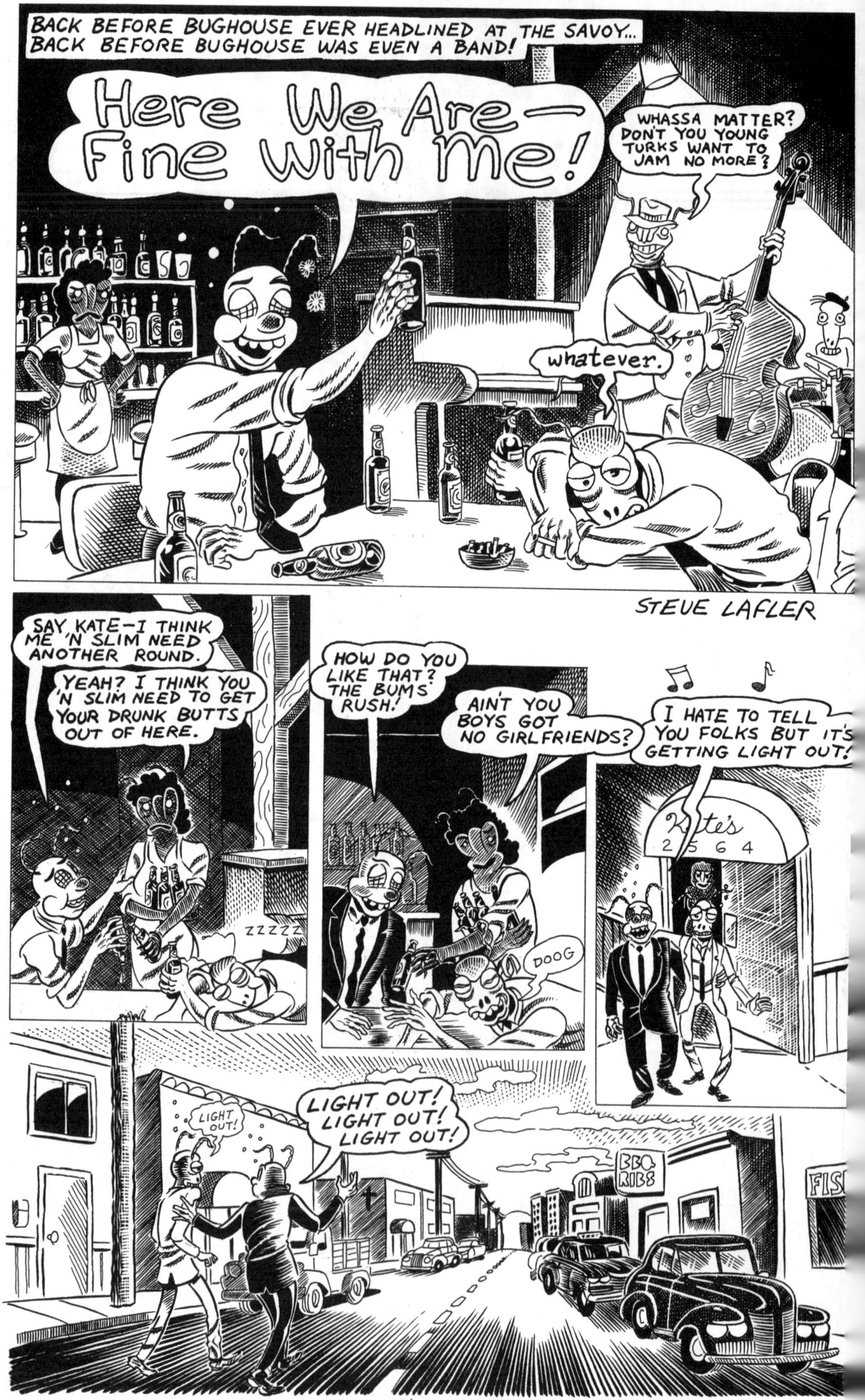
BACK BEFORE BUGHOUSE EVER HEADLINED AT THE SAVOY...
BACK BEFORE BUGHOUSE WAS EVEN A BAND!
Here We Are— Fine With Me!
WHASSA MATTER? DON'T YOU YOUNG TURKS WANT TO JAM NO MORE?
whatever.
STEVE LAFLER
SAY KATE—I THINK ME 'N SLIM NEED ANOTHER ROUND.
YEAH? I THINK YOU 'N SLIM NEED TO GET YOUR DRUNK BUTTS OUT OF HERE.
ZZZZZ
HOW DO YOU LIKE THAT? THE BUMS' RUSH!
AIN'T YOU BOYS GOT NO GIRLFRIENDS?
DOOG
I HATE TO TELL YOU FOLKS BUT IT'S GETTING LIGHT OUT!
Kate's
2564
LIGHT OUT!
LIGHT OUT! LIGHT OUT! LIGHT OUT!
BBQ RIBS
FIS

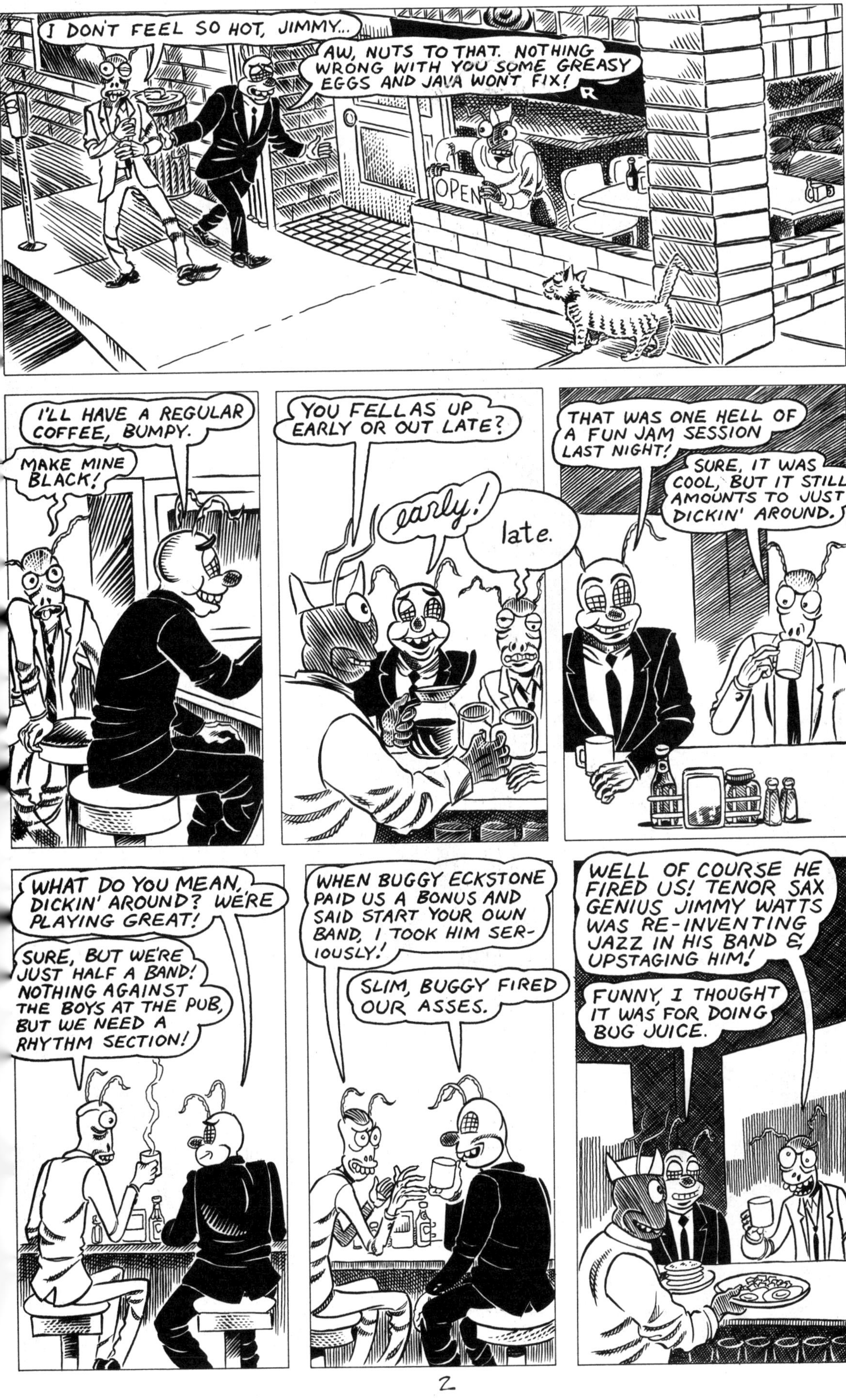

I DON'T FEEL SO HOT, JIMMY...
AW, NUTS TO THAT. NOTHING WRONG WITH YOU SOME GREASY EGGS AND JAVA WON'T FIX!
OPEN
I'LL HAVE A REGULAR COFFEE, BUMPY.
MAKE MINE BLACK!
YOU FELLAS UP EARLY OR OUT LATE?
early!
late.
THAT WAS ONE HELL OF A FUN JAM SESSION LAST NIGHT!
SURE, IT WAS COOL, BUT IT STILL AMOUNTS TO JUST DICKIN' AROUND.
WHAT DO YOU MEAN, DICKIN' AROUND? WE'RE PLAYING GREAT!
SURE, BUT WE'RE JUST HALF A BAND! NOTHING AGAINST THE BOYS AT THE PUB, BUT WE NEED A RHYTHM SECTION!
WHEN BUGGY ECKSTONE PAID US A BONUS AND SAID START YOUR OWN BAND, I TOOK HIM SERIOUSLY!
SLIM, BUGGY FIRED OUR ASSES.
WELL OF COURSE HE FIRED US! TENOR SAX GENIUS JIMMY WATTS WAS RE-INVENTING JAZZ IN HIS BAND & UPSTAGING HIM!
FUNNY, I THOUGHT IT WAS FOR DOING BUG JUICE.

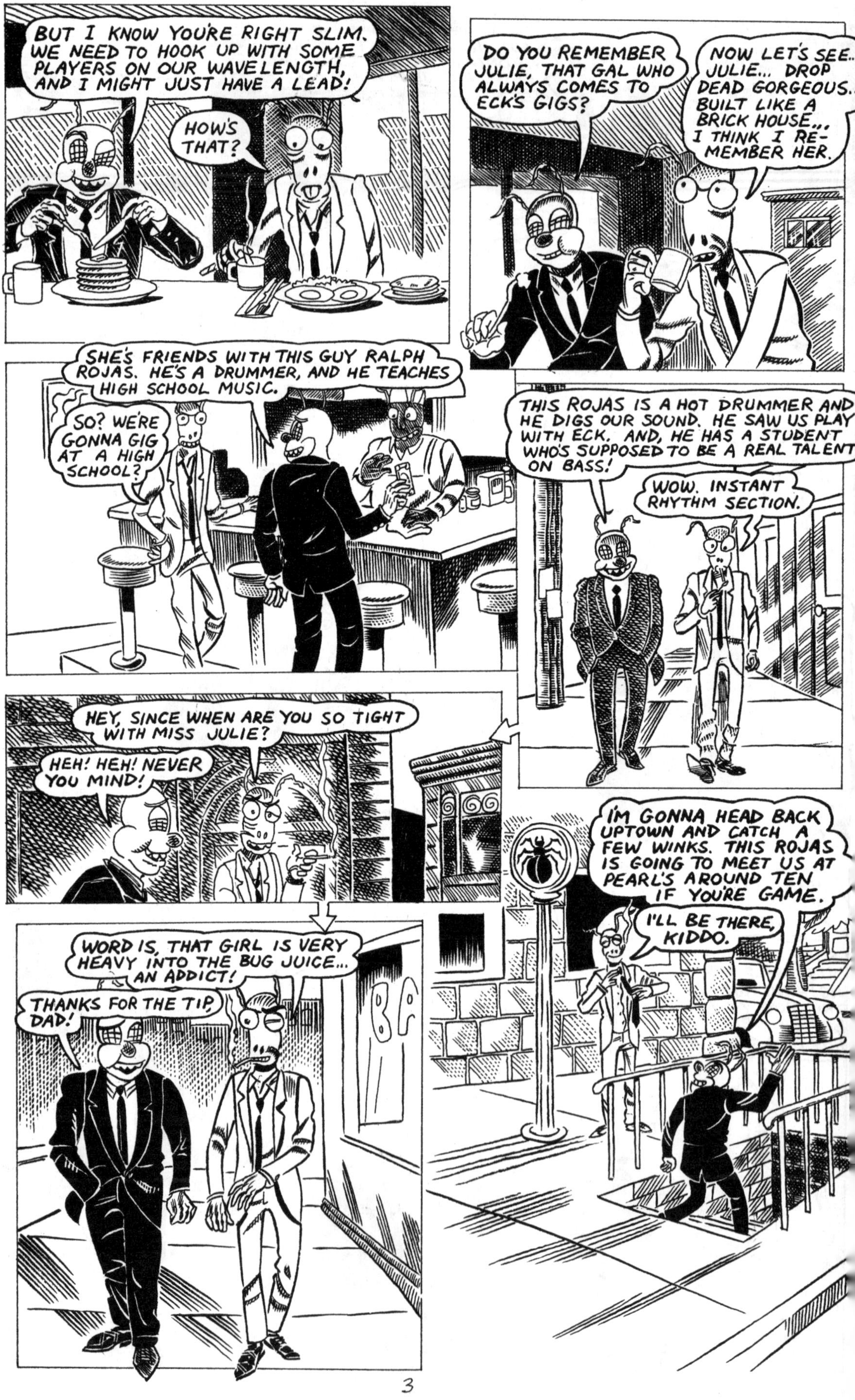
BUT I KNOW YOU'RE RIGHT SLIM. WE NEED TO HOOK UP WITH SOME PLAYERS ON OUR WAVELENGTH, AND I MIGHT JUST HAVE A LEAD!
HOW'S THAT?
DO YOU REMEMBER JULIE, THAT GAL WHO ALWAYS COMES TO ECK'S GIGS?
NOW LET'S SEE... JULIE... DROP DEAD GORGEOUS... BUILT LIKE A BRICK HOUSE... I THINK I REMEMBER HER.
SHE'S FRIENDS WITH THIS GUY RALPH ROJAS. HE'S A DRUMMER, AND HE TEACHES HIGH SCHOOL MUSIC.
SO? WE'RE GONNA GIG AT A HIGH SCHOOL?
THIS ROJAS IS A HOT DRUMMER AND HE DIGS OUR SOUND. HE SAW US PLAY WITH ECK. AND, HE HAS A STUDENT WHO'S SUPPOSED TO BE A REAL TALENT ON BASS!
WOW. INSTANT RHYTHM SECTION.
HEY, SINCE WHEN ARE YOU SO TIGHT WITH MISS JULIE?
HEH! HEH! NEVER YOU MIND!
WORD IS, THAT GIRL IS VERY HEAVY INTO THE BUG JUICE... AN ADDICT!
THANKS FOR THE TIP, DAD!
I'M GONNA HEAD BACK UPTOWN AND CATCH A FEW WINKS. THIS ROJAS IS GOING TO MEET US AT PEARL'S AROUND TEN IF YOU'RE GAME.
I'LL BE THERE, KIDDO.

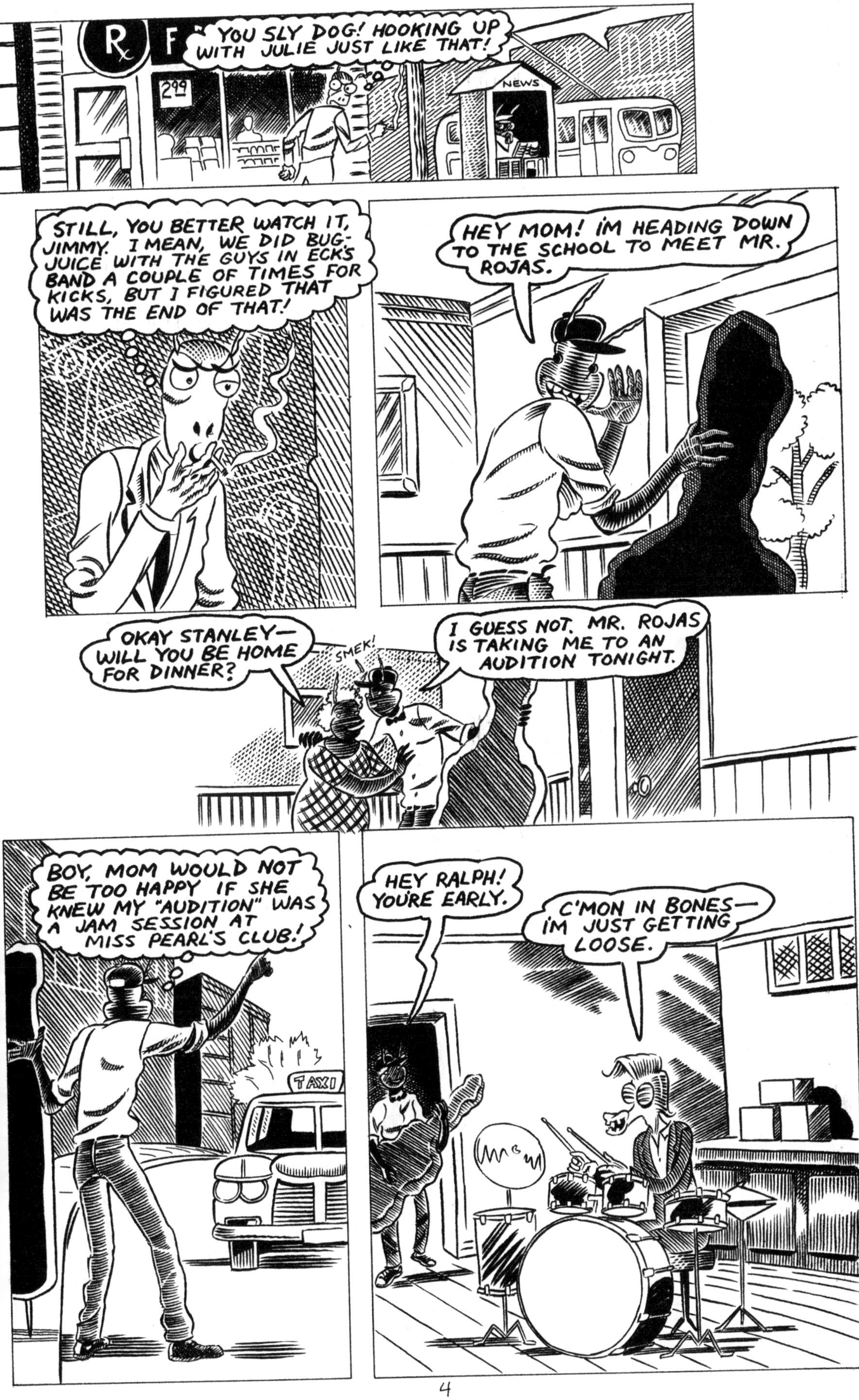
YOU SLY DOG! HOOKING UP WITH JULIE JUST LIKE THAT!
NEWS
STILL, YOU BETTER WATCH IT, JIMMY. I MEAN, WE DID BUG-JUICE WITH THE GUYS IN ECK'S BAND A COUPLE OF TIMES FOR KICKS, BUT I FIGURED THAT WAS THE END OF THAT!
HEY MOM! I'M HEADING DOWN TO THE SCHOOL TO MEET MR. ROJAS.
OKAY STANLEY— WILL YOU BE HOME FOR DINNER?
SMEK!
I GUESS NOT. MR. ROJAS IS TAKING ME TO AN AUDITION TONIGHT.
BOY, MOM WOULD NOT BE TOO HAPPY IF SHE KNEW MY "AUDITION" WAS A JAM SESSION AT MISS PEARL'S CLUB!
TAXI
HEY RALPH! YOU'RE EARLY.
C'MON IN BONES— I'M JUST GETTING LOOSE.

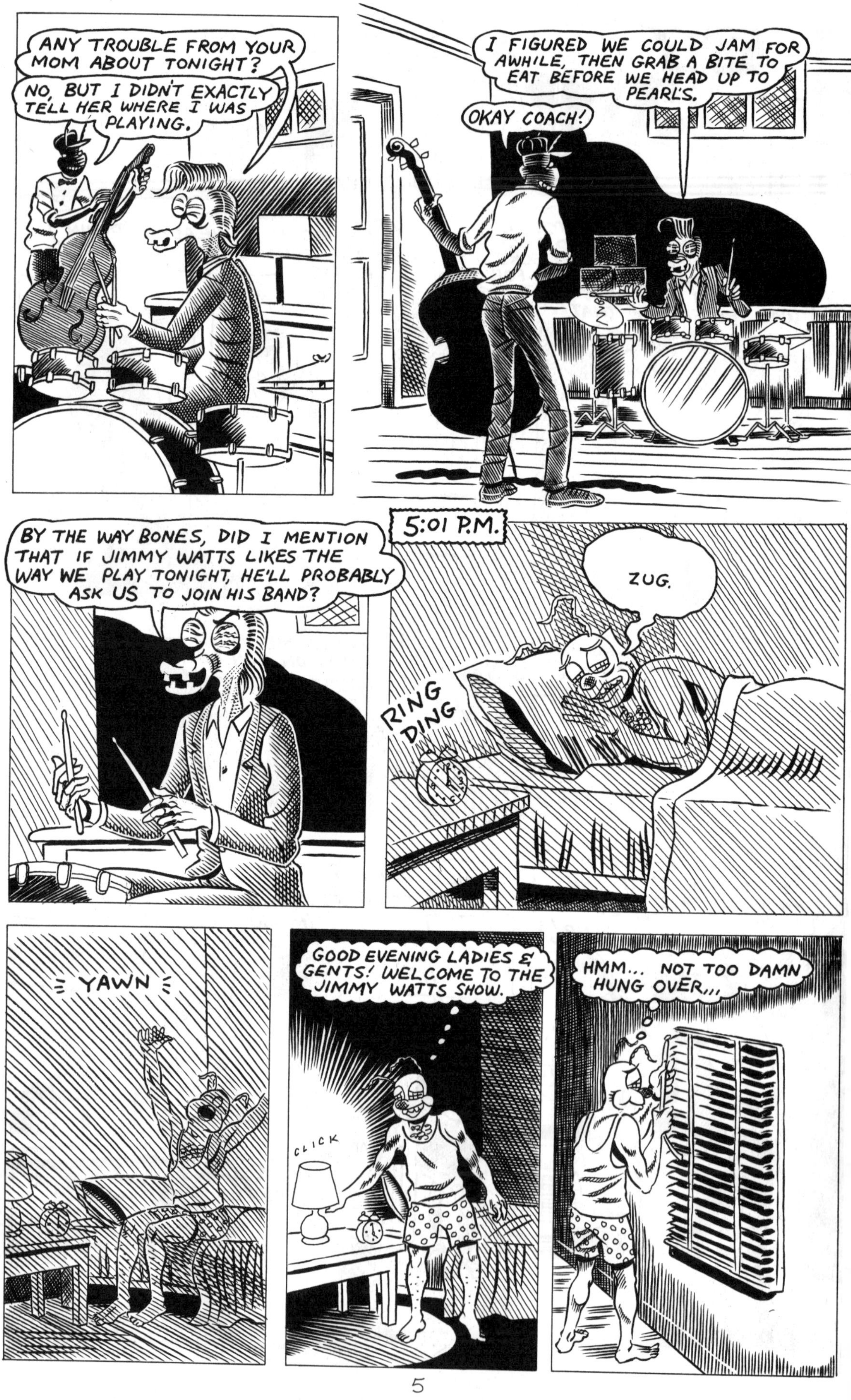
ANY TROUBLE FROM YOUR MOM ABOUT TONIGHT?
NO, BUT I DIDN'T EXACTLY TELL HER WHERE I WAS PLAYING.
I FIGURED WE COULD JAM FOR AWHILE, THEN GRAB A BITE TO EAT BEFORE WE HEAD UP TO PEARL'S.
OKAY COACH!
BY THE WAY BONES, DID I MENTION THAT IF JIMMY WATTS LIKES THE WAY WE PLAY TONIGHT, HE'LL PROBABLY ASK US TO JOIN HIS BAND?
5:01 P.M.
ZUG.
RING DING
YAWN
GOOD EVENING LADIES & GENTS! WELCOME TO THE JIMMY WATTS SHOW.
CLICK
HMM... NOT TOO DAMN HUNG OVER...

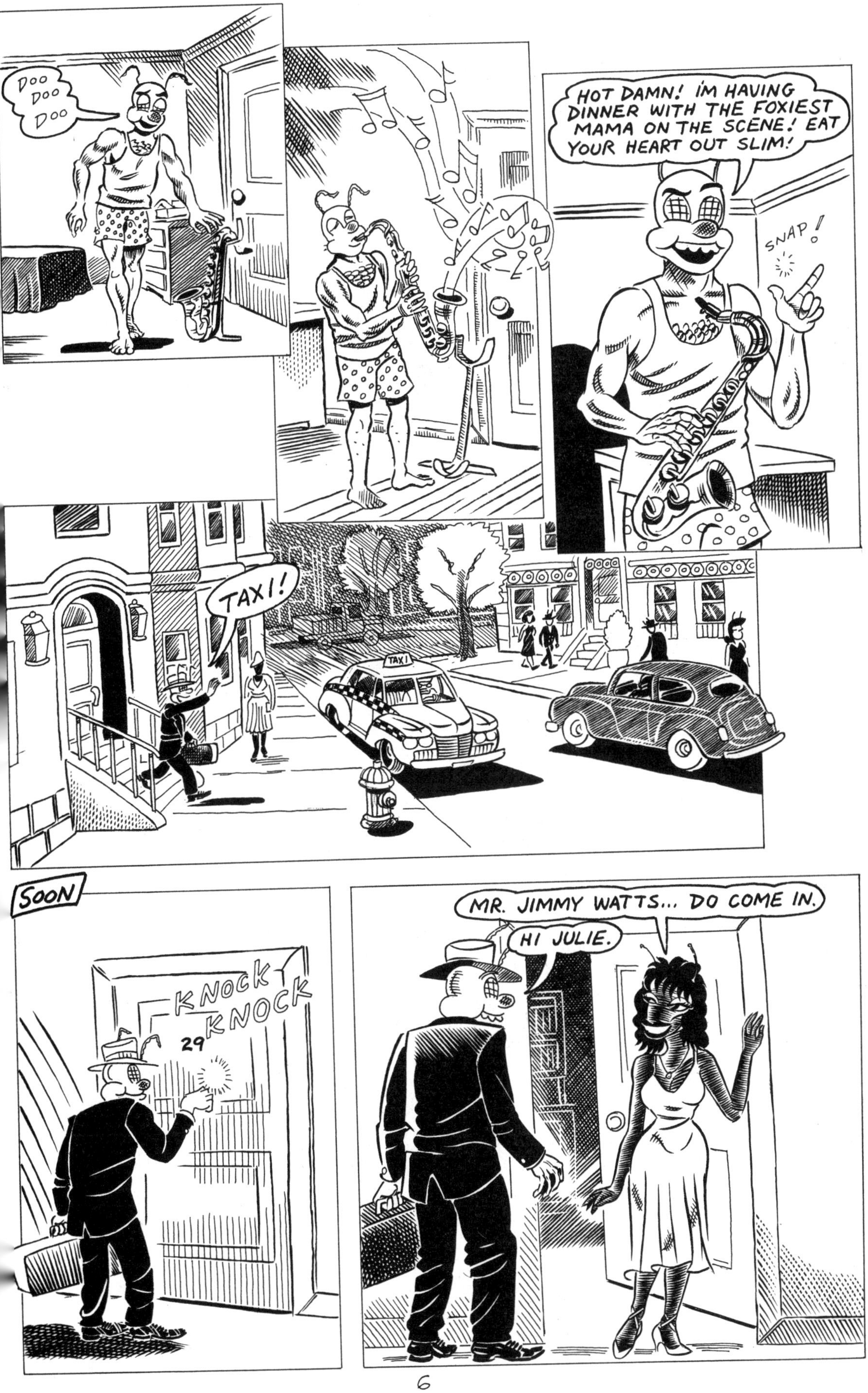
DOO DOO DOO
HOT DAMN! I'M HAVING DINNER WITH THE FOXIEST MAMA ON THE SCENE! EAT YOUR HEART OUT SLIM!
SNAP!
TAXI!
TAXI
SOON
KNOCK KNOCK
29
MR. JIMMY WATTS... DO COME IN.
HI JULIE.

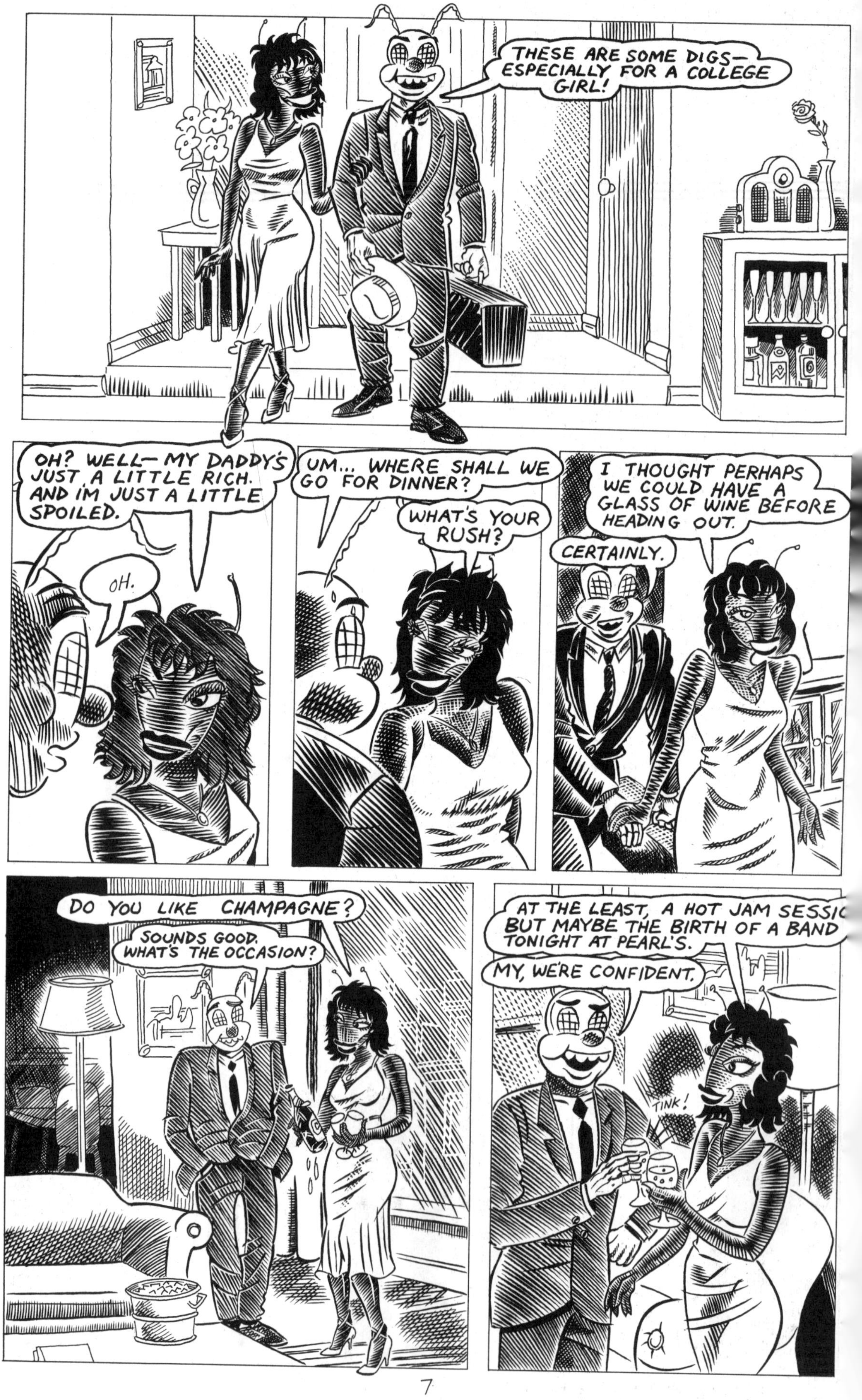

THESE ARE SOME DIGS— ESPECIALLY FOR A COLLEGE GIRL!
OH? WELL— MY DADDY'S JUST A LITTLE RICH. AND I'M JUST A LITTLE SPOILED.
OH.
UM... WHERE SHALL WE GO FOR DINNER?
WHAT'S YOUR RUSH?
I THOUGHT PERHAPS WE COULD HAVE A GLASS OF WINE BEFORE HEADING OUT.
CERTAINLY.
DO YOU LIKE CHAMPAGNE?
SOUNDS GOOD. WHAT'S THE OCCASION?
AT THE LEAST, A HOT JAM SESSIC
BUT MAYBE THE BIRTH OF A BAND
TONIGHT AT PEARL'S.
MY, WE'RE CONFIDENT.
TINK!

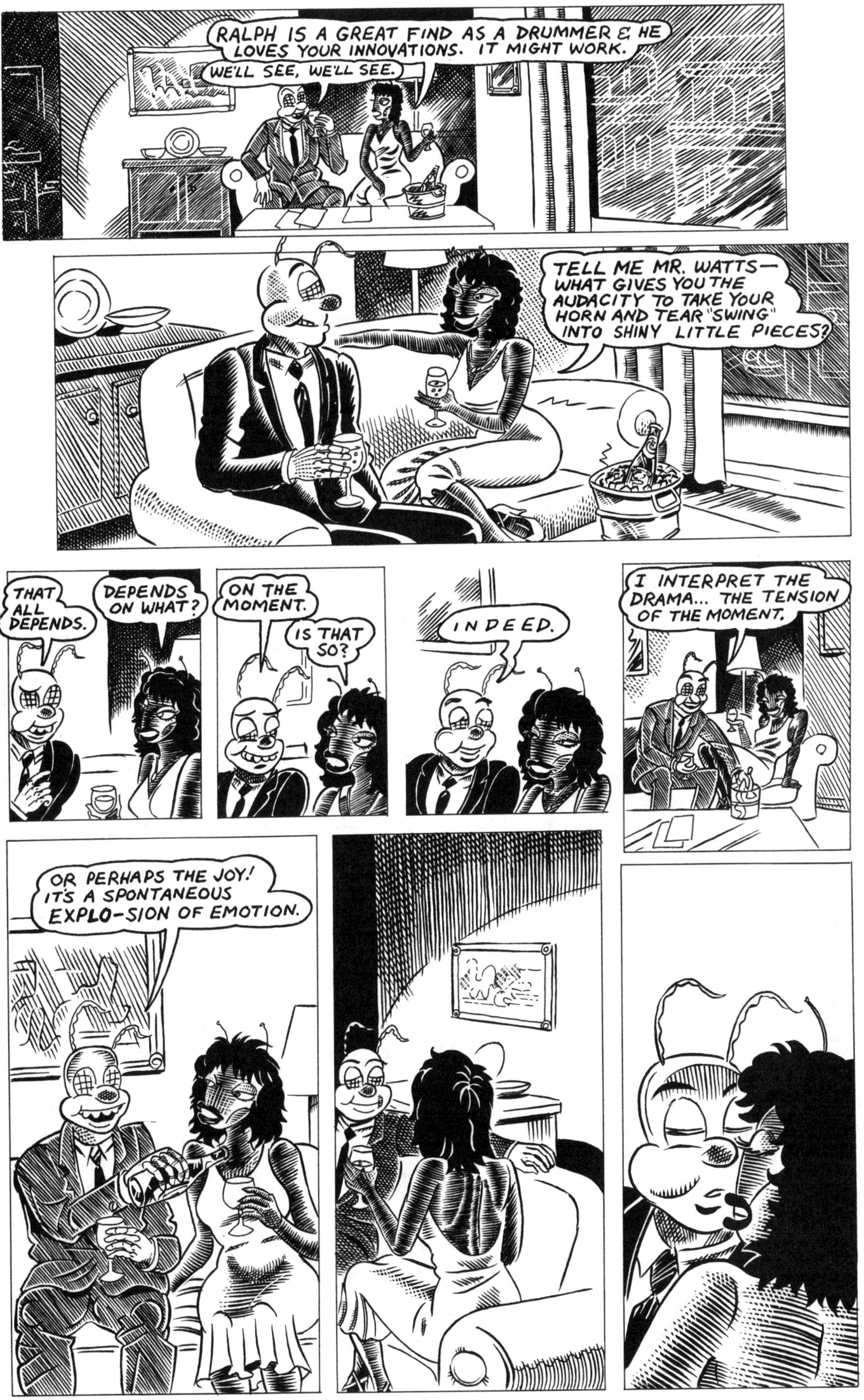
RALPH IS A GREAT FIND AS A DRUMMER & HE LOVES YOUR INNOVATIONS. IT MIGHT WORK.
WE'LL SEE, WE'LL SEE.
TELL ME MR. WATTS— WHAT GIVES YOU THE AUDACITY TO TAKE YOUR HORN AND TEAR "SWING" INTO SHINY LITTLE PIECES?
THAT ALL DEPENDS.
DEPENDS ON WHAT?
ON THE MOMENT.
IS THAT SO?
INDEED.
I INTERPRET THE DRAMA... THE TENSION OF THE MOMENT.
OR PERHAPS THE JOY! IT'S A SPONTANEOUS EXPLO-SION OF EMOTION.

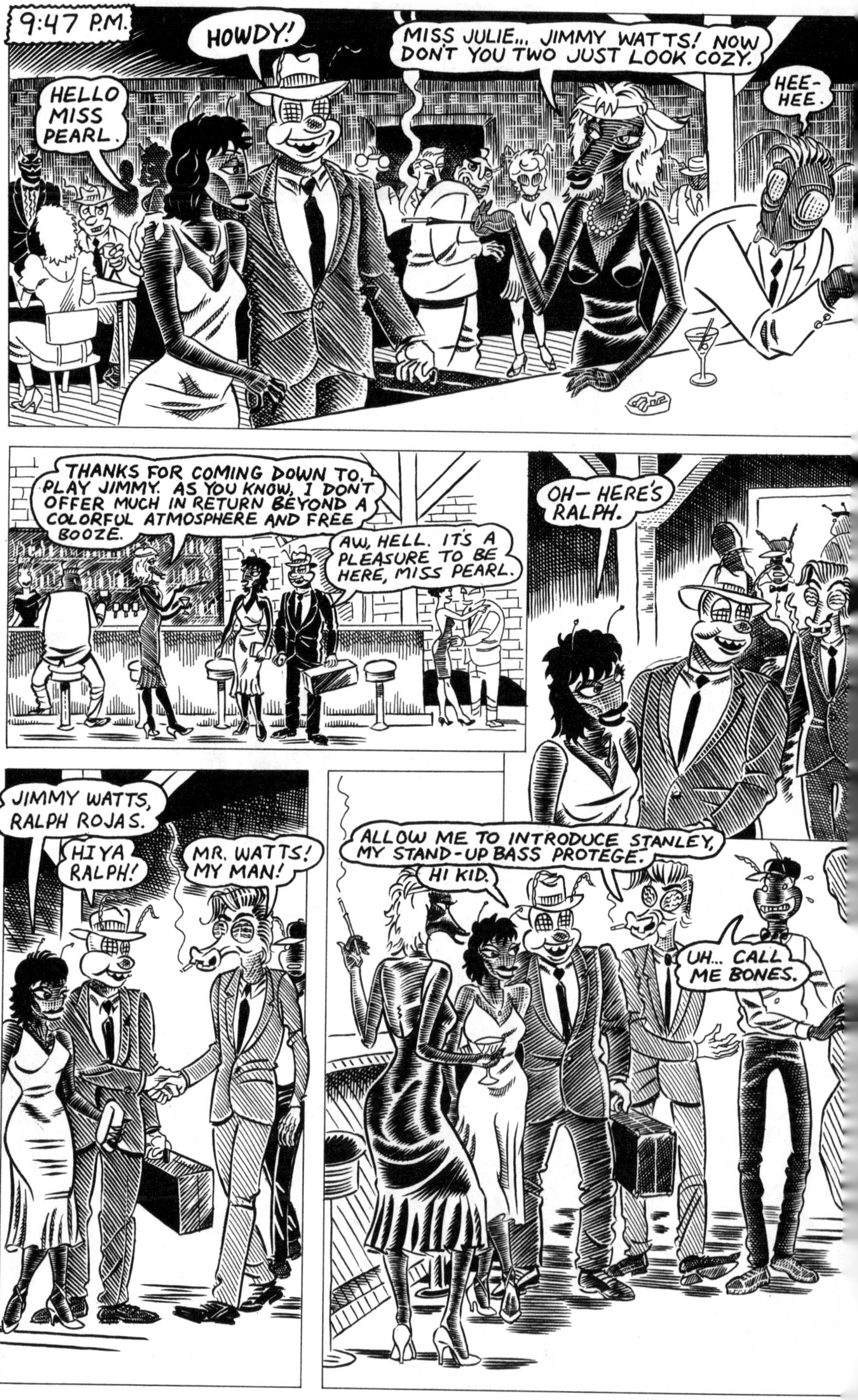

9:47 P.M.
HELLO MISS PEARL.
HOWDY!
MISS JULIE... JIMMY WATTS! NOW DON'T YOU TWO JUST LOOK COZY.
HEE-HEE.
THANKS FOR COMING DOWN TO PLAY JIMMY. AS YOU KNOW, I DON'T OFFER MUCH IN RETURN BEYOND A COLORFUL ATMOSPHERE AND FREE BOOZE.
AW, HELL. IT'S A PLEASURE TO BE HERE, MISS PEARL.
OH- HERE'S RALPH.
JIMMY WATTS, RALPH ROJAS.
HIYA RALPH!
MR. WATTS! MY MAN!
ALLOW ME TO INTRODUCE STANLEY, MY STAND-UP BASS PROTEGE.
HI KID.
UH... CALL ME BONES.

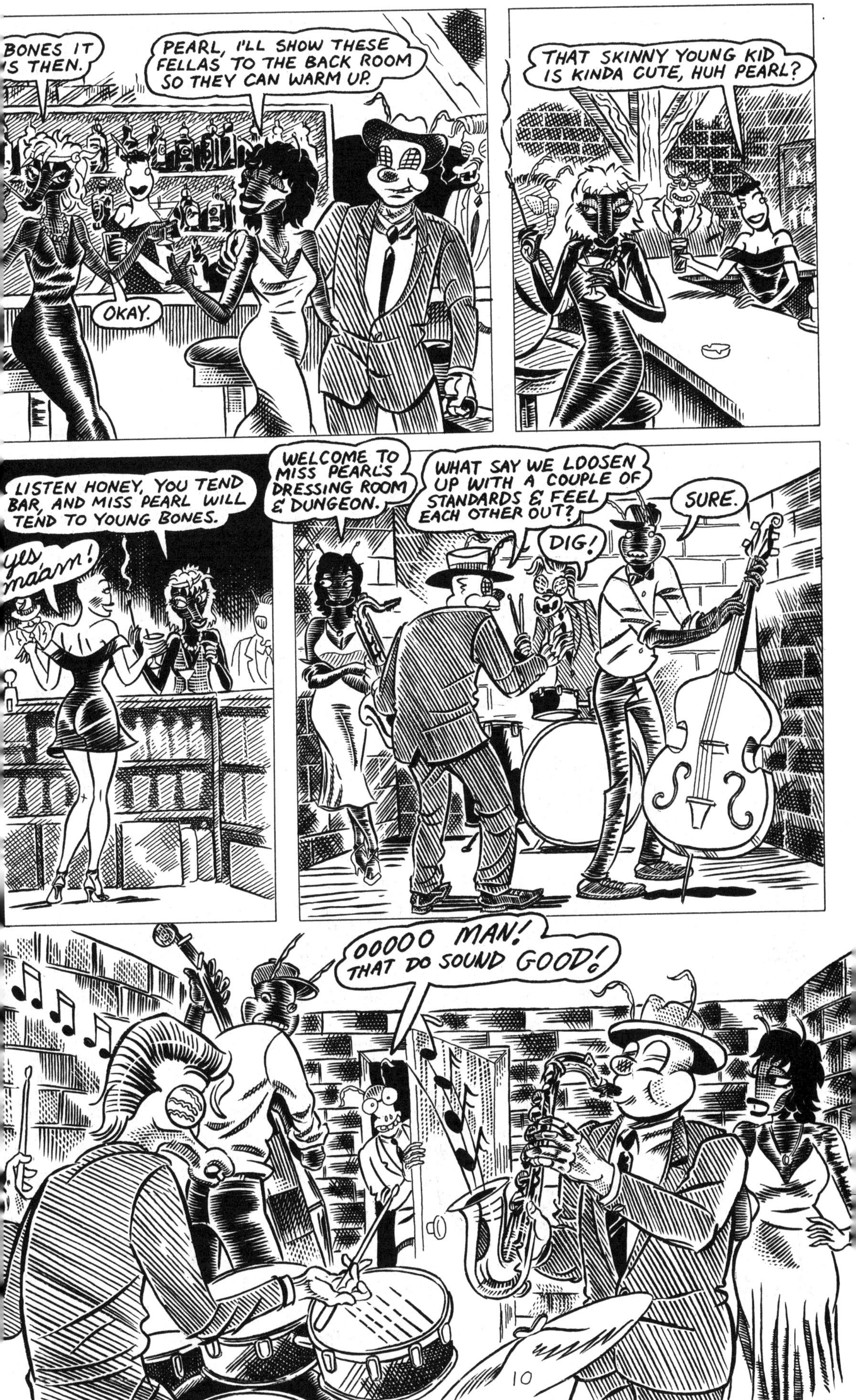

BONES IT 'S THEN.
PEARL, I'LL SHOW THESE FELLAS TO THE BACK ROOM SO THEY CAN WARM UP.
OKAY.
THAT SKINNY YOUNG KID IS KINDA CUTE, HUH PEARL?
LISTEN HONEY, YOU TEND BAR, AND MISS PEARL WILL TEND TO YOUNG BONES.
yes ma'am!
WELCOME TO MISS PEARL'S DRESSING ROOM & DUNGEON.
WHAT SAY WE LOOSEN UP WITH A COUPLE OF STANDARDS & FEEL EACH OTHER OUT?
DIG!
SURE.
OOOOO MAN! THAT DO SOUND GOOD!

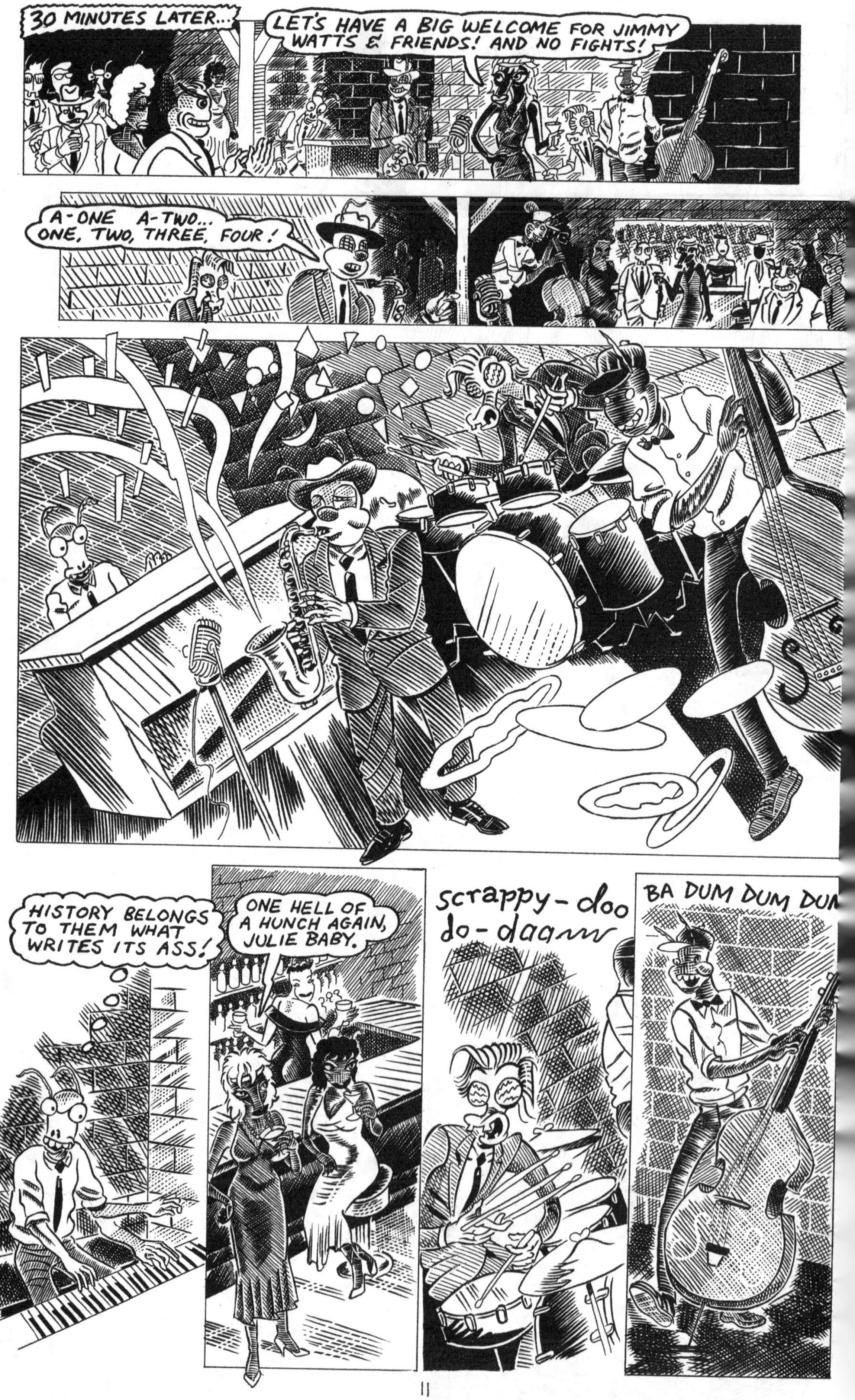
30 MINUTES LATER...
LET'S HAVE A BIG WELCOME FOR JIMMY WATTS & FRIENDS! AND NO FIGHTS!
A-ONE A-TWO... ONE, TWO, THREE, FOUR!
HISTORY BELONGS TO THEM WHAT WRITES ITS ASS!
ONE HELL OF A HUNCH AGAIN, JULIE BABY.
scrappy-doo do-daaaw
BA DUM DUM DUM

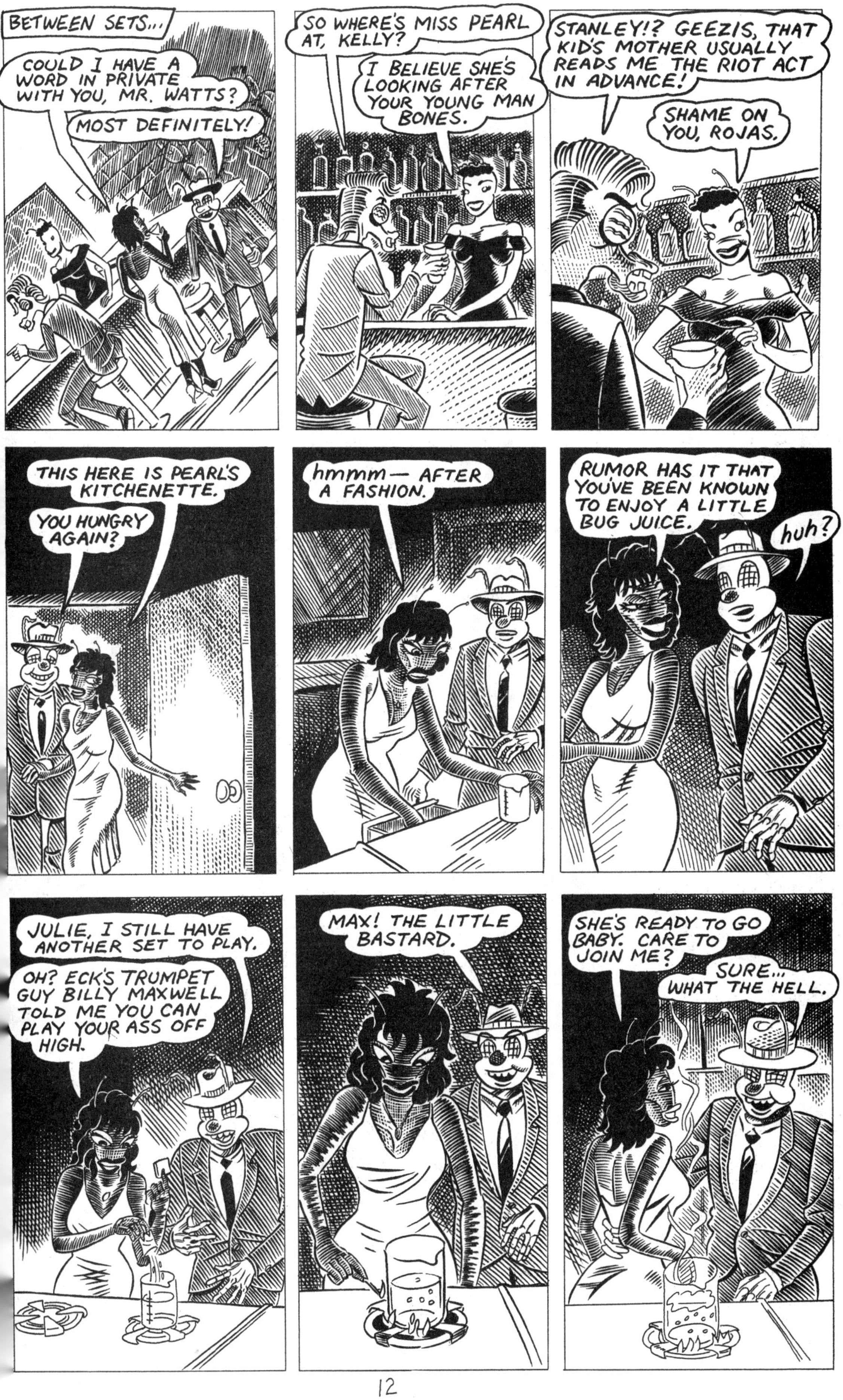
BETWEEN SETS...
COULD I HAVE A WORD IN PRIVATE WITH YOU, MR. WATTS?
MOST DEFINITELY!
SO WHERE'S MISS PEARL AT, KELLY?
I BELIEVE SHE'S LOOKING AFTER YOUR YOUNG MAN BONES.
STANLEY!? GEEZIS, THAT KID'S MOTHER USUALLY READS ME THE RIOT ACT IN ADVANCE!
SHAME ON YOU, ROJAS.
THIS HERE IS PEARL'S KITCHENETTE.
YOU HUNGRY AGAIN?
hmmm— AFTER A FASHION.
RUMOR HAS IT THAT YOU'VE BEEN KNOWN TO ENJOY A LITTLE BUG JUICE.
huh?
JULIE, I STILL HAVE ANOTHER SET TO PLAY.
OH? ECK'S TRUMPET GUY BILLY MAXWELL TOLD ME YOU CAN PLAY YOUR ASS OFF HIGH.
MAX! THE LITTLE BASTARD.
SHE'S READY TO GO BABY. CARE TO JOIN ME?
SURE... WHAT THE HELL.

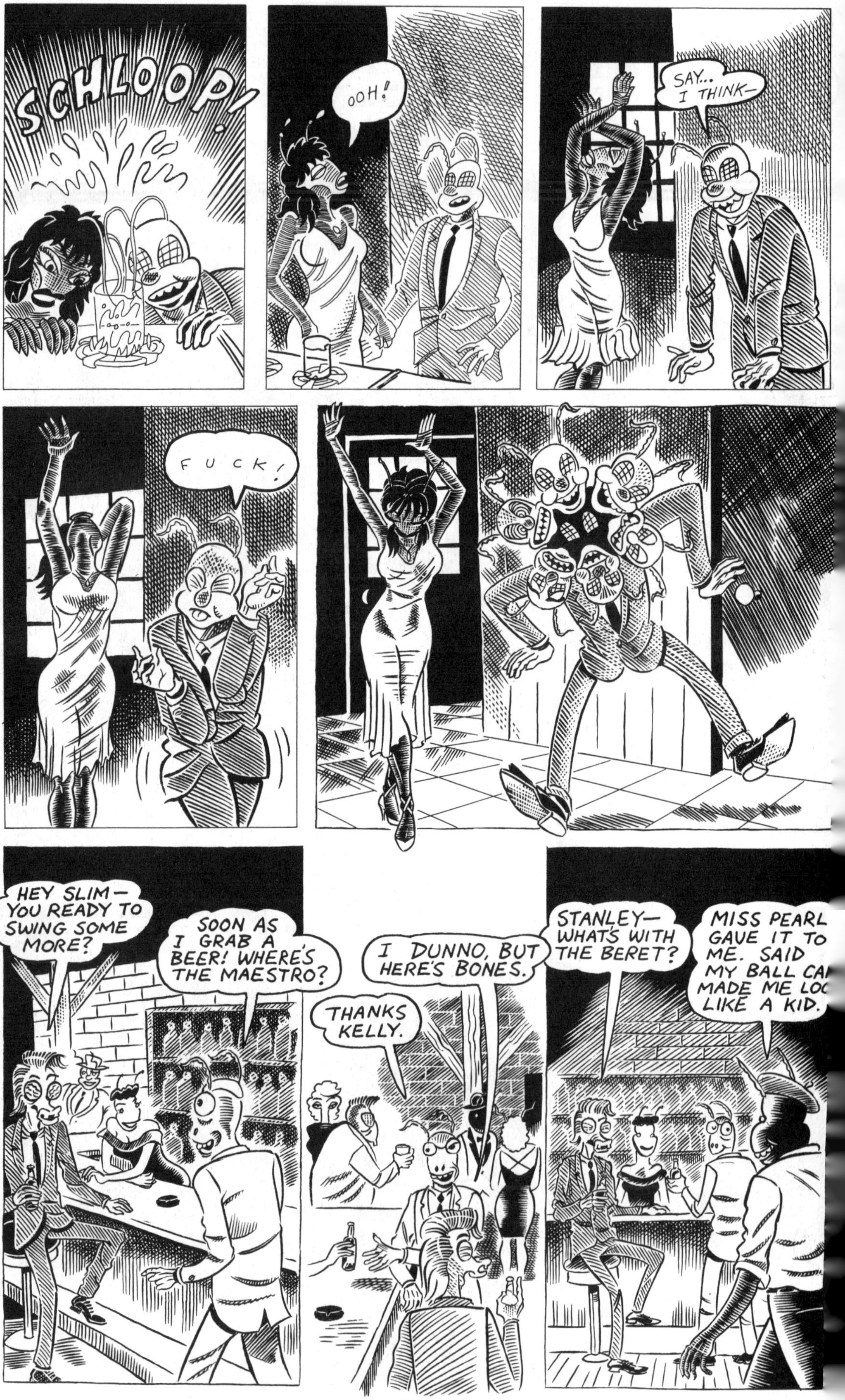

SCHLOOP!
OOH!
SAY... I THINK—
FUCK!
HEY SLIM— YOU READY TO SWING SOME MORE?
SOON AS I GRAB A BEER! WHERE'S THE MAESTRO?
I DUNNO, BUT HERE'S BONES.
THANKS KELLY.
STANLEY— WHAT'S WITH THE BERET?
MISS PEARL GAVE IT TO ME. SAID MY BALL CA MADE ME LOO LIKE A KID.

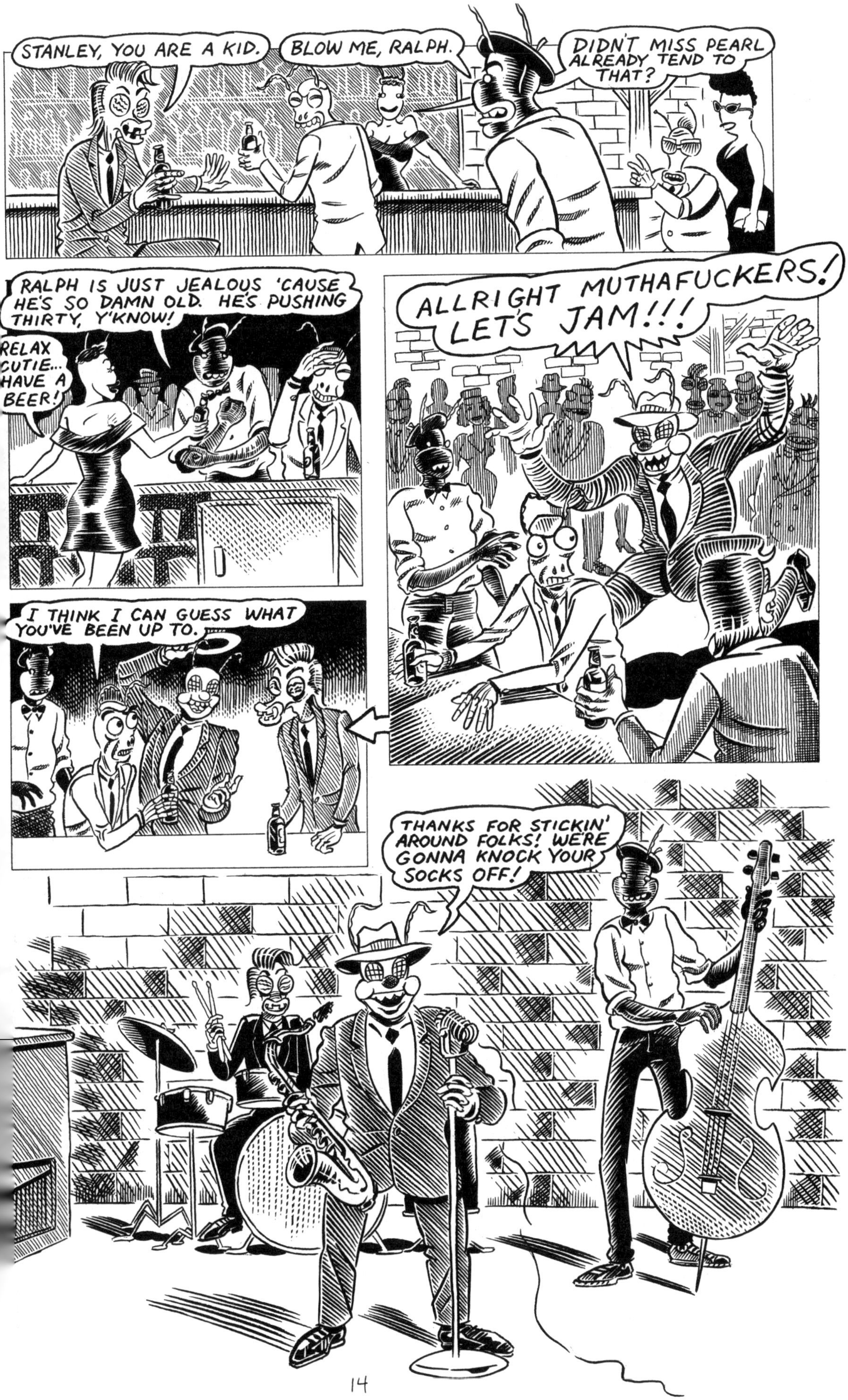
STANLEY, YOU ARE A KID.
BLOW ME, RALPH.
DIDN'T MISS PEARL ALREADY TEND TO THAT?
RALPH IS JUST JEALOUS 'CAUSE HE'S SO DAMN OLD. HE'S PUSHING THIRTY, Y'KNOW!
RELAX CUTIE... HAVE A BEER!
I THINK I CAN GUESS WHAT YOU'VE BEEN UP TO.
ALLRIGHT MUTHAFUCKERS! LET'S JAM!!!
THANKS FOR STICKIN' AROUND FOLKS! WE'RE GONNA KNOCK YOUR SOCKS OFF!

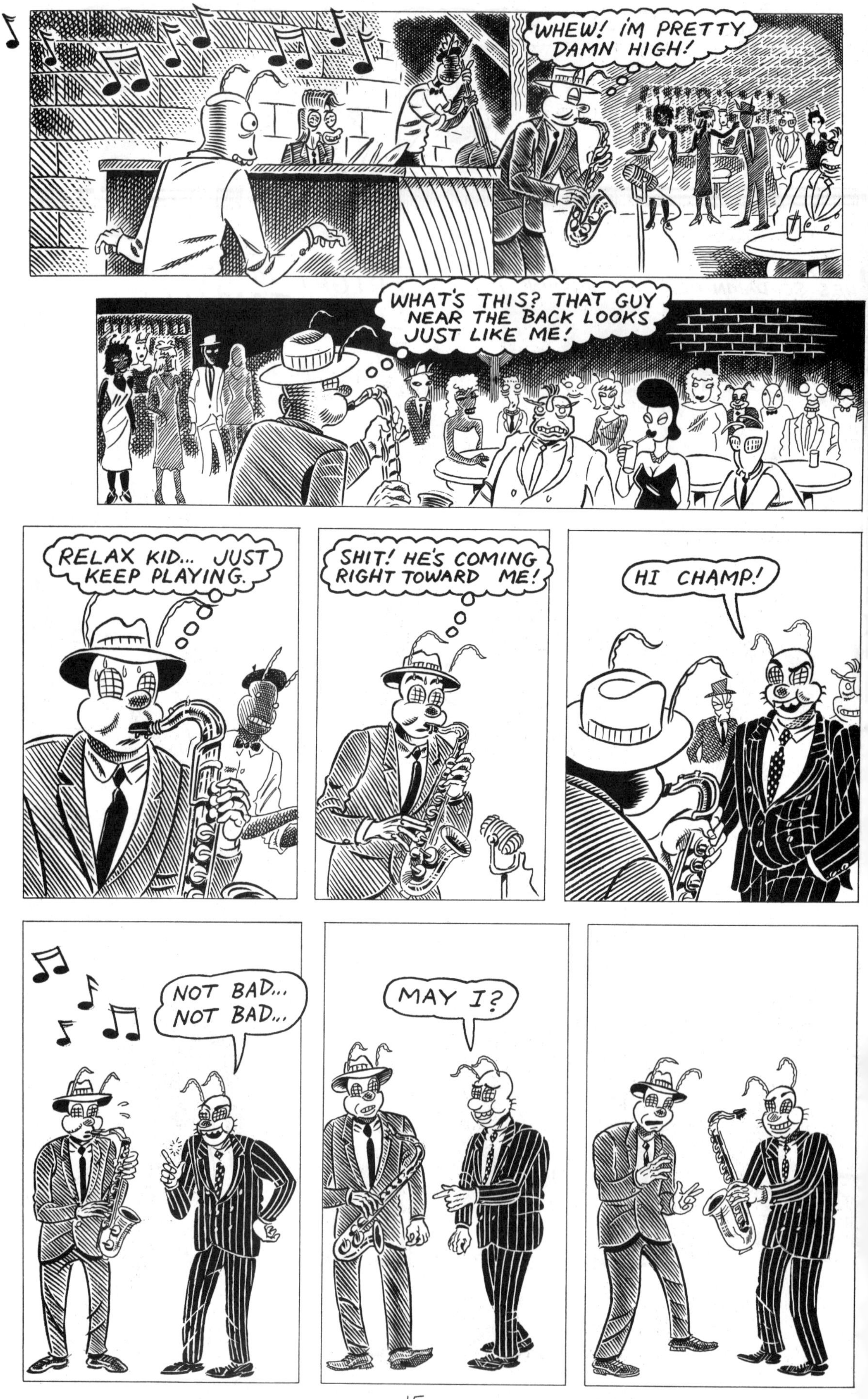
WHEW! I'M PRETTY DAMN HIGH!
WHAT'S THIS? THAT GUY NEAR THE BACK LOOKS JUST LIKE ME!
RELAX KID... JUST KEEP PLAYING.
SHIT! HE'S COMING RIGHT TOWARD ME!
HI CHAMP!
NOT BAD... NOT BAD...
MAY I?

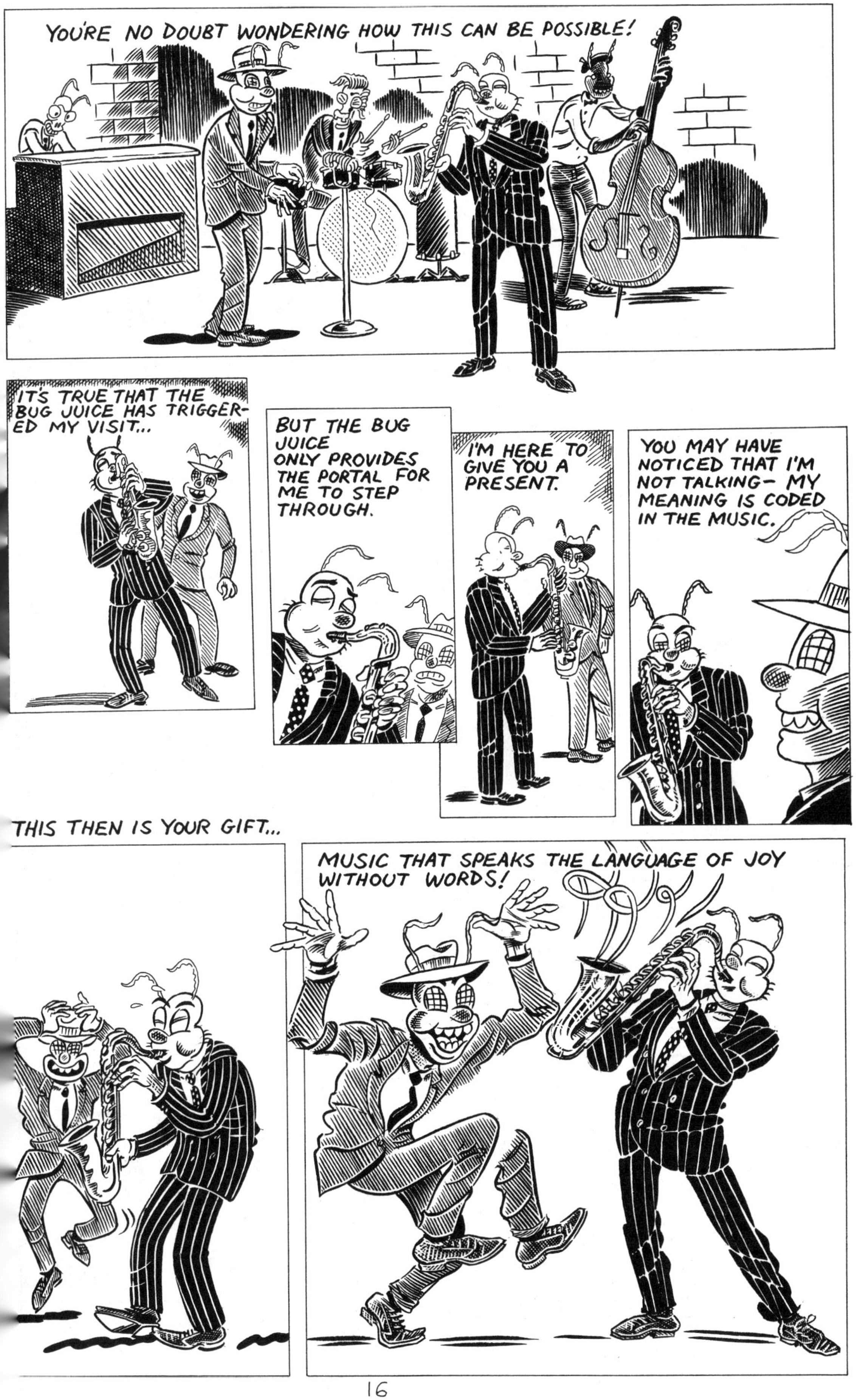
YOU'RE NO DOUBT WONDERING HOW THIS CAN BE POSSIBLE!
IT'S TRUE THAT THE BUG JUICE HAS TRIGGER-ED MY VISIT...
BUT THE BUG JUICE ONLY PROVIDES THE PORTAL FOR ME TO STEP THROUGH.
I'M HERE TO GIVE YOU A PRESENT.
YOU MAY HAVE NOTICED THAT I'M NOT TALKING– MY MEANING IS CODED IN THE MUSIC.
THIS THEN IS YOUR GIFT...
MUSIC THAT SPEAKS THE LANGUAGE OF JOY WITHOUT WORDS!

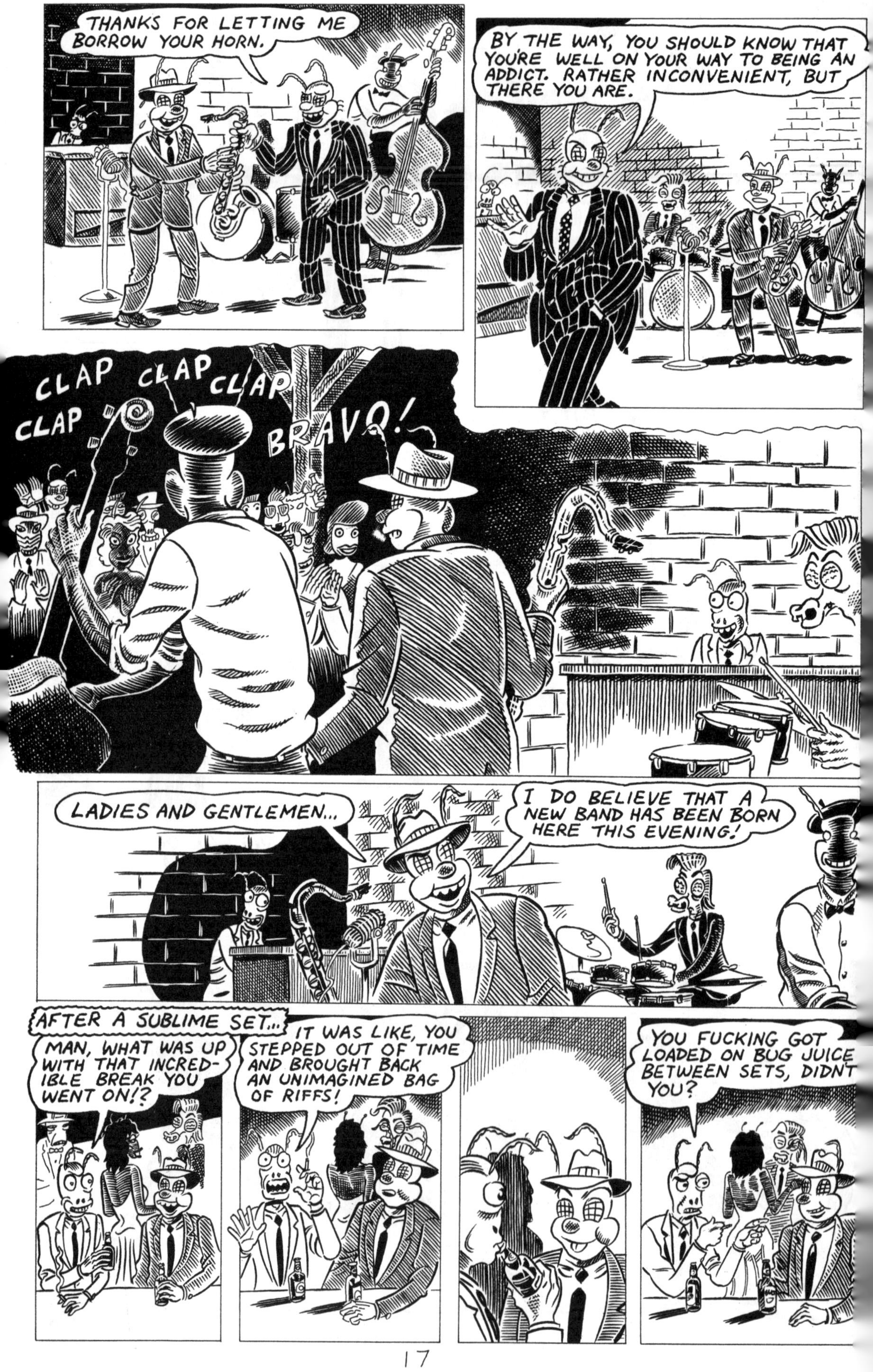
THANKS FOR LETTING ME BORROW YOUR HORN.
BY THE WAY, YOU SHOULD KNOW THAT YOU'RE WELL ON YOUR WAY TO BEING AN ADDICT. RATHER INCONVENIENT, BUT THERE YOU ARE.
CLAP CLAP CLAP CLAP
BRAVO!
LADIES AND GENTLEMEN...
I DO BELIEVE THAT A NEW BAND HAS BEEN BORN HERE THIS EVENING!
AFTER A SUBLIME SET...
MAN, WHAT WAS UP WITH THAT INCREDIBLE BREAK YOU WENT ON!?
IT WAS LIKE, YOU STEPPED OUT OF TIME AND BROUGHT BACK AN UNIMAGINED BAG OF RIFFS!
YOU FUCKING GOT LOADED ON BUG JUICE BETWEEN SETS, DIDN'T YOU?

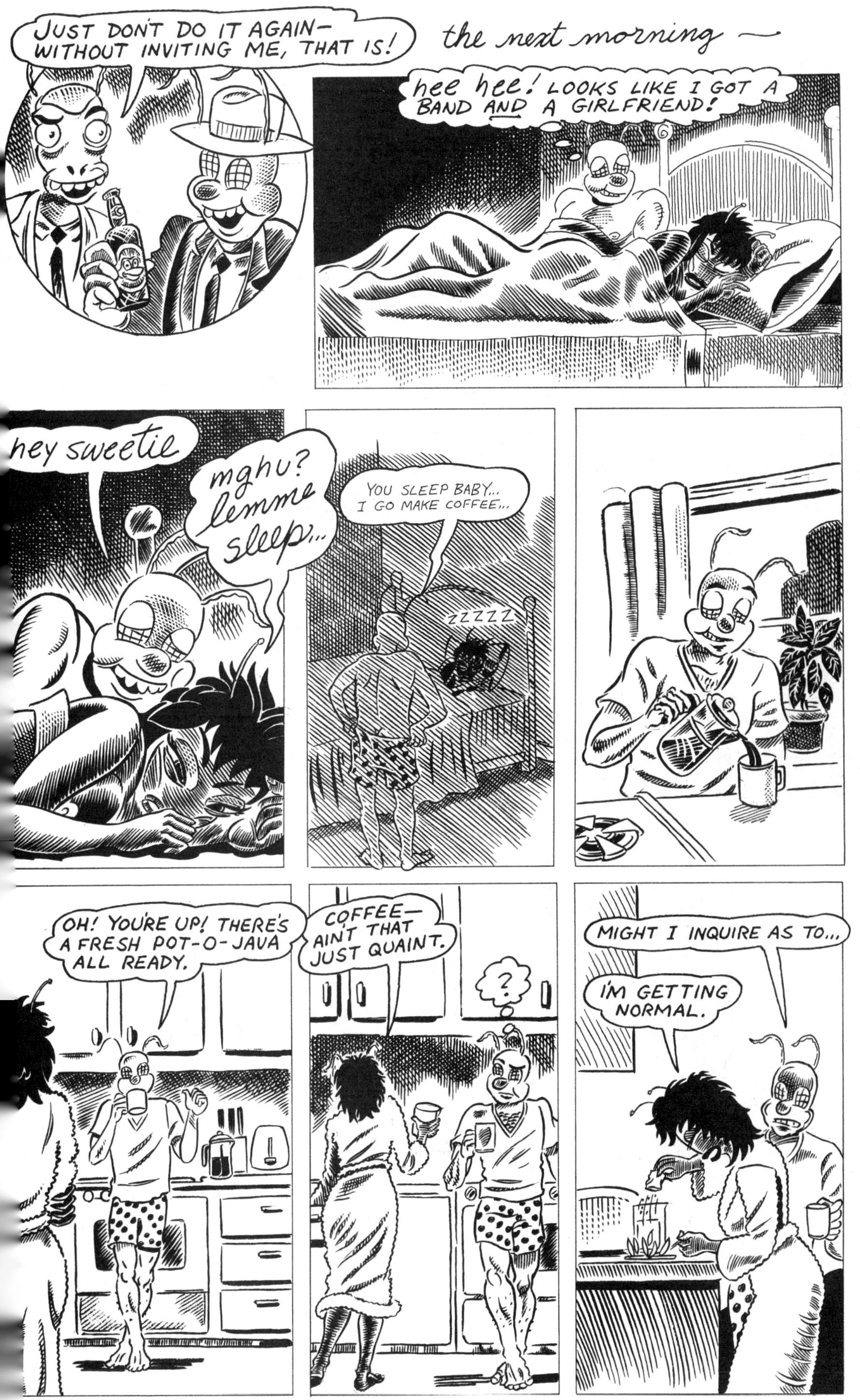
JUST DON'T DO IT AGAIN-
WITHOUT INVITING ME, THAT IS!
the next morning ~
hee hee! LOOKS LIKE I GOT A BAND AND A GIRLFRIEND!
hey sweetie
mghu? lemme sleep...
YOU SLEEP BABY... I GO MAKE COFFEE...
ZZZZZ
OH! YOU'RE UP! THERE'S A FRESH POT-O-JAVA ALL READY.
COFFEE- AIN'T THAT JUST QUAINT.
?
MIGHT I INQUIRE AS TO...
I'M GETTING NORMAL.

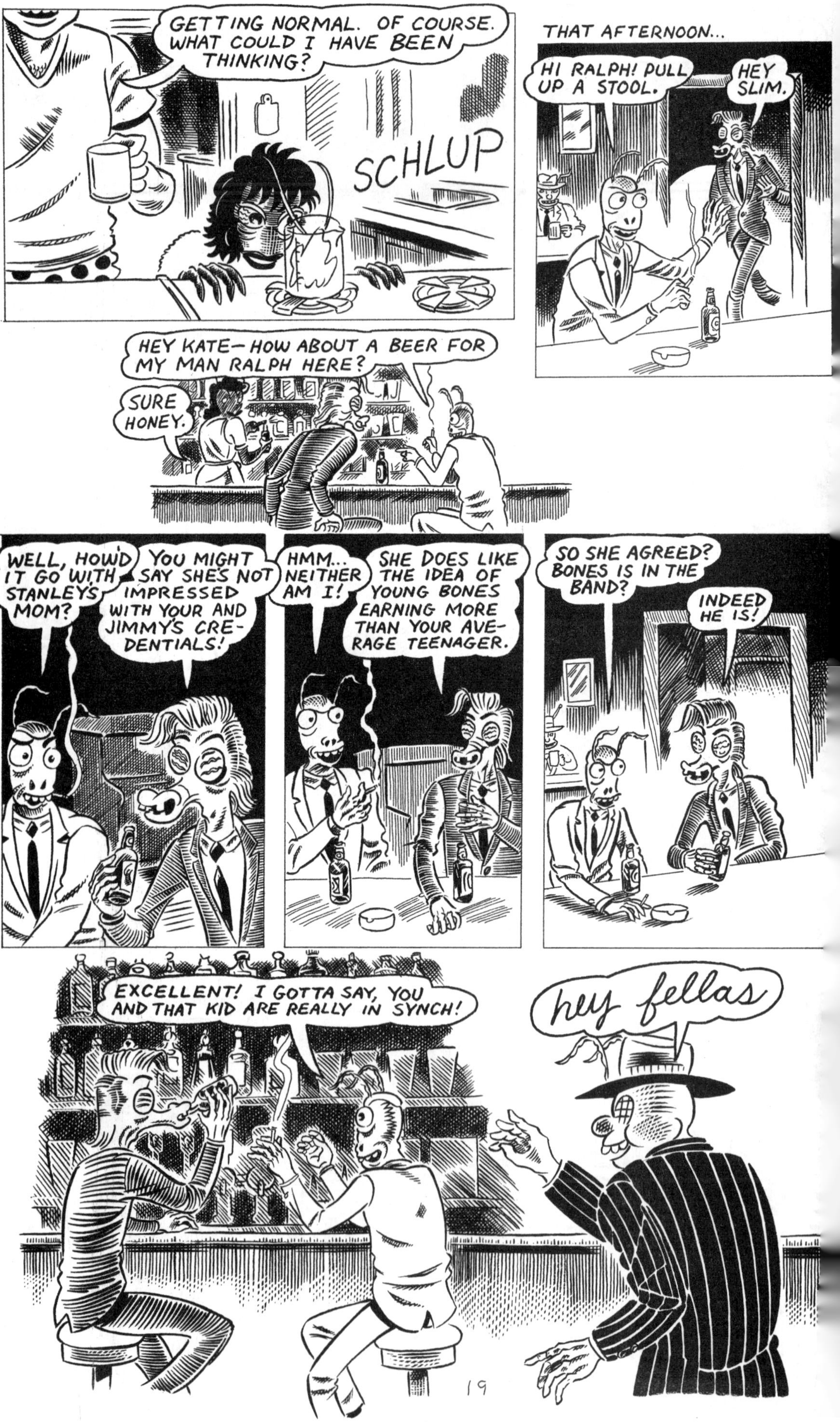

GETTING NORMAL. OF COURSE. WHAT COULD I HAVE BEEN THINKING?
SCHLUP
THAT AFTERNOON...
HI RALPH! PULL UP A STOOL.
HEY SLIM.
HEY KATE— HOW ABOUT A BEER FOR MY MAN RALPH HERE?
SURE HONEY.
WELL, HOW'D IT GO WITH STANLEY'S MOM?
YOU MIGHT SAY SHE'S NOT IMPRESSED WITH YOUR AND JIMMY'S CRE-DENTIALS!
HMM... NEITHER AM I!
SHE DOES LIKE THE IDEA OF YOUNG BONES EARNING MORE THAN YOUR AVE-RAGE TEENAGER.
SO SHE AGREED? BONES IS IN THE BAND?
INDEED HE IS!
EXCELLENT! I GOTTA SAY, YOU AND THAT KID ARE REALLY IN SYNCH!
hey fellas

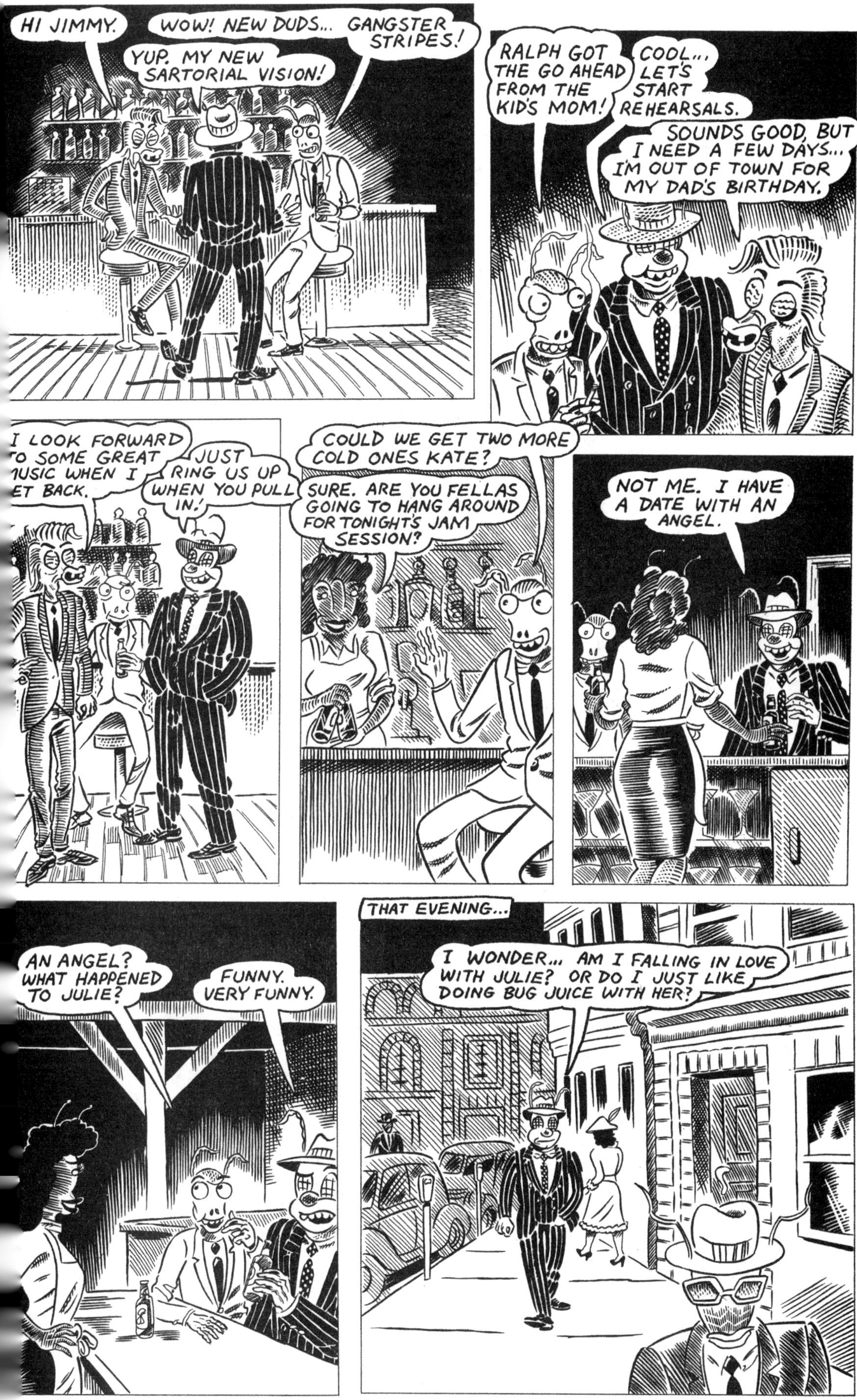
HI JIMMY.
WOW! NEW DUDS... GANGSTER STRIPES!
YUP. MY NEW SARTORIAL VISION!
RALPH GOT THE GO AHEAD FROM THE KID'S MOM!
COOL... LET'S START REHEARSALS.
SOUNDS GOOD, BUT I NEED A FEW DAYS... I'M OUT OF TOWN FOR MY DAD'S BIRTHDAY.
I LOOK FORWARD TO SOME GREAT MUSIC WHEN I GET BACK.
JUST RING US UP WHEN YOU PULL IN!
COULD WE GET TWO MORE COLD ONES KATE?
SURE. ARE YOU FELLAS GOING TO HANG AROUND FOR TONIGHT'S JAM SESSION?
NOT ME. I HAVE A DATE WITH AN ANGEL.
AN ANGEL? WHAT HAPPENED TO JULIE?
FUNNY. VERY FUNNY.
THAT EVENING...
I WONDER... AM I FALLING IN LOVE WITH JULIE? OR DO I JUST LIKE DOING BUG JUICE WITH HER?

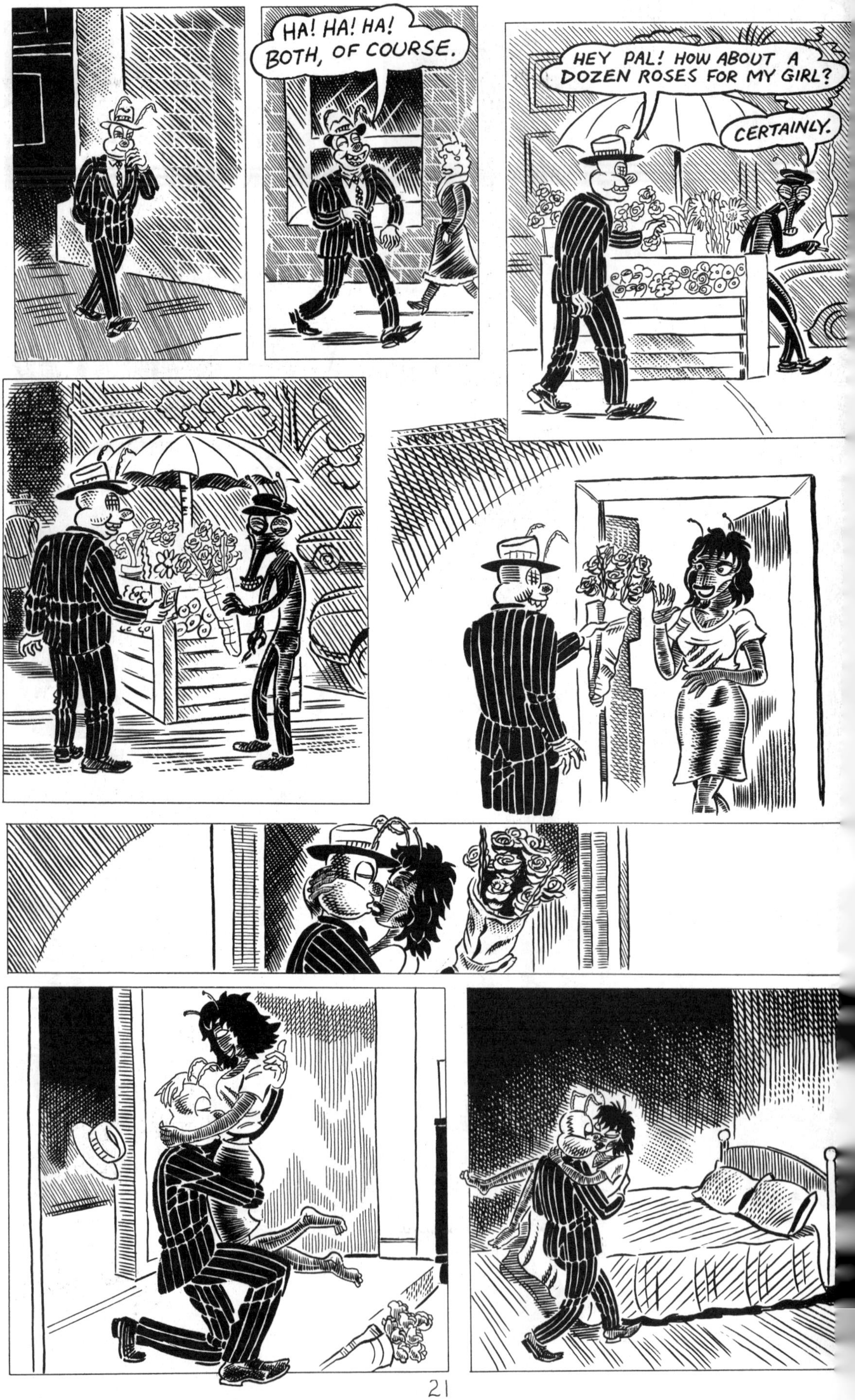
HA! HA! HA!
BOTH, OF COURSE.
HEY PAL! HOW ABOUT A DOZEN ROSES FOR MY GIRL?
CERTAINLY.

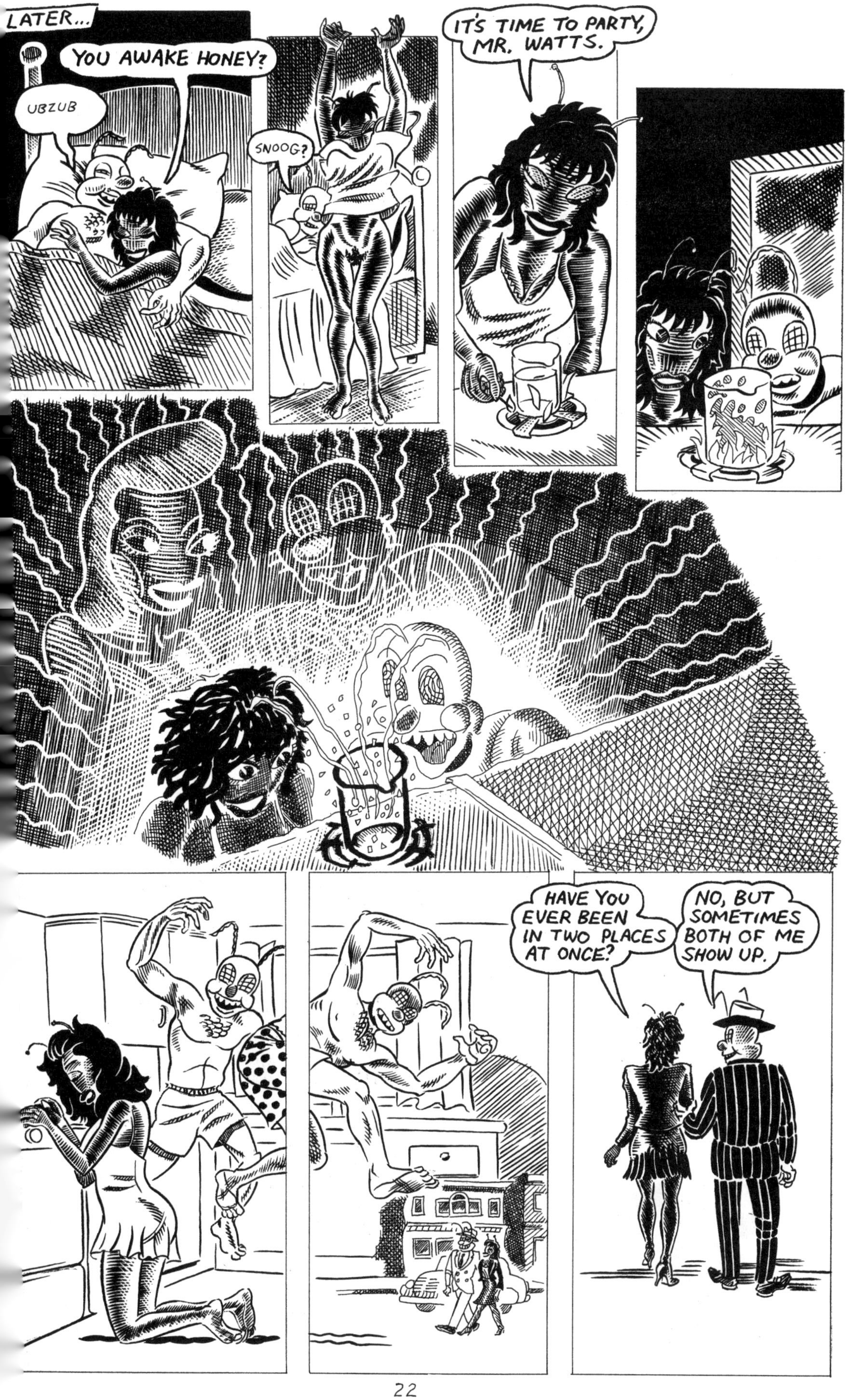
LATER...
YOU AWAKE HONEY?
UBZUB
SNOOG?
IT'S TIME TO PARTY, MR. WATTS.
HAVE YOU EVER BEEN IN TWO PLACES AT ONCE?
NO, BUT SOMETIMES BOTH OF ME SHOW UP.

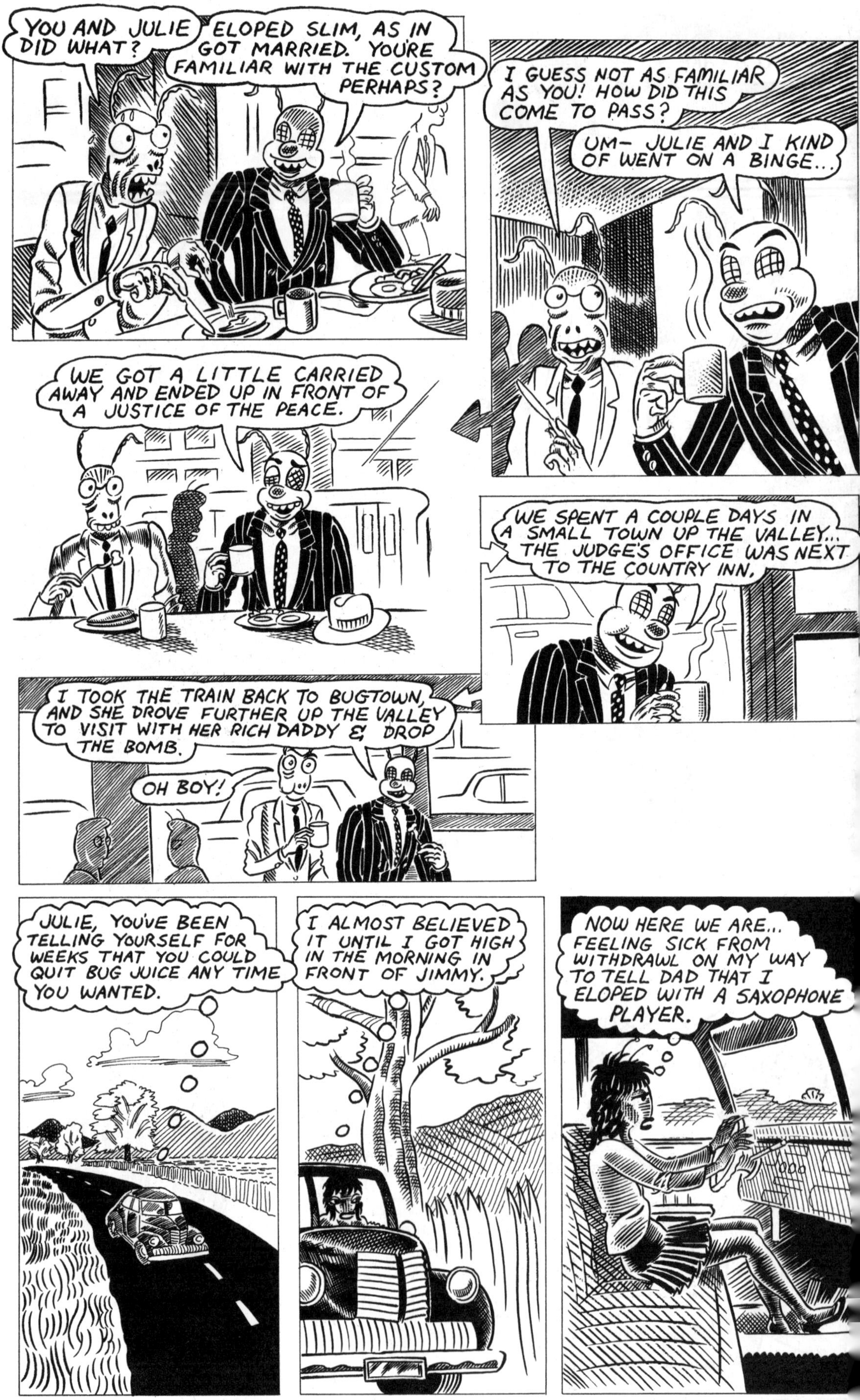
YOU AND JULIE DID WHAT?
ELOPED SLIM, AS IN GOT MARRIED. YOU'RE FAMILIAR WITH THE CUSTOM PERHAPS?
I GUESS NOT AS FAMILIAR AS YOU! HOW DID THIS COME TO PASS?
UM- JULIE AND I KIND OF WENT ON A BINGE...
WE GOT A LITTLE CARRIED AWAY AND ENDED UP IN FRONT OF A JUSTICE OF THE PEACE.
WE SPENT A COUPLE DAYS IN A SMALL TOWN UP THE VALLEY... THE JUDGE'S OFFICE WAS NEXT TO THE COUNTRY INN,
I TOOK THE TRAIN BACK TO BUGTOWN, AND SHE DROVE FURTHER UP THE VALLEY TO VISIT WITH HER RICH DADDY & DROP THE BOMB.
OH BOY!
JULIE, YOU'VE BEEN TELLING YOURSELF FOR WEEKS THAT YOU COULD QUIT BUG JUICE ANY TIME YOU WANTED.
I ALMOST BELIEVED IT UNTIL I GOT HIGH IN THE MORNING IN FRONT OF JIMMY.
NOW HERE WE ARE... FEELING SICK FROM WITHDRAWL ON MY WAY TO TELL DAD THAT I ELOPED WITH A SAXOPHONE PLAYER.

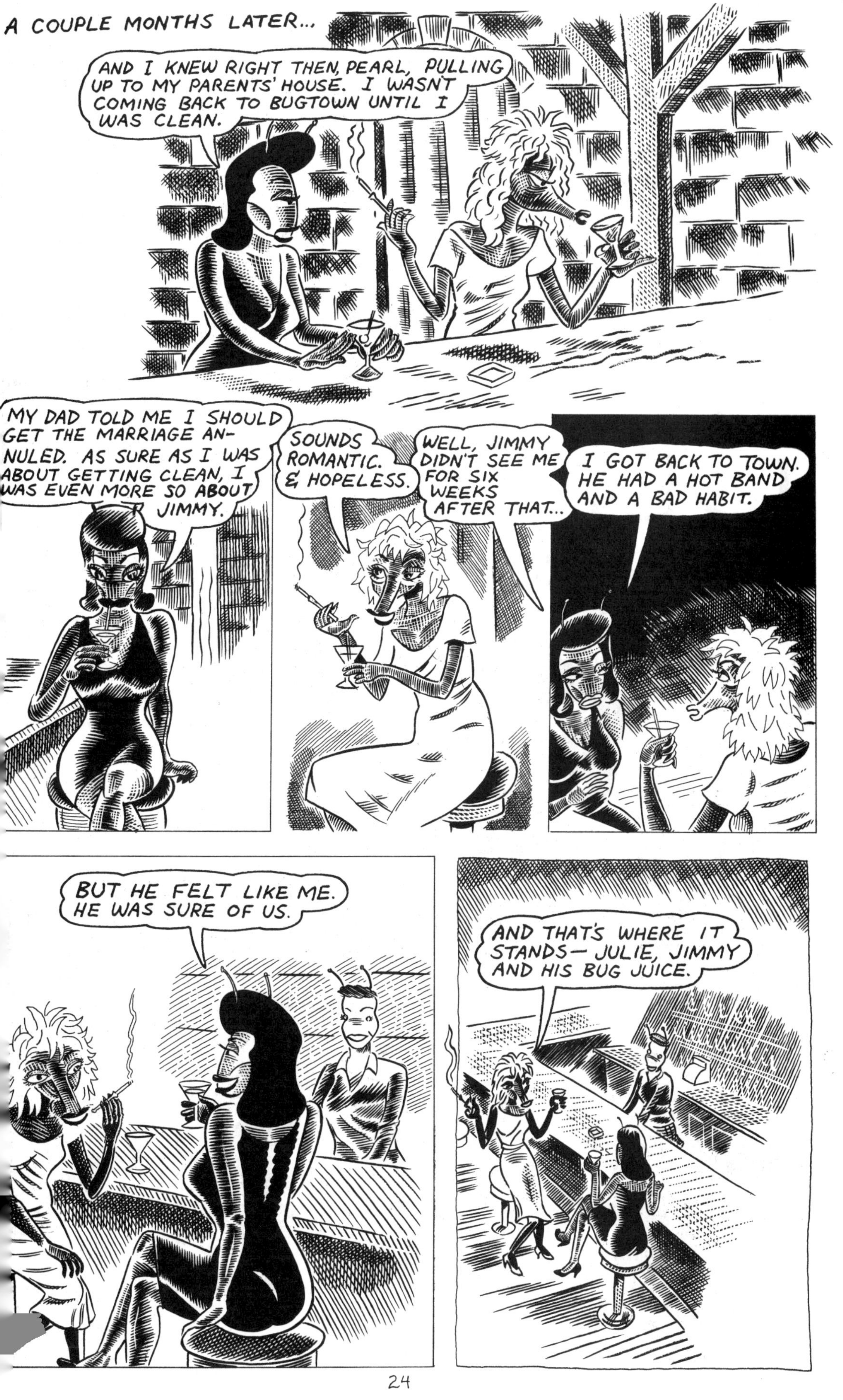
A COUPLE MONTHS LATER...
AND I KNEW RIGHT THEN, PEARL, PULLING UP TO MY PARENTS' HOUSE. I WASN'T COMING BACK TO BUGTOWN UNTIL I WAS CLEAN.
MY DAD TOLD ME I SHOULD GET THE MARRIAGE AN-NULED. AS SURE AS I WAS ABOUT GETTING CLEAN, I WAS EVEN MORE SO ABOUT JIMMY.
SOUNDS ROMANTIC. & HOPELESS.
WELL, JIMMY DIDN'T SEE ME FOR SIX WEEKS AFTER THAT...
I GOT BACK TO TOWN. HE HAD A HOT BAND AND A BAD HABIT.
BUT HE FELT LIKE ME. HE WAS SURE OF US.
AND THAT'S WHERE IT STANDS— JULIE, JIMMY AND HIS BUG JUICE.

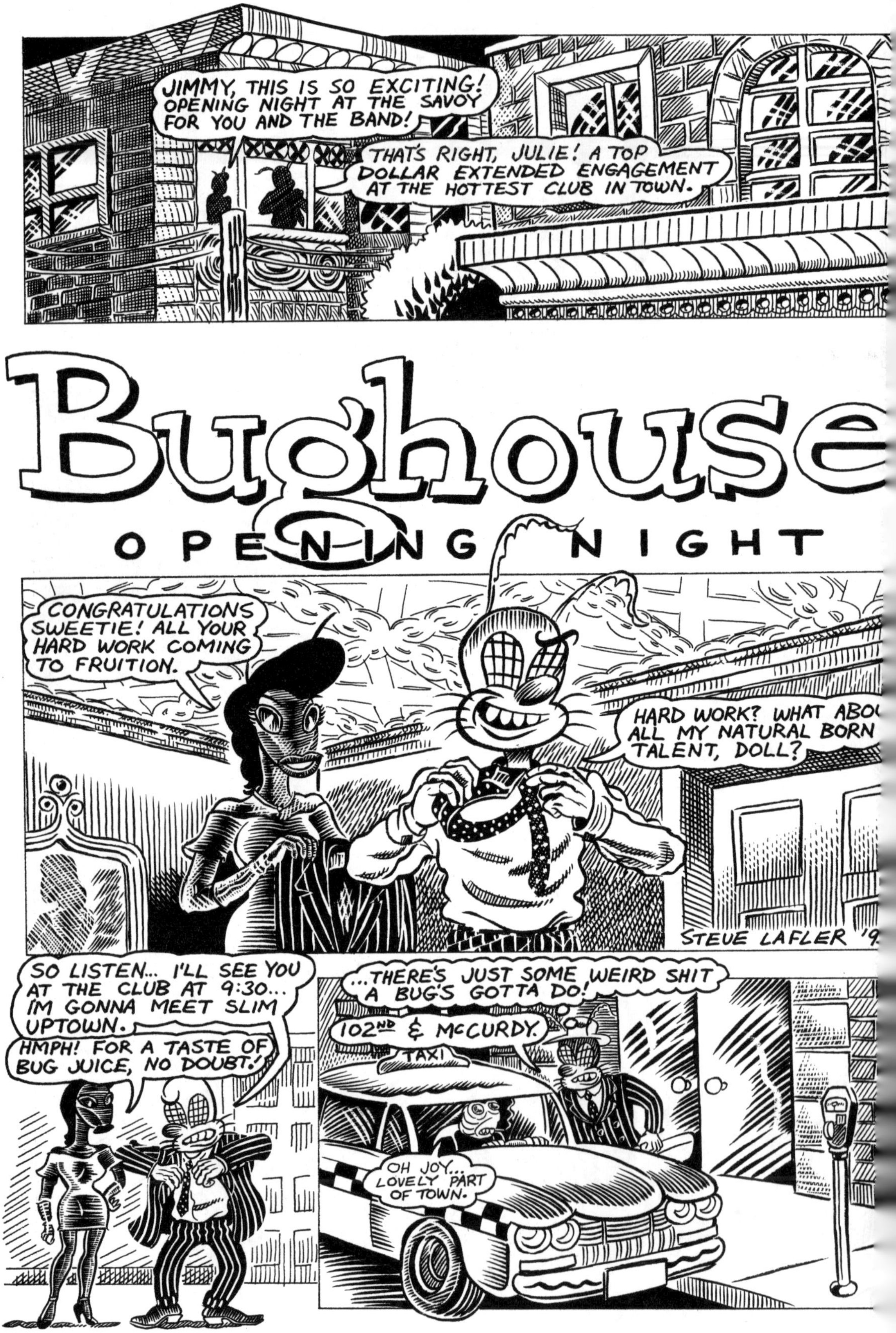
JIMMY, THIS IS SO EXCITING! OPENING NIGHT AT THE SAVOY FOR YOU AND THE BAND!
THAT'S RIGHT, JULIE! A TOP DOLLAR EXTENDED ENGAGEMENT AT THE HOTTEST CLUB IN TOWN.
Bughouse
OPENING NIGHT
CONGRATULATIONS SWEETIE! ALL YOUR HARD WORK COMING TO FRUITION.
HARD WORK? WHAT ABOU ALL MY NATURAL BORN TALENT, DOLL?
STEVE LAFLER '9
SO LISTEN... I'LL SEE YOU AT THE CLUB AT 9:30... I'M GONNA MEET SLIM UPTOWN.
HMPH! FOR A TASTE OF BUG JUICE, NO DOUBT!
...THERE'S JUST SOME WEIRD SHIT A BUG'S GOTTA DO!
102ND & McCURDY.
TAXI
OH JOY... LOVELY PART OF TOWN.

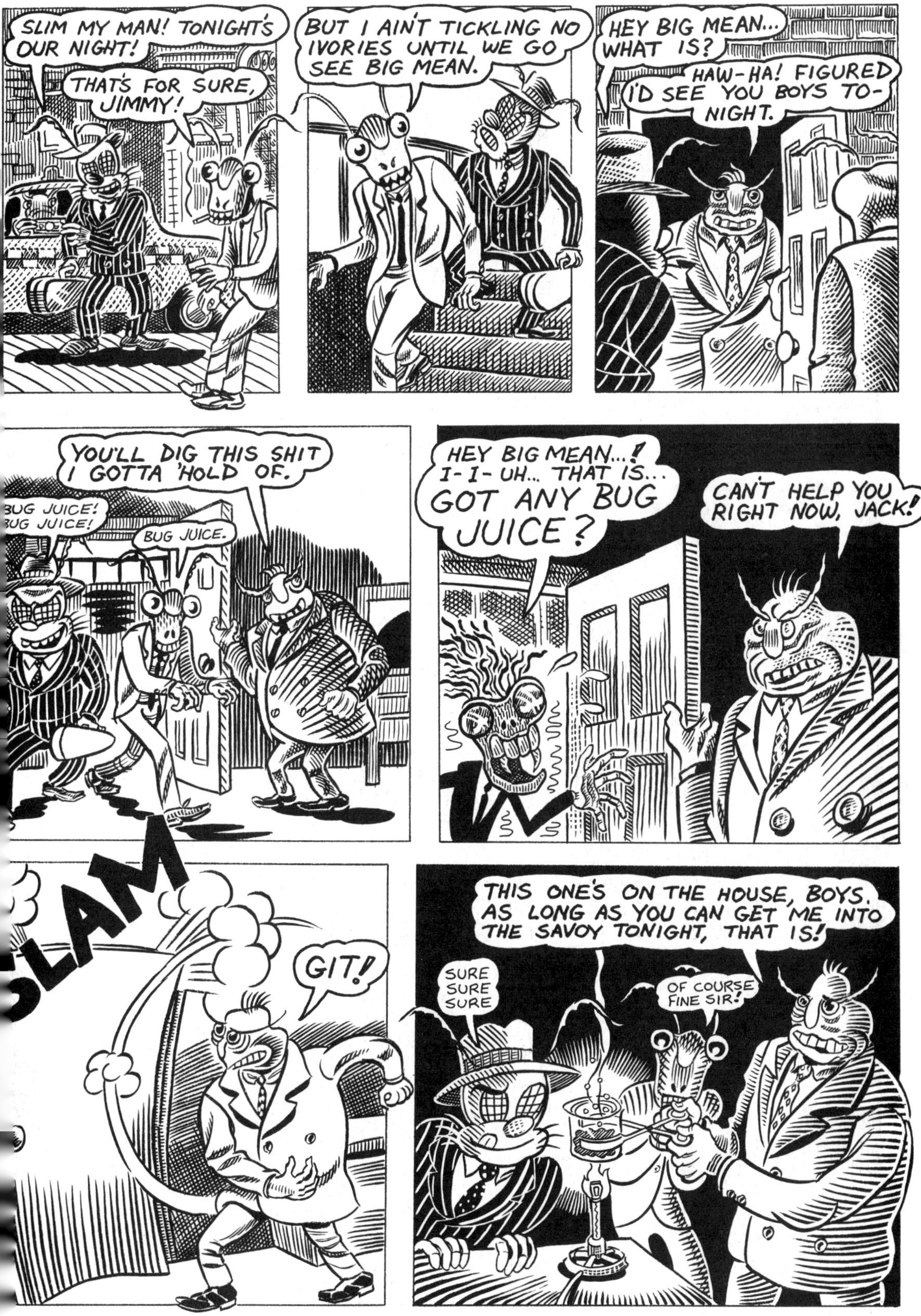
SLIM MY MAN! TONIGHT'S OUR NIGHT!
THAT'S FOR SURE, JIMMY!
BUT I AIN'T TICKLING NO IVORIES UNTIL WE GO SEE BIG MEAN.
HEY BIG MEAN... WHAT IS?
HAW-HA! FIGURED I'D SEE YOU BOYS TO-NIGHT.
YOU'LL DIG THIS SHIT I GOTTA 'HOLD OF.
BUG JUICE! BUG JUICE!
BUG JUICE.
HEY BIG MEAN...! I-I-UH... THAT IS... GOT ANY BUG JUICE?
CAN'T HELP YOU RIGHT NOW, JACK!
SLAM
GIT!
THIS ONE'S ON THE HOUSE, BOYS. AS LONG AS YOU CAN GET ME INTO THE SAVOY TONIGHT, THAT IS!
SURE SURE SURE
OF COURSE FINE SIR!

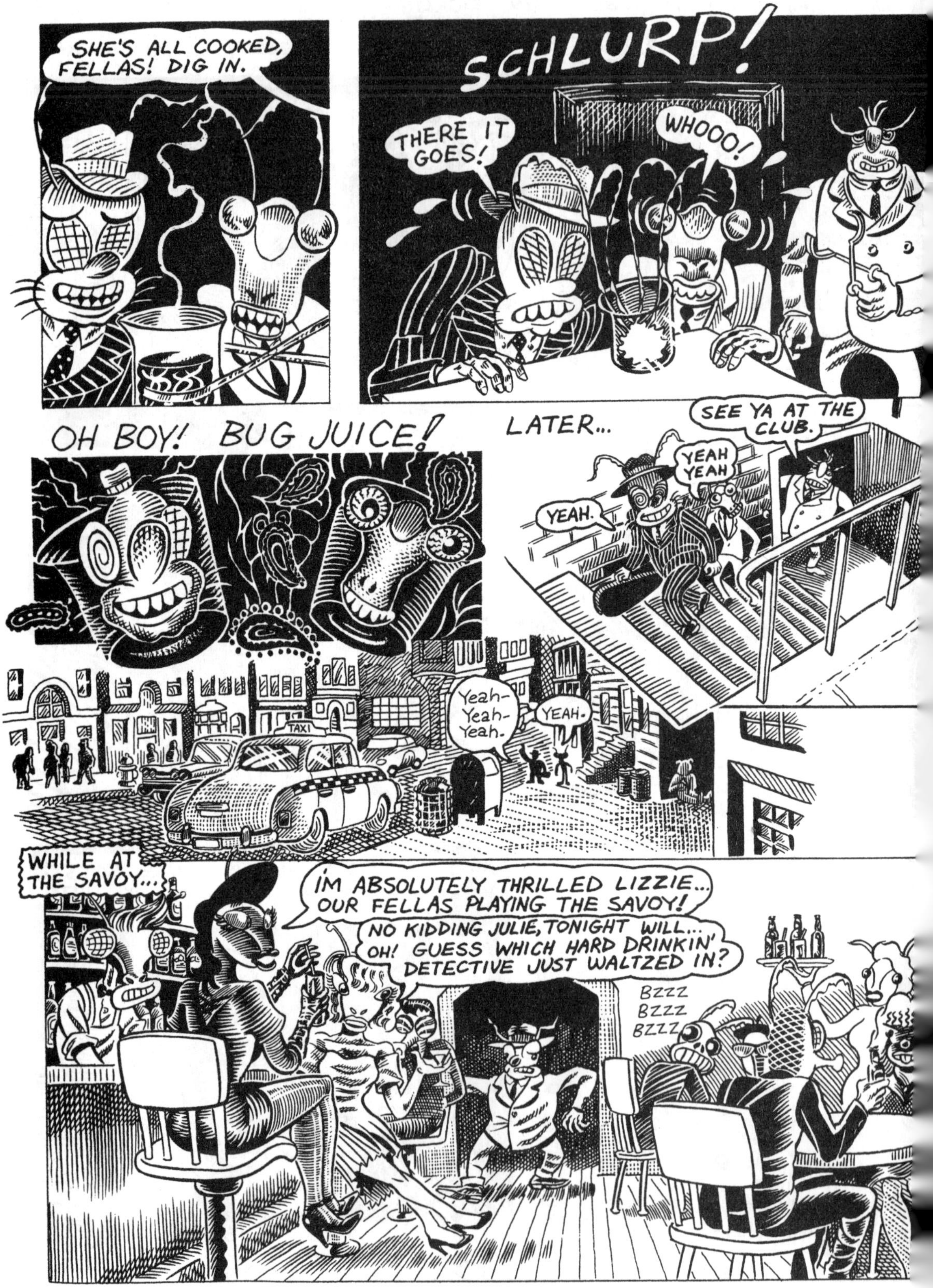
SHE'S ALL COOKED, FELLAS! DIG IN.
SCHLURP!
THERE IT GOES!
WHOOO!
OH BOY! BUG JUICE!
LATER...
SEE YA AT THE CLUB.
YEAH YEAH
YEAH.
Yeah-Yeah-Yeah.
YEAH.
TAXI
WHILE AT THE SAVOY...
I'M ABSOLUTELY THRILLED LIZZIE... OUR FELLAS PLAYING THE SAVOY!
NO KIDDING JULIE, TONIGHT WILL... OH! GUESS WHICH HARD DRINKIN' DETECTIVE JUST WALTZED IN?
BZZZ BZZZ BZZZ

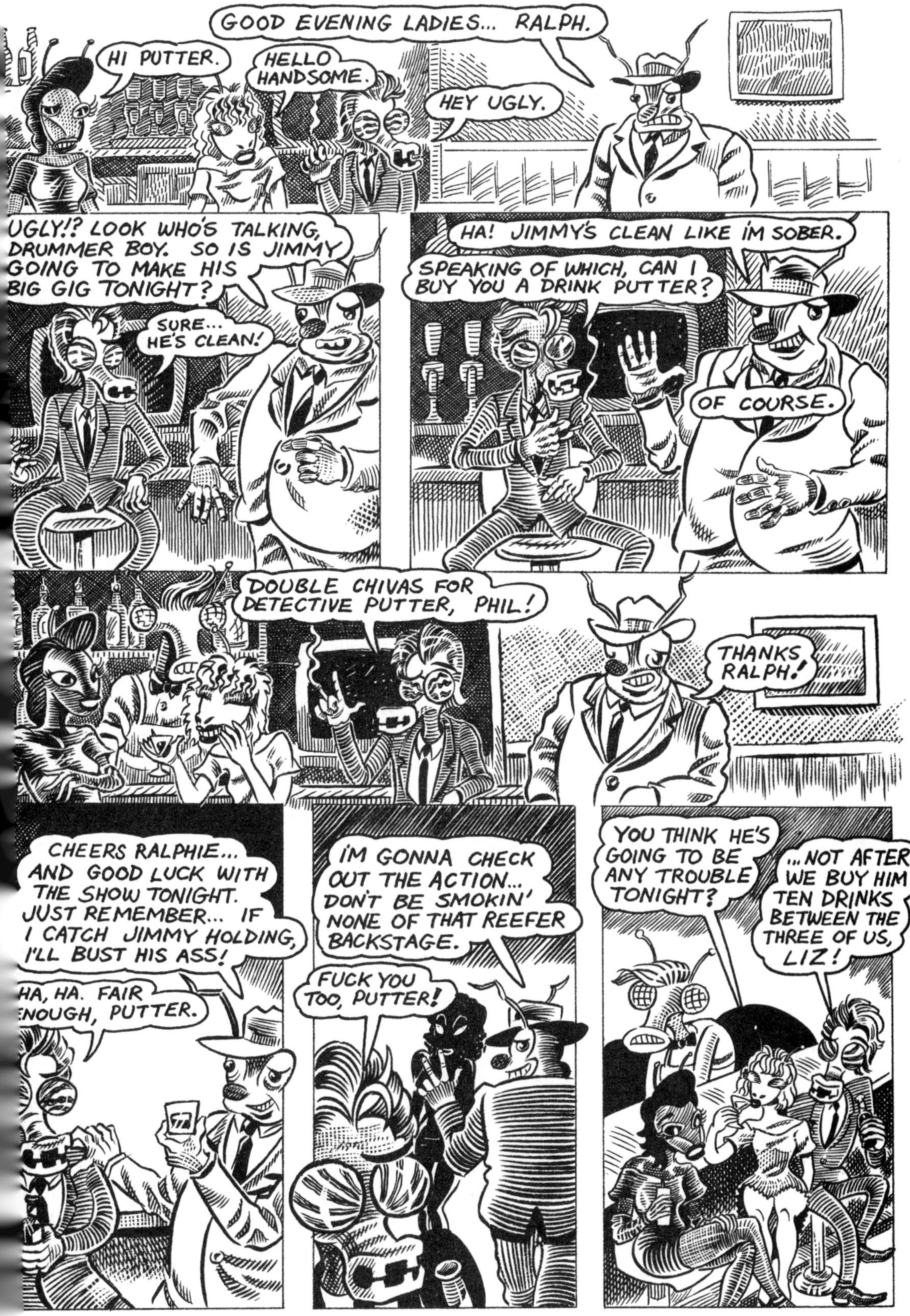
GOOD EVENING LADIES... RALPH.
HI PUTTER.
HELLO HANDSOME.
HEY UGLY.
UGLY!? LOOK WHO'S TALKING, DRUMMER BOY. SO IS JIMMY GOING TO MAKE HIS BIG GIG TONIGHT?
SURE... HE'S CLEAN!
HA! JIMMY'S CLEAN LIKE I'M SOBER.
SPEAKING OF WHICH, CAN I BUY YOU A DRINK PUTTER?
OF COURSE.
DOUBLE CHIVAS FOR DETECTIVE PUTTER, PHIL!
THANKS RALPH!
CHEERS RALPHIE... AND GOOD LUCK WITH THE SHOW TONIGHT. JUST REMEMBER... IF I CATCH JIMMY HOLDING, I'LL BUST HIS ASS!
HA, HA. FAIR ENOUGH, PUTTER.
I'M GONNA CHECK OUT THE ACTION... DON'T BE SMOKIN' NONE OF THAT REEFER BACKSTAGE.
FUCK YOU TOO, PUTTER!
YOU THINK HE'S GOING TO BE ANY TROUBLE TONIGHT?
...NOT AFTER WE BUY HIM TEN DRINKS BETWEEN THE THREE OF US, LIZ!

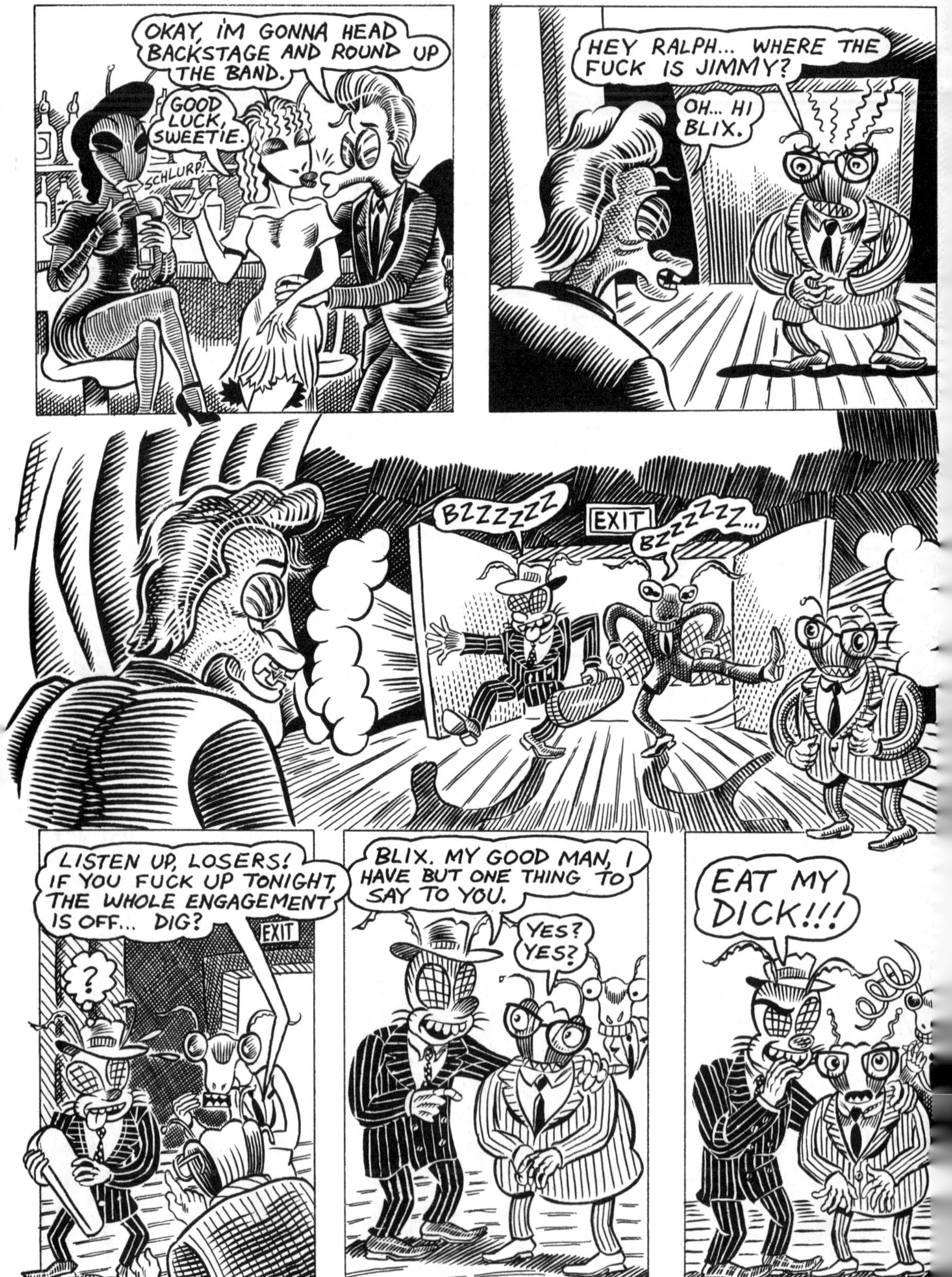
OKAY, I'M GONNA HEAD BACKSTAGE AND ROUND UP THE BAND.
GOOD LUCK, SWEETIE.
SCHLURP!
HEY RALPH... WHERE THE FUCK IS JIMMY?
OH... HI BLIX.
BZZZZZZ
EXIT
BZZZZZZ...
LISTEN UP, LOSERS! IF YOU FUCK UP TONIGHT, THE WHOLE ENGAGEMENT IS OFF... DIG?
?
EXIT
BLIX. MY GOOD MAN, I HAVE BUT ONE THING TO SAY TO YOU.
YES? YES?
EAT MY DICK!!!

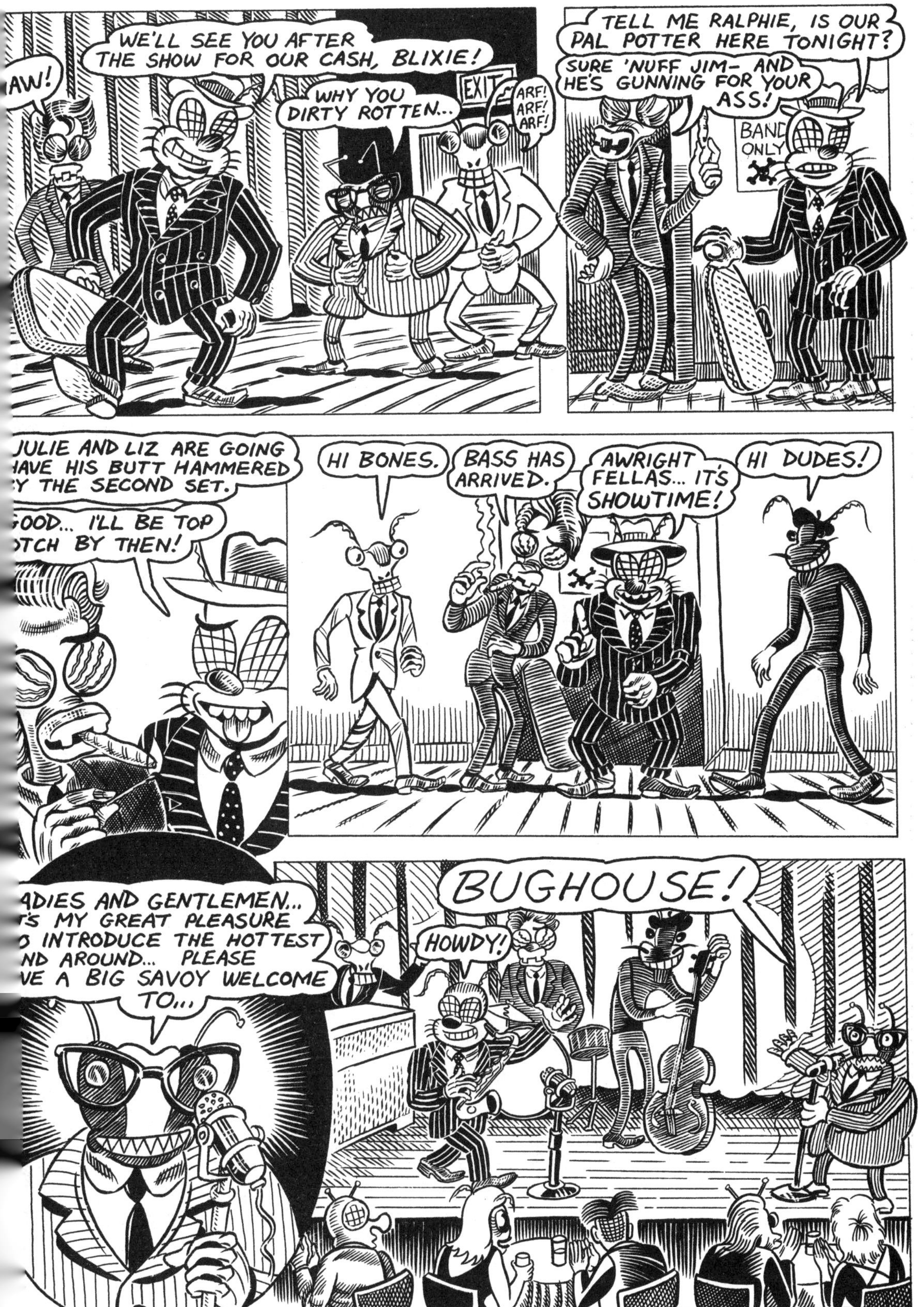

AW!
WE'LL SEE YOU AFTER THE SHOW FOR OUR CASH, BLIXIE!
WHY YOU DIRTY ROTTEN...
EXIT
ARF! ARF! ARF!
TELL ME RALPHIE, IS OUR PAL POTTER HERE TONIGHT?
SURE 'NUFF JIM- AND HE'S GUNNING FOR YOUR ASS!
BAND ONLY
JULIE AND LIZ ARE GOING HAVE HIS BUTT HAMMERED Y THE SECOND SET.
GOOD... I'LL BE TOP OTCH BY THEN!
HI BONES.
BASS HAS ARRIVED.
AWRIGHT FELLAS... IT'S SHOWTIME!
HI DUDES!
ADIES AND GENTLEMEN... T'S MY GREAT PLEASURE O INTRODUCE THE HOTTEST ND AROUND... PLEASE VE A BIG SAVOY WELCOME TO...
HOWDY!
BUGHOUSE!

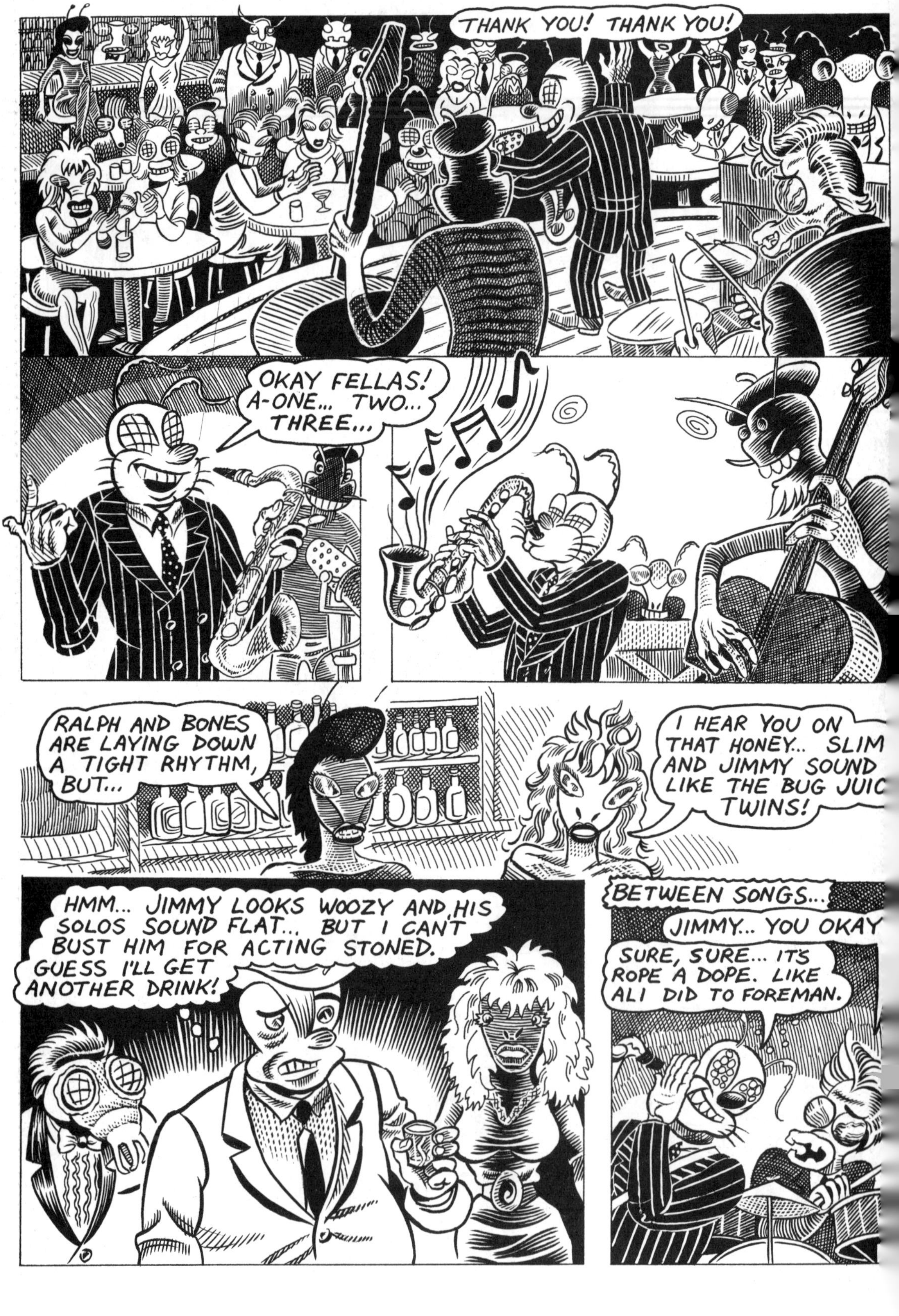
THANK YOU! THANK YOU!
OKAY FELLAS! A-ONE... TWO... THREE...
RALPH AND BONES ARE LAYING DOWN A TIGHT RHYTHM, BUT...
I HEAR YOU ON THAT HONEY... SLIM AND JIMMY SOUND LIKE THE BUG JUIC
TWINS!
HMM... JIMMY LOOKS WOOZY AND HIS SOLOS SOUND FLAT... BUT I CAN'T BUST HIM FOR ACTING STONED.
GUESS I'LL GET ANOTHER DRINK!
BETWEEN SONGS...
JIMMY... YOU OKAY
SURE, SURE... IT'S ROPE A DOPE. LIKE ALI DID TO FOREMAN.

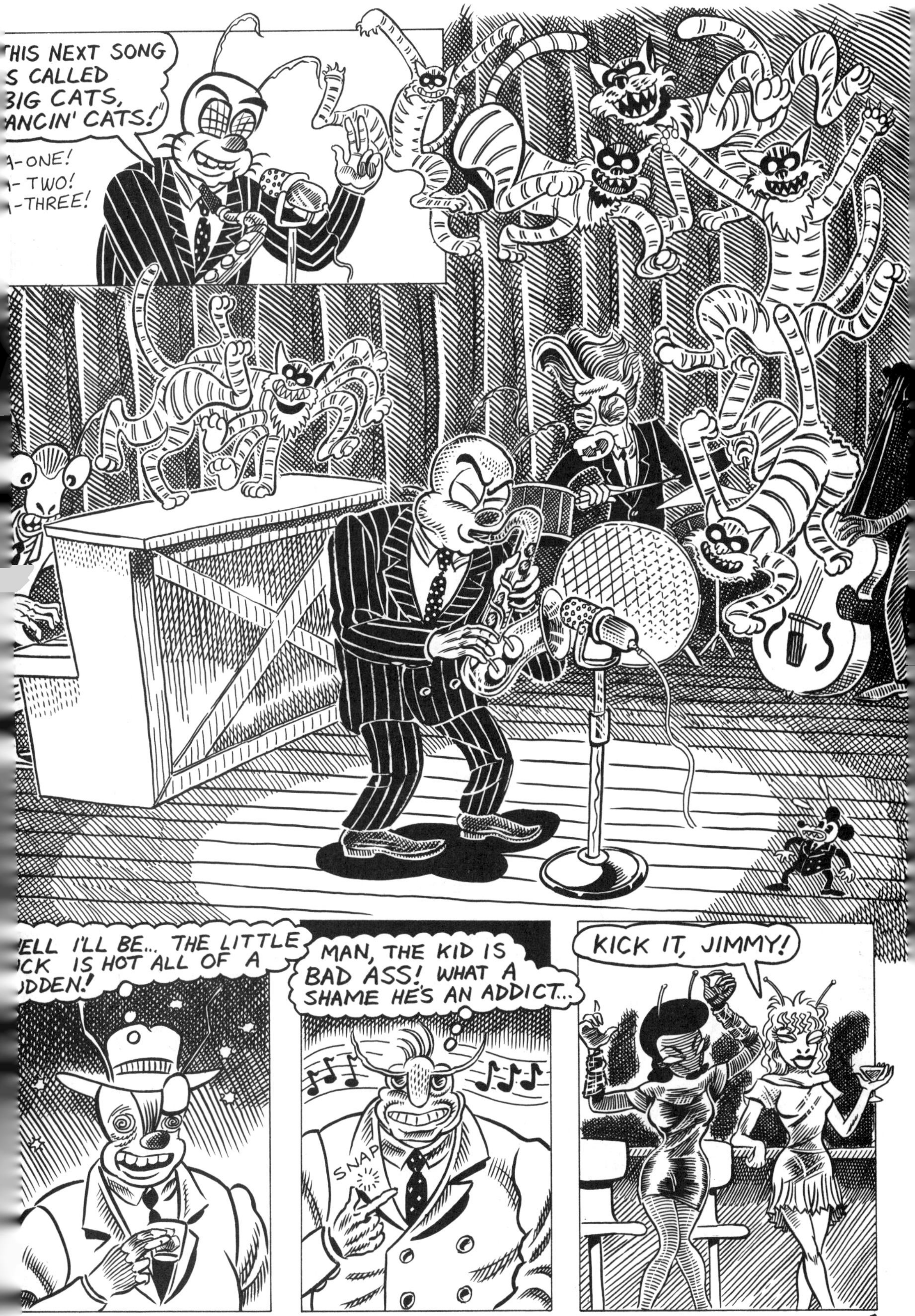

THIS NEXT SONG
S CALLED
BIG CATS,
ANCIN' CATS!
A-ONE!
-TWO!
-THREE!
ELL I'LL BE... THE LITTLE
CK IS HOT ALL OF A
DDEN!
MAN, THE KID IS BAD ASS! WHAT A SHAME HE'S AN ADDICT...
SNAP
KICK IT, JIMMY!

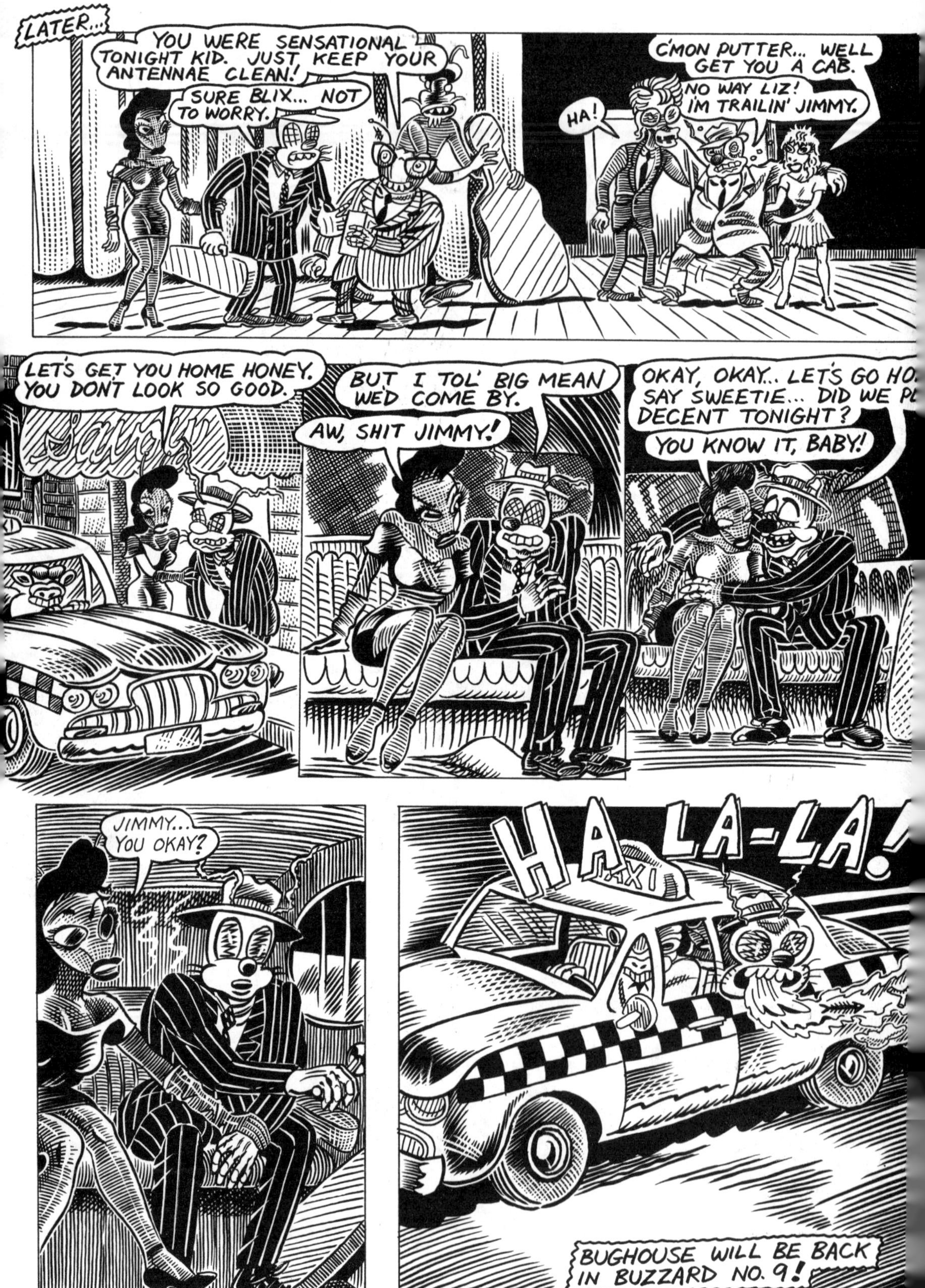
LATER...
YOU WERE SENSATIONAL TONIGHT KID. JUST KEEP YOUR ANTENNAE CLEAN!
SURE BLIX... NOT TO WORRY.
C'MON PUTTER... WE'LL GET YOU A CAB.
HA!
NO WAY LIZ! I'M TRAILIN' JIMMY.
LET'S GET YOU HOME HONEY. YOU DON'T LOOK SO GOOD.
BUT I TOL' BIG MEAN WE'D COME BY.
AW, SHIT JIMMY!
OKAY, OKAY... LET'S GO HO
SAY SWEETIE... DID WE P
DECENT TONIGHT?
YOU KNOW IT, BABY!
JIMMY... YOU OKAY?
HA LA-LA!
TAXI
BUGHOUSE WILL BE BACK IN BUZZARD NO. 9!

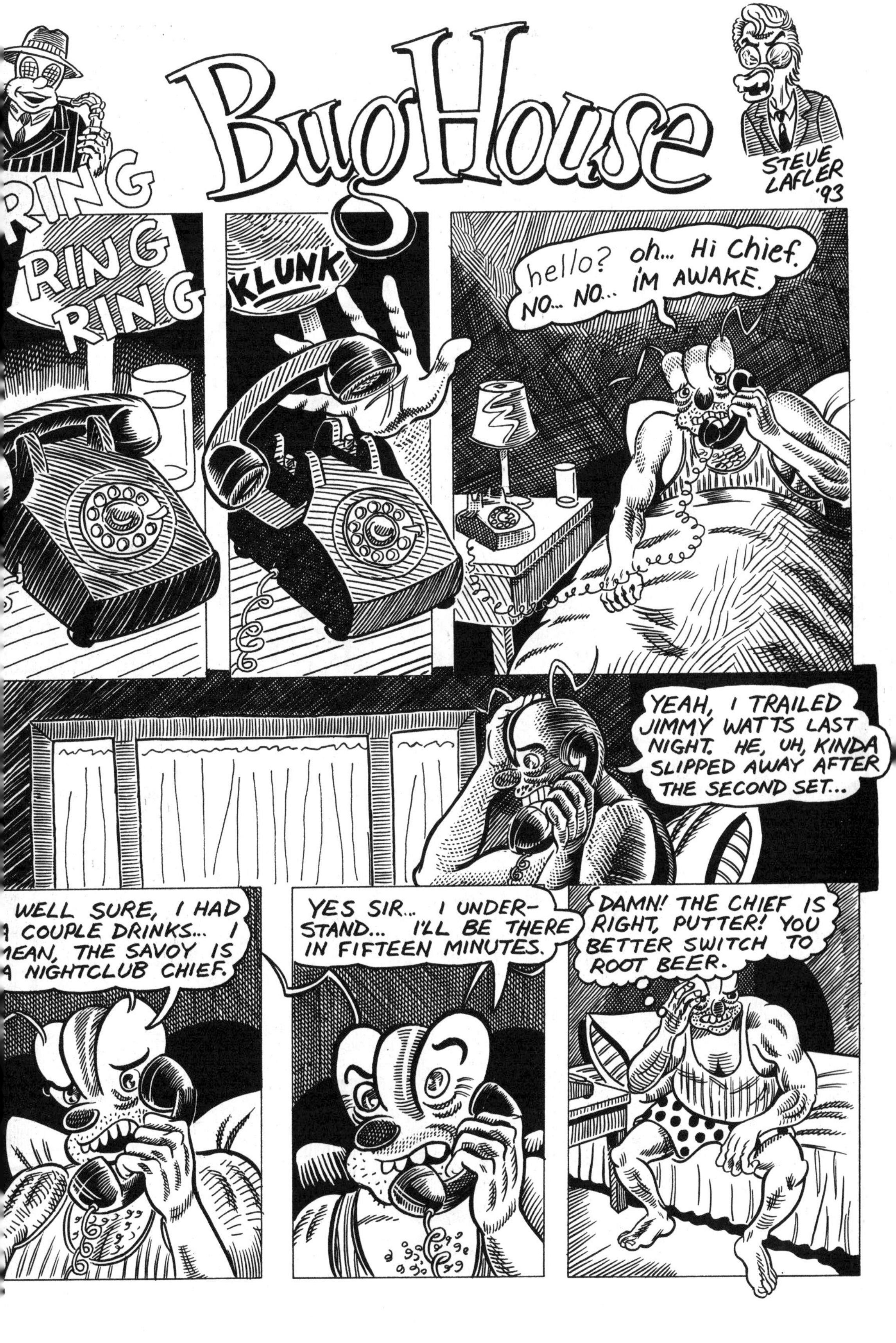
BugHouse
STEVE LAFLER '93
RING RING RING RING
KLUNK
hello? oh... Hi Chief. NO... NO... IM AWAKE.
YEAH, I TRAILED JIMMY WATTS LAST NIGHT. HE, UH, KINDA SLIPPED AWAY AFTER THE SECOND SET...
WELL SURE, I HAD A COUPLE DRINKS... I MEAN, THE SAVOY IS A NIGHTCLUB CHIEF.
YES SIR... I UNDERSTAND... I'LL BE THERE IN FIFTEEN MINUTES.
DAMN! THE CHIEF IS RIGHT, PUTTER! YOU BETTER SWITCH TO ROOT BEER.

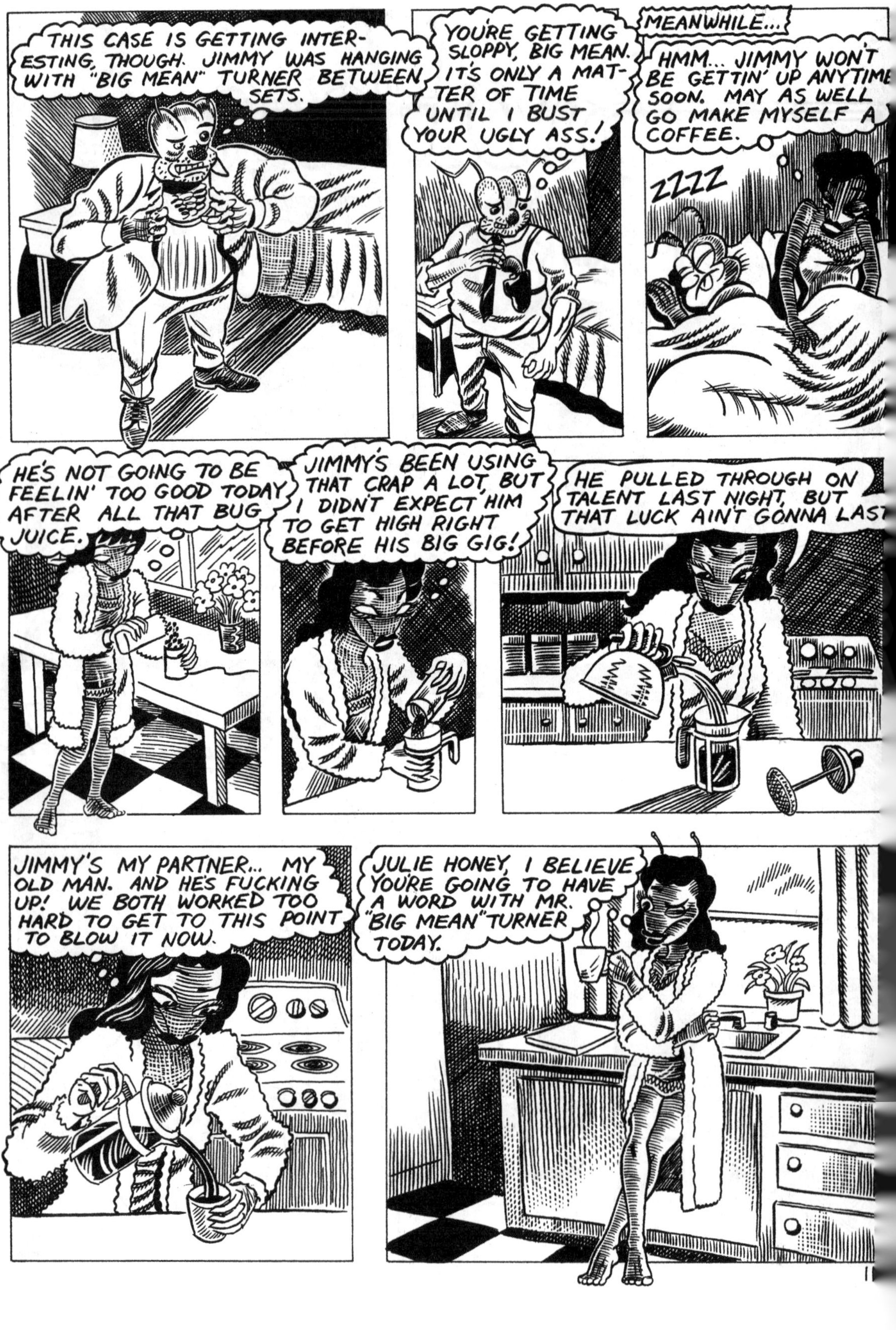
THIS CASE IS GETTING INTERESTING, THOUGH. JIMMY WAS HANGING WITH "BIG MEAN" TURNER BETWEEN SETS.
YOU'RE GETTING SLOPPY, BIG MEAN. IT'S ONLY A MATTER OF TIME UNTIL I BUST YOUR UGLY ASS!
MEANWHILE...
HMM... JIMMY WON'T BE GETTIN' UP ANYTIME SOON. MAY AS WELL GO MAKE MYSELF A COFFEE.
ZZZZ
HE'S NOT GOING TO BE FEELIN' TOO GOOD TODAY AFTER ALL THAT BUG JUICE.
JIMMY'S BEEN USING THAT CRAP A LOT, BUT I DIDN'T EXPECT HIM TO GET HIGH RIGHT BEFORE HIS BIG GIG!
HE PULLED THROUGH ON TALENT LAST NIGHT, BUT THAT LUCK AIN'T GONNA LAST
JIMMY'S MY PARTNER... MY OLD MAN. AND HE'S FUCKING UP! WE BOTH WORKED TOO HARD TO GET TO THIS POINT TO BLOW IT NOW.
JULIE HONEY, I BELIEVE YOU'RE GOING TO HAVE A WORD WITH MR. "BIG MEAN" TURNER TODAY.

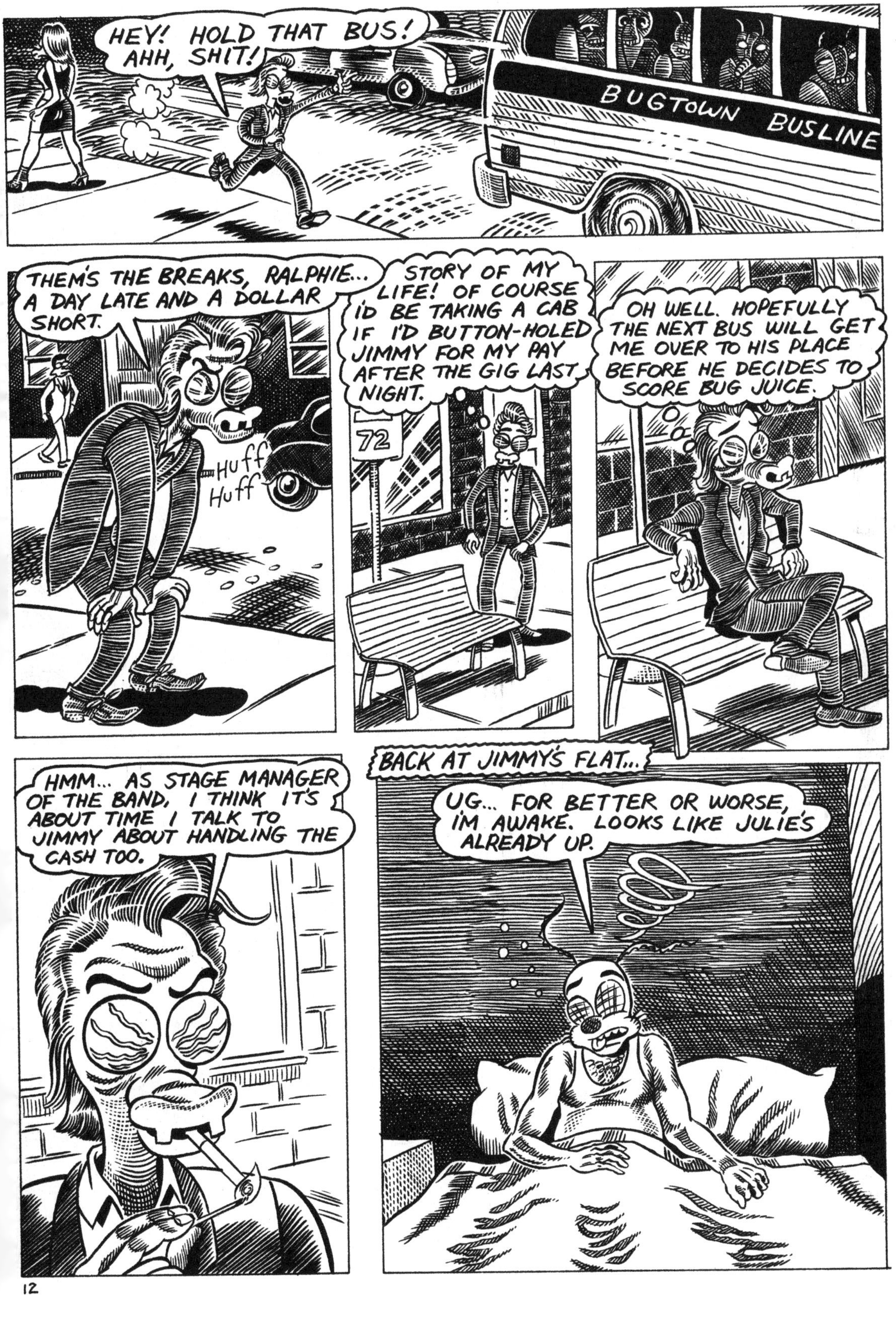
HEY! HOLD THAT BUS! AHH, SHIT!
BUGTOWN BUSLINE
THEM'S THE BREAKS, RALPHIE... A DAY LATE AND A DOLLAR SHORT.
Huff Huff
STORY OF MY LIFE! OF COURSE I'D BE TAKING A CAB IF I'D BUTTON-HOLED JIMMY FOR MY PAY AFTER THE GIG LAST NIGHT.
72
OH WELL. HOPEFULLY THE NEXT BUS WILL GET ME OVER TO HIS PLACE BEFORE HE DECIDES TO SCORE BUG JUICE.
HMM... AS STAGE MANAGER OF THE BAND, I THINK IT'S ABOUT TIME I TALK TO JIMMY ABOUT HANDLING THE CASH TOO.
BACK AT JIMMY'S FLAT...
UG... FOR BETTER OR WORSE, I'M AWAKE. LOOKS LIKE JULIE'S ALREADY UP.

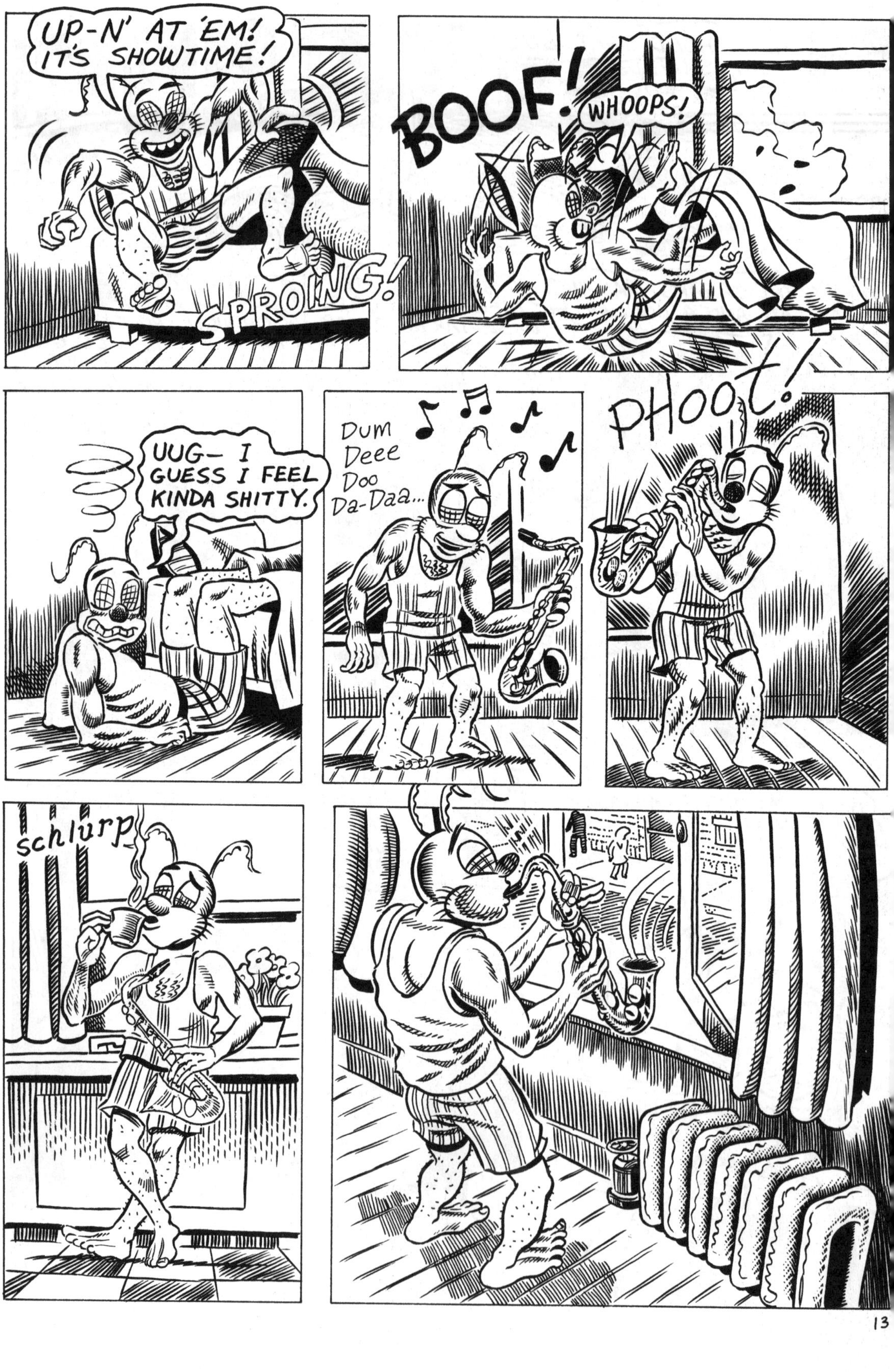
UP-N' AT 'EM! IT'S SHOWTIME!
SPROING!
BOOF!
WHOOPS!
UUG— I GUESS I FEEL KINDA SHITTY.
Dum Deee Doo Da-Daa...
PHOOT!
schlurp

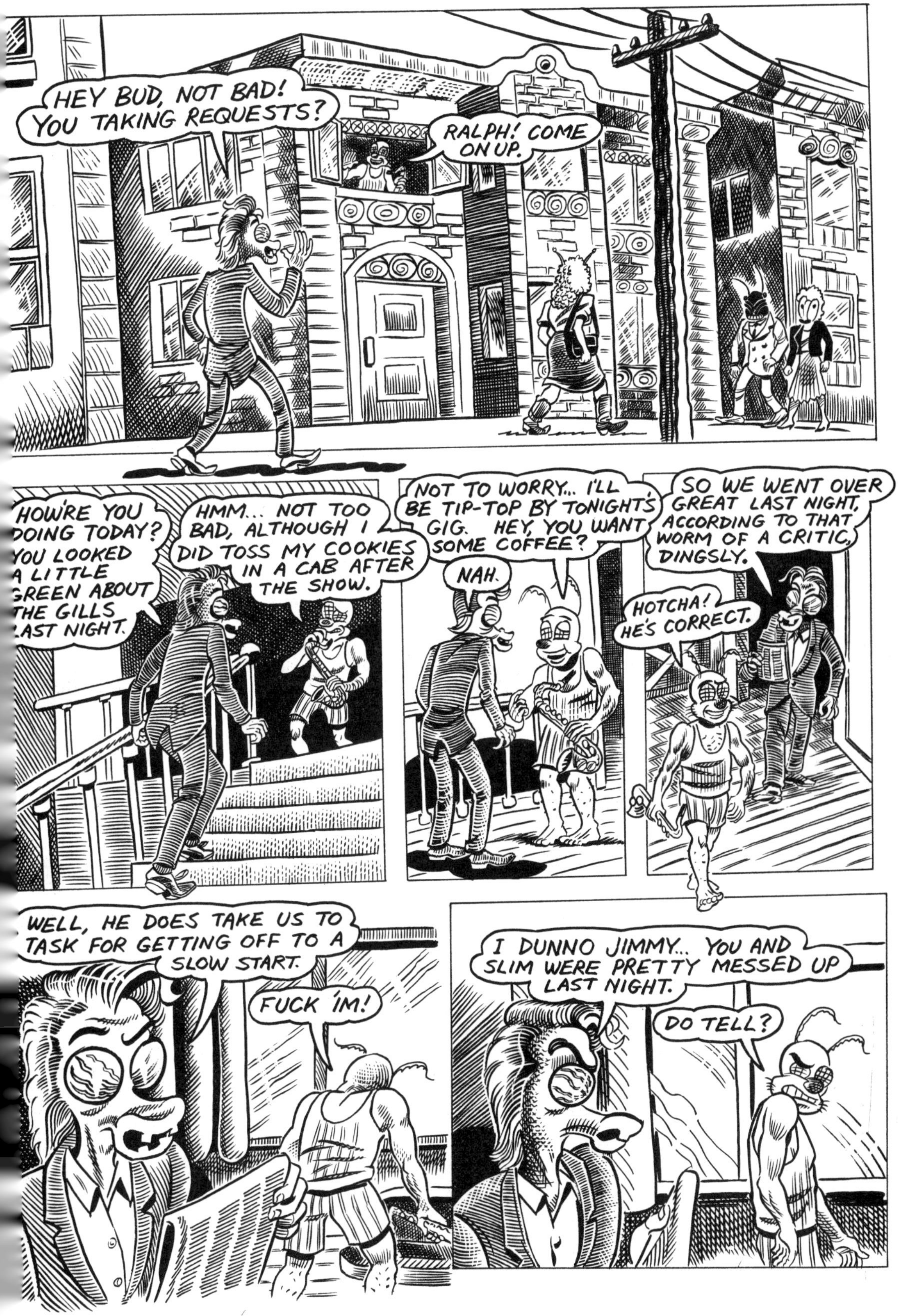
HEY BUD, NOT BAD! YOU TAKING REQUESTS?
RALPH! COME ON UP.
HOW'RE YOU DOING TODAY? YOU LOOKED A LITTLE GREEN ABOUT THE GILLS LAST NIGHT.
HMM... NOT TOO BAD, ALTHOUGH I DID TOSS MY COOKIES IN A CAB AFTER THE SHOW.
NOT TO WORRY... I'LL BE TIP-TOP BY TONIGHT'S GIG. HEY, YOU WANT SOME COFFEE?
NAH.
SO WE WENT OVER GREAT LAST NIGHT, ACCORDING TO THAT WORM OF A CRITIC, DINGSLY.
HOTCHA! HE'S CORRECT.
WELL, HE DOES TAKE US TO TASK FOR GETTING OFF TO A SLOW START.
FUCK 'IM!
I DUNNO JIMMY... YOU AND SLIM WERE PRETTY MESSED UP LAST NIGHT.
DO TELL?

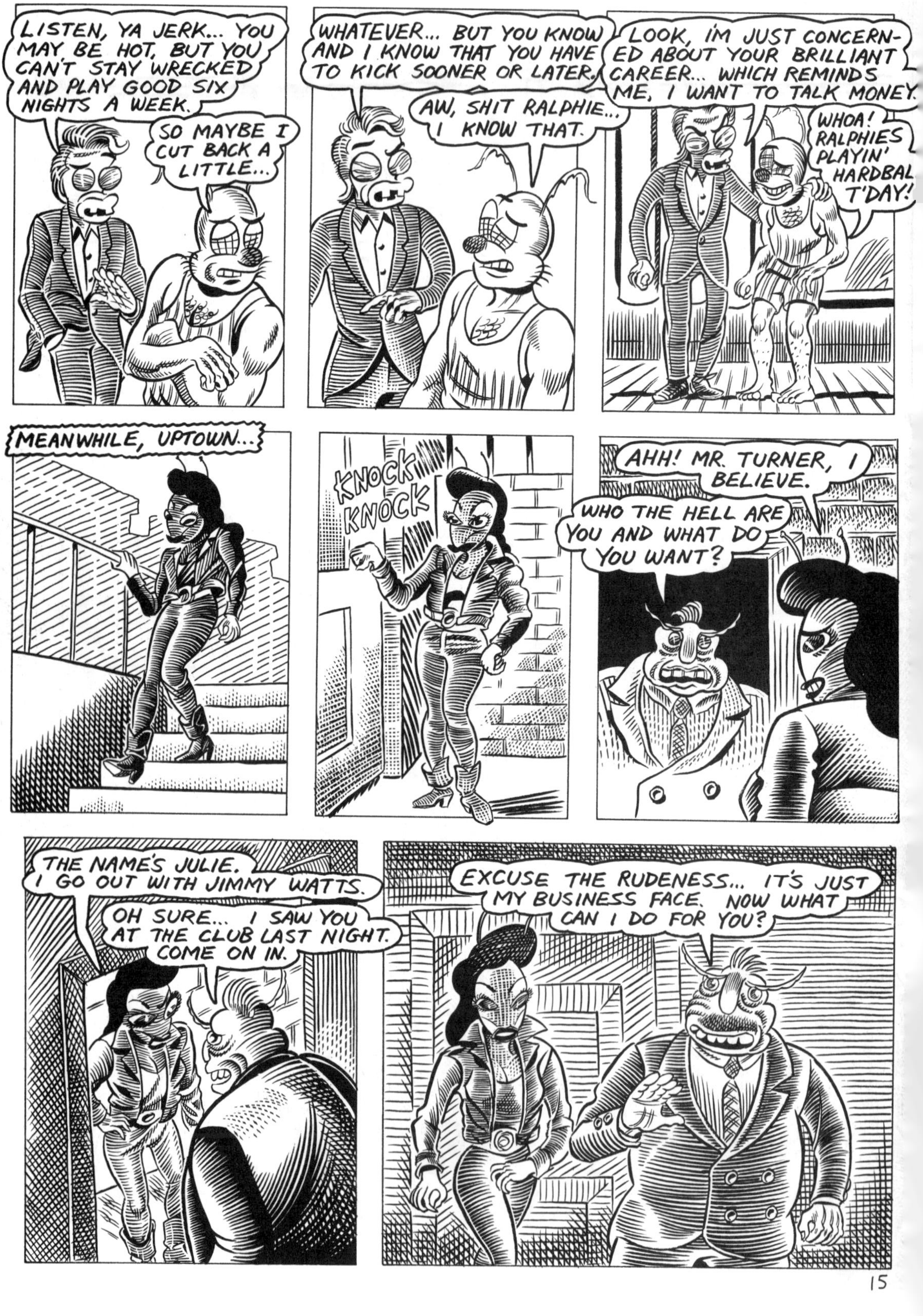
LISTEN, YA JERK... YOU MAY BE HOT, BUT YOU CAN'T STAY WRECKED AND PLAY GOOD SIX NIGHTS A WEEK.
SO MAYBE I CUT BACK A LITTLE...
WHATEVER... BUT YOU KNOW AND I KNOW THAT YOU HAVE TO KICK SOONER OR LATER.
AW, SHIT RALPHIE... I KNOW THAT.
LOOK, I'M JUST CONCERNED ABOUT YOUR BRILLIANT CAREER... WHICH REMINDS ME, I WANT TO TALK MONEY.
WHOA! RALPHIES PLAYIN' HARDBAL T'DAY!
MEANWHILE, UPTOWN...
KNOCK KNOCK
AHH! MR. TURNER, I BELIEVE.
WHO THE HELL ARE YOU AND WHAT DO YOU WANT?
THE NAME'S JULIE. I GO OUT WITH JIMMY WATTS.
OH SURE... I SAW YOU AT THE CLUB LAST NIGHT. COME ON IN.
EXCUSE THE RUDENESS... IT'S JUST MY BUSINESS FACE. NOW WHAT CAN I DO FOR YOU?

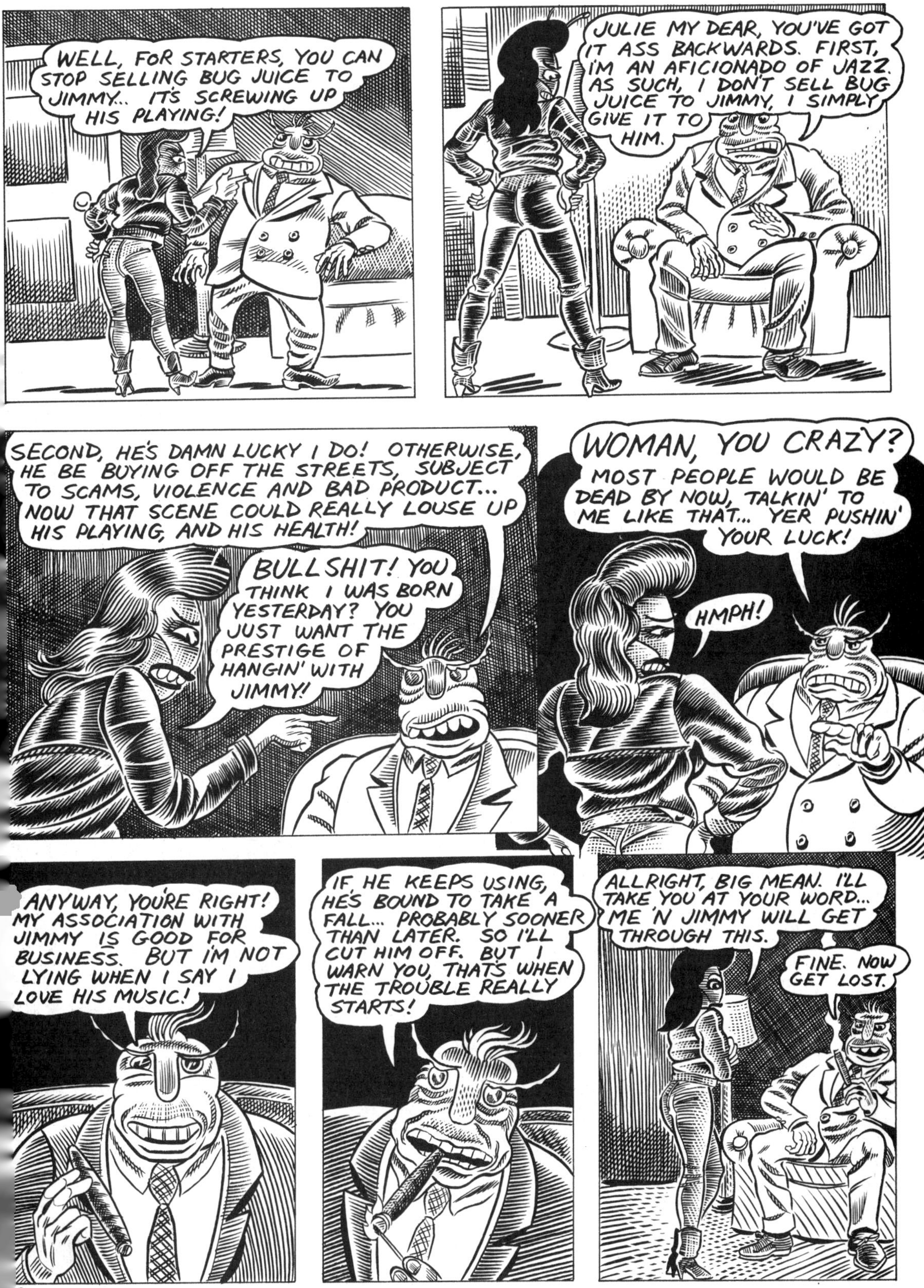
WELL, FOR STARTERS, YOU CAN STOP SELLING BUG JUICE TO JIMMY... IT'S SCREWING UP HIS PLAYING!
JULIE MY DEAR, YOU'VE GOT IT ASS BACKWARDS. FIRST, I'M AN AFICIONADO OF JAZZ. AS SUCH, I DON'T SELL BUG JUICE TO JIMMY, I SIMPLY GIVE IT TO HIM.
SECOND, HE'S DAMN LUCKY I DO! OTHERWISE, HE BE BUYING OFF THE STREETS, SUBJECT TO SCAMS, VIOLENCE AND BAD PRODUCT... NOW THAT SCENE COULD REALLY LOUSE UP HIS PLAYING, AND HIS HEALTH!
BULLSHIT! YOU THINK I WAS BORN YESTERDAY? YOU JUST WANT THE PRESTIGE OF HANGIN' WITH JIMMY!
WOMAN, YOU CRAZY? MOST PEOPLE WOULD BE DEAD BY NOW, TALKIN' TO ME LIKE THAT... YER PUSHIN' YOUR LUCK!
HMPH!
ANYWAY, YOU'RE RIGHT! MY ASSOCIATION WITH JIMMY IS GOOD FOR BUSINESS. BUT I'M NOT LYING WHEN I SAY I LOVE HIS MUSIC!
IF HE KEEPS USING, HE'S BOUND TO TAKE A FALL... PROBABLY SOONER THAN LATER. SO I'LL CUT HIM OFF. BUT I WARN YOU, THAT'S WHEN THE TROUBLE REALLY STARTS!
ALLRIGHT, BIG MEAN. I'LL TAKE YOU AT YOUR WORD... ME 'N JIMMY WILL GET THROUGH THIS.
FINE. NOW GET LOST.

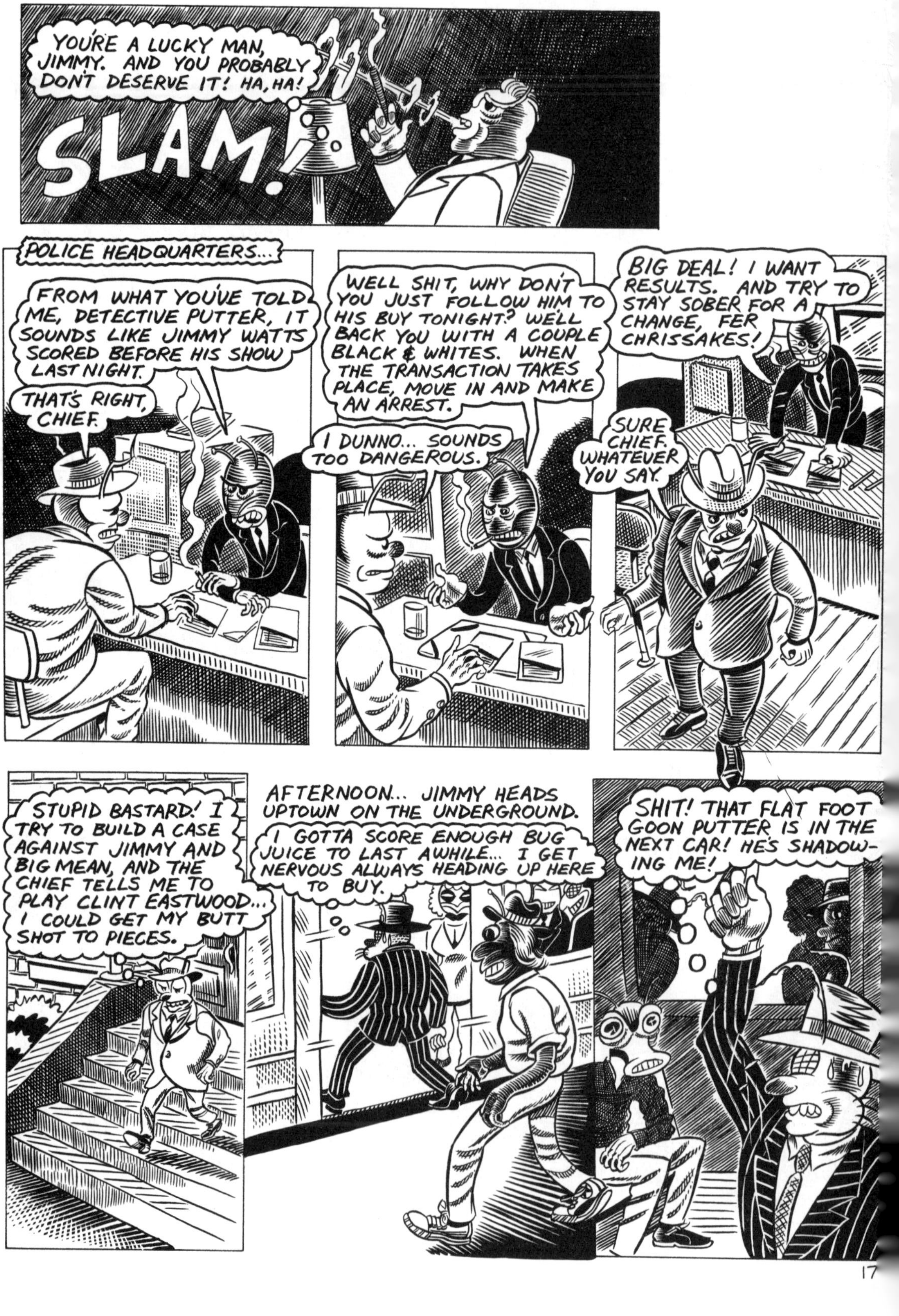
YOU'RE A LUCKY MAN, JIMMY. AND YOU PROBABLY DON'T DESERVE IT! HA, HA!
SLAM!
POLICE HEADQUARTERS...
FROM WHAT YOU'VE TOLD ME, DETECTIVE PUTTER, IT SOUNDS LIKE JIMMY WATTS SCORED BEFORE HIS SHOW LAST NIGHT.
THAT'S RIGHT, CHIEF.
WELL SHIT, WHY DON'T YOU JUST FOLLOW HIM TO HIS BUY TONIGHT? WE'LL BACK YOU WITH A COUPLE BLACK & WHITES. WHEN THE TRANSACTION TAKES PLACE, MOVE IN AND MAKE AN ARREST.
I DUNNO... SOUNDS TOO DANGEROUS.
BIG DEAL! I WANT RESULTS. AND TRY TO STAY SOBER FOR A CHANGE, FER CHRISSAKES!
SURE CHIEF. WHATEVER YOU SAY.
STUPID BASTARD! I TRY TO BUILD A CASE AGAINST JIMMY AND BIG MEAN, AND THE CHIEF TELLS ME TO PLAY CLINT EASTWOOD... I COULD GET MY BUTT SHOT TO PIECES.
AFTERNOON... JIMMY HEADS UPTOWN ON THE UNDERGROUND.
I GOTTA SCORE ENOUGH BUG JUICE TO LAST AWHILE... I GET NERVOUS ALWAYS HEADING UP HERE TO BUY.
SHIT! THAT FLAT FOOT GOON PUTTER IS IN THE NEXT CAR! HE'S SHADOWING ME!

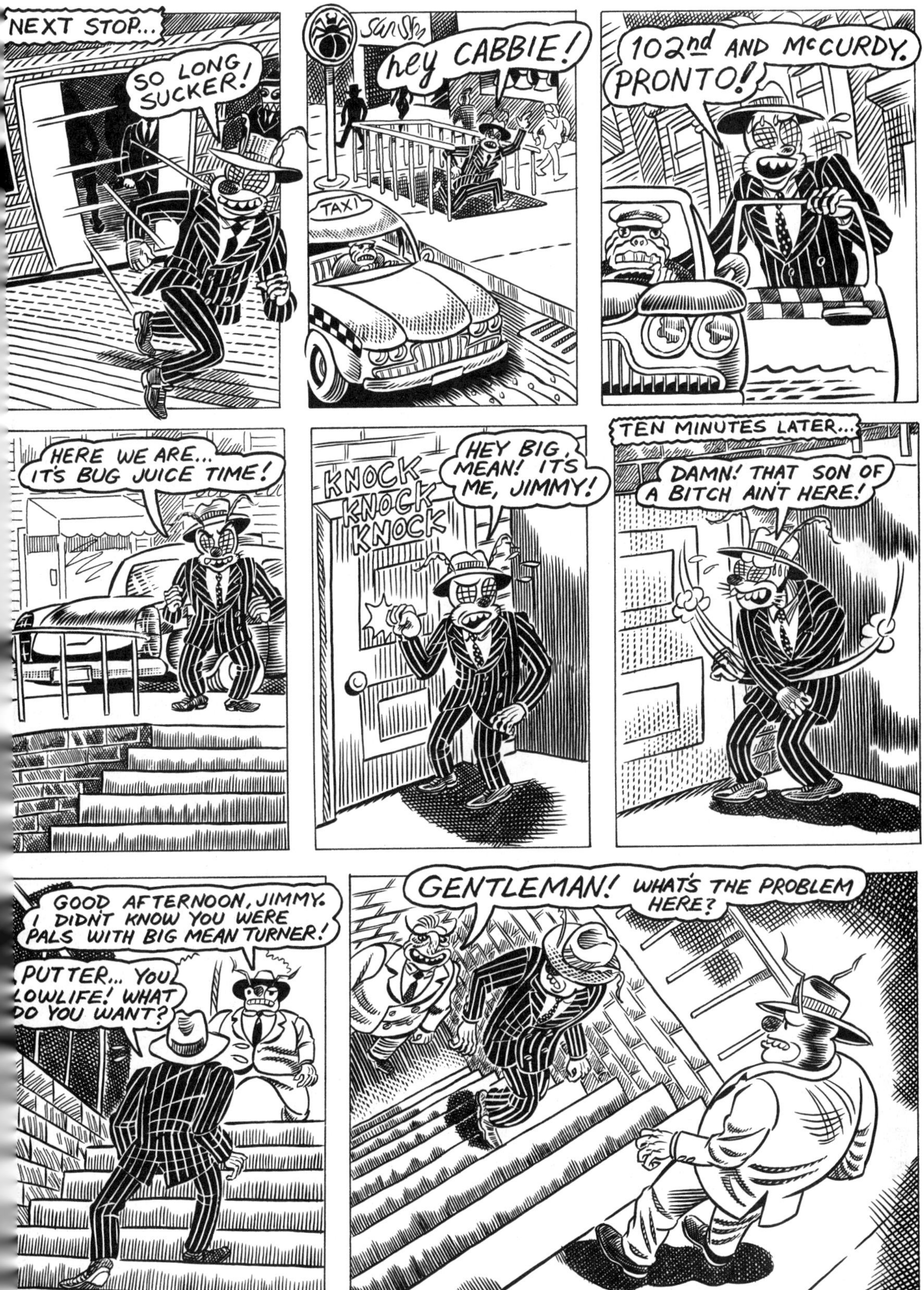

NEXT STOP...
SO LONG SUCKER!
SAN SAN
hey CABBIE!
TAXI
102nd AND McCURDY. PRONTO!
HERE WE ARE... IT'S BUG JUICE TIME!
KNOCK KNOCK KNOCK
HEY BIG MEAN! IT'S ME, JIMMY!
TEN MINUTES LATER...
DAMN! THAT SON OF A BITCH AIN'T HERE!
GOOD AFTERNOON, JIMMY. I DIDN'T KNOW YOU WERE PALS WITH BIG MEAN TURNER!
PUTTER... YOU LOWLIFE! WHAT DO YOU WANT?
GENTLEMAN! WHAT'S THE PROBLEM HERE?

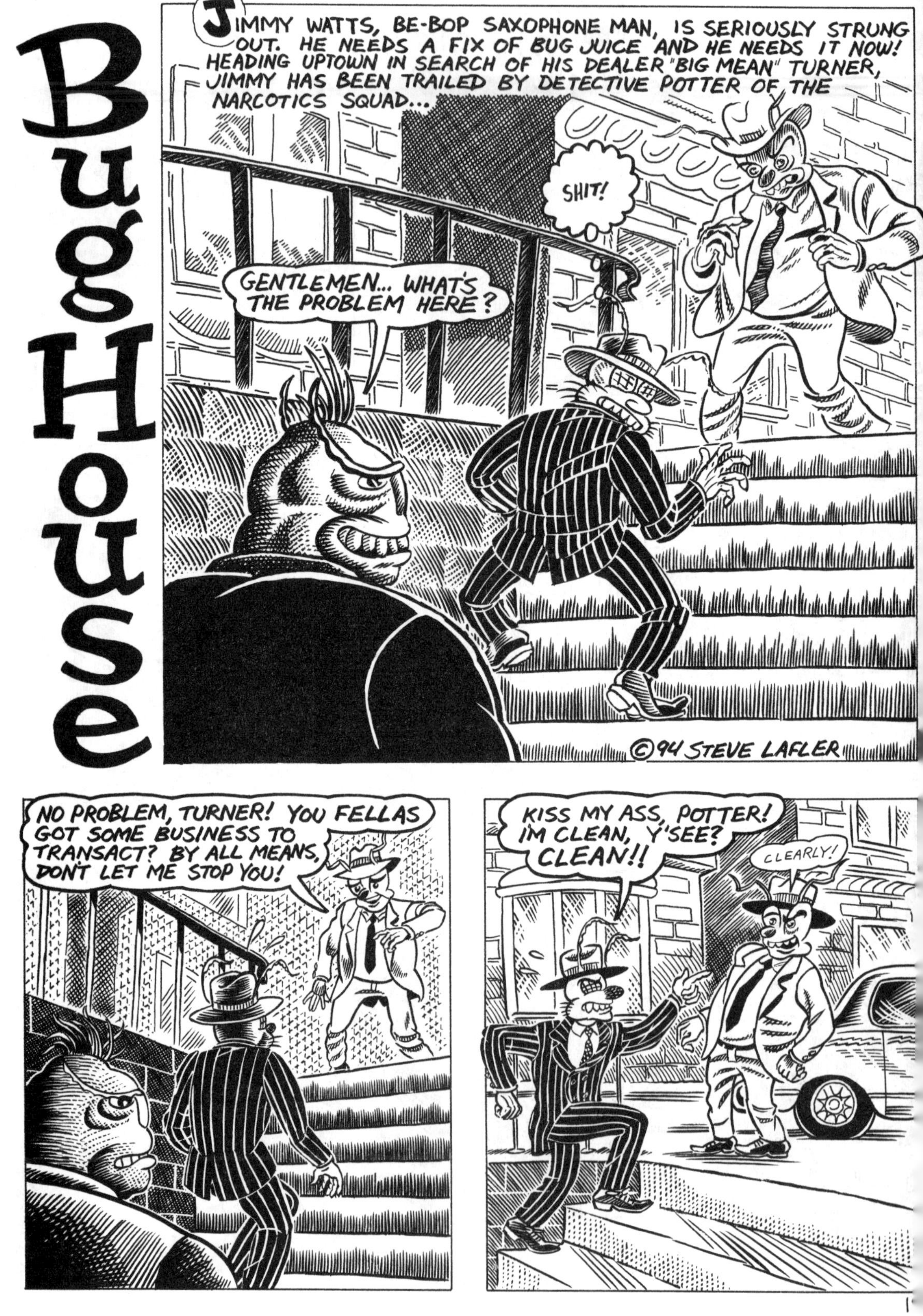
BugHouse
JIMMY WATTS, BE-BOP SAXOPHONE MAN, IS SERIOUSLY STRUNG OUT. HE NEEDS A FIX OF BUG JUICE AND HE NEEDS IT NOW! HEADING UPTOWN IN SEARCH OF HIS DEALER "BIG MEAN" TURNER, JIMMY HAS BEEN TRAILED BY DETECTIVE POTTER OF THE NARCOTICS SQUAD...
SHIT!
GENTLEMEN... WHAT'S THE PROBLEM HERE?
©94 STEVE LAFLER
NO PROBLEM, TURNER! YOU FELLAS GOT SOME BUSINESS TO TRANSACT? BY ALL MEANS, DON'T LET ME STOP YOU!
KISS MY ASS, POTTER! I'M CLEAN, Y'SEE? CLEAN!!
CLEARLY!

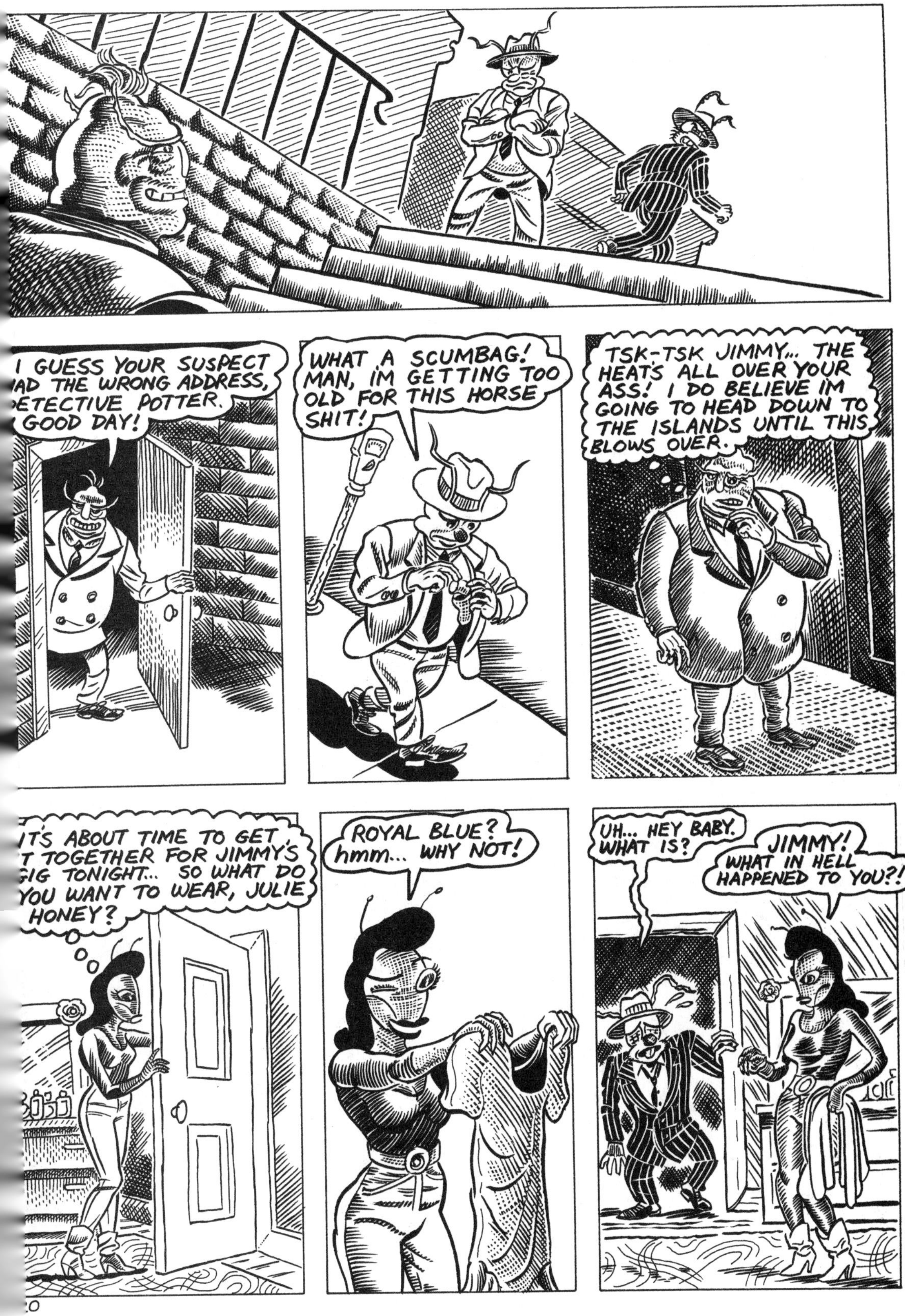
I GUESS YOUR SUSPECT
AD THE WRONG ADDRESS,
ETECTIVE POTTER.
GOOD DAY!
WHAT A SCUMBAG! MAN, IM GETTING TOO OLD FOR THIS HORSE SHIT!
TSK-TSK JIMMY... THE HEAT'S ALL OVER YOUR ASS! I DO BELIEVE IM GOING TO HEAD DOWN TO THE ISLANDS UNTIL THIS BLOWS OVER.
IT'S ABOUT TIME TO GET
T TOGETHER FOR JIMMY'S
GIG TONIGHT... SO WHAT DO
YOU WANT TO WEAR, JULIE
HONEY?
ROYAL BLUE? hmm... WHY NOT!
UH... HEY BABY. WHAT IS?
JIMMY! WHAT IN HELL HAPPENED TO YOU?!

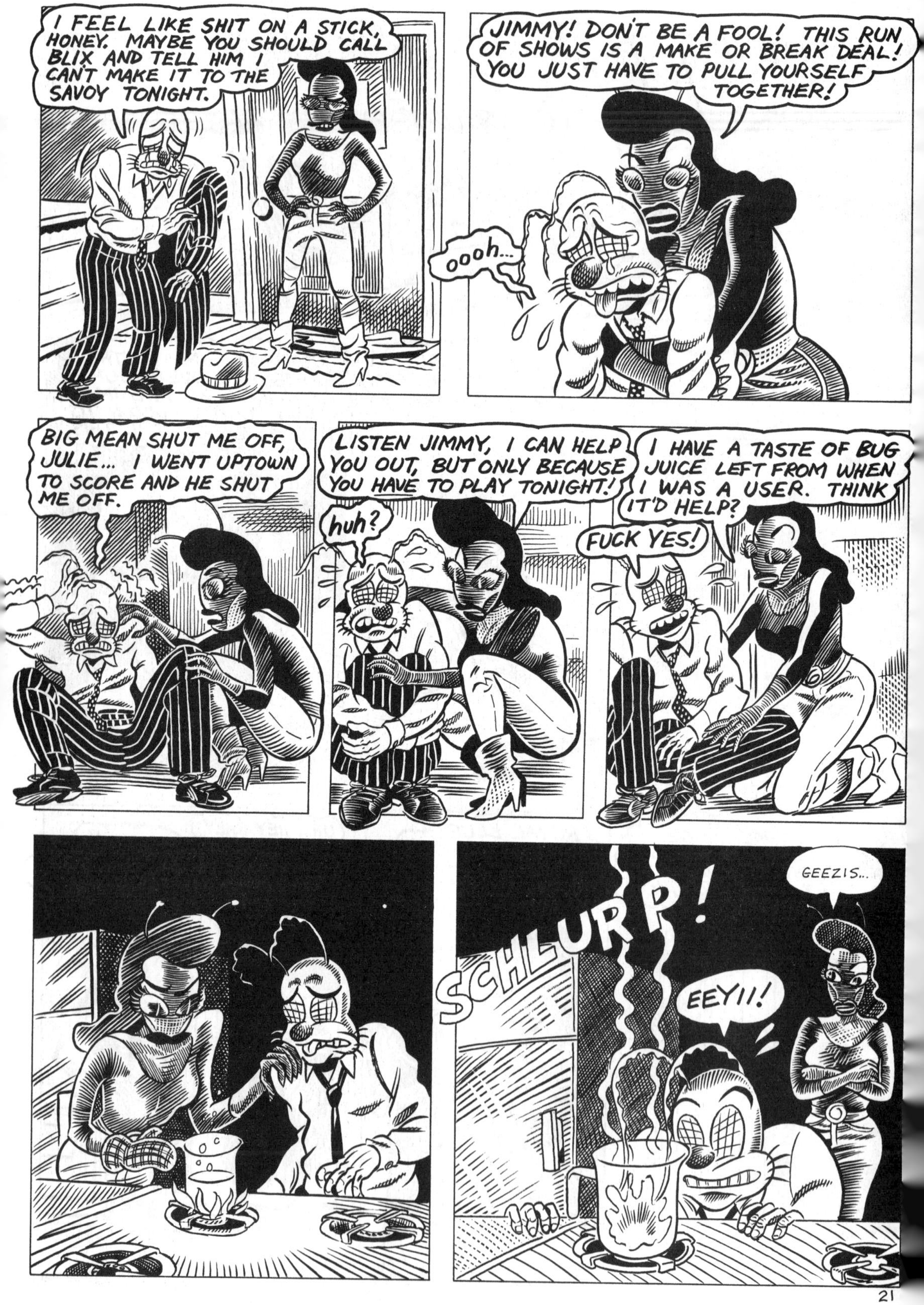

I FEEL LIKE SHIT ON A STICK, HONEY. MAYBE YOU SHOULD CALL BLIX AND TELL HIM I CAN'T MAKE IT TO THE SAVOY TONIGHT.
JIMMY! DON'T BE A FOOL! THIS RUN OF SHOWS IS A MAKE OR BREAK DEAL! YOU JUST HAVE TO PULL YOURSELF TOGETHER!
oooh...
BIG MEAN SHUT ME OFF, JULIE... I WENT UPTOWN TO SCORE AND HE SHUT ME OFF.
LISTEN JIMMY, I CAN HELP YOU OUT, BUT ONLY BECAUSE YOU HAVE TO PLAY TONIGHT!
huh?
I HAVE A TASTE OF BUG JUICE LEFT FROM WHEN I WAS A USER. THINK IT'D HELP?
FUCK YES!
SCHLURP!
GEEZIS...
EEYII!

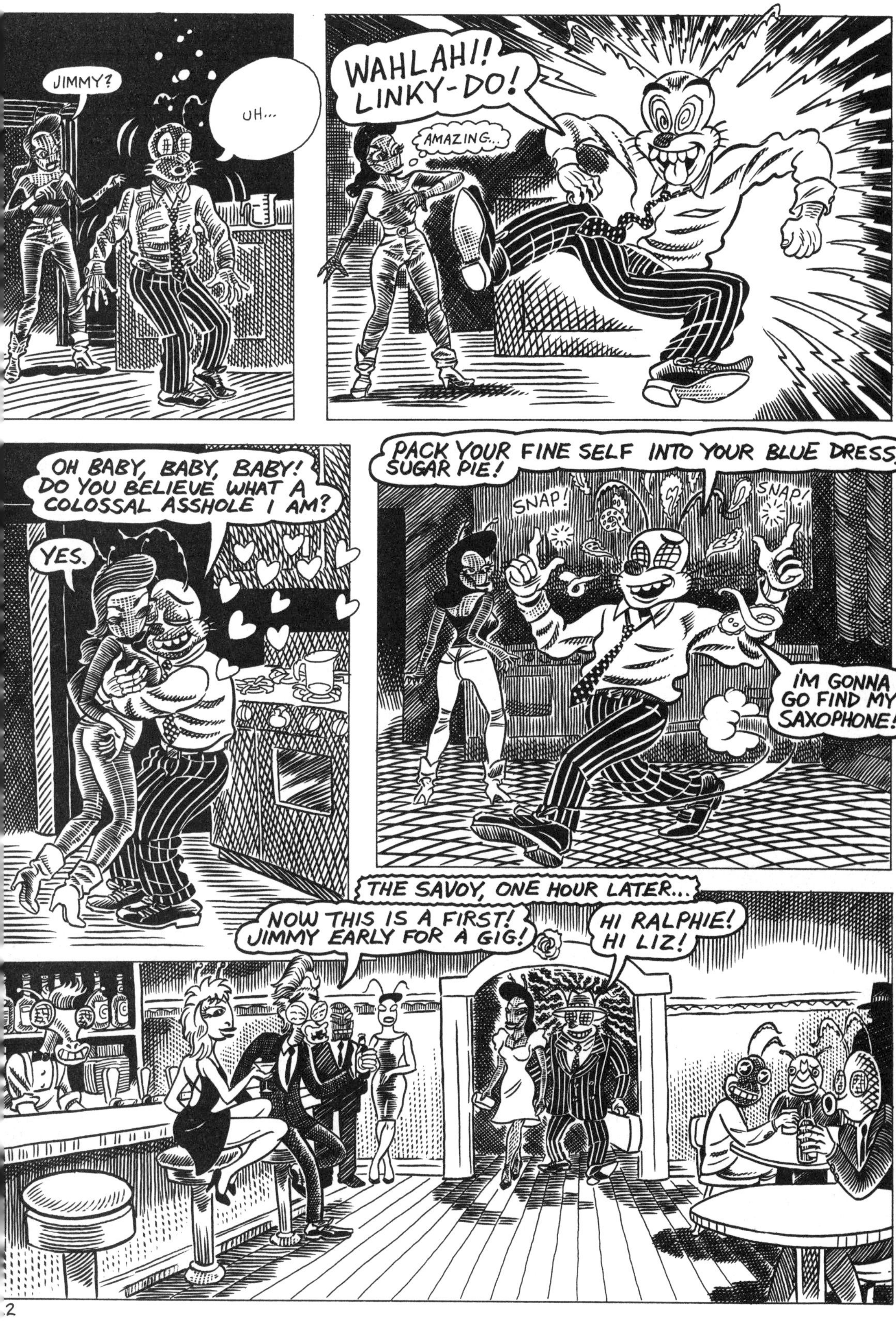
JIMMY?
UH...
WAHLAH!! LINKY-DO!
AMAZING...
OH BABY, BABY, BABY! DO YOU BELIEVE WHAT A COLOSSAL ASSHOLE I AM?
YES.
PACK YOUR FINE SELF INTO YOUR BLUE DRESS, SUGAR PIE!
SNAP!
SNAP!
I'M GONNA GO FIND MY SAXOPHONE!
THE SAVOY, ONE HOUR LATER...
NOW THIS IS A FIRST! JIMMY EARLY FOR A GIG!
HI RALPHIE! HI LIZ!

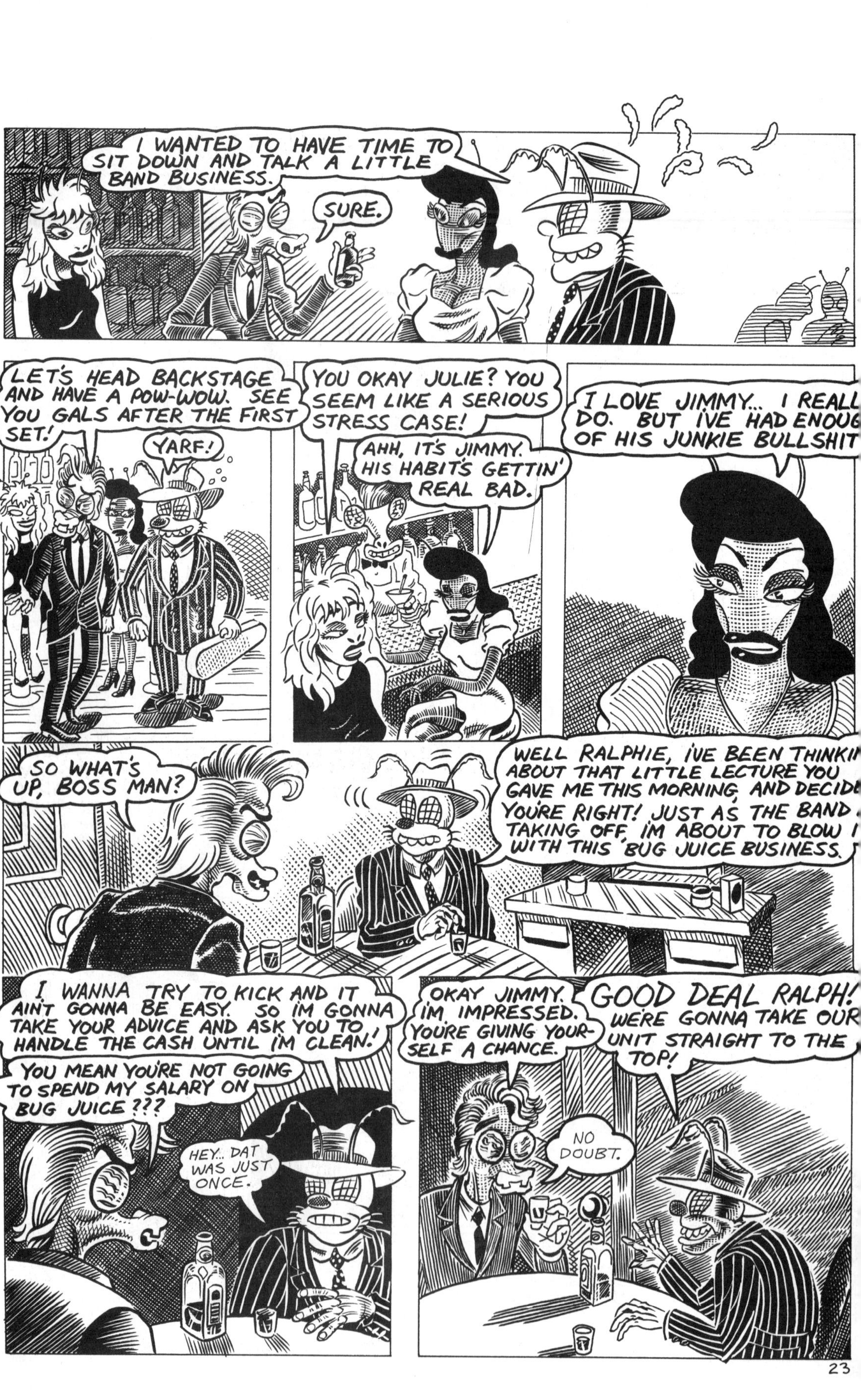
I WANTED TO HAVE TIME TO SIT DOWN AND TALK A LITTLE BAND BUSINESS.
SURE.
LET'S HEAD BACKSTAGE AND HAVE A POW-WOW. SEE YOU GALS AFTER THE FIRST SET!
YARF!
YOU OKAY JULIE? YOU SEEM LIKE A SERIOUS STRESS CASE!
AHH, IT'S JIMMY. HIS HABIT'S GETTIN' REAL BAD.
I LOVE JIMMY... I REALL DO. BUT I'VE HAD ENOUG OF HIS JUNKIE BULLSHIT
SO WHAT'S UP, BOSS MAN?
WELL RALPHIE, I'VE BEEN THINKI ABOUT THAT LITTLE LECTURE YOU GAVE ME THIS MORNING, AND DECID YOU'RE RIGHT! JUST AS THE BAND TAKING OFF, I'M ABOUT TO BLOW I WITH THIS 'BUG JUICE BUSINESS.
I WANNA TRY TO KICK AND IT AIN'T GONNA BE EASY. SO I'M GONNA TAKE YOUR ADVICE AND ASK YOU TO HANDLE THE CASH UNTIL I'M CLEAN!
YOU MEAN YOU'RE NOT GOING TO SPEND MY SALARY ON BUG JUICE???
HEY... DAT WAS JUST ONCE.
OKAY JIMMY. I'M IMPRESSED. YOU'RE GIVING YOURSELF A CHANCE.
GOOD DEAL RALPH! WE'RE GONNA TAKE OUR UNIT STRAIGHT TO THE TOP!
NO DOUBT.

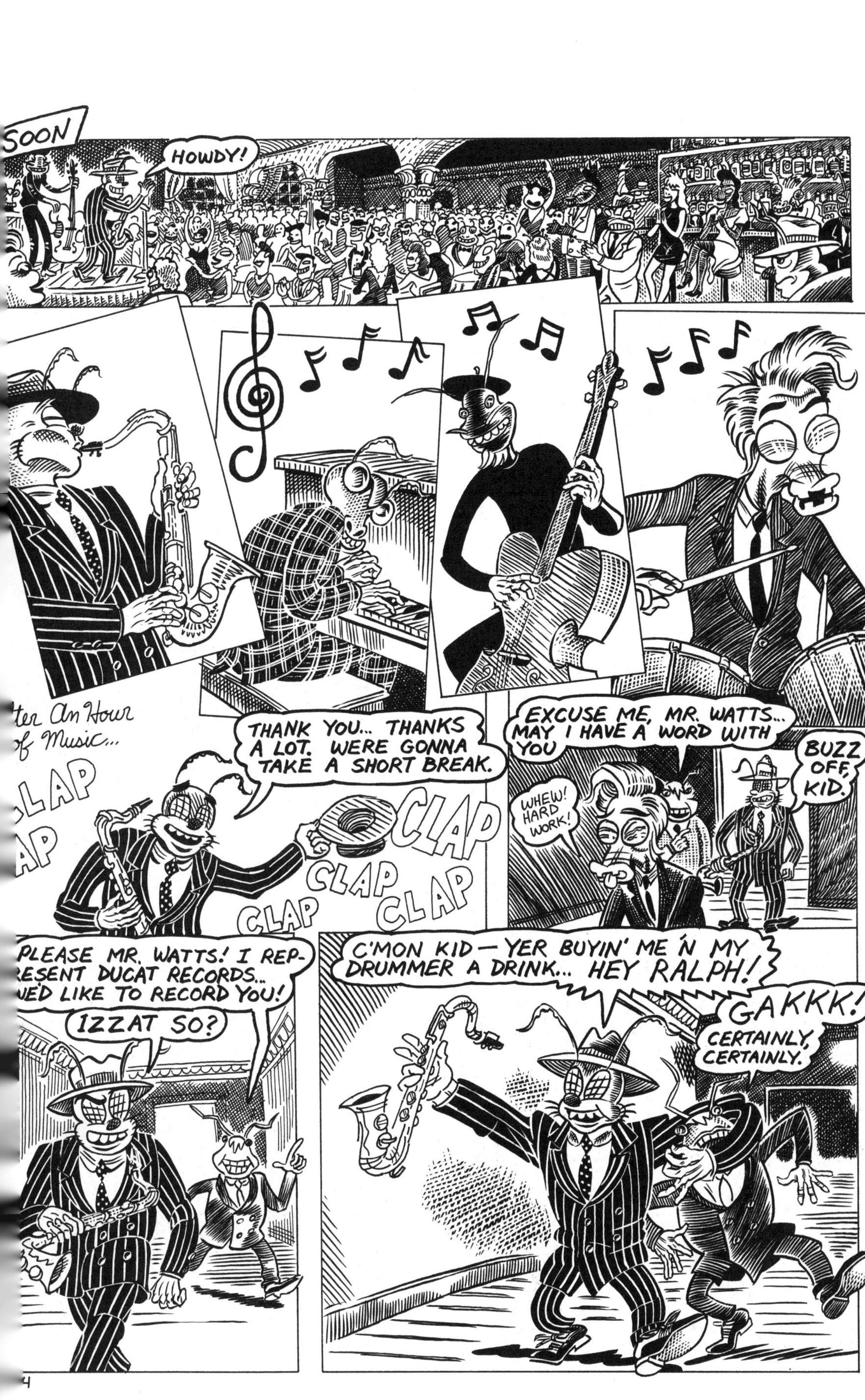

SOON
HOWDY!
...ter An Hour of Music...
THANK YOU... THANKS A LOT. WERE GONNA TAKE A SHORT BREAK.
CLAP CLAP
CLAP CLAP CLAP CLAP
EXCUSE ME, MR. WATTS... MAY I HAVE A WORD WITH YOU
WHEW! HARD WORK!
BUZZ OFF, KID.
PLEASE MR. WATTS! I REPRESENT DUCAT RECORDS... WE'D LIKE TO RECORD YOU!
IZZAT SO?
C'MON KID — YER BUYIN' ME 'N MY DRUMMER A DRINK... HEY RALPH!
GAKKK!
CERTAINLY, CERTAINLY.

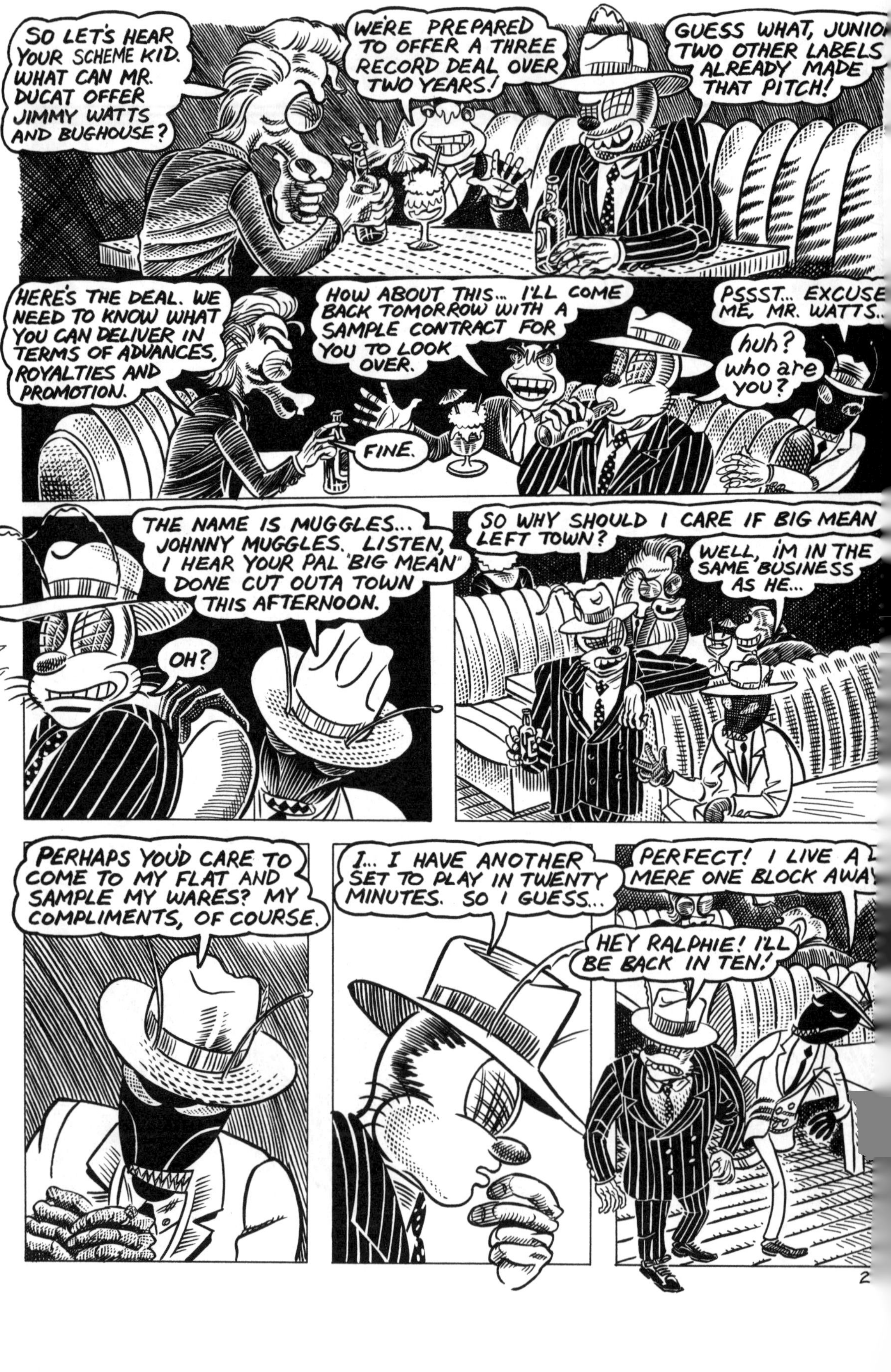
SO LET'S HEAR YOUR SCHEME KID. WHAT CAN MR. DUCAT OFFER JIMMY WATTS AND BUGHOUSE?
WE'RE PREPARED TO OFFER A THREE RECORD DEAL OVER TWO YEARS!
GUESS WHAT, JUNIO TWO OTHER LABELS ALREADY MADE THAT PITCH!
HERE'S THE DEAL. WE NEED TO KNOW WHAT YOU CAN DELIVER IN TERMS OF ADVANCES, ROYALTIES AND PROMOTION.
HOW ABOUT THIS... I'LL COME BACK TOMORROW WITH A SAMPLE CONTRACT FOR YOU TO LOOK OVER.
FINE.
PSSST... EXCUSE ME, MR. WATTS...
huh? who are you?
THE NAME IS MUGGLES... JOHNNY MUGGLES. LISTEN, I HEAR YOUR PAL "BIG MEAN" DONE CUT OUTA TOWN THIS AFTERNOON.
OH?
SO WHY SHOULD I CARE IF BIG MEAN LEFT TOWN?
WELL, I'M IN THE SAME BUSINESS AS HE...
PERHAPS YOU'D CARE TO COME TO MY FLAT AND SAMPLE MY WARES? MY COMPLIMENTS, OF COURSE.
I... I HAVE ANOTHER SET TO PLAY IN TWENTY MINUTES. SO I GUESS...
PERFECT! I LIVE A MERE ONE BLOCK AWA
HEY RALPHIE! I'LL BE BACK IN TEN!

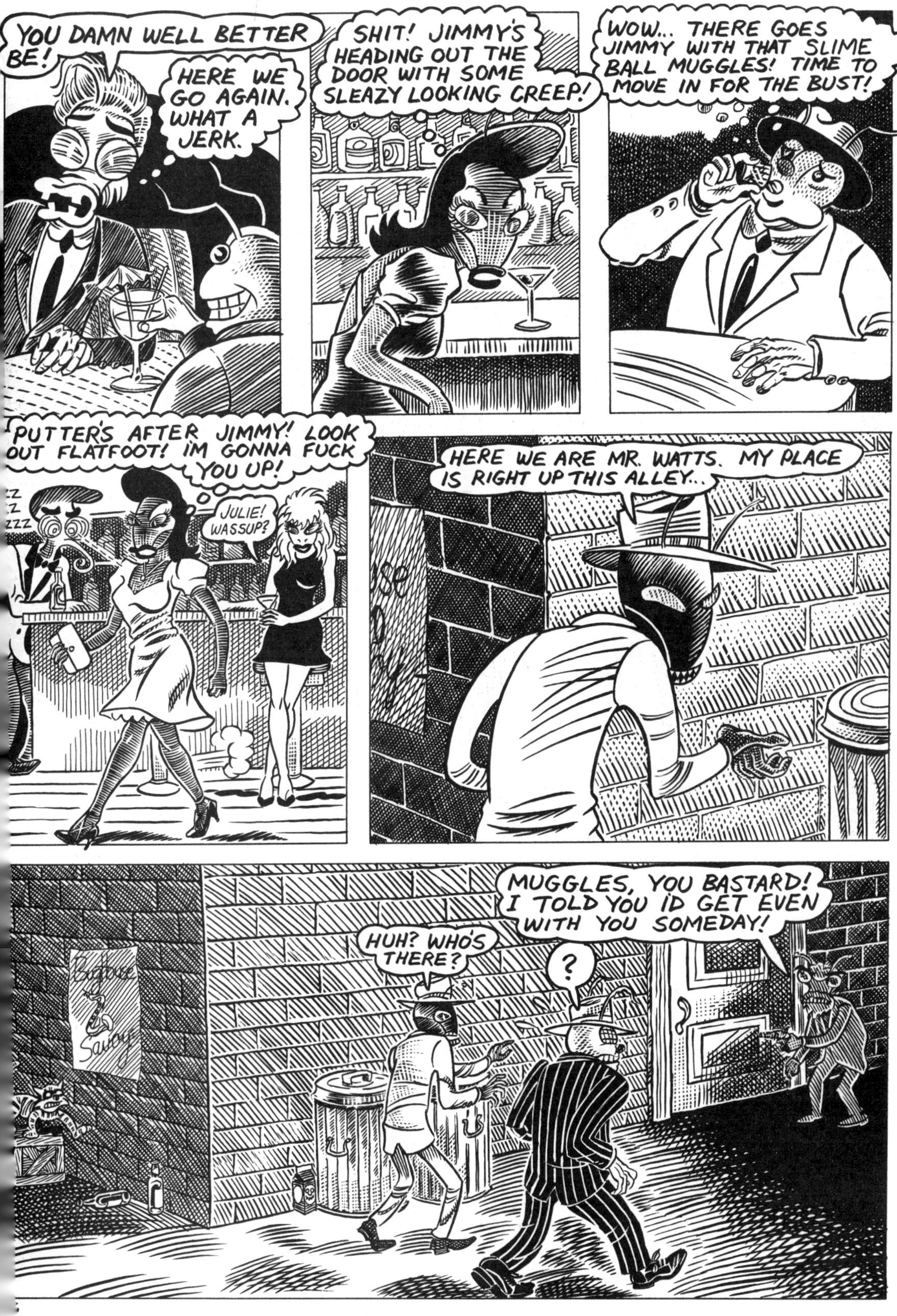
YOU DAMN WELL BETTER BE!
HERE WE GO AGAIN. WHAT A JERK.
SHIT! JIMMY'S HEADING OUT THE DOOR WITH SOME SLEAZY LOOKING CREEP!
WOW... THERE GOES JIMMY WITH THAT SLIME BALL MUGGLES! TIME TO MOVE IN FOR THE BUST!
PUTTER'S AFTER JIMMY! LOOK OUT FLATFOOT! IM GONNA FUCK YOU UP!
JULIE! WASSUP?
ZZ Z ZZZ
HERE WE ARE MR. WATTS. MY PLACE IS RIGHT UP THIS ALLEY...
HUH? WHO'S THERE?
?
MUGGLES, YOU BASTARD! I TOLD YOU ID GET EVEN WITH YOU SOMEDAY!

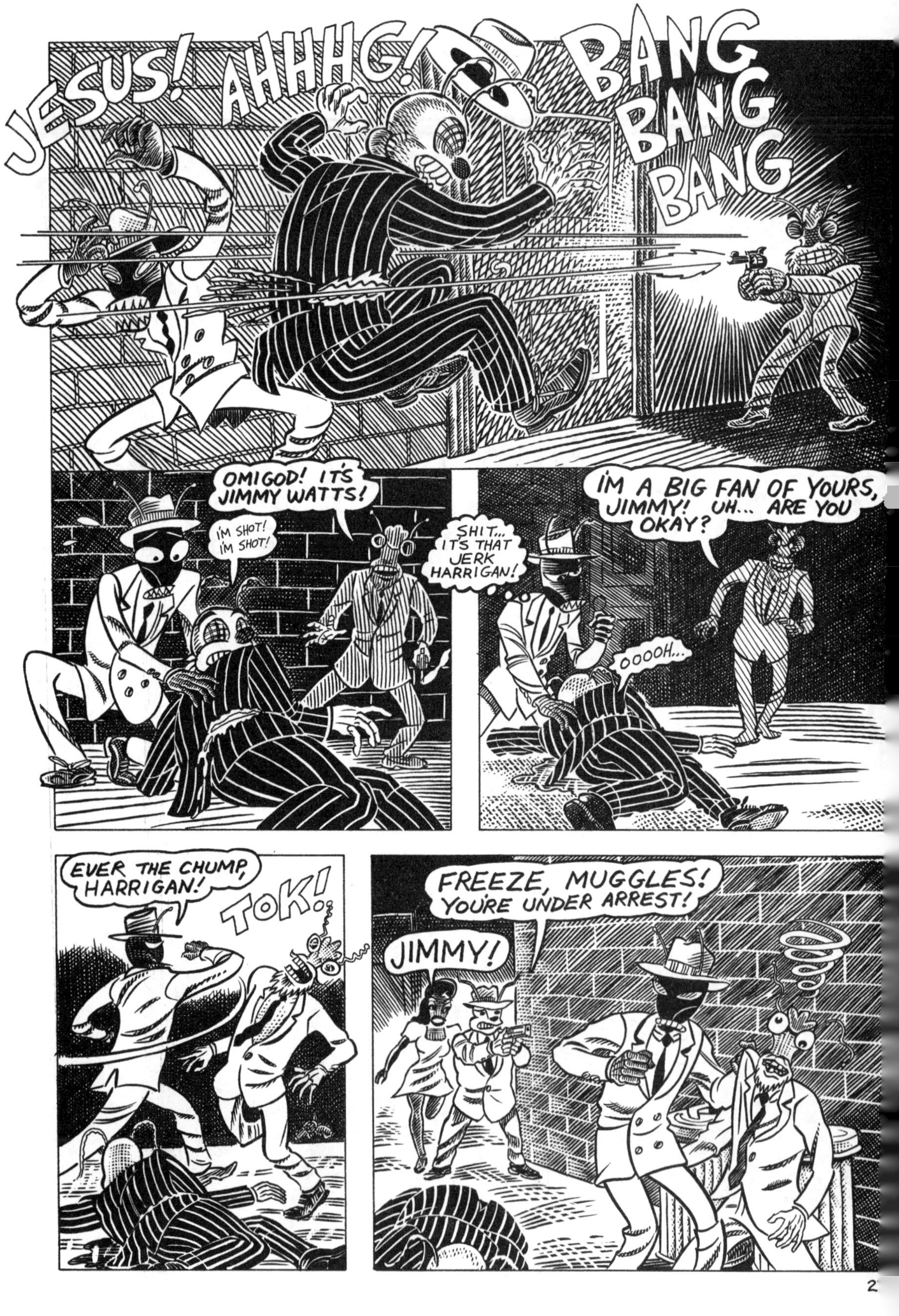
JESUS!
AHHHG!
BANG
BANG
BANG
OMIGOD! IT'S JIMMY WATTS!
I'M SHOT! I'M SHOT!
SHIT... IT'S THAT JERK HARRIGAN!
I'M A BIG FAN OF YOURS, JIMMY! UH... ARE YOU OKAY?
OOOOH...
EVER THE CHUMP, HARRIGAN!
TOK!
FREEZE, MUGGLES! YOU'RE UNDER ARREST!
JIMMY!

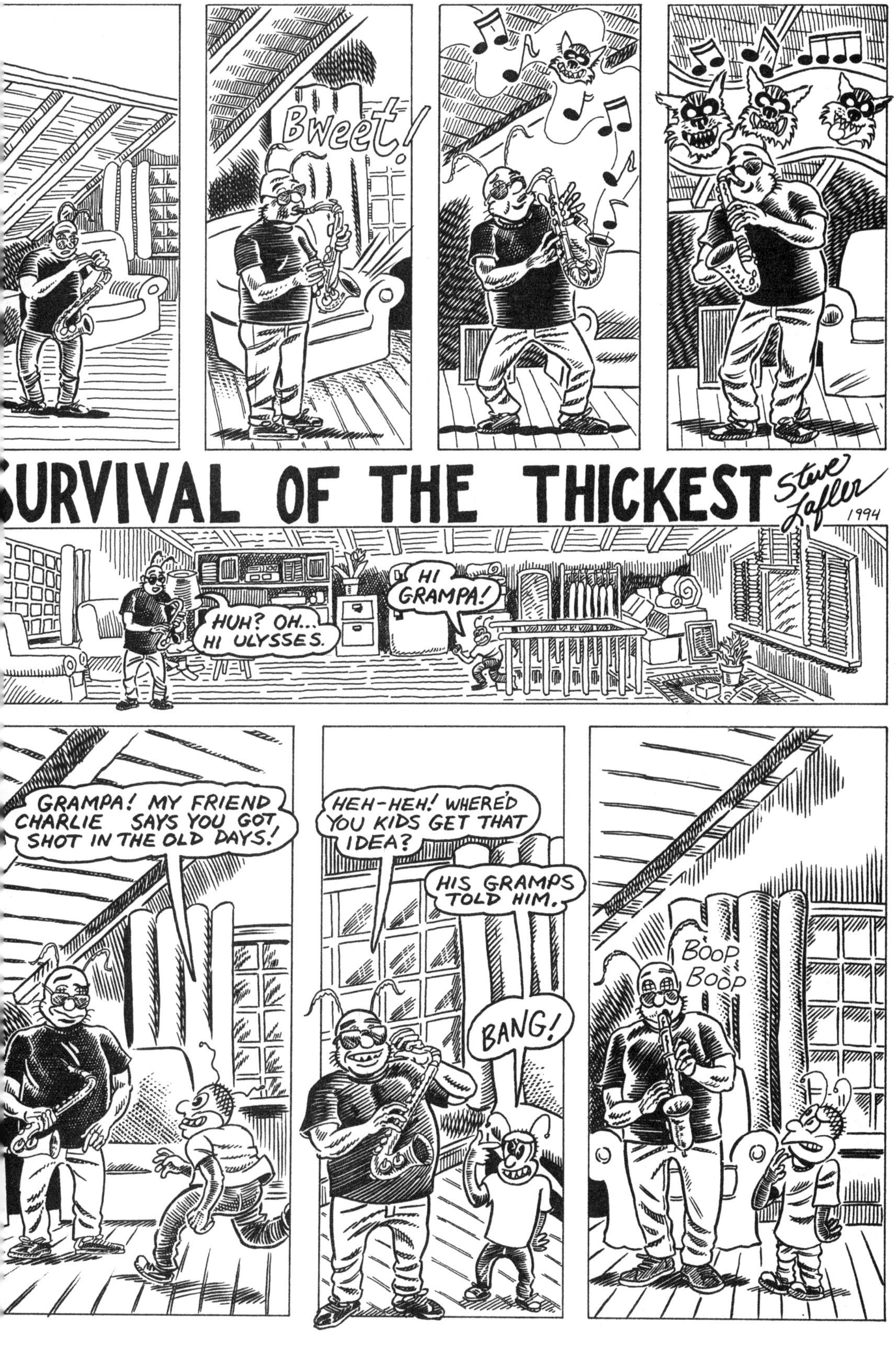
Bweet!
SURVIVAL OF THE THICKEST
Steve Lafler 1994
HI GRAMPA!
HUH? OH... HI ULYSSES.
GRAMPA! MY FRIEND CHARLIE SAYS YOU GOT SHOT IN THE OLD DAYS!
HEH-HEH! WHERE'D YOU KIDS GET THAT IDEA?
HIS GRAMPS TOLD HIM.
BANG!
BOOP BOOP

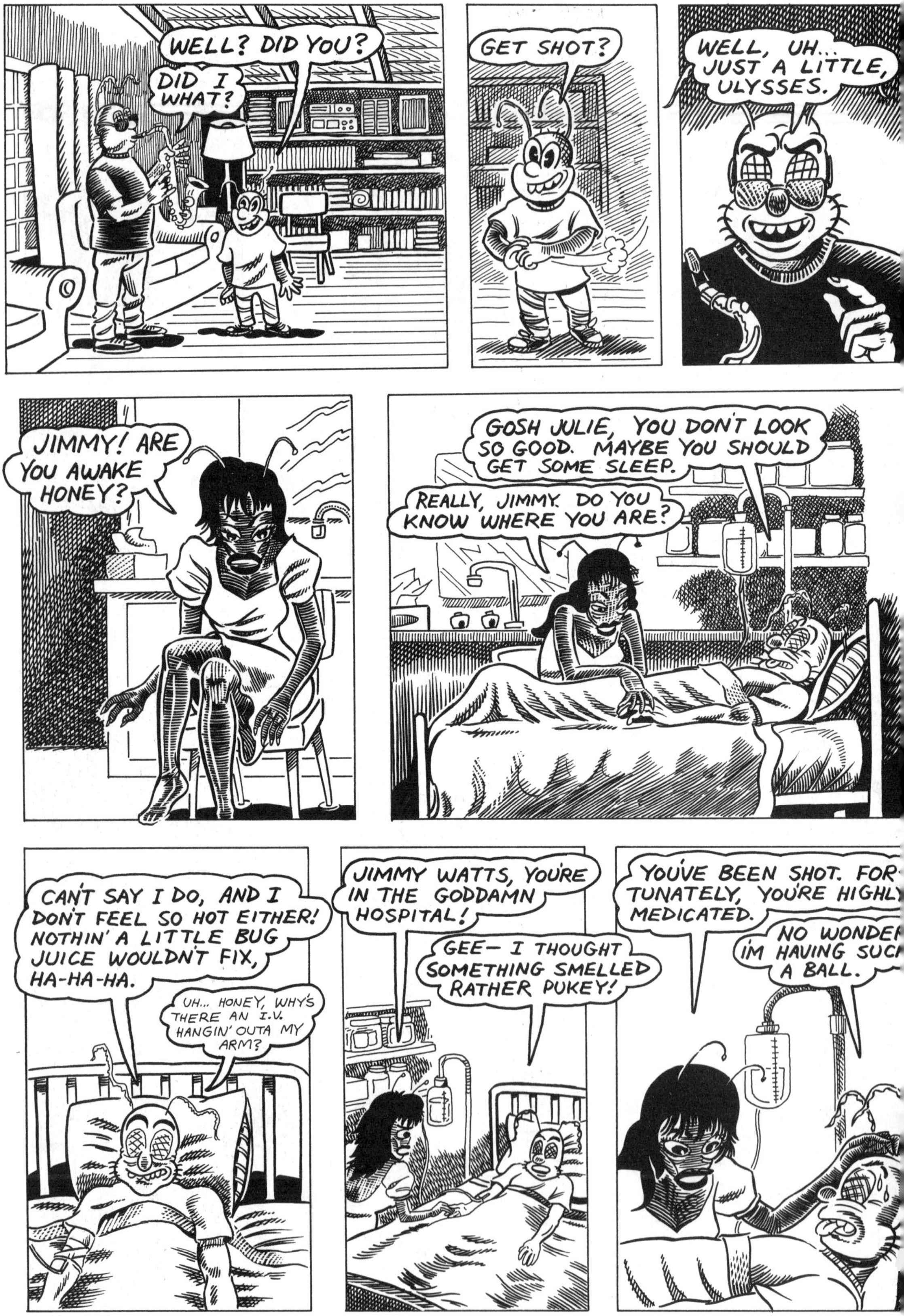
DID I WHAT?
WELL? DID YOU?
GET SHOT?
WELL, UH... JUST A LITTLE, ULYSSES.
JIMMY! ARE YOU AWAKE HONEY?
GOSH JULIE, YOU DON'T LOOK SO GOOD. MAYBE YOU SHOULD GET SOME SLEEP.
REALLY, JIMMY. DO YOU KNOW WHERE YOU ARE?
CAN'T SAY I DO, AND I DON'T FEEL SO HOT EITHER! NOTHIN' A LITTLE BUG JUICE WOULDN'T FIX, HA-HA-HA.
UH... HONEY, WHY'S THERE AN I.V. HANGIN' OUTA MY ARM?
JIMMY WATTS, YOU'RE IN THE GODDAMN HOSPITAL!
GEE— I THOUGHT SOMETHING SMELLED RATHER PUKEY!
YOU'VE BEEN SHOT. FORTUNATELY, YOU'RE HIGHLY MEDICATED.
NO WONDER I'M HAVING SUCH A BALL.

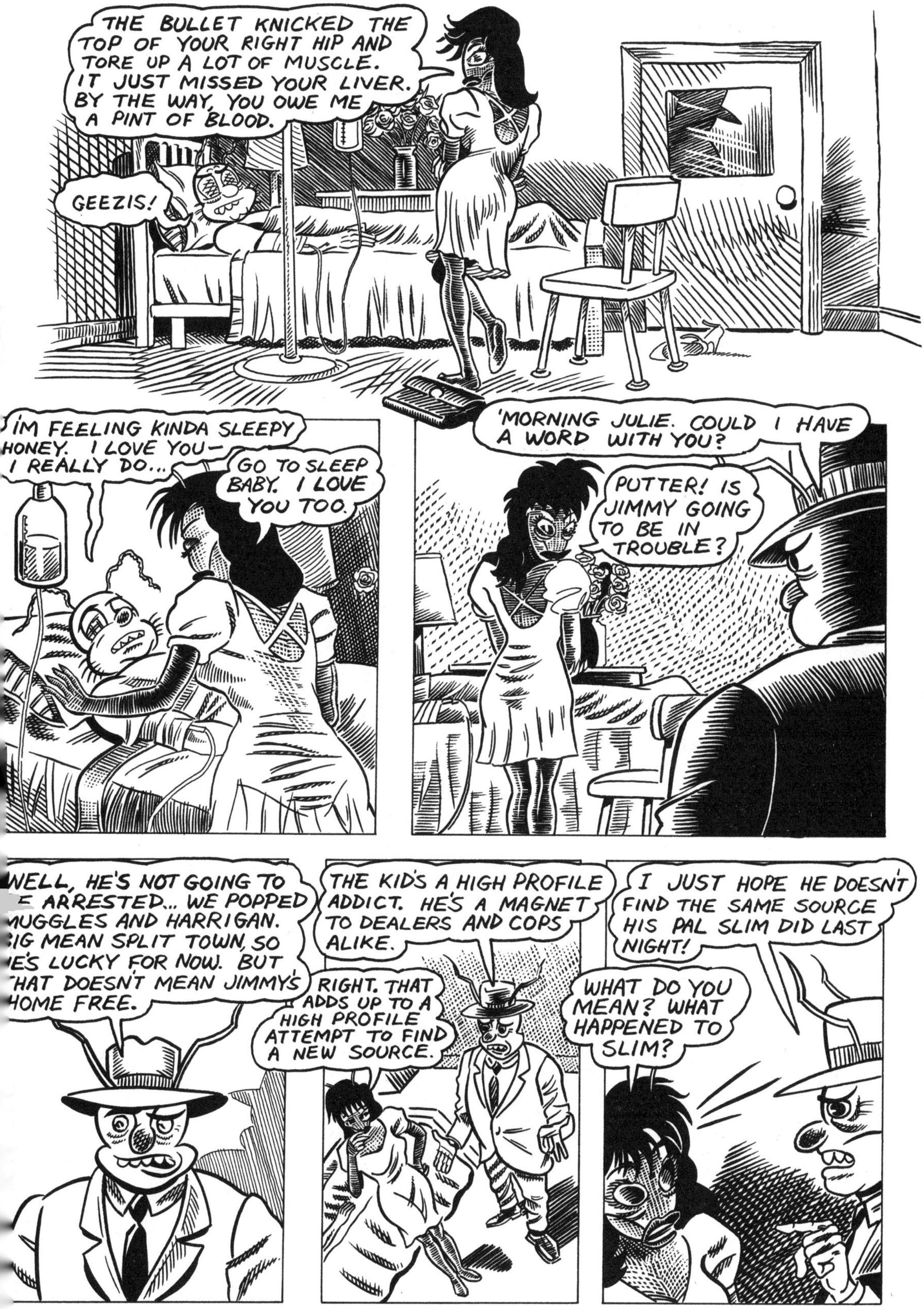
THE BULLET KNICKED THE TOP OF YOUR RIGHT HIP AND TORE UP A LOT OF MUSCLE. IT JUST MISSED YOUR LIVER. BY THE WAY, YOU OWE ME A PINT OF BLOOD.
GEEZIS!
I'M FEELING KINDA SLEEPY HONEY. I LOVE YOU— I REALLY DO...
GO TO SLEEP BABY. I LOVE YOU TOO.
'MORNING JULIE. COULD I HAVE A WORD WITH YOU?
PUTTER! IS JIMMY GOING TO BE IN TROUBLE?
WELL, HE'S NOT GOING TO E ARRESTED... WE POPPED MUGGLES AND HARRIGAN. IG MEAN SPLIT TOWN, SO E'S LUCKY FOR NOW. BUT HAT DOESN'T MEAN JIMMY'S HOME FREE.
THE KID'S A HIGH PROFILE ADDICT. HE'S A MAGNET TO DEALERS AND COPS ALIKE.
RIGHT. THAT ADDS UP TO A HIGH PROFILE ATTEMPT TO FIND A NEW SOURCE.
I JUST HOPE HE DOESN'T FIND THE SAME SOURCE HIS PAL SLIM DID LAST NIGHT!
WHAT DO YOU MEAN? WHAT HAPPENED TO SLIM?

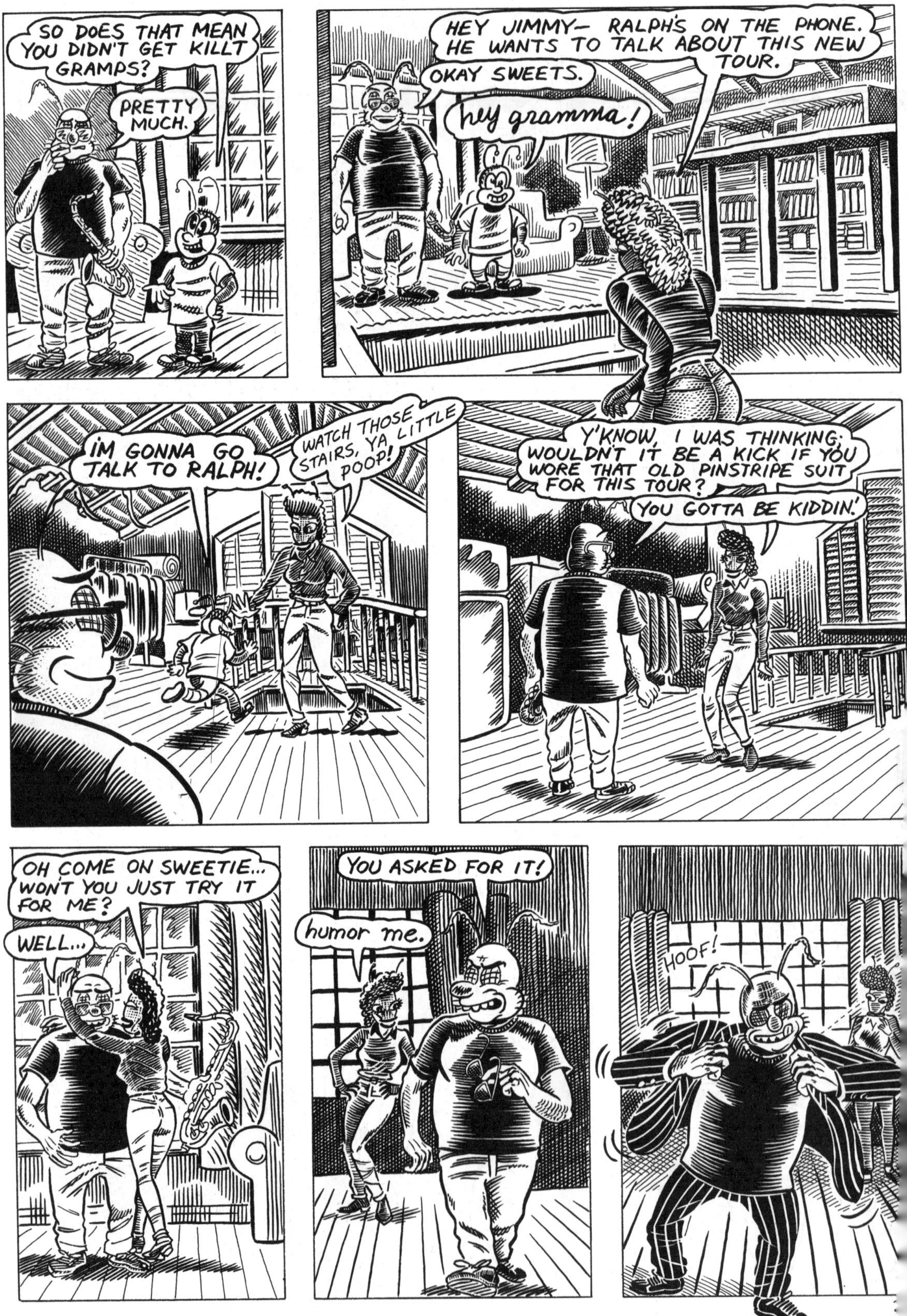

SO DOES THAT MEAN YOU DIDN'T GET KILLT GRAMPS?
PRETTY MUCH.
HEY JIMMY— RALPH'S ON THE PHONE. HE WANTS TO TALK ABOUT THIS NEW TOUR.
OKAY SWEETS.
hey gramma!
I'M GONNA GO TALK TO RALPH!
WATCH THOSE STAIRS, YA LITTLE POOP!
Y'KNOW, I WAS THINKING; WOULDN'T IT BE A KICK IF YOU WORE THAT OLD PINSTRIPE SUIT FOR THIS TOUR?
YOU GOTTA BE KIDDIN'
OH COME ON SWEETIE... WON'T YOU JUST TRY IT FOR ME?
WELL...
YOU ASKED FOR IT!
humor me.
HOOF!

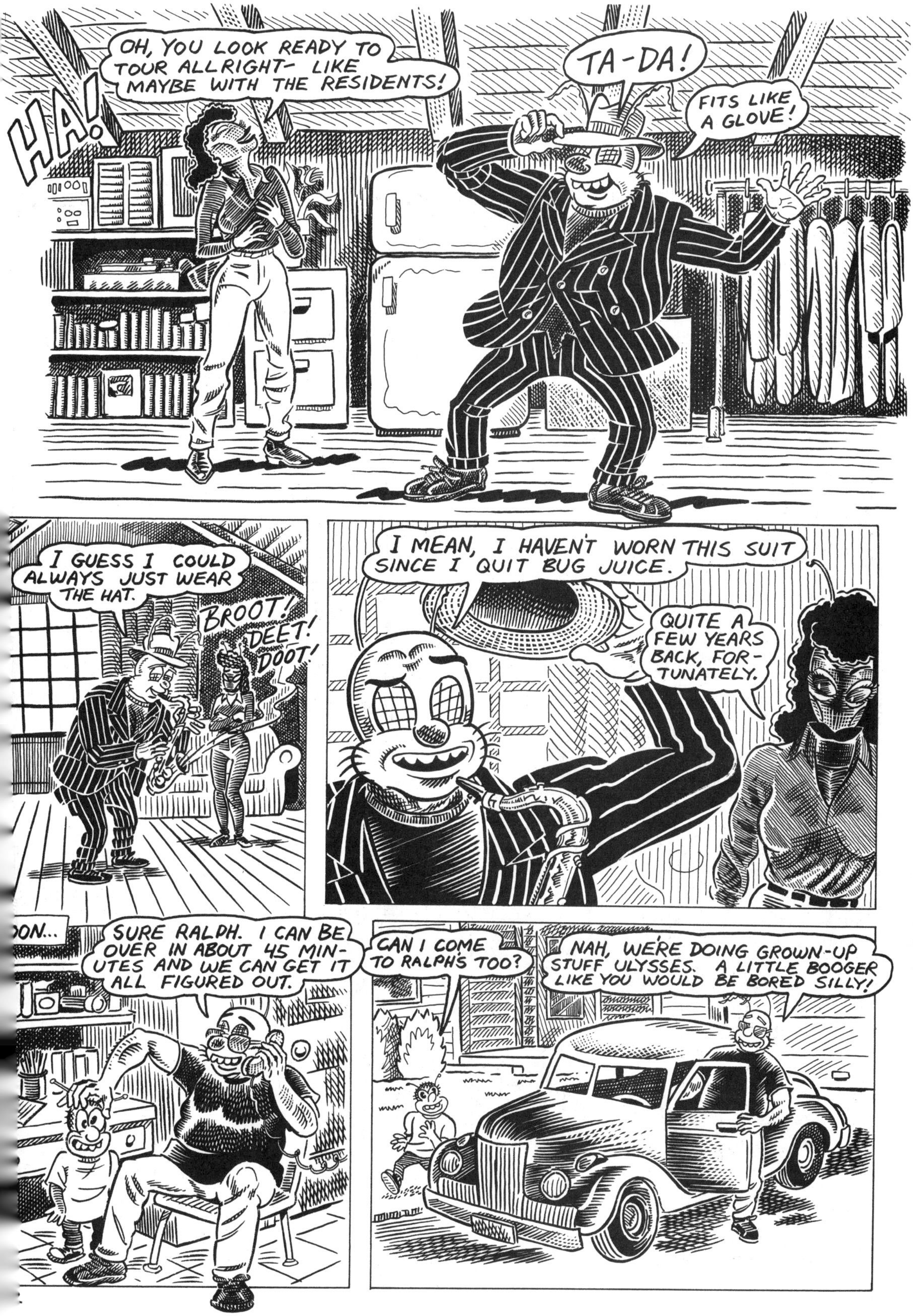
HA!
OH, YOU LOOK READY TO TOUR ALLRIGHT- LIKE MAYBE WITH THE RESIDENTS!
TA-DA!
FITS LIKE A GLOVE!
I GUESS I COULD ALWAYS JUST WEAR THE HAT.
BROOT! DEET! DOOT!
I MEAN, I HAVEN'T WORN THIS SUIT SINCE I QUIT BUG JUICE.
QUITE A FEW YEARS BACK, FORTUNATELY.
...OON...
SURE RALPH. I CAN BE OVER IN ABOUT 45 MINUTES AND WE CAN GET IT ALL FIGURED OUT.
CAN I COME TO RALPH'S TOO?
NAH, WE'RE DOING GROWN-UP STUFF ULYSSES. A LITTLE BOOGER LIKE YOU WOULD BE BORED SILLY!

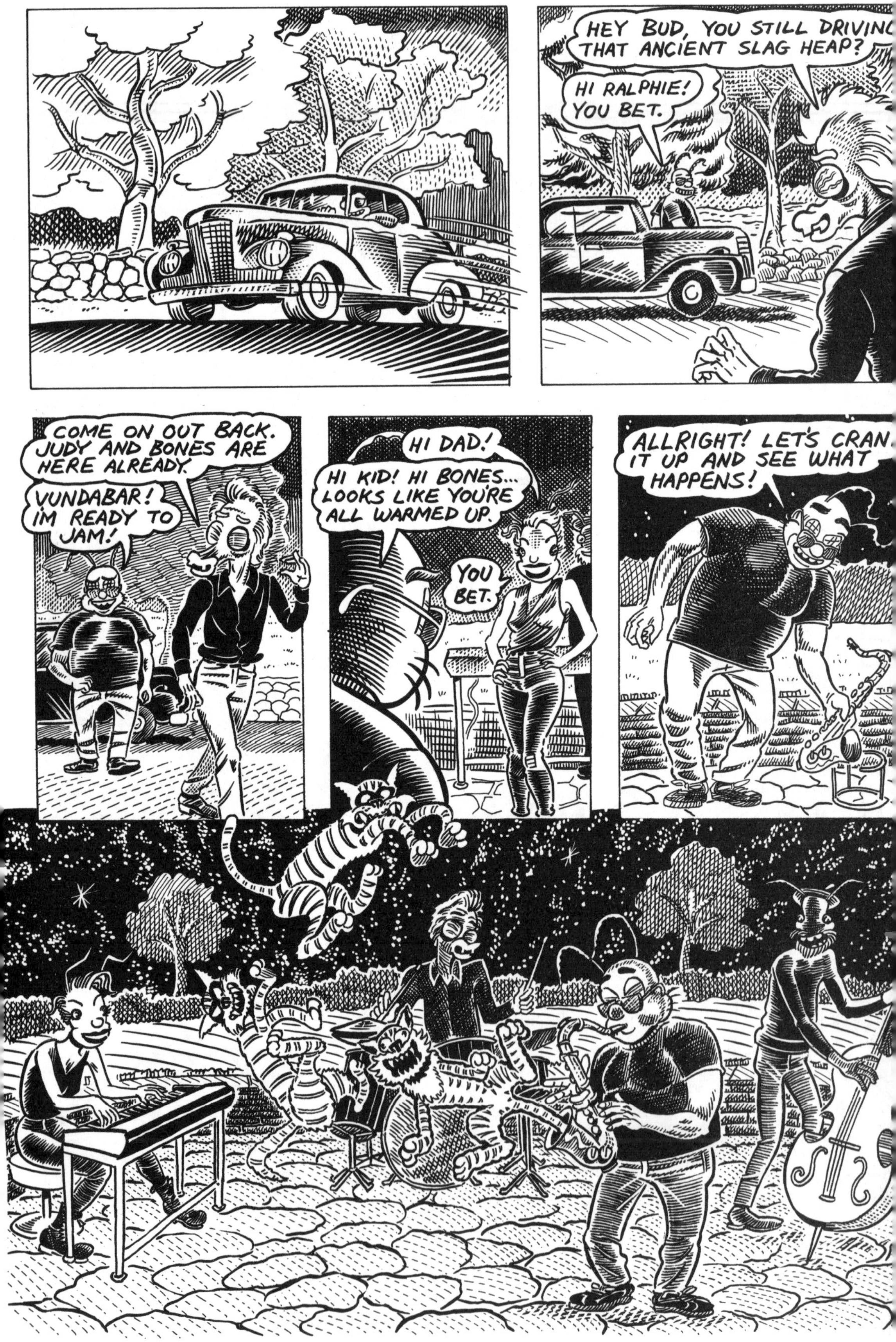
HEY BUD, YOU STILL DRIVING THAT ANCIENT SLAG HEAP?
HI RALPHIE! YOU BET.
COME ON OUT BACK. JUDY AND BONES ARE HERE ALREADY.
VUNDABAR! I'M READY TO JAM!
HI DAD!
HI KID! HI BONES... LOOKS LIKE YOU'RE ALL WARMED UP.
YOU BET.
ALLRIGHT! LET'S CRAN IT UP AND SEE WHAT HAPPENS!

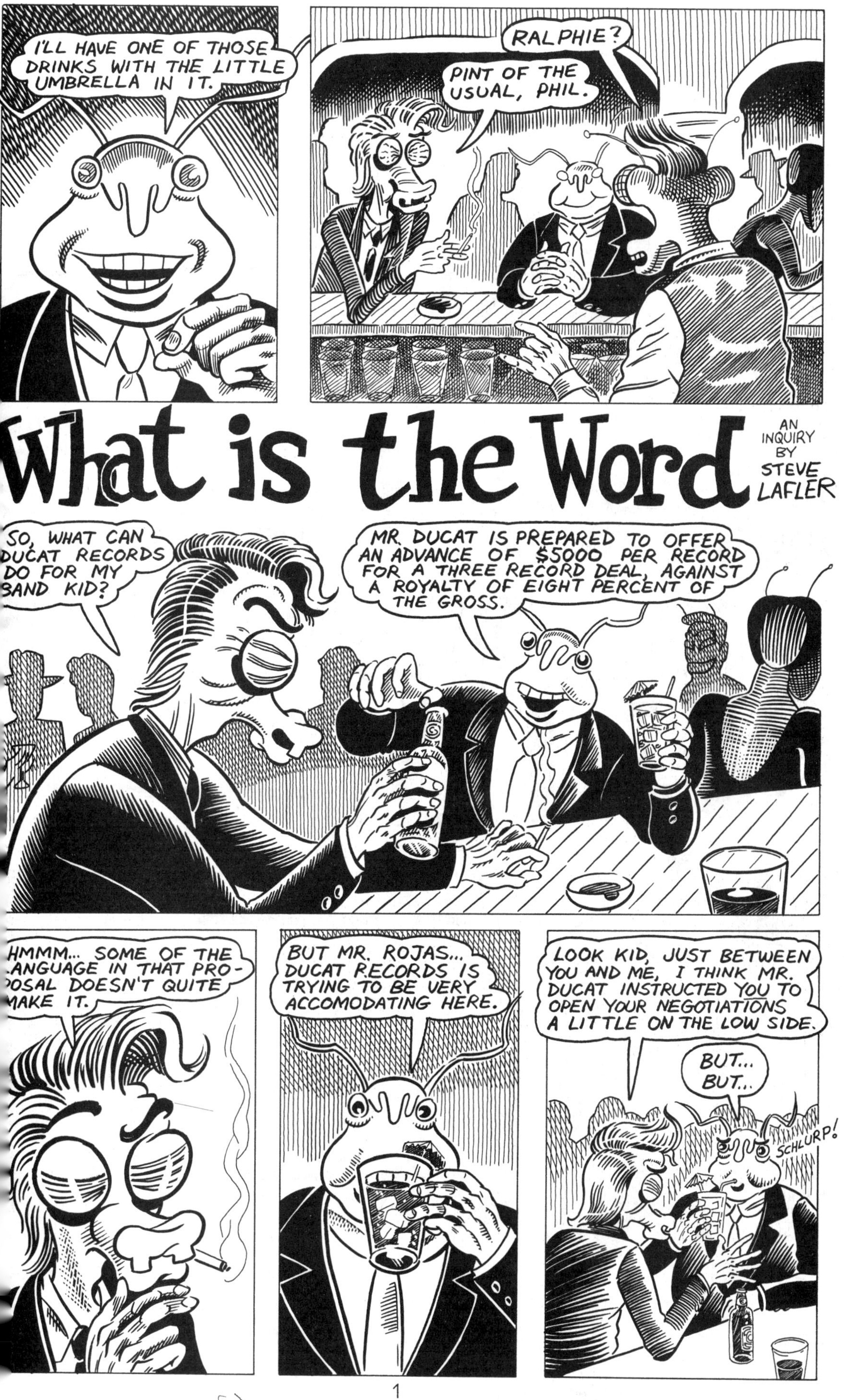
I'LL HAVE ONE OF THOSE DRINKS WITH THE LITTLE UMBRELLA IN IT.
RALPHIE?
PINT OF THE USUAL, PHIL.
What is the Word
AN INQUIRY BY STEVE LAFLER
SO, WHAT CAN DUCAT RECORDS DO FOR MY BAND KID?
MR. DUCAT IS PREPARED TO OFFER AN ADVANCE OF $5000 PER RECORD FOR A THREE RECORD DEAL, AGAINST A ROYALTY OF EIGHT PERCENT OF THE GROSS.
HMMM... SOME OF THE LANGUAGE IN THAT PROPOSAL DOESN'T QUITE MAKE IT.
BUT MR. ROJAS... DUCAT RECORDS IS TRYING TO BE VERY ACCOMODATING HERE.
LOOK KID, JUST BETWEEN YOU AND ME, I THINK MR. DUCAT INSTRUCTED YOU TO OPEN YOUR NEGOTIATIONS A LITTLE ON THE LOW SIDE.
BUT... BUT...
SCHLURP!

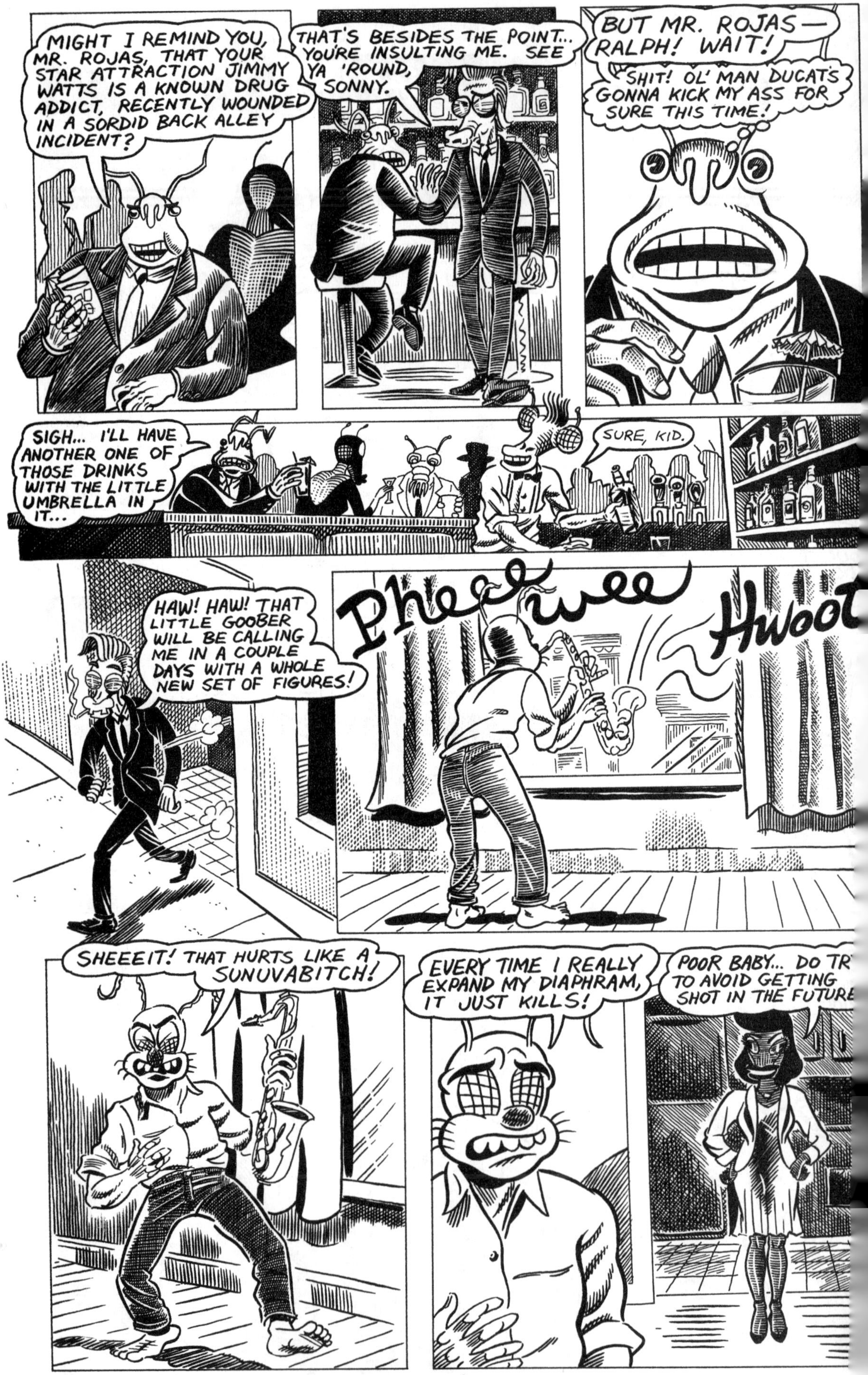
MIGHT I REMIND YOU, MR. ROJAS, THAT YOUR STAR ATTRACTION JIMMY WATTS IS A KNOWN DRUG ADDICT, RECENTLY WOUNDED IN A SORDID BACK ALLEY INCIDENT?
THAT'S BESIDES THE POINT... YOU'RE INSULTING ME. SEE YA 'ROUND, SONNY.
BUT MR. ROJAS— RALPH! WAIT!
SHIT! OL' MAN DUCAT'S GONNA KICK MY ASS FOR SURE THIS TIME!
SIGH... I'LL HAVE ANOTHER ONE OF THOSE DRINKS WITH THE LITTLE UMBRELLA IN IT...
SURE, KID.
HAW! HAW! THAT LITTLE GOOBER WILL BE CALLING ME IN A COUPLE DAYS WITH A WHOLE NEW SET OF FIGURES!
Pheeewee
Hwoot
SHEEEIT! THAT HURTS LIKE A SUNUVABITCH!
EVERY TIME I REALLY EXPAND MY DIAPHRAM, IT JUST KILLS!
POOR BABY... DO TR
TO AVOID GETTING
SHOT IN THE FUTURE

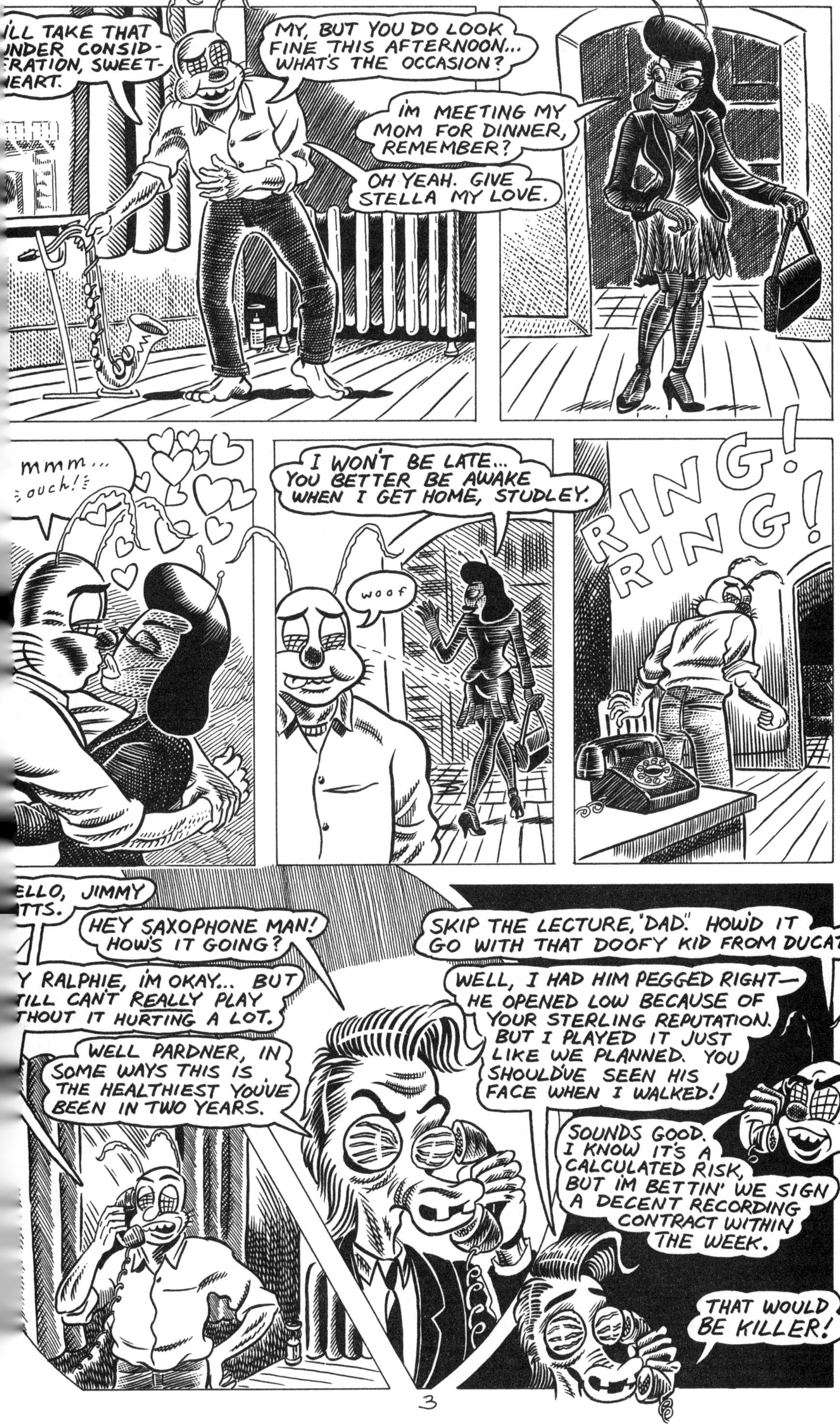
ILL TAKE THAT UNDER CONSID-ERATION, SWEET-HEART.
MY, BUT YOU DO LOOK FINE THIS AFTERNOON... WHAT'S THE OCCASION?
IM MEETING MY MOM FOR DINNER, REMEMBER?
OH YEAH. GIVE STELLA MY LOVE.
mmm... ouch!
I WON'T BE LATE... YOU BETTER BE AWAKE WHEN I GET HOME, STUDLEY.
woof
RING! RING!
ELLO, JIMMY TTS.
HEY SAXOPHONE MAN! HOW'S IT GOING?
Y RALPHIE, IM OKAY... BUT TILL CAN'T REALLY PLAY THOUT IT HURTING A LOT.
WELL PARDNER, IN SOME WAYS THIS IS THE HEALTHIEST YOU'VE BEEN IN TWO YEARS.
SKIP THE LECTURE, "DAD." HOW'D IT GO WITH THAT DOOFY KID FROM DUCAT?
WELL, I HAD HIM PEGGED RIGHT— HE OPENED LOW BECAUSE OF YOUR STERLING REPUTATION. BUT I PLAYED IT JUST LIKE WE PLANNED. YOU SHOULD'VE SEEN HIS FACE WHEN I WALKED!
SOUNDS GOOD. I KNOW IT'S A CALCULATED RISK, BUT IM BETTIN' WE SIGN A DECENT RECORDING CONTRACT WITHIN THE WEEK.
THAT WOULD BE KILLER!

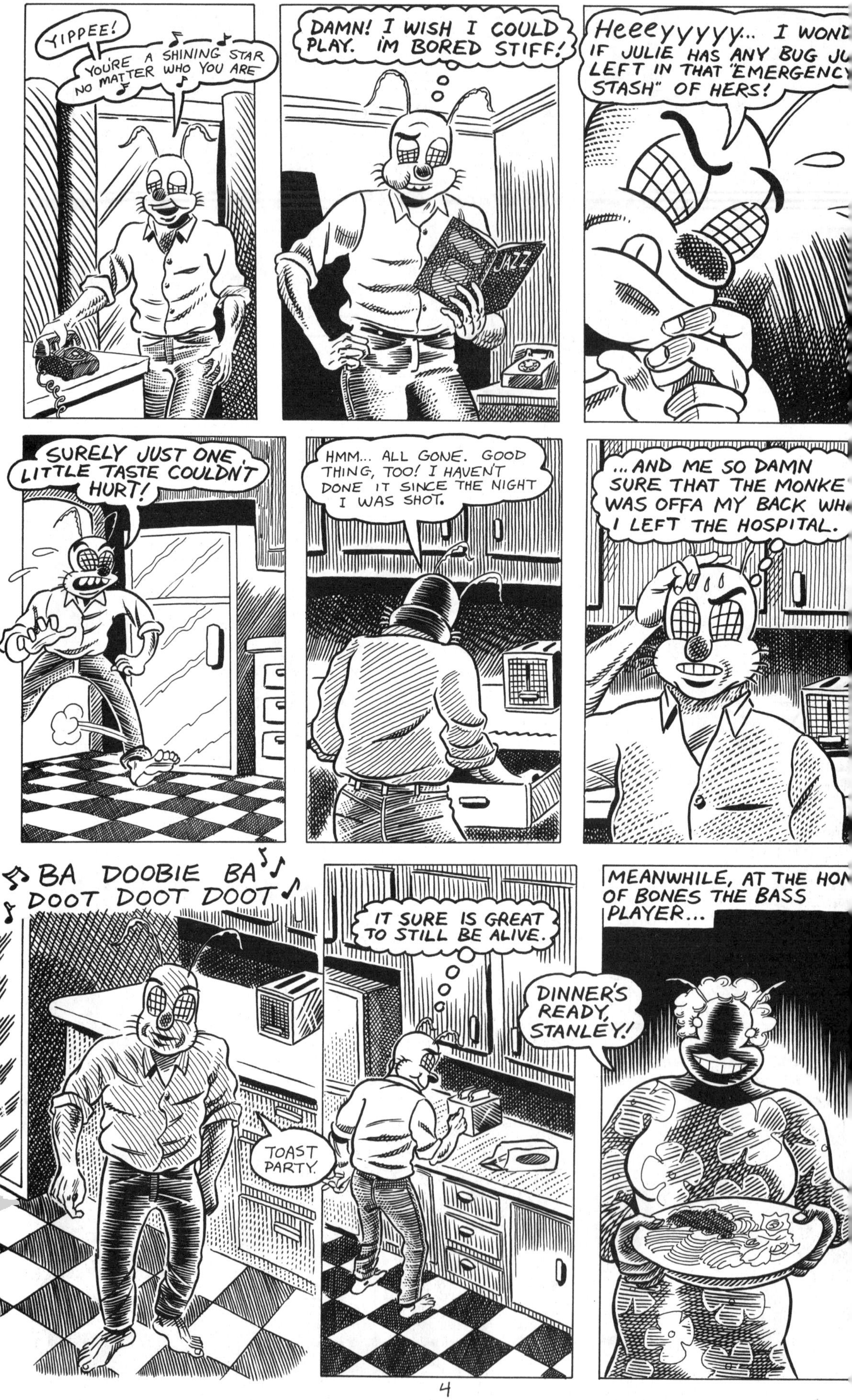
YIPPEE!
YOU'RE A SHINING STAR NO MATTER WHO YOU ARE
DAMN! I WISH I COULD PLAY. IM BORED STIFF!
JAZZ
Heeeyyyyy... I WOND IF JULIE HAS ANY BUG JU LEFT IN THAT "EMERGENC STASH" OF HERS!
SURELY JUST ONE LITTLE TASTE COULDN'T HURT!
HMM... ALL GONE. GOOD THING, TOO! I HAVEN'T DONE IT SINCE THE NIGHT I WAS SHOT.
...AND ME SO DAMN SURE THAT THE MONKE WAS OFFA MY BACK WH I LEFT THE HOSPITAL.
BA DOOBIE BA DOOT DOOT DOOT
IT SURE IS GREAT TO STILL BE ALIVE.
TOAST PARTY.
MEANWHILE, AT THE HO OF BONES THE BASS PLAYER...
DINNER'S READY, STANLEY!

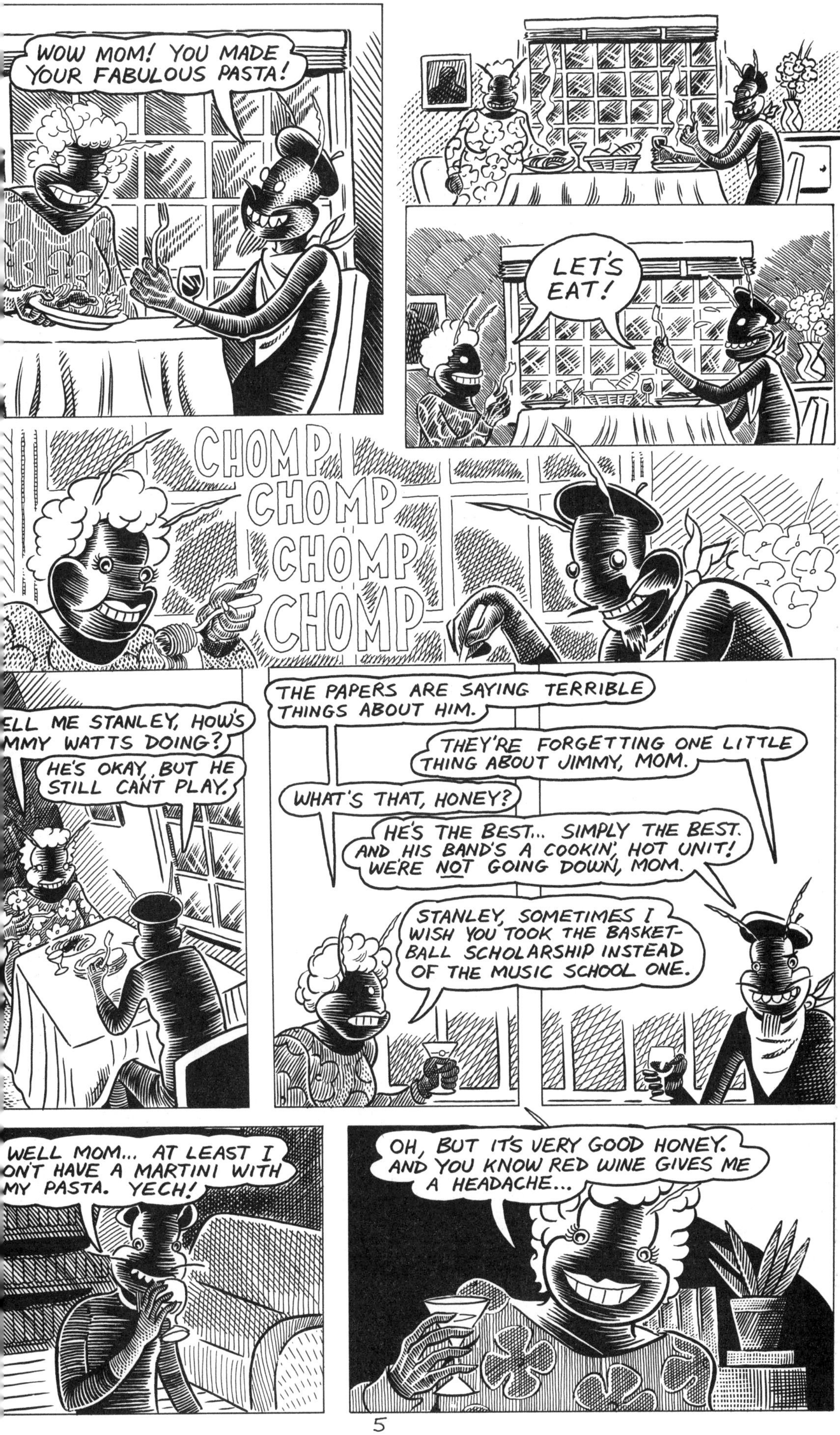

WOW MOM! YOU MADE YOUR FABULOUS PASTA!
LET'S EAT!
CHOMP CHOMP CHOMP CHOMP
ELL ME STANLEY, HOW'S MMY WATTS DOING?
HE'S OKAY, BUT HE STILL CAN'T PLAY.
THE PAPERS ARE SAYING TERRIBLE THINGS ABOUT HIM.
THEY'RE FORGETTING ONE LITTLE THING ABOUT JIMMY, MOM.
WHAT'S THAT, HONEY?
HE'S THE BEST... SIMPLY THE BEST. AND HIS BAND'S A COOKIN' HOT UNIT! WE'RE NOT GOING DOWN, MOM.
STANLEY, SOMETIMES I WISH YOU TOOK THE BASKET-BALL SCHOLARSHIP INSTEAD OF THE MUSIC SCHOOL ONE.
WELL MOM... AT LEAST I ON'T HAVE A MARTINI WITH MY PASTA. YECH!
OH, BUT IT'S VERY GOOD HONEY. AND YOU KNOW RED WINE GIVES ME A HEADACHE...

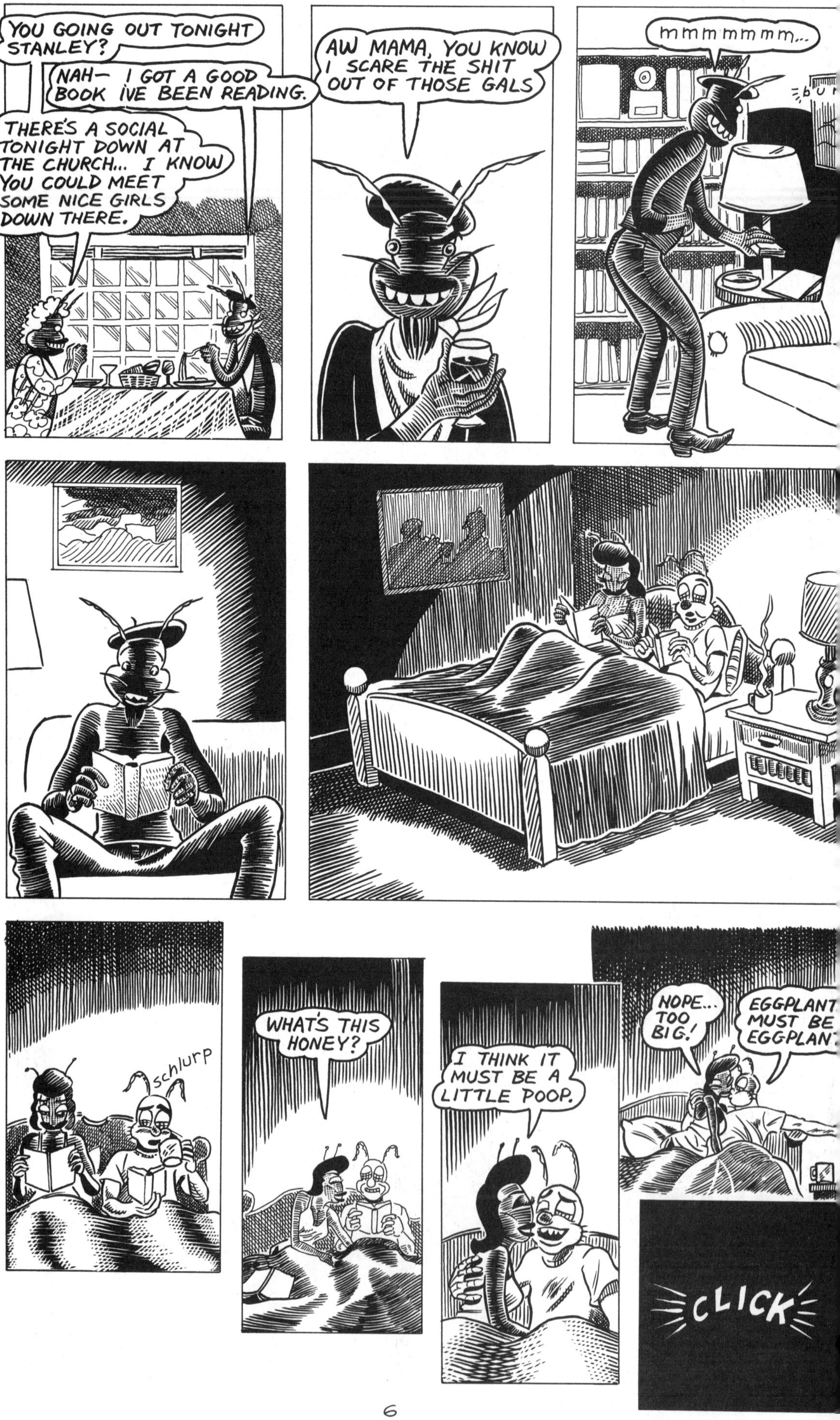
YOU GOING OUT TONIGHT STANLEY?
NAH— I GOT A GOOD BOOK I'VE BEEN READING.
THERE'S A SOCIAL TONIGHT DOWN AT THE CHURCH... I KNOW YOU COULD MEET SOME NICE GIRLS DOWN THERE.
AW MAMA, YOU KNOW I SCARE THE SHIT OUT OF THOSE GALS
mmmmmmm...
schlurp
WHAT'S THIS HONEY?
I THINK IT MUST BE A LITTLE POOP.
NOPE... TOO BIG!
EGGPLANT MUST BE EGGPLANT
CLICK

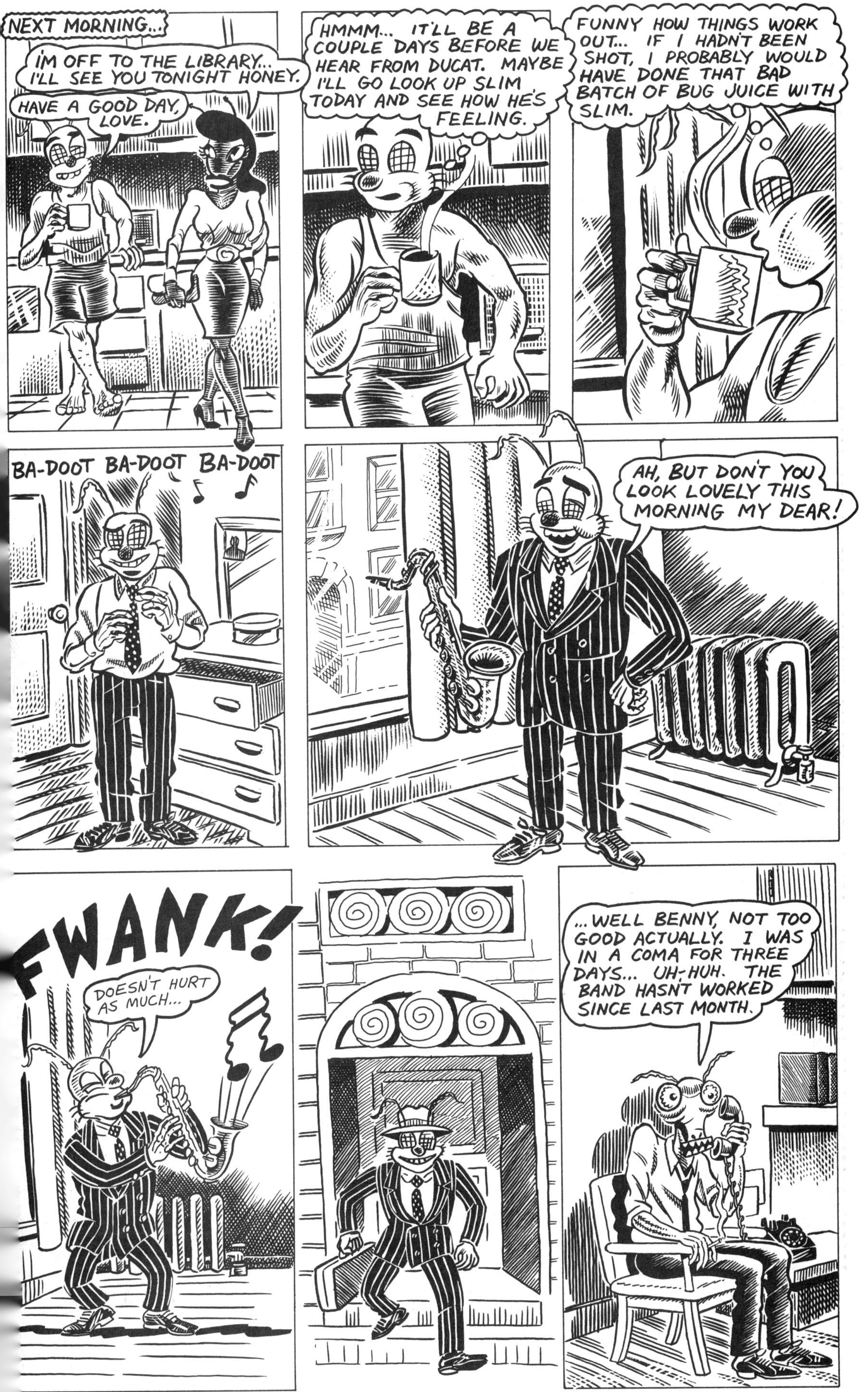
NEXT MORNING...
I'M OFF TO THE LIBRARY... I'LL SEE YOU TONIGHT HONEY.
HAVE A GOOD DAY, LOVE.
HMMM... IT'LL BE A COUPLE DAYS BEFORE WE HEAR FROM DUCAT. MAYBE I'LL GO LOOK UP SLIM TODAY AND SEE HOW HE'S FEELING.
FUNNY HOW THINGS WORK OUT... IF I HADN'T BEEN SHOT, I PROBABLY WOULD HAVE DONE THAT BAD BATCH OF BUG JUICE WITH SLIM.
BA-DOOT BA-DOOT BA-DOOT
AH, BUT DON'T YOU LOOK LOVELY THIS MORNING MY DEAR!
FWANK!
DOESN'T HURT AS MUCH...
...WELL BENNY, NOT TOO GOOD ACTUALLY. I WAS IN A COMA FOR THREE DAYS... UH-HUH. THE BAND HASN'T WORKED SINCE LAST MONTH.

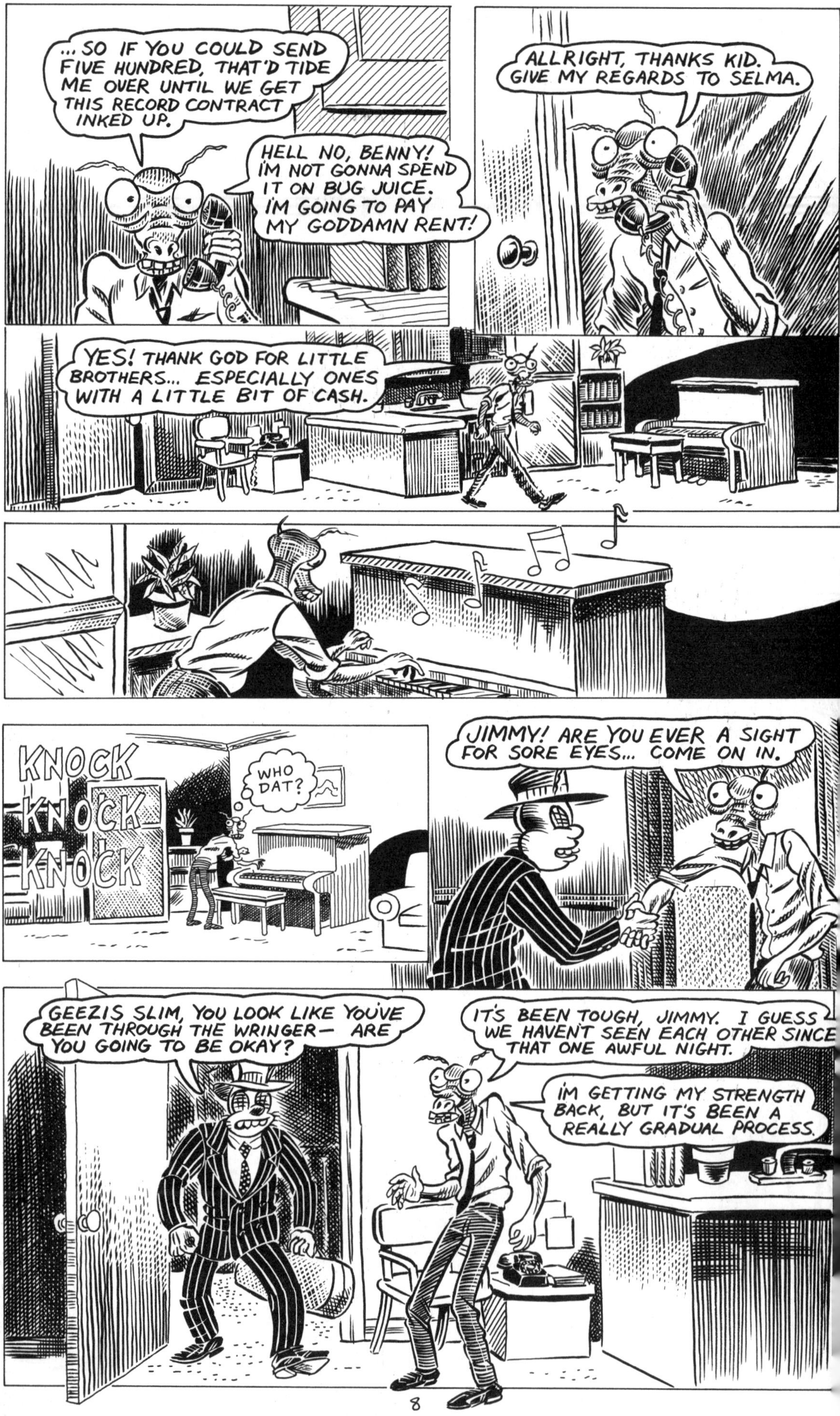
...SO IF YOU COULD SEND FIVE HUNDRED, THAT'D TIDE ME OVER UNTIL WE GET THIS RECORD CONTRACT INKED UP.
HELL NO, BENNY! I'M NOT GONNA SPEND IT ON BUG JUICE. I'M GOING TO PAY MY GODDAMN RENT!
ALLRIGHT, THANKS KID. GIVE MY REGARDS TO SELMA.
YES! THANK GOD FOR LITTLE BROTHERS... ESPECIALLY ONES WITH A LITTLE BIT OF CASH.
KNOCK KNOCK KNOCK
WHO DAT?
JIMMY! ARE YOU EVER A SIGHT FOR SORE EYES... COME ON IN.
GEEZIS SLIM, YOU LOOK LIKE YOU'VE BEEN THROUGH THE WRINGER— ARE YOU GOING TO BE OKAY?
IT'S BEEN TOUGH, JIMMY. I GUESS WE HAVEN'T SEEN EACH OTHER SINCE THAT ONE AWFUL NIGHT.
I'M GETTING MY STRENGTH BACK, BUT IT'S BEEN A REALLY GRADUAL PROCESS.

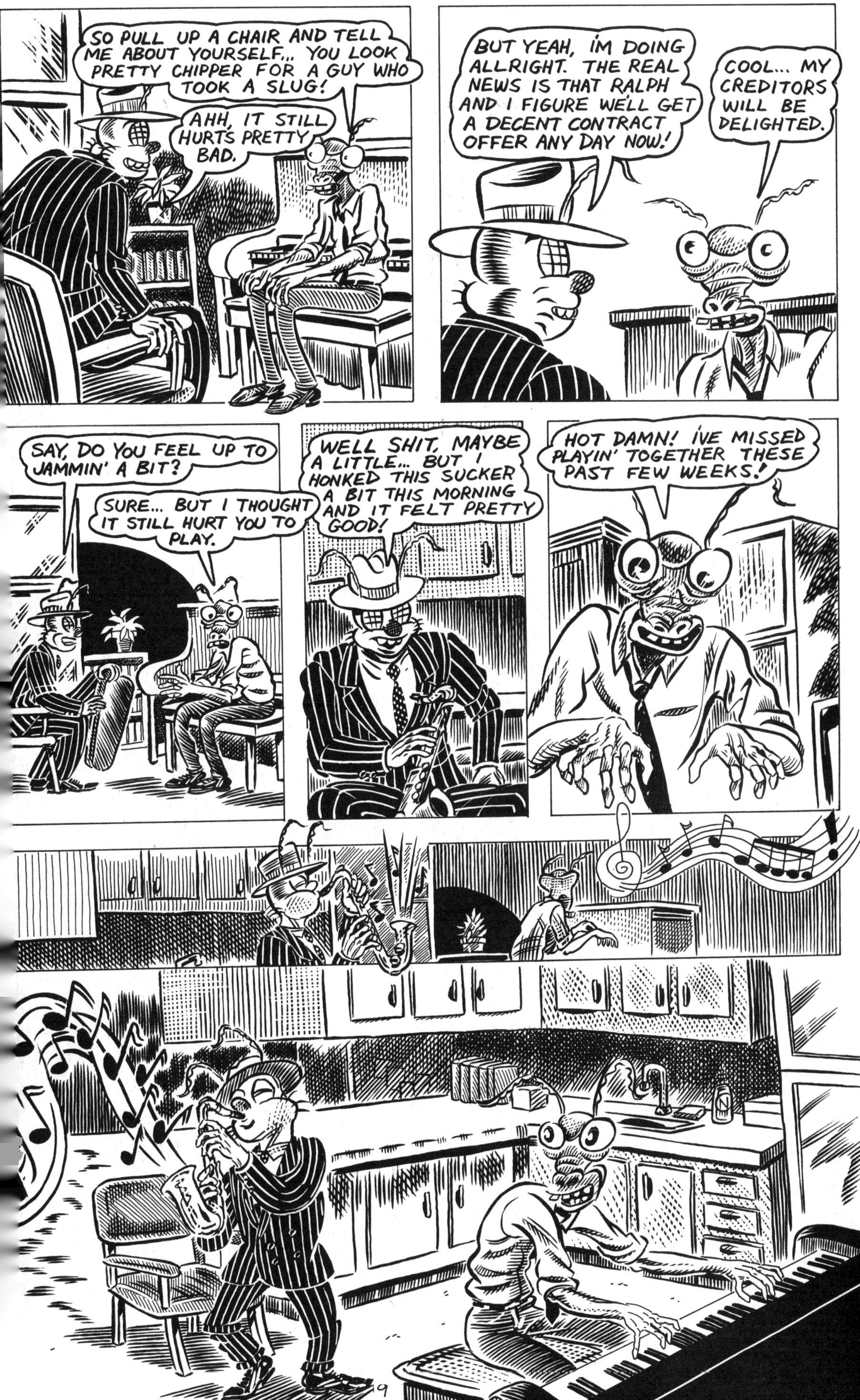

SO PULL UP A CHAIR AND TELL ME ABOUT YOURSELF... YOU LOOK PRETTY CHIPPER FOR A GUY WHO TOOK A SLUG!
AHH, IT STILL HURTS PRETTY BAD.
BUT YEAH, I'M DOING ALLRIGHT. THE REAL NEWS IS THAT RALPH AND I FIGURE WE'LL GET A DECENT CONTRACT OFFER ANY DAY NOW!
COOL... MY CREDITORS WILL BE DELIGHTED.
SAY, DO YOU FEEL UP TO JAMMIN' A BIT?
SURE... BUT I THOUGHT IT STILL HURT YOU TO PLAY.
WELL SHIT, MAYBE A LITTLE... BUT I HONKED THIS SUCKER A BIT THIS MORNING AND IT FELT PRETTY GOOD!
HOT DAMN! I'VE MISSED PLAYIN' TOGETHER THESE PAST FEW WEEKS!

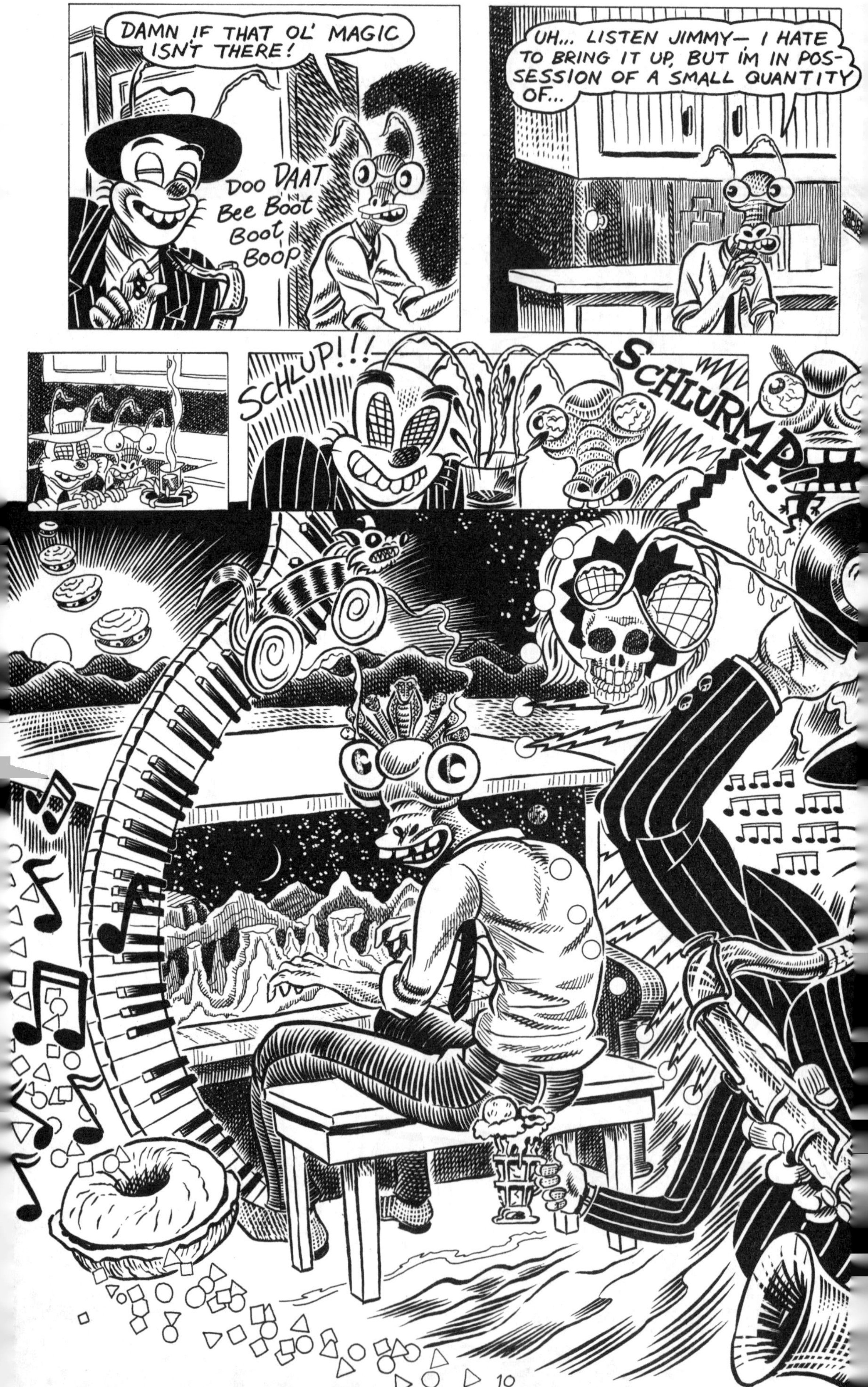

DAMN IF THAT OL' MAGIC ISN'T THERE!
DOO DAAT Bee Boot Boot Boop
UH... LISTEN JIMMY— I HATE TO BRING IT UP, BUT I'M IN POSSESSION OF A SMALL QUANTITY OF...
SCHLUP!!!
SCHLURMP!!

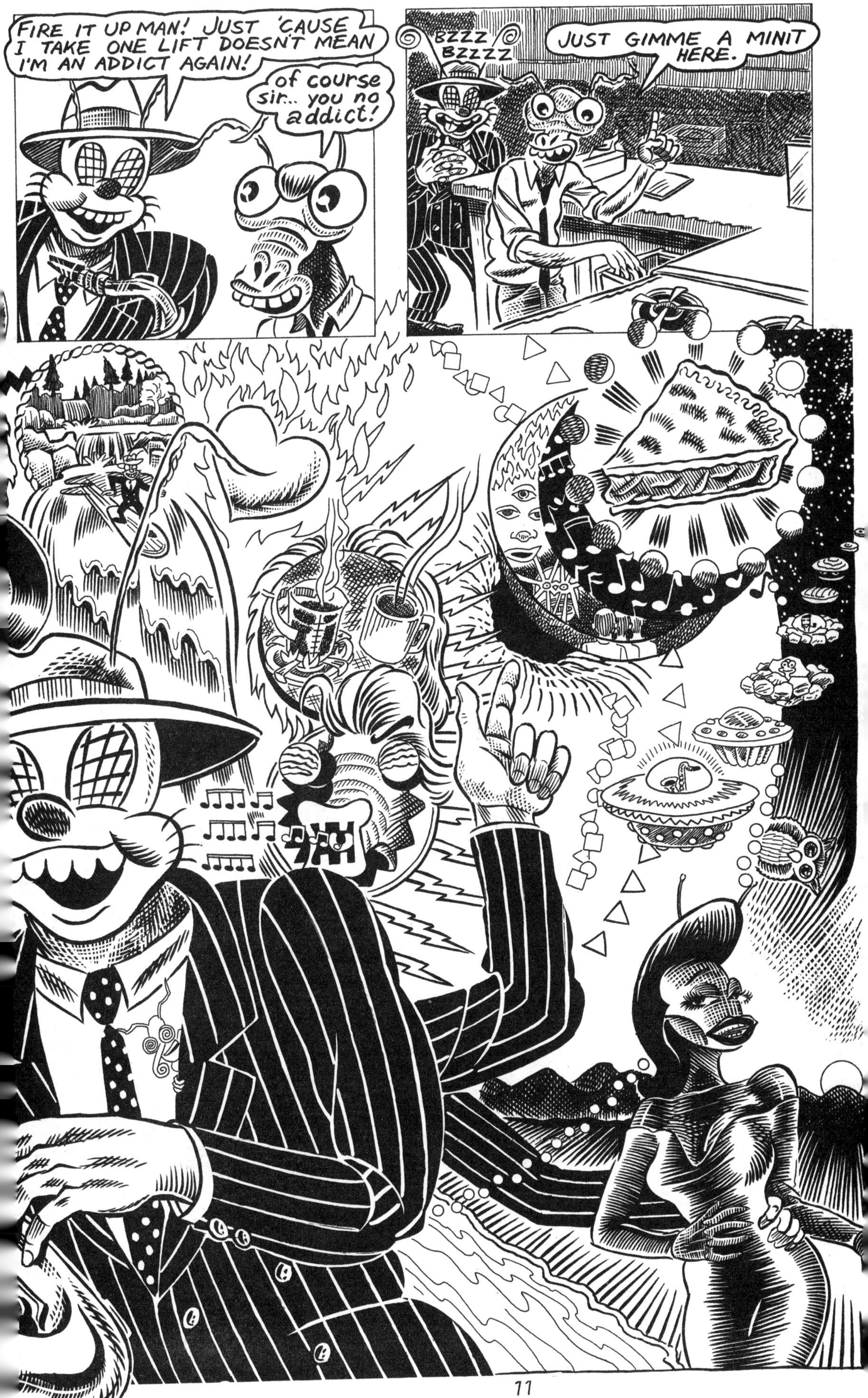
FIRE IT UP MAN! JUST 'CAUSE I TAKE ONE LIFT DOESN'T MEAN I'M AN ADDICT AGAIN!
of course sir... you no addict!
BZZZ BZZZZ
JUST GIMME A MINIT HERE.

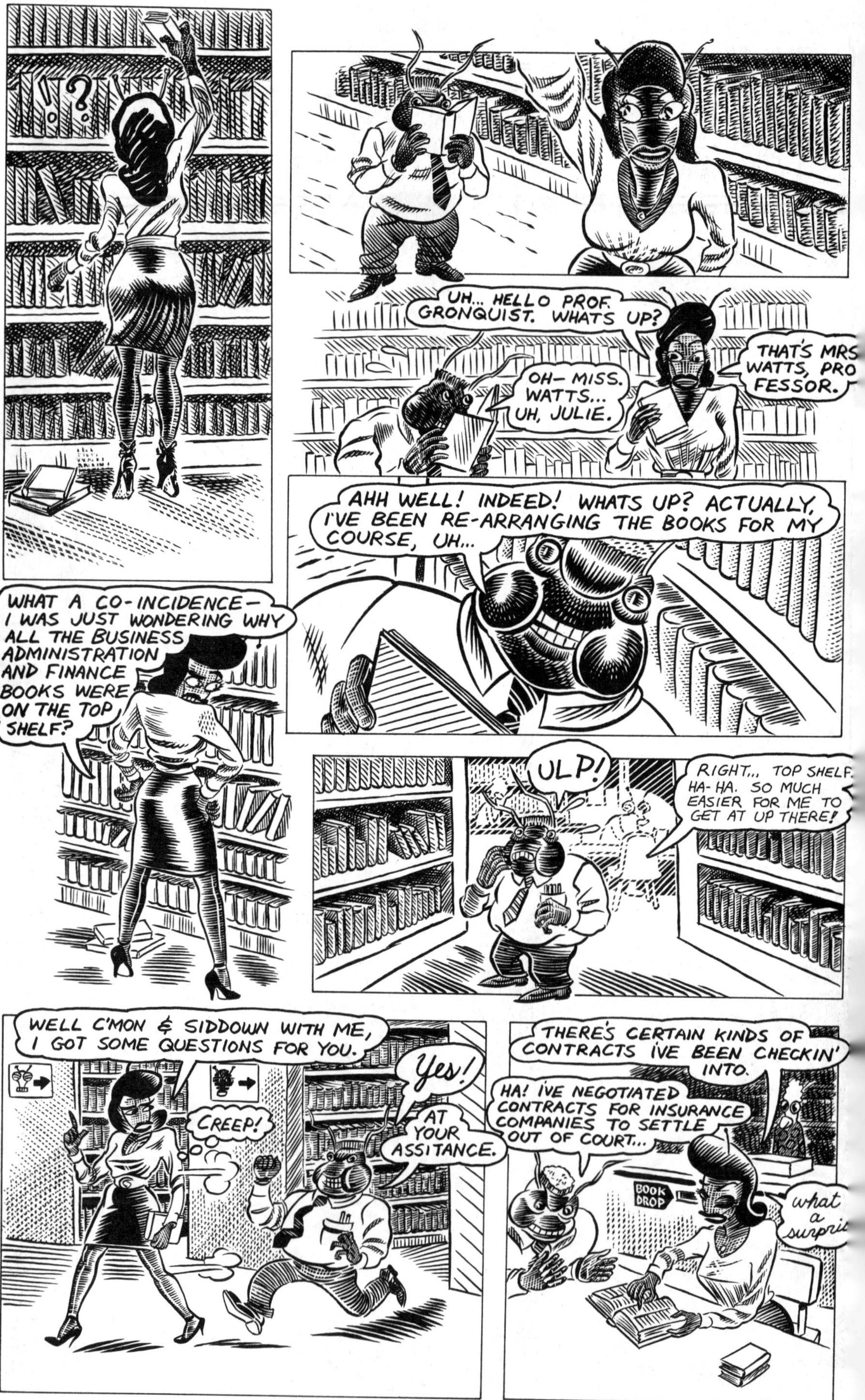
UH... HELLO PROF. GRONQUIST. WHATS UP?
OH— MISS. WATTS... UH, JULIE.
THAT'S MRS WATTS, PROFESSOR.
AHH WELL! INDEED! WHATS UP? ACTUALLY, I'VE BEEN RE-ARRANGING THE BOOKS FOR MY COURSE, UH...
WHAT A CO-INCIDENCE— I WAS JUST WONDERING WHY ALL THE BUSINESS ADMINISTRATION AND FINANCE BOOKS WERE ON THE TOP SHELF?
ULP!
RIGHT... TOP SHELF. HA-HA. SO MUCH EASIER FOR ME TO GET AT UP THERE!
WELL C'MON & SIDDOWN WITH ME, I GOT SOME QUESTIONS FOR YOU.
CREEP!
Yes!
AT YOUR ASSITANCE.
THERE'S CERTAIN KINDS OF CONTRACTS I'VE BEEN CHECKIN' INTO.
HA! I'VE NEGOTIATED CONTRACTS FOR INSURANCE COMPANIES TO SETTLE OUT OF COURT...
BOOK DROP
what a surpri

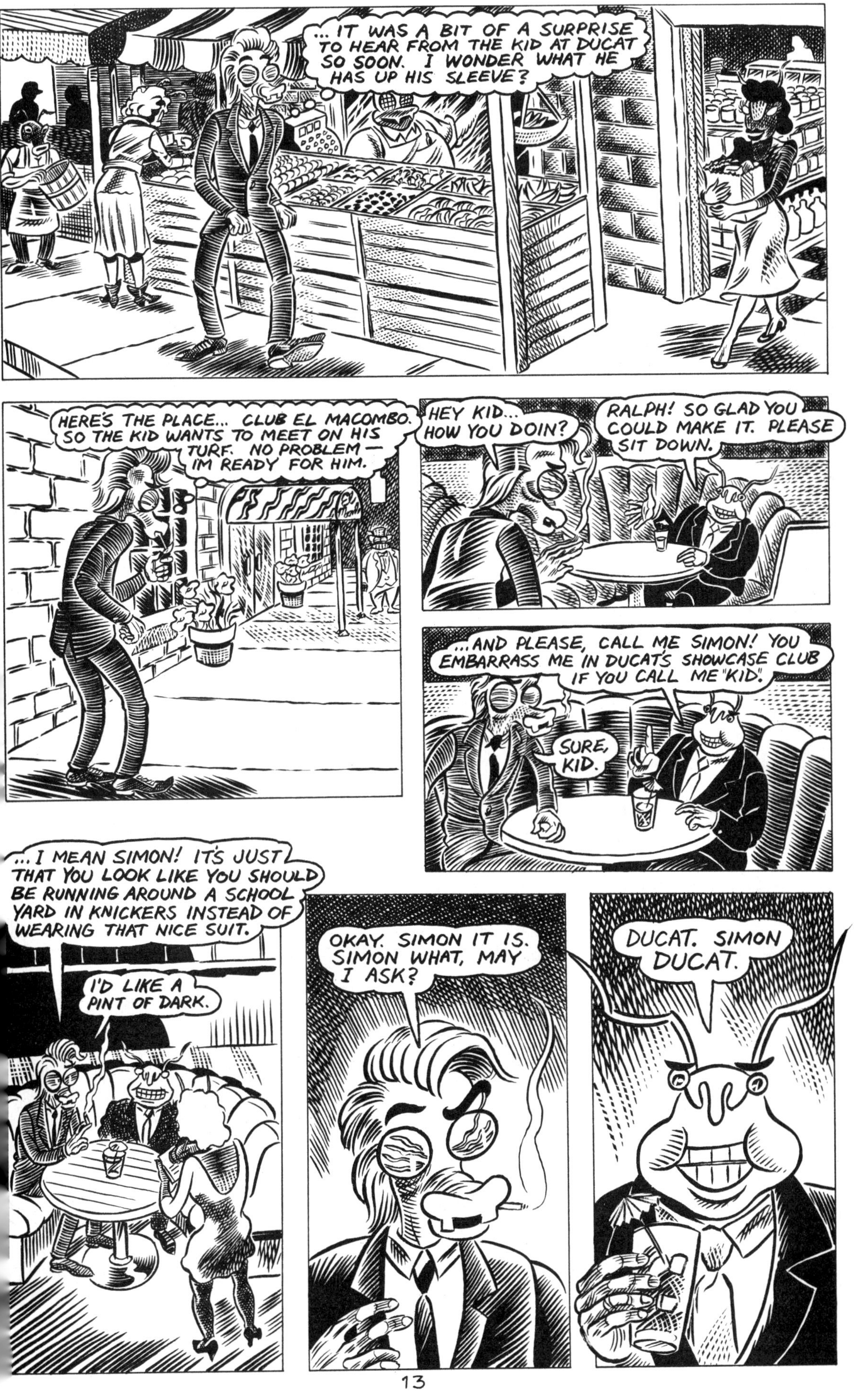

... IT WAS A BIT OF A SURPRISE TO HEAR FROM THE KID AT DUCAT SO SOON. I WONDER WHAT HE HAS UP HIS SLEEVE?
HERE'S THE PLACE... CLUB EL MACOMBO. SO THE KID WANTS TO MEET ON HIS TURF. NO PROBLEM — IM READY FOR HIM.
HEY KID... HOW YOU DOIN?
RALPH! SO GLAD YOU COULD MAKE IT. PLEASE SIT DOWN.
...AND PLEASE, CALL ME SIMON! YOU EMBARRASS ME IN DUCAT'S SHOWCASE CLUB IF YOU CALL ME "KID".
SURE, KID.
...I MEAN SIMON! IT'S JUST THAT YOU LOOK LIKE YOU SHOULD BE RUNNING AROUND A SCHOOL YARD IN KNICKERS INSTEAD OF WEARING THAT NICE SUIT.
I'D LIKE A PINT OF DARK.
OKAY. SIMON IT IS. SIMON WHAT, MAY I ASK?
DUCAT. SIMON DUCAT.

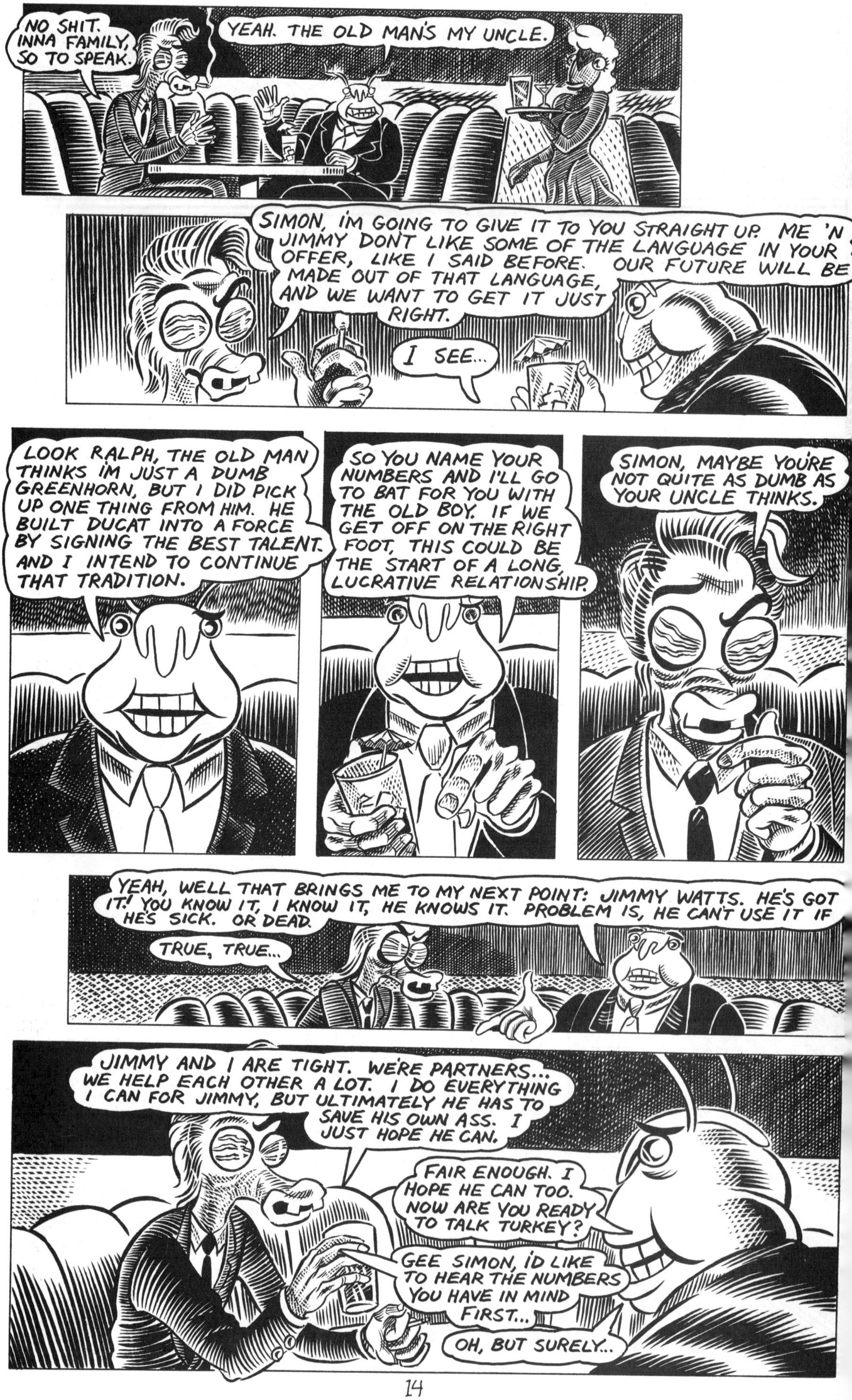

NO SHIT. INNA FAMILY, SO TO SPEAK.
YEAH. THE OLD MAN'S MY UNCLE.
SIMON, I'M GOING TO GIVE IT TO YOU STRAIGHT UP. ME 'N JIMMY DON'T LIKE SOME OF THE LANGUAGE IN YOUR OFFER, LIKE I SAID BEFORE. OUR FUTURE WILL BE MADE OUT OF THAT LANGUAGE, AND WE WANT TO GET IT JUST RIGHT.
I SEE...
LOOK RALPH, THE OLD MAN THINKS I'M JUST A DUMB GREENHORN, BUT I DID PICK UP ONE THING FROM HIM. HE BUILT DUCAT INTO A FORCE BY SIGNING THE BEST TALENT. AND I INTEND TO CONTINUE THAT TRADITION.
SO YOU NAME YOUR NUMBERS AND I'LL GO TO BAT FOR YOU WITH THE OLD BOY. IF WE GET OFF ON THE RIGHT FOOT, THIS COULD BE THE START OF A LONG, LUCRATIVE RELATIONSHIP.
SIMON, MAYBE YOU'RE NOT QUITE AS DUMB AS YOUR UNCLE THINKS.
YEAH, WELL THAT BRINGS ME TO MY NEXT POINT: JIMMY WATTS. HE'S GOT IT! YOU KNOW IT, I KNOW IT, HE KNOWS IT. PROBLEM IS, HE CAN'T USE IT IF HE'S SICK. OR DEAD.
TRUE, TRUE...
JIMMY AND I ARE TIGHT. WE'RE PARTNERS... WE HELP EACH OTHER A LOT. I DO EVERYTHING I CAN FOR JIMMY, BUT ULTIMATELY HE HAS TO SAVE HIS OWN ASS. I JUST HOPE HE CAN.
FAIR ENOUGH. I HOPE HE CAN TOO. NOW ARE YOU READY TO TALK TURKEY?
GEE SIMON, I'D LIKE TO HEAR THE NUMBERS YOU HAVE IN MIND FIRST...
OH, BUT SURELY...

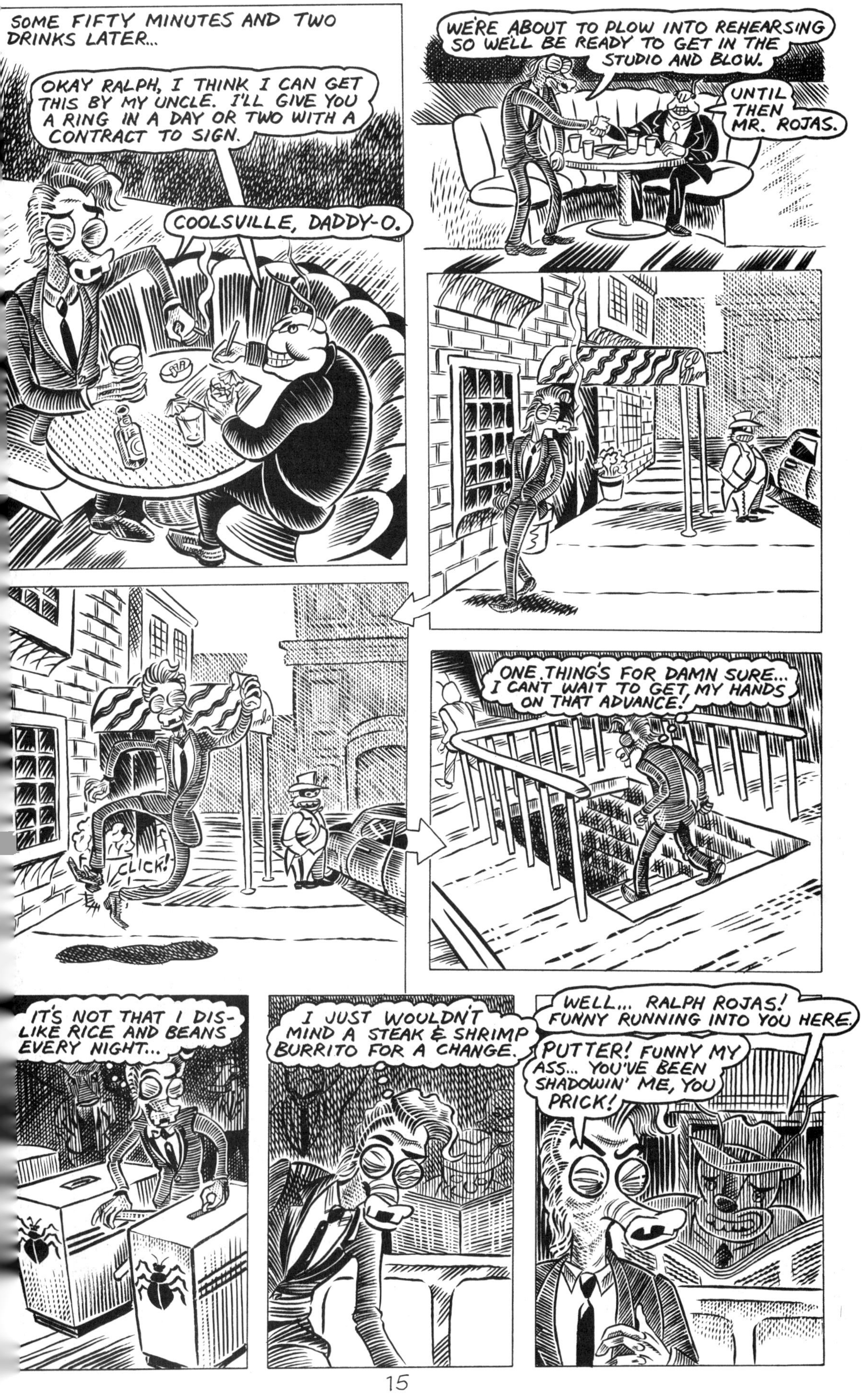
SOME FIFTY MINUTES AND TWO DRINKS LATER...
OKAY RALPH, I THINK I CAN GET THIS BY MY UNCLE. I'LL GIVE YOU A RING IN A DAY OR TWO WITH A CONTRACT TO SIGN.
COOLSVILLE, DADDY-O.
WE'RE ABOUT TO PLOW INTO REHEARSING SO WE'LL BE READY TO GET IN THE STUDIO AND BLOW.
UNTIL THEN MR. ROJAS.
CLICK!
ONE THING'S FOR DAMN SURE... I CAN'T WAIT TO GET MY HANDS ON THAT ADVANCE!
IT'S NOT THAT I DISLIKE RICE AND BEANS EVERY NIGHT...
I JUST WOULDN'T MIND A STEAK & SHRIMP BURRITO FOR A CHANGE.
WELL... RALPH ROJAS! FUNNY RUNNING INTO YOU HERE.
PUTTER! FUNNY MY ASS... YOU'VE BEEN SHADOWIN' ME, YOU PRICK!

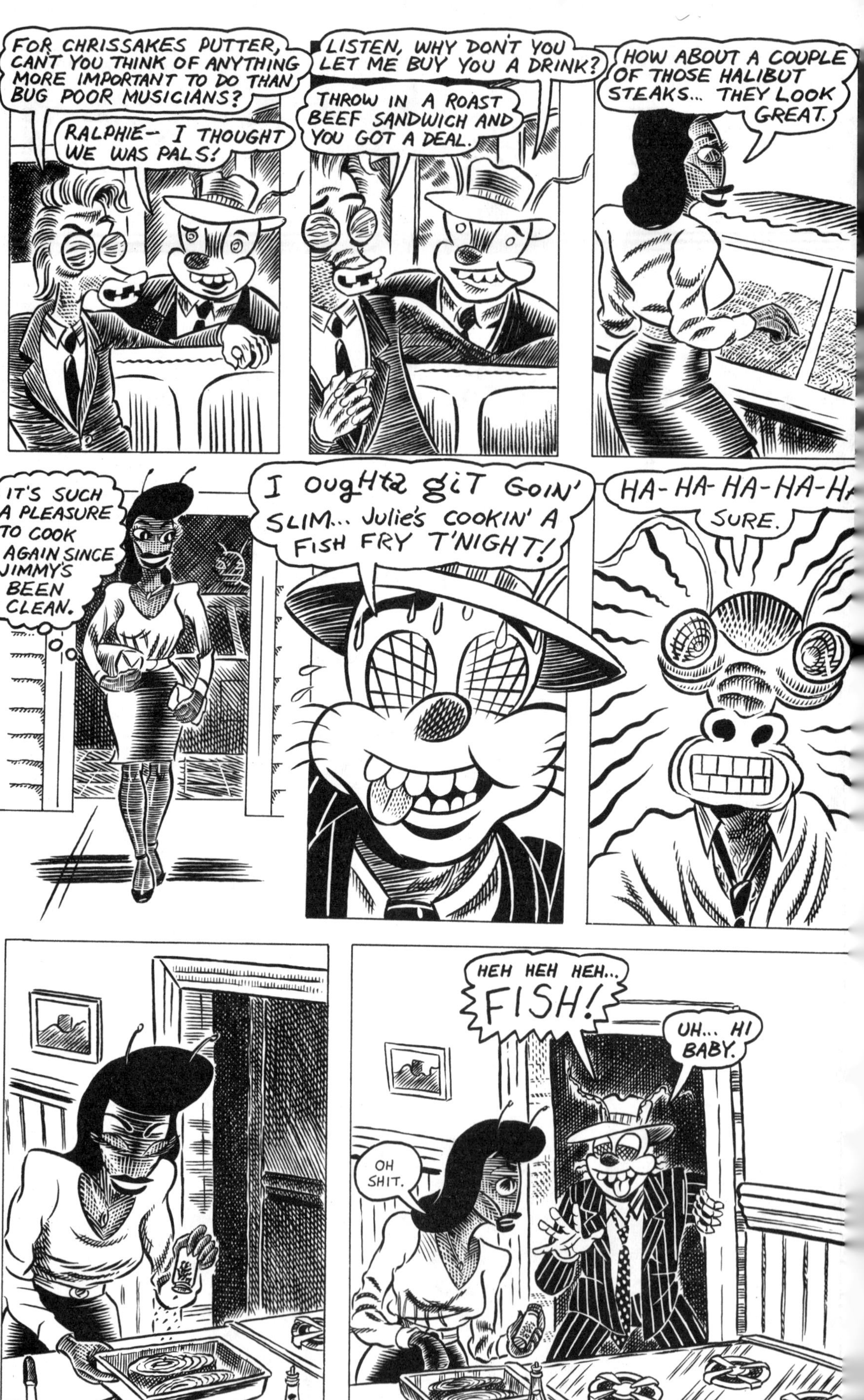
FOR CHRISSAKES PUTTER, CAN'T YOU THINK OF ANYTHING MORE IMPORTANT TO DO THAN BUG POOR MUSICIANS?
RALPHIE— I THOUGHT WE WAS PALS!
LISTEN, WHY DON'T YOU LET ME BUY YOU A DRINK?
THROW IN A ROAST BEEF SANDWICH AND YOU GOT A DEAL.
HOW ABOUT A COUPLE OF THOSE HALIBUT STEAKS... THEY LOOK GREAT.
IT'S SUCH A PLEASURE TO COOK AGAIN SINCE JIMMY'S BEEN CLEAN.
I oughta git Goin' SLIM... Julie's cookin' A FISH FRY T'NIGHT!
HA-HA-HA-HA-HA
SURE.
HEH HEH HEH... FISH!
UH... HI BABY.
OH SHIT.

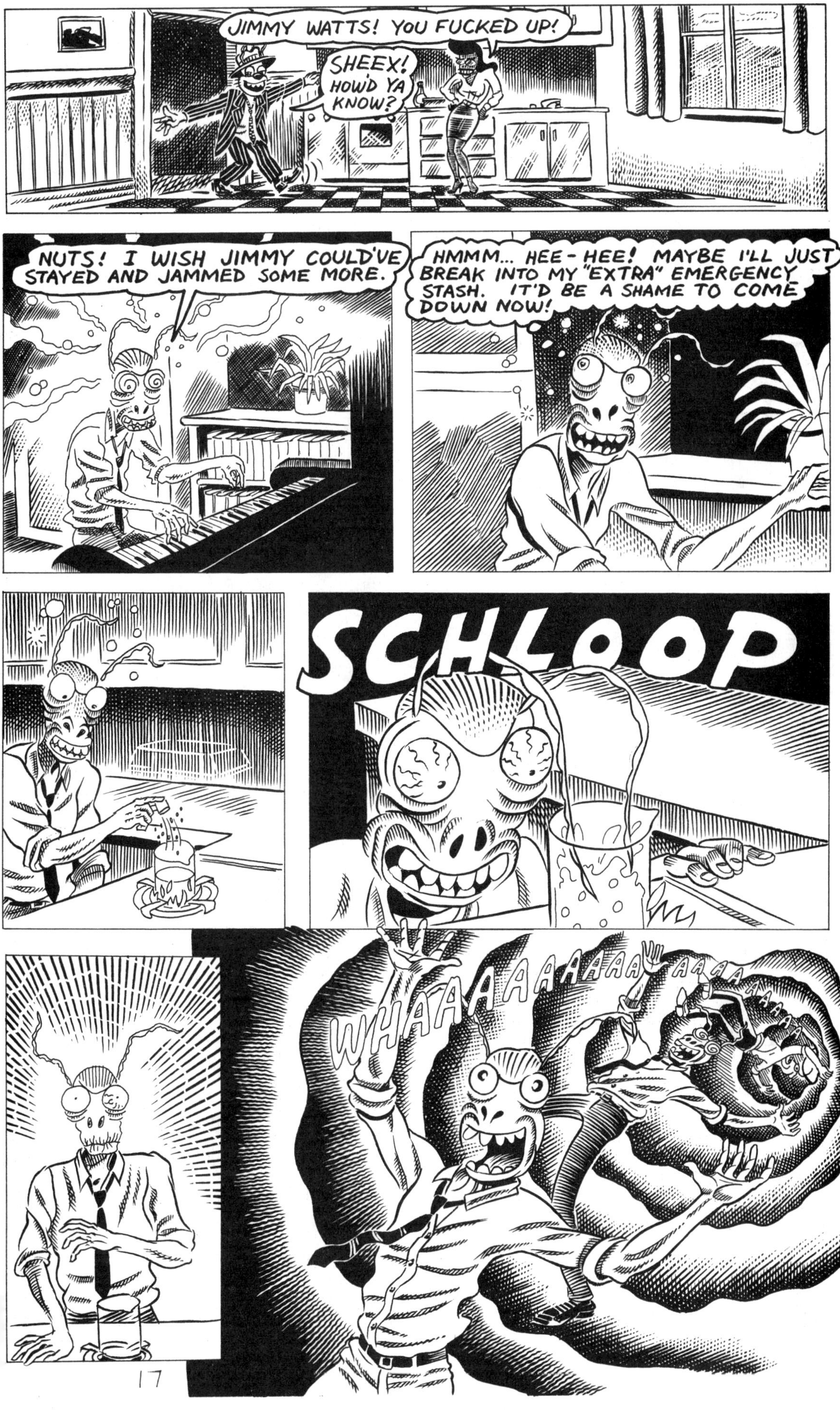

JIMMY WATTS! YOU FUCKED UP!
SHEEX! HOW'D YA KNOW?
NUTS! I WISH JIMMY COULD'VE STAYED AND JAMMED SOME MORE.
HMMM... HEE-HEE! MAYBE I'LL JUST BREAK INTO MY "EXTRA" EMERGENCY STASH. IT'D BE A SHAME TO COME DOWN NOW!
SCHLOOP
WHAAAAAAAAAAAAAAA

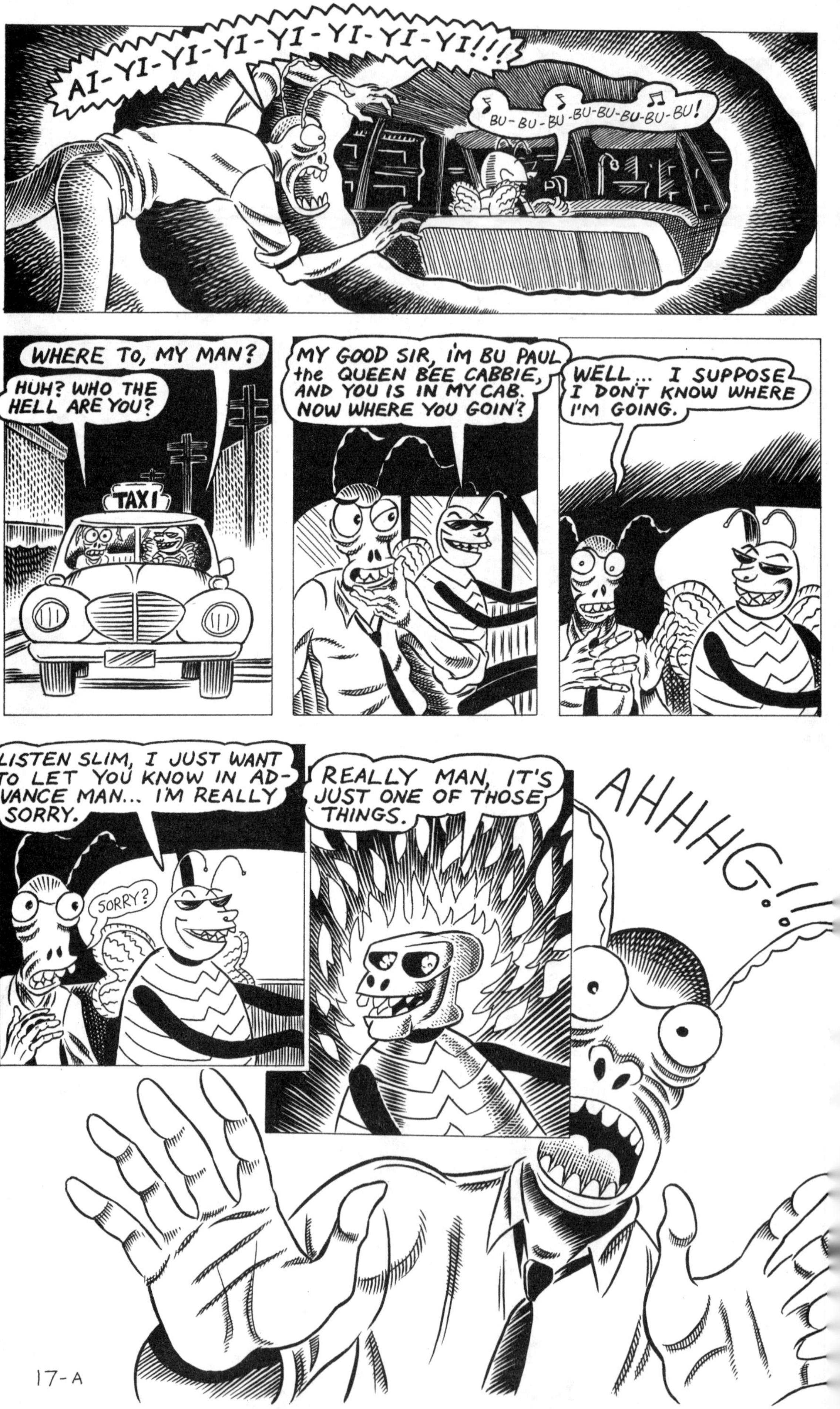
AI-YI-YI-YI-YI-YI-YI-YI!!!
BU-BU-BU-BU-BU-BU-BU-BU!
WHERE TO, MY MAN?
HUH? WHO THE HELL ARE YOU?
TAXI
MY GOOD SIR, I'M BU PAUL the QUEEN BEE CABBIE, AND YOU IS IN MY CAB. NOW WHERE YOU GOIN'?
WELL... I SUPPOSE I DON'T KNOW WHERE I'M GOING.
LISTEN SLIM, I JUST WANT TO LET YOU KNOW IN ADVANCE MAN... I'M REALLY SORRY.
SORRY?
REALLY MAN, IT'S JUST ONE OF THOSE THINGS.
AHHHG!!!

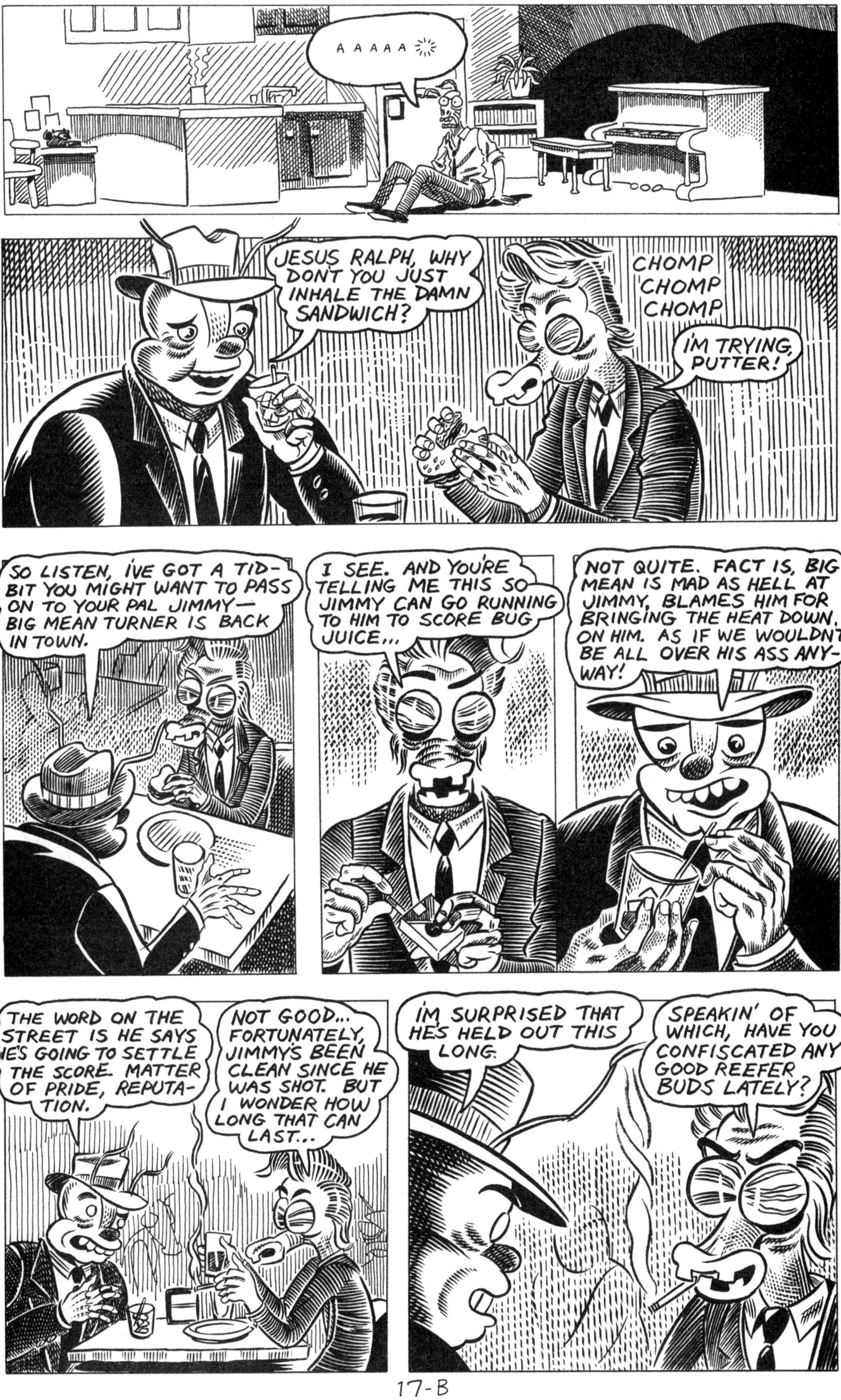
A A A A A
JESUS RALPH, WHY DON'T YOU JUST INHALE THE DAMN SANDWICH?
CHOMP CHOMP CHOMP
I'M TRYING, PUTTER!
SO LISTEN, I'VE GOT A TID-BIT YOU MIGHT WANT TO PASS ON TO YOUR PAL JIMMY— BIG MEAN TURNER IS BACK IN TOWN.
I SEE. AND YOU'RE TELLING ME THIS SO JIMMY CAN GO RUNNING TO HIM TO SCORE BUG JUICE...
NOT QUITE. FACT IS, BIG MEAN IS MAD AS HELL AT JIMMY, BLAMES HIM FOR BRINGING THE HEAT DOWN ON HIM. AS IF WE WOULDN'T BE ALL OVER HIS ASS ANY-WAY!
THE WORD ON THE STREET IS HE SAYS HE'S GOING TO SETTLE THE SCORE. MATTER OF PRIDE, REPUTA-TION.
NOT GOOD... FORTUNATELY, JIMMY'S BEEN CLEAN SINCE HE WAS SHOT. BUT I WONDER HOW LONG THAT CAN LAST...
I'M SURPRISED THAT HE'S HELD OUT THIS LONG.
SPEAKIN' OF WHICH, HAVE YOU CONFISCATED ANY GOOD REEFER BUDS LATELY?

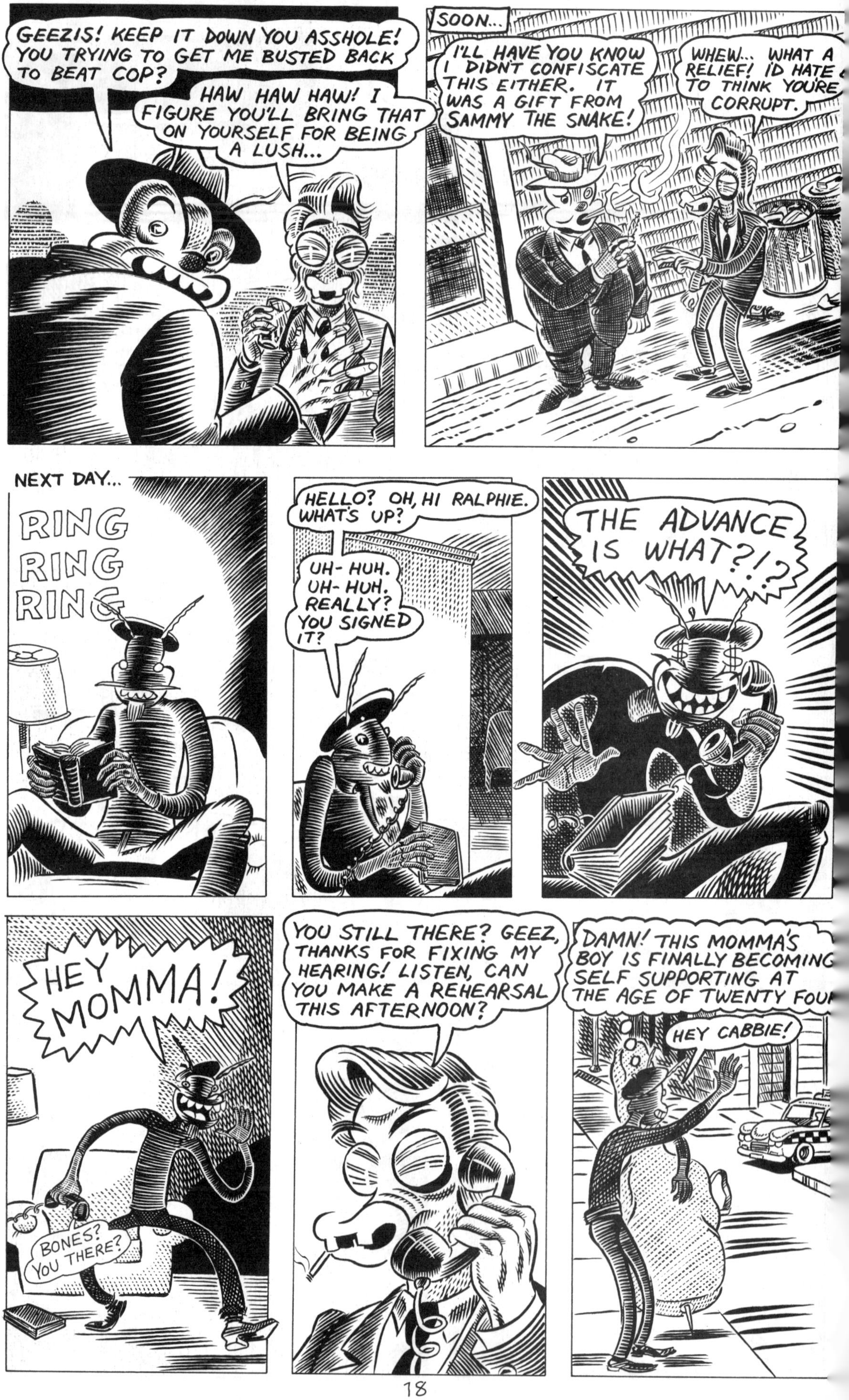
GEEZIS! KEEP IT DOWN YOU ASSHOLE! YOU TRYING TO GET ME BUSTED BACK TO BEAT COP?
HAW HAW HAW! I FIGURE YOU'LL BRING THAT ON YOURSELF FOR BEING A LUSH...
SOON...
I'LL HAVE YOU KNOW I DIDN'T CONFISCATE THIS EITHER. IT WAS A GIFT FROM SAMMY THE SNAKE!
WHEW... WHAT A RELIEF! I'D HATE TO THINK YOU'RE CORRUPT.
NEXT DAY...
RING
RING
RING
HELLO? OH, HI RALPHIE. WHAT'S UP?
UH-HUH. UH-HUH. REALLY? YOU SIGNED IT?
THE ADVANCE IS WHAT?!?
HEY MOMMA!
BONES? YOU THERE?
YOU STILL THERE? GEEZ, THANKS FOR FIXING MY HEARING! LISTEN, CAN YOU MAKE A REHEARSAL THIS AFTERNOON?
DAMN! THIS MOMMA'S BOY IS FINALLY BECOMING SELF SUPPORTING AT THE AGE OF TWENTY FOUR
HEY CABBIE!

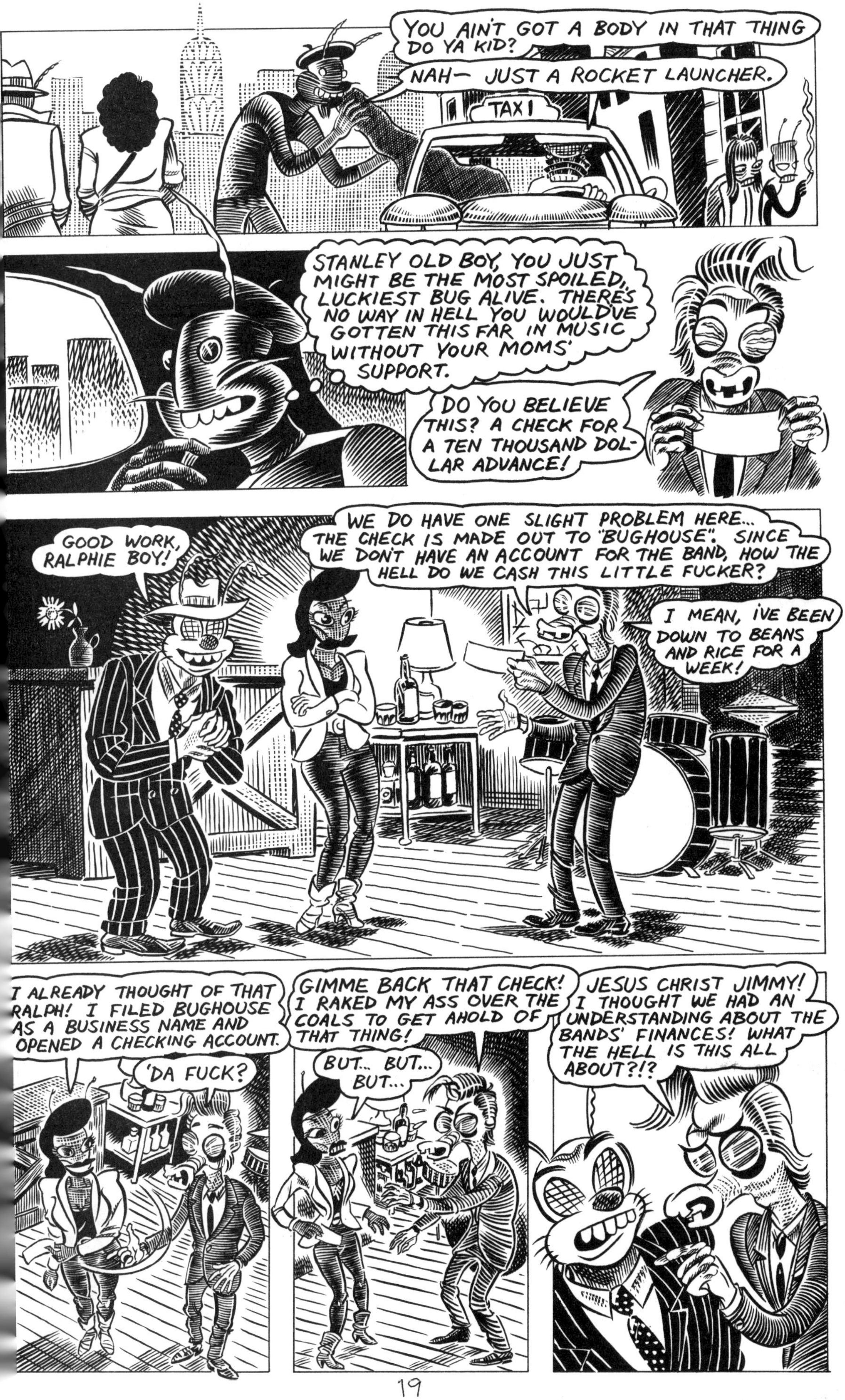
YOU AIN'T GOT A BODY IN THAT THING DO YA KID?
NAH— JUST A ROCKET LAUNCHER.
TAXI
STANLEY OLD BOY, YOU JUST MIGHT BE THE MOST SPOILED, LUCKIEST BUG ALIVE. THERE'S NO WAY IN HELL YOU WOULD'VE GOTTEN THIS FAR IN MUSIC WITHOUT YOUR MOMS' SUPPORT.
DO YOU BELIEVE THIS? A CHECK FOR A TEN THOUSAND DOL-LAR ADVANCE!
GOOD WORK, RALPHIE BOY!
WE DO HAVE ONE SLIGHT PROBLEM HERE... THE CHECK IS MADE OUT TO "BUGHOUSE". SINCE WE DON'T HAVE AN ACCOUNT FOR THE BAND, HOW THE HELL DO WE CASH THIS LITTLE FUCKER?
I MEAN, I'VE BEEN DOWN TO BEANS AND RICE FOR A WEEK!
I ALREADY THOUGHT OF THAT RALPH! I FILED BUGHOUSE AS A BUSINESS NAME AND OPENED A CHECKING ACCOUNT.
'DA FUCK?
GIMME BACK THAT CHECK! I RAKED MY ASS OVER THE COALS TO GET AHOLD OF THAT THING!
BUT... BUT... BUT...
JESUS CHRIST JIMMY! I THOUGHT WE HAD AN UNDERSTANDING ABOUT THE BANDS' FINANCES! WHAT THE HELL IS THIS ALL ABOUT?!?

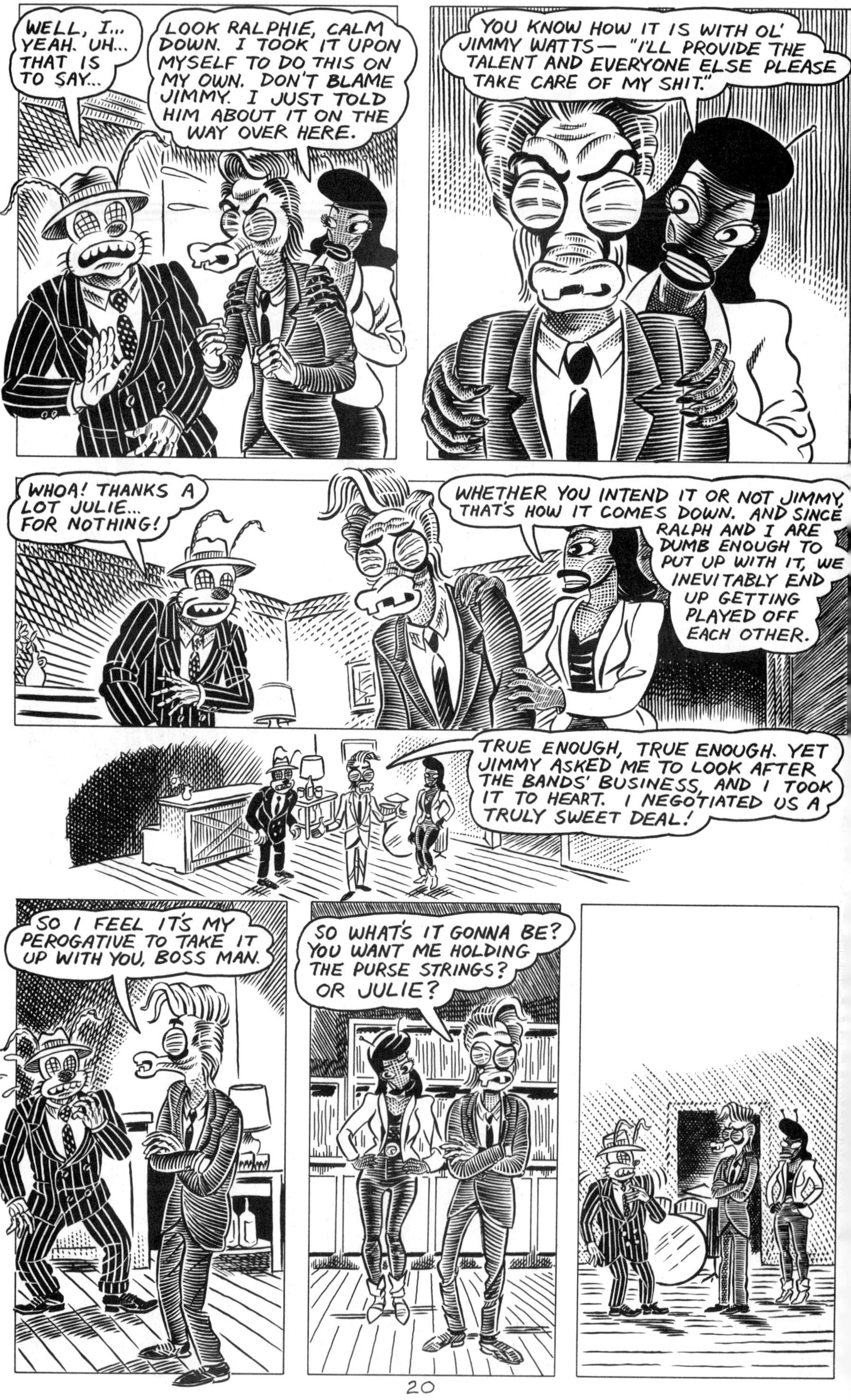
WELL, I... YEAH. UH... THAT IS TO SAY...
LOOK RALPHIE, CALM DOWN. I TOOK IT UPON MYSELF TO DO THIS ON MY OWN. DON'T BLAME JIMMY. I JUST TOLD HIM ABOUT IT ON THE WAY OVER HERE.
YOU KNOW HOW IT IS WITH OL' JIMMY WATTS— "I'LL PROVIDE THE TALENT AND EVERYONE ELSE PLEASE TAKE CARE OF MY SHIT."
WHOA! THANKS A LOT JULIE... FOR NOTHING!
WHETHER YOU INTEND IT OR NOT JIMMY, THAT'S HOW IT COMES DOWN. AND SINCE RALPH AND I ARE DUMB ENOUGH TO PUT UP WITH IT, WE INEVITABLY END UP GETTING PLAYED OFF EACH OTHER.
TRUE ENOUGH, TRUE ENOUGH. YET JIMMY ASKED ME TO LOOK AFTER THE BANDS' BUSINESS, AND I TOOK IT TO HEART. I NEGOTIATED US A TRULY SWEET DEAL!
SO I FEEL IT'S MY PEROGATIVE TO TAKE IT UP WITH YOU, BOSS MAN.
SO WHAT'S IT GONNA BE? YOU WANT ME HOLDING THE PURSE STRINGS? OR JULIE?

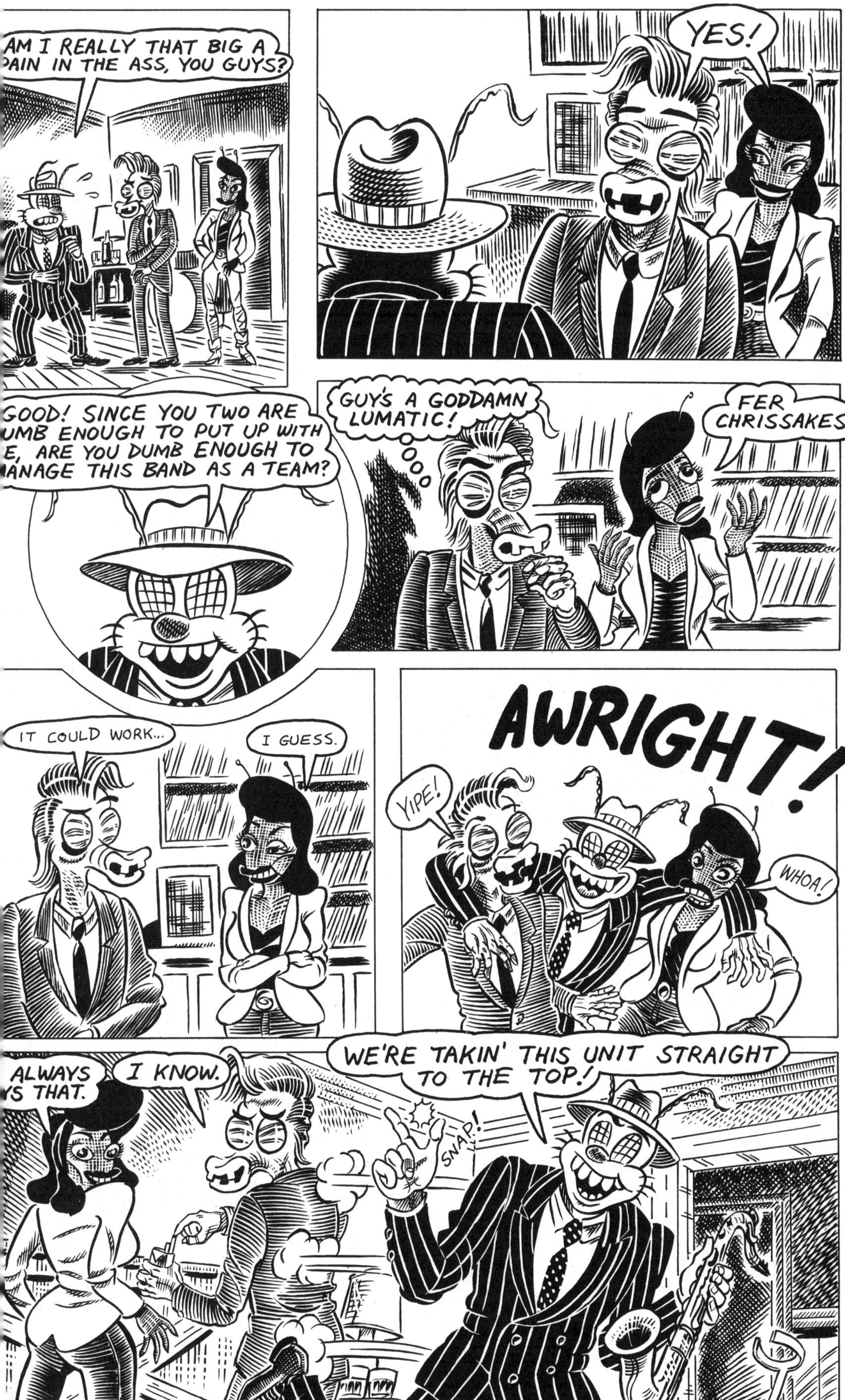
AM I REALLY THAT BIG A
PAIN IN THE ASS, YOU GUYS?
YES!
GOOD! SINCE YOU TWO ARE
UMB ENOUGH TO PUT UP WITH
E, ARE YOU DUMB ENOUGH TO
ANAGE THIS BAND AS A TEAM?
GUY'S A GODDAMN LUMATIC!
FER CHRISSAKES.
IT COULD WORK...
I GUESS.
AWRIGHT!
YIPE!
WHOA!
ALWAYS
YS THAT.
I KNOW.
WE'RE TAKIN' THIS UNIT STRAIGHT TO THE TOP!
SNAP!

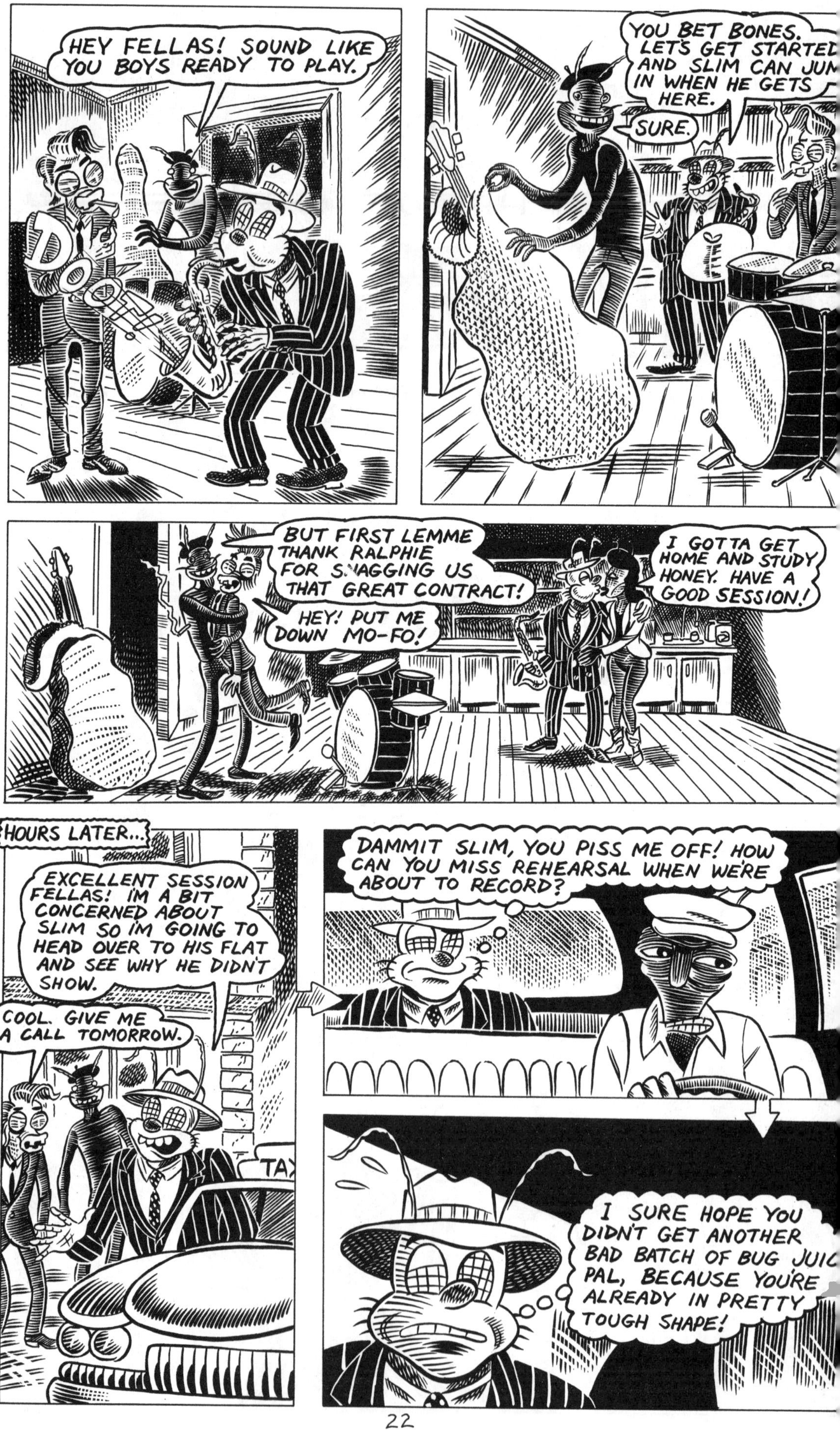
HEY FELLAS! SOUND LIKE YOU BOYS READY TO PLAY.
DOO
YOU BET BONES. LET'S GET STARTED AND SLIM CAN JUM IN WHEN HE GETS HERE.
SURE.
BUT FIRST LEMME THANK RALPHIE FOR SNAGGING US THAT GREAT CONTRACT!
HEY! PUT ME DOWN MO-FO!
I GOTTA GET HOME AND STUDY HONEY. HAVE A GOOD SESSION!
HOURS LATER...
EXCELLENT SESSION FELLAS! I'M A BIT CONCERNED ABOUT SLIM SO I'M GOING TO HEAD OVER TO HIS FLAT AND SEE WHY HE DIDN'T SHOW.
COOL. GIVE ME A CALL TOMORROW.
TAX
DAMMIT SLIM, YOU PISS ME OFF! HOW CAN YOU MISS REHEARSAL WHEN WE'RE ABOUT TO RECORD?
I SURE HOPE YOU DIDN'T GET ANOTHER BAD BATCH OF BUG JUIC PAL, BECAUSE YOU'RE ALREADY IN PRETTY TOUGH SHAPE!

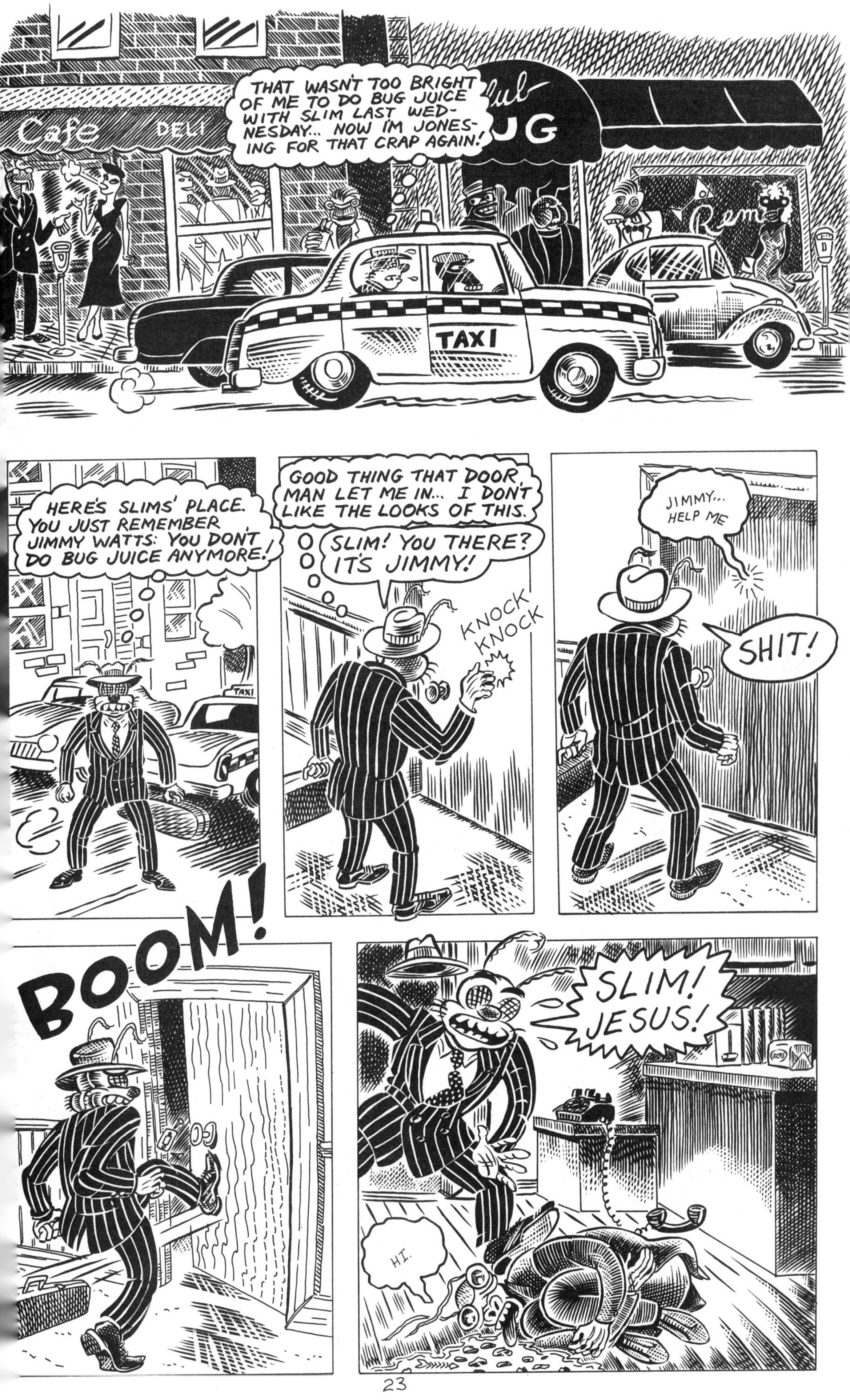
THAT WASN'T TOO BRIGHT OF ME TO DO BUG JUICE WITH SLIM LAST WEDNESDAY... NOW I'M JONESING FOR THAT CRAP AGAIN!
Cafe
DELI
TAXI
HERE'S SLIMS' PLACE. YOU JUST REMEMBER JIMMY WATTS: YOU DON'T DO BUG JUICE ANYMORE!
TAXI
GOOD THING THAT DOOR, MAN LET ME IN... I DON'T LIKE THE LOOKS OF THIS.
SLIM! YOU THERE? IT'S JIMMY!
KNOCK KNOCK
JIMMY... HELP ME
SHIT!
BOOM!
SLIM! JESUS!
HI.

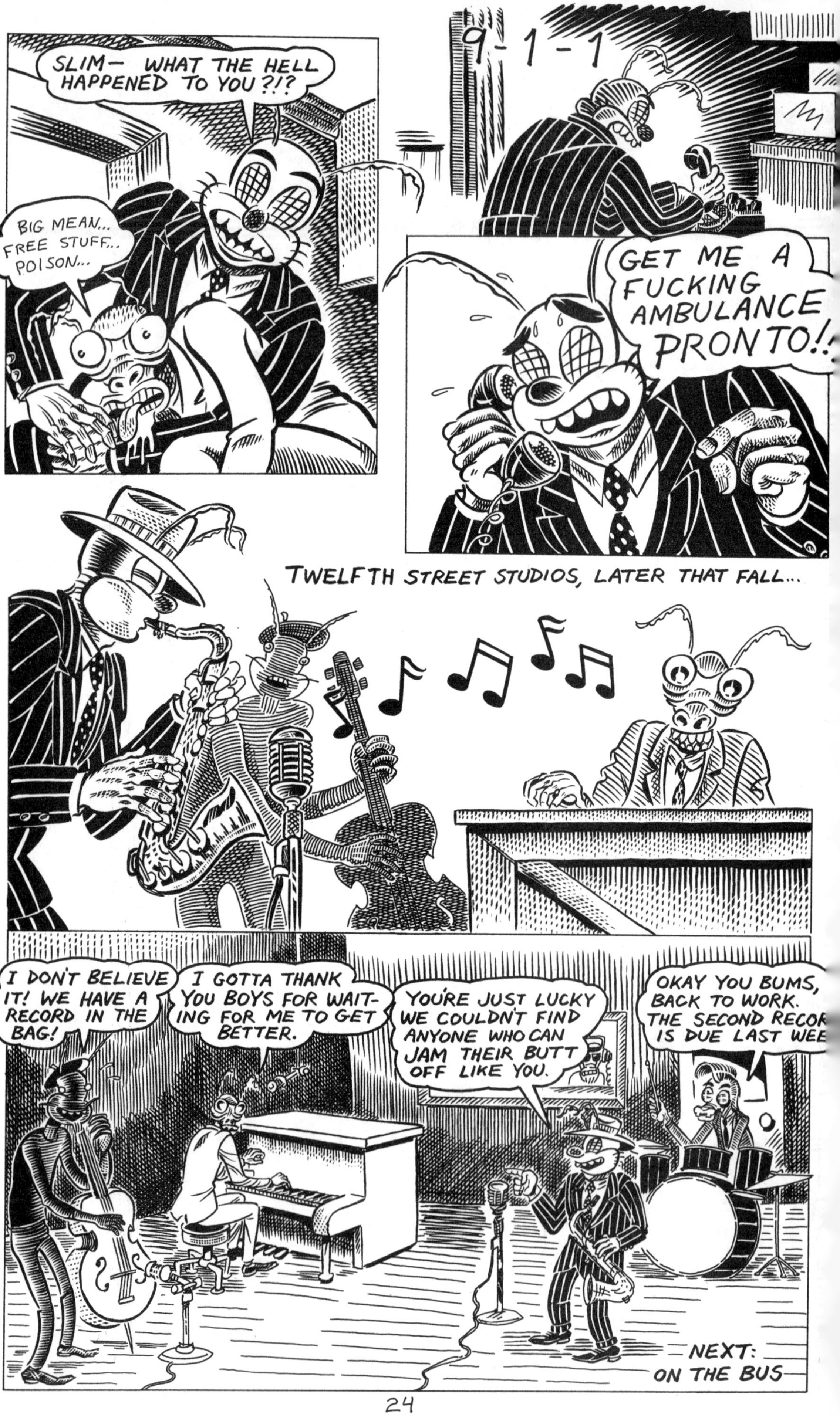
SLIM— WHAT THE HELL HAPPENED TO YOU?!?
BIG MEAN... FREE STUFF... POISON...
9-1-1
GET ME A FUCKING AMBULANCE PRONTO!!
TWELFTH STREET STUDIOS, LATER THAT FALL...
I DON'T BELIEVE IT! WE HAVE A RECORD IN THE BAG!
I GOTTA THANK YOU BOYS FOR WAITING FOR ME TO GET BETTER.
YOU'RE JUST LUCKY WE COULDN'T FIND ANYONE WHO CAN JAM THEIR BUTT OFF LIKE YOU.
OKAY YOU BUMS, BACK TO WORK. THE SECOND RECOR IS DUE LAST WEE
NEXT: ON THE BUS

BugHouse Part III: On the Road

SO THE KID FROM DUCAT RECORDS GAVE ME THE DATES FOR OUR FIRST NATIONAL TOUR... I GUESS IT'S TIME TO PICK UP SOME KIND OF VAN OR SMALL TRUCK.

NO PROBLEM... MY COUSIN EDDIE HAS A LINE ON A VEHICLE FOR US.

BUT THERE'S SOMETHING ELSE ABOUT TOURING THAT WORRIES ME, JIMMY.

OH? AND WHAT MIGHT THAT BE?

UH, WELL... I KNOW YOU'RE BETWEEN HABITS RIGHT NOW, AND I COMMEND YOU FOR IT...

BETWEEN HABITS?! I KICKED SLIM!

OKAY, SO YOU KICKED. THE POINT IS, I STILL HAVE A LITTLE HABIT. IF I TRY TO STOP BUG JUICE NOW, I'LL FALL TO PIECES. I'D HARDLY BE ABLE TO TRAVEL AND PLAY WELL BECAUSE I'D BE TOO SICK.

HMMM... I UNDERSTAND THAT. BUT I GOTTA ASK YOU TO BE COOL ABOUT IT. FOR THE BAND, AND FOR ME BECAUSE I'M REALLY TRYING TO STAY CLEAN.

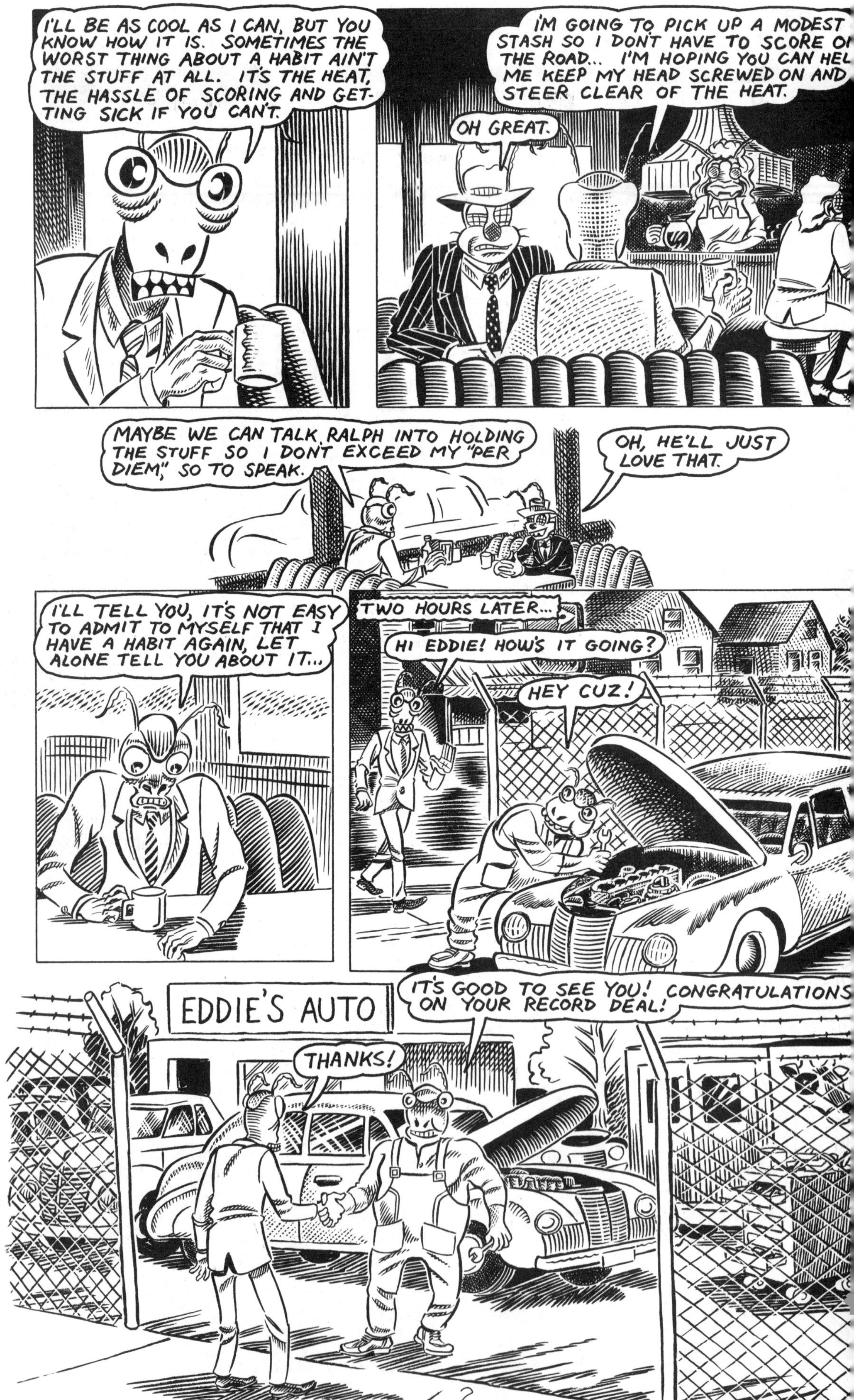
I'LL BE AS COOL AS I CAN, BUT YOU KNOW HOW IT IS. SOMETIMES THE WORST THING ABOUT A HABIT AIN'T THE STUFF AT ALL. IT'S THE HEAT, THE HASSLE OF SCORING AND GETTING SICK IF YOU CAN'T.
I'M GOING TO PICK UP A MODEST STASH SO I DON'T HAVE TO SCORE O
THE ROAD... I'M HOPING YOU CAN HEL
ME KEEP MY HEAD SCREWED ON AND STEER CLEAR OF THE HEAT.
OH GREAT.
MAYBE WE CAN TALK RALPH INTO HOLDING THE STUFF SO I DON'T EXCEED MY "PER DIEM," SO TO SPEAK.
OH, HE'LL JUST LOVE THAT.
I'LL TELL YOU, IT'S NOT EASY TO ADMIT TO MYSELF THAT I HAVE A HABIT AGAIN, LET ALONE TELL YOU ABOUT IT...
TWO HOURS LATER...
HI EDDIE! HOW'S IT GOING?
HEY CUZ!
EDDIE'S AUTO
IT'S GOOD TO SEE YOU! CONGRATULATIONS ON YOUR RECORD DEAL!
THANKS!

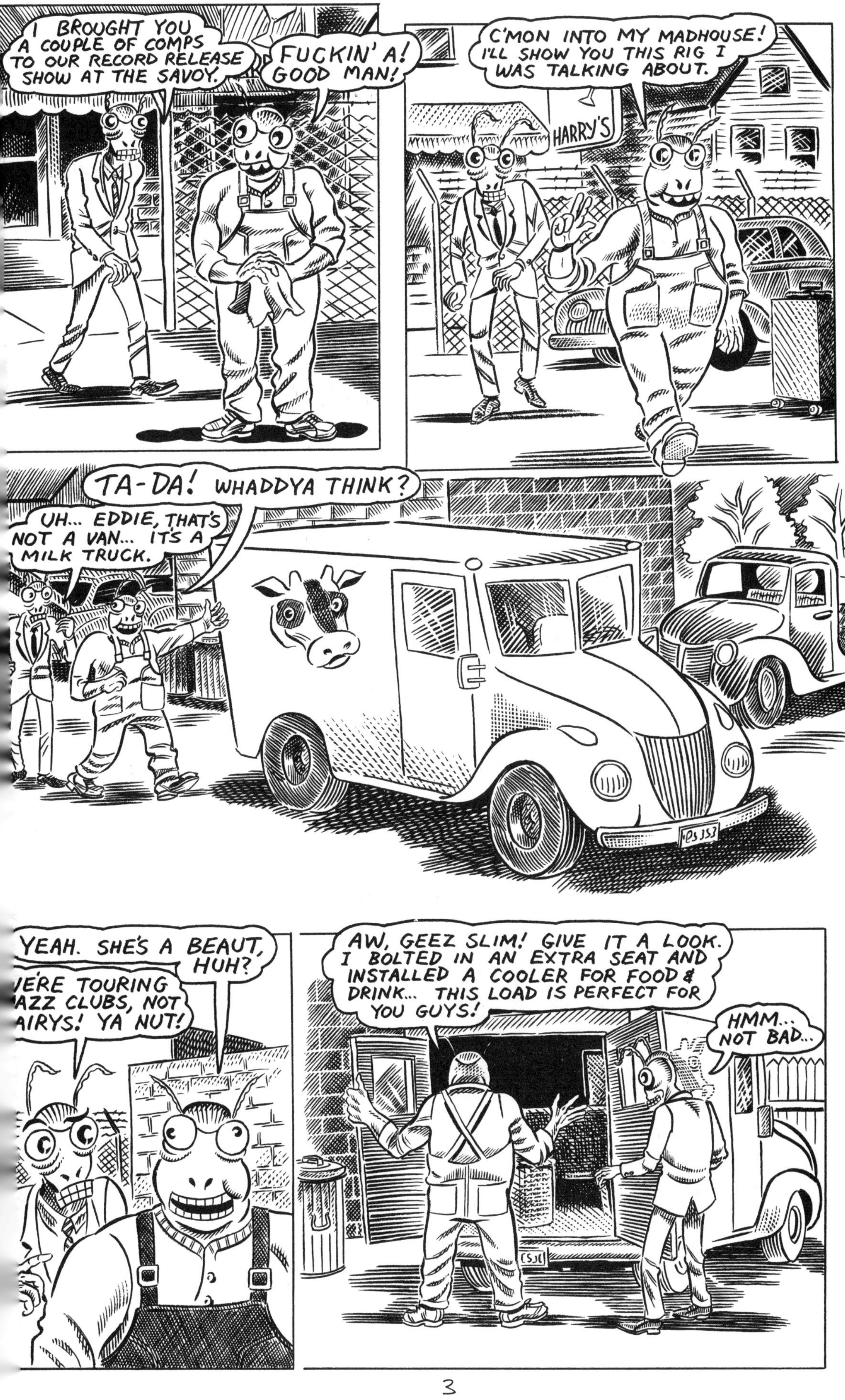
I BROUGHT YOU A COUPLE OF COMPS TO OUR RECORD RELEASE SHOW AT THE SAVOY.
FUCKIN' A! GOOD MAN!
C'MON INTO MY MADHOUSE! I'LL SHOW YOU THIS RIG I WAS TALKING ABOUT.
HARRY'S
TA-DA! WHADDYA THINK?
UH... EDDIE, THAT'S NOT A VAN... IT'S A MILK TRUCK.
YEAH. SHE'S A BEAUT, HUH?
WE'RE TOURING JAZZ CLUBS, NOT DAIRYS! YA NUT!
AW, GEEZ SLIM! GIVE IT A LOOK. I BOLTED IN AN EXTRA SEAT AND INSTALLED A COOLER FOR FOOD & DRINK... THIS LOAD IS PERFECT FOR YOU GUYS!
HMM... NOT BAD...

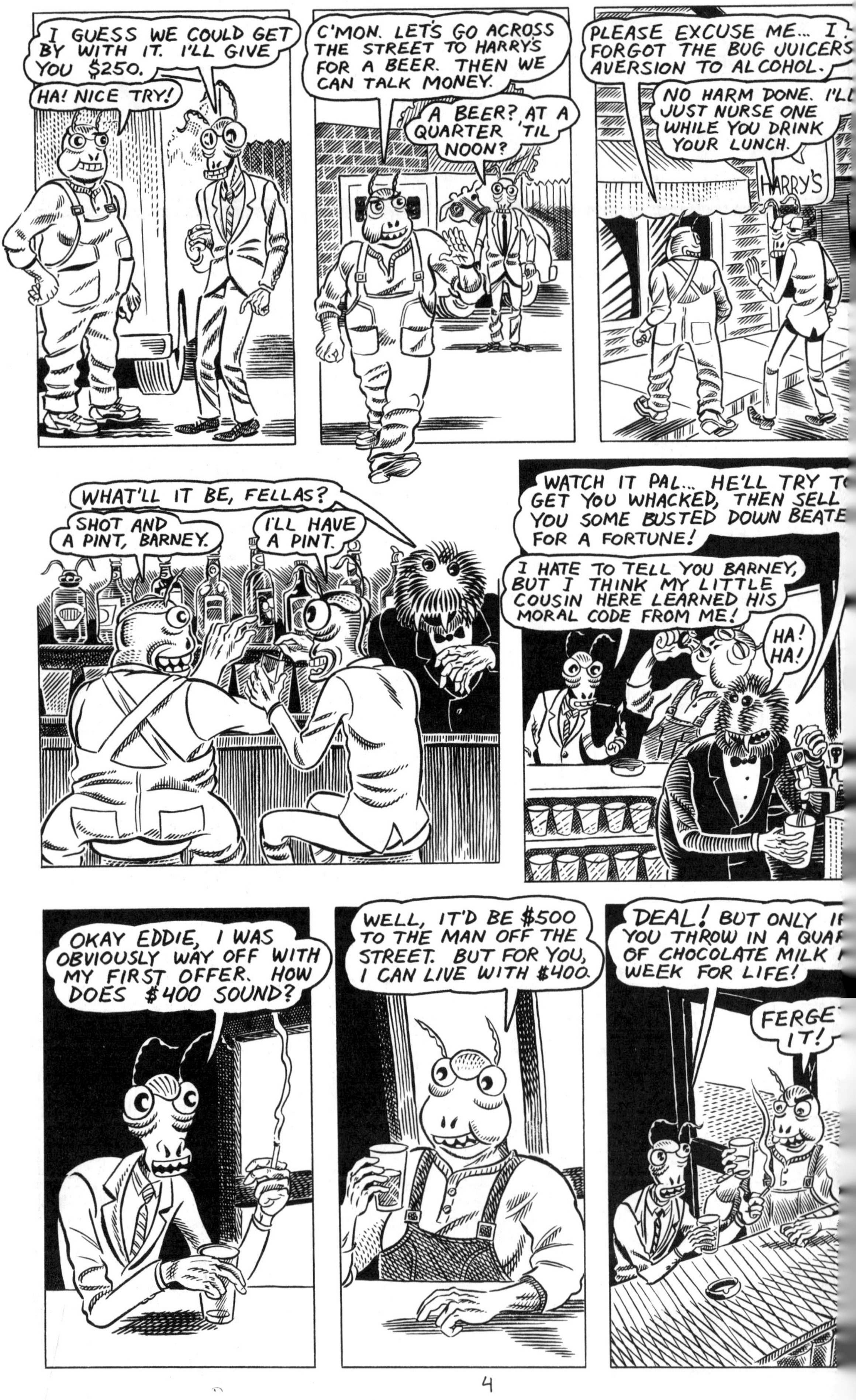
I GUESS WE COULD GET BY WITH IT. I'LL GIVE YOU $250.
HA! NICE TRY!
C'MON. LET'S GO ACROSS THE STREET TO HARRY'S FOR A BEER. THEN WE CAN TALK MONEY.
A BEER? AT A QUARTER 'TIL NOON?
PLEASE EXCUSE ME... I... FORGOT THE BUG JUICER'S AVERSION TO ALCOHOL.
NO HARM DONE. I'LL JUST NURSE ONE WHILE YOU DRINK YOUR LUNCH.
HARRY'S
WHAT'LL IT BE, FELLAS?
SHOT AND A PINT, BARNEY.
I'LL HAVE A PINT.
WATCH IT PAL... HE'LL TRY TO GET YOU WHACKED, THEN SELL YOU SOME BUSTED DOWN BEATE
FOR A FORTUNE!
I HATE TO TELL YOU BARNEY, BUT I THINK MY LITTLE COUSIN HERE LEARNED HIS MORAL CODE FROM ME!
HA! HA!
OKAY EDDIE, I WAS OBVIOUSLY WAY OFF WITH MY FIRST OFFER. HOW DOES $400 SOUND?
WELL, IT'D BE $500 TO THE MAN OFF THE STREET. BUT FOR YOU, I CAN LIVE WITH $400.
DEAL! BUT ONLY I
YOU THROW IN A QUA
OF CHOCOLATE MILK
WEEK FOR LIFE!
FERGE
IT!

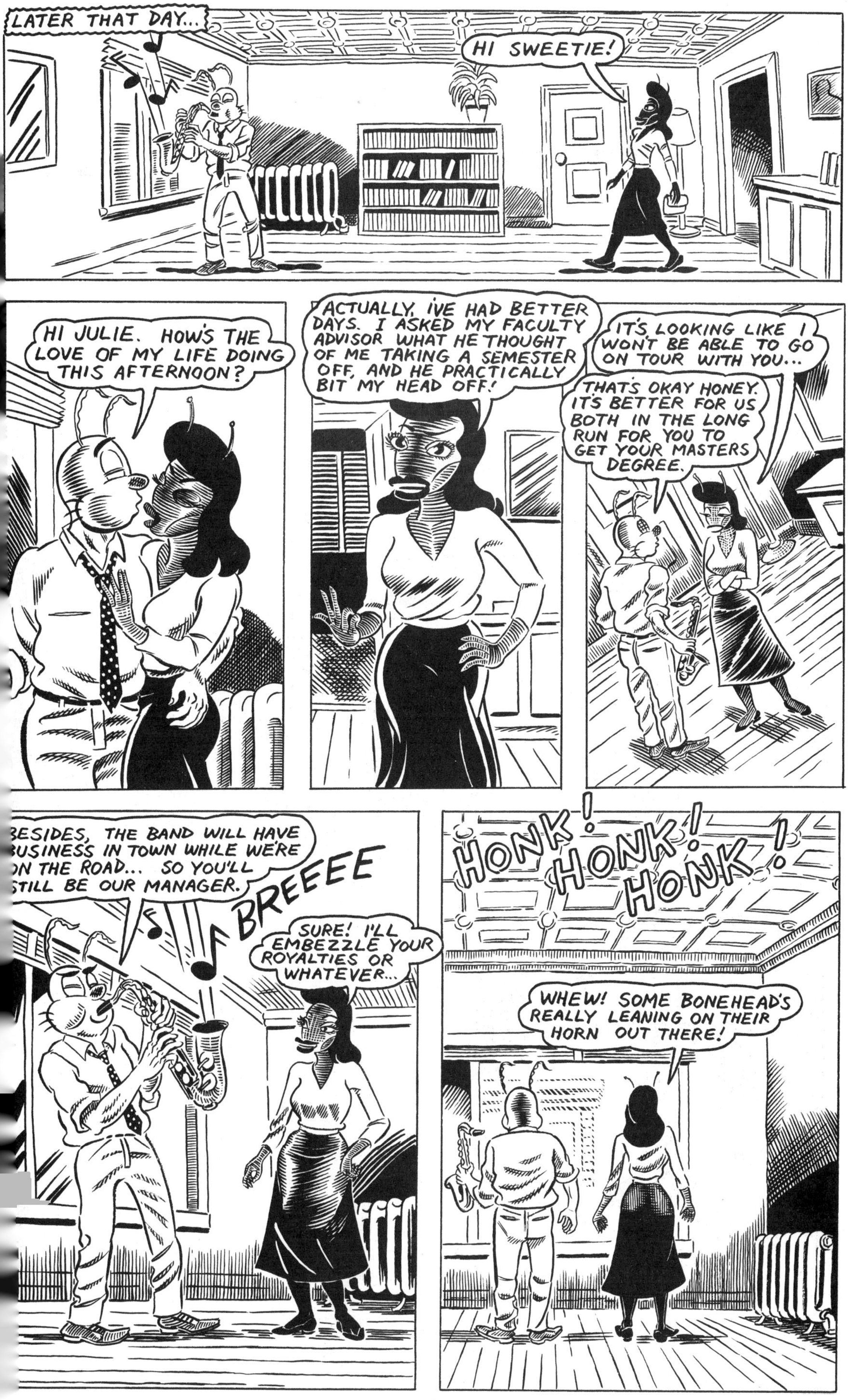
LATER THAT DAY...
HI SWEETIE!
HI JULIE. HOW'S THE LOVE OF MY LIFE DOING THIS AFTERNOON?
ACTUALLY, I'VE HAD BETTER DAYS. I ASKED MY FACULTY ADVISOR WHAT HE THOUGHT OF ME TAKING A SEMESTER OFF, AND HE PRACTICALLY BIT MY HEAD OFF!
IT'S LOOKING LIKE I WON'T BE ABLE TO GO ON TOUR WITH YOU...
THAT'S OKAY HONEY. IT'S BETTER FOR US BOTH IN THE LONG RUN FOR YOU TO GET YOUR MASTERS DEGREE.
BESIDES, THE BAND WILL HAVE BUSINESS IN TOWN WHILE WE'RE ON THE ROAD... SO YOU'LL STILL BE OUR MANAGER.
BREEEEE
SURE! I'LL EMBEZZLE YOUR ROYALTIES OR WHATEVER...
HONK! HONK! HONK!
WHEW! SOME BONEHEAD'S REALLY LEANING ON THEIR HORN OUT THERE!

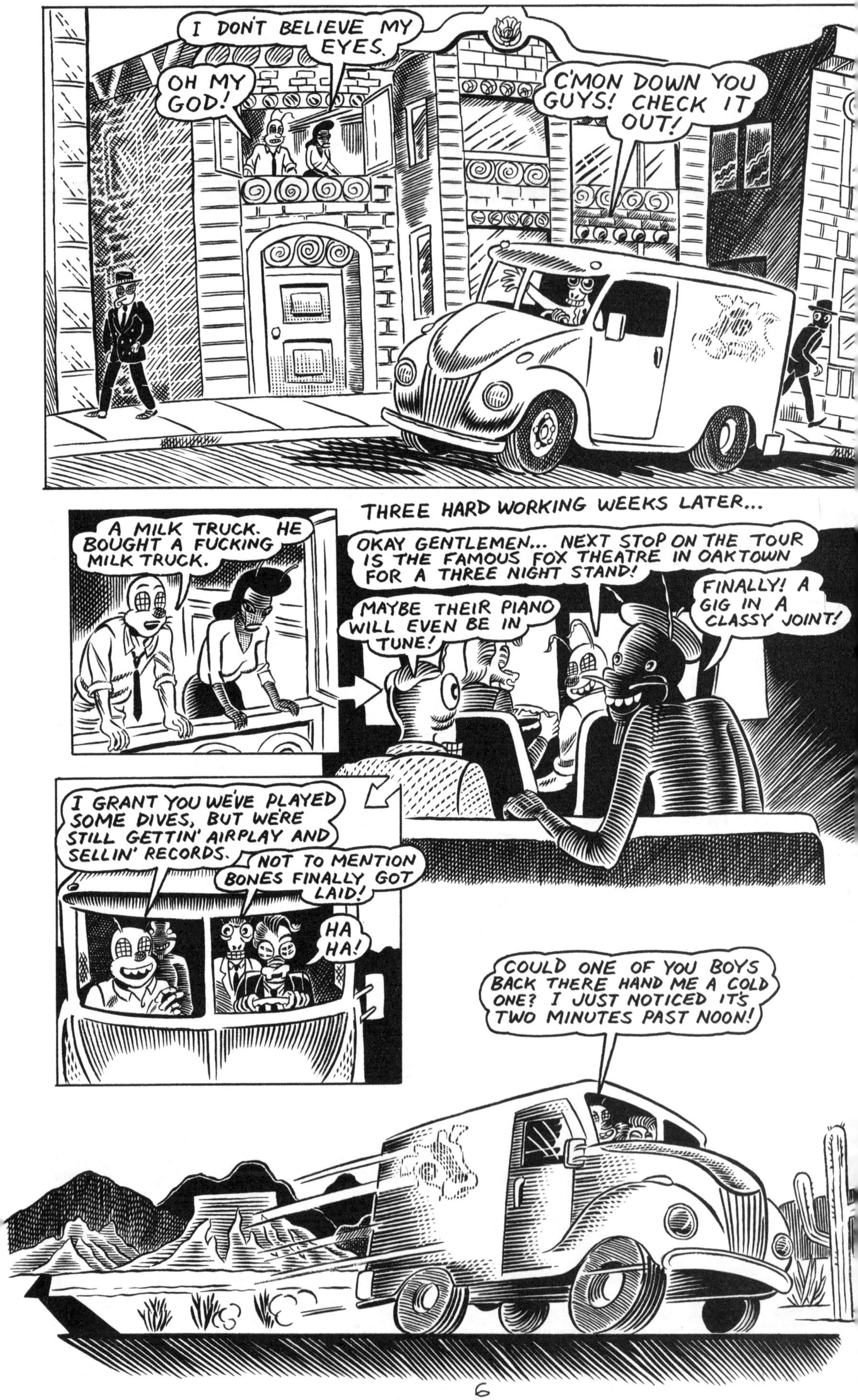
I DON'T BELIEVE MY EYES.
OH MY GOD!
C'MON DOWN YOU GUYS! CHECK IT OUT!
A MILK TRUCK. HE BOUGHT A FUCKING MILK TRUCK.
THREE HARD WORKING WEEKS LATER...
OKAY GENTLEMEN... NEXT STOP ON THE TOUR IS THE FAMOUS FOX THEATRE IN OAKTOWN FOR A THREE NIGHT STAND!
MAYBE THEIR PIANO WILL EVEN BE IN TUNE!
FINALLY! A GIG IN A CLASSY JOINT!
I GRANT YOU WE'VE PLAYED SOME DIVES, BUT WE'RE STILL GETTIN' AIRPLAY AND SELLIN' RECORDS.
NOT TO MENTION BONES FINALLY GOT LAID!
HA HA!
COULD ONE OF YOU BOYS BACK THERE HAND ME A COLD ONE? I JUST NOTICED IT'S TWO MINUTES PAST NOON!

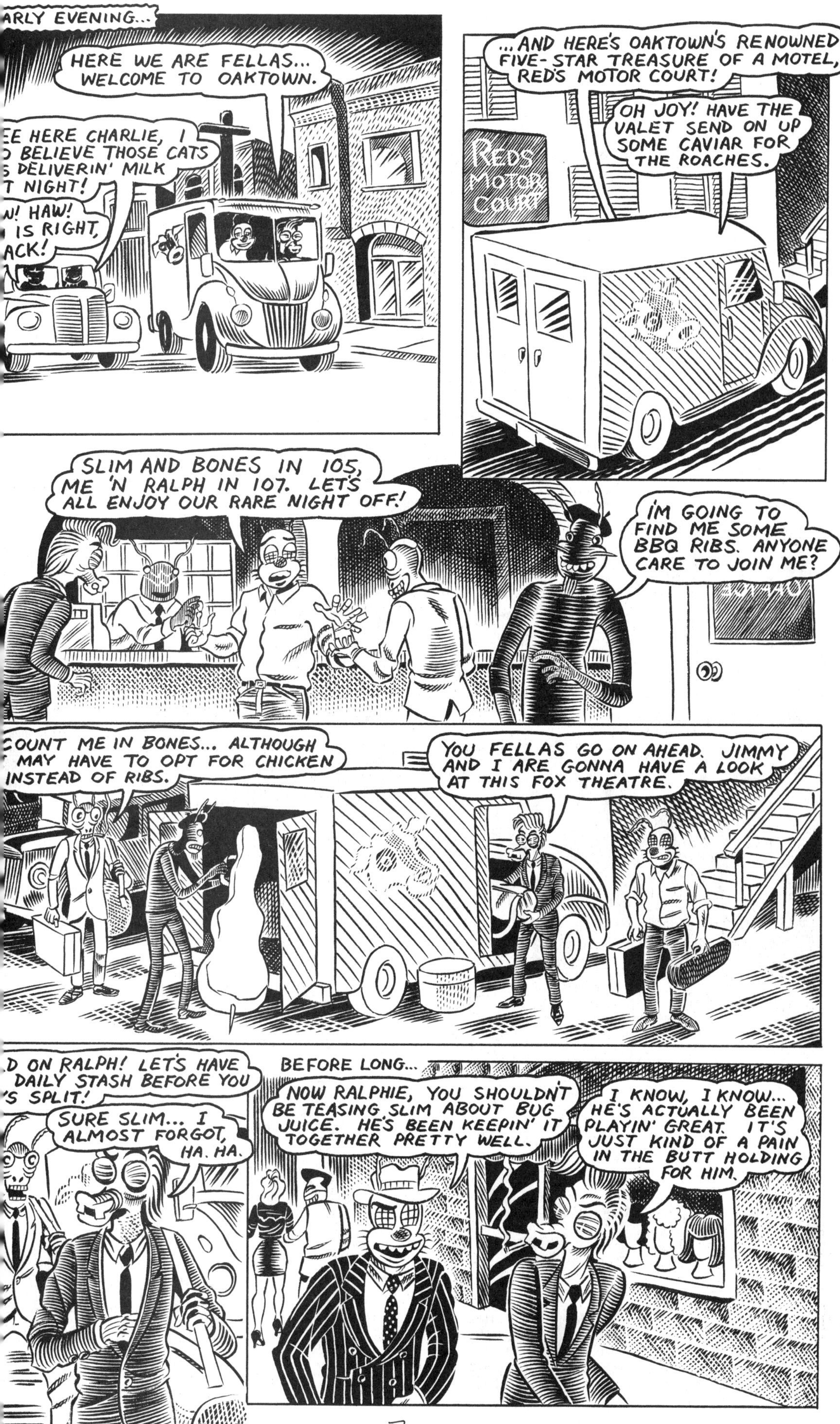
ARLY EVENING...
HERE WE ARE FELLAS... WELCOME TO OAKTOWN.
EE HERE CHARLIE, I
D BELIEVE THOSE CATS
S DELIVERIN' MILK
T NIGHT!
W! HAW!
IS RIGHT,
ACK!
...AND HERE'S OAKTOWN'S RENOWNED FIVE-STAR TREASURE OF A MOTEL, RED'S MOTOR COURT!
OH JOY! HAVE THE VALET SEND ON UP SOME CAVIAR FOR THE ROACHES.
RED'S MOTOR COURT
SLIM AND BONES IN 105, ME 'N RALPH IN 107. LET'S ALL ENJOY OUR RARE NIGHT OFF!
I'M GOING TO FIND ME SOME BBQ RIBS. ANYONE CARE TO JOIN ME?
COUNT ME IN BONES... ALTHOUGH
MAY HAVE TO OPT FOR CHICKEN
INSTEAD OF RIBS.
YOU FELLAS GO ON AHEAD. JIMMY AND I ARE GONNA HAVE A LOOK AT THIS FOX THEATRE.
D ON RALPH! LET'S HAVE
DAILY STASH BEFORE YOU
'S SPLIT!
SURE SLIM... I ALMOST FORGOT, HA. HA.
BEFORE LONG...
NOW RALPHIE, YOU SHOULDN'T BE TEASING SLIM ABOUT BUG JUICE. HE'S BEEN KEEPIN' IT TOGETHER PRETTY WELL.
I KNOW, I KNOW... HE'S ACTUALLY BEEN PLAYIN' GREAT. IT'S JUST KIND OF A PAIN IN THE BUTT HOLDING FOR HIM.

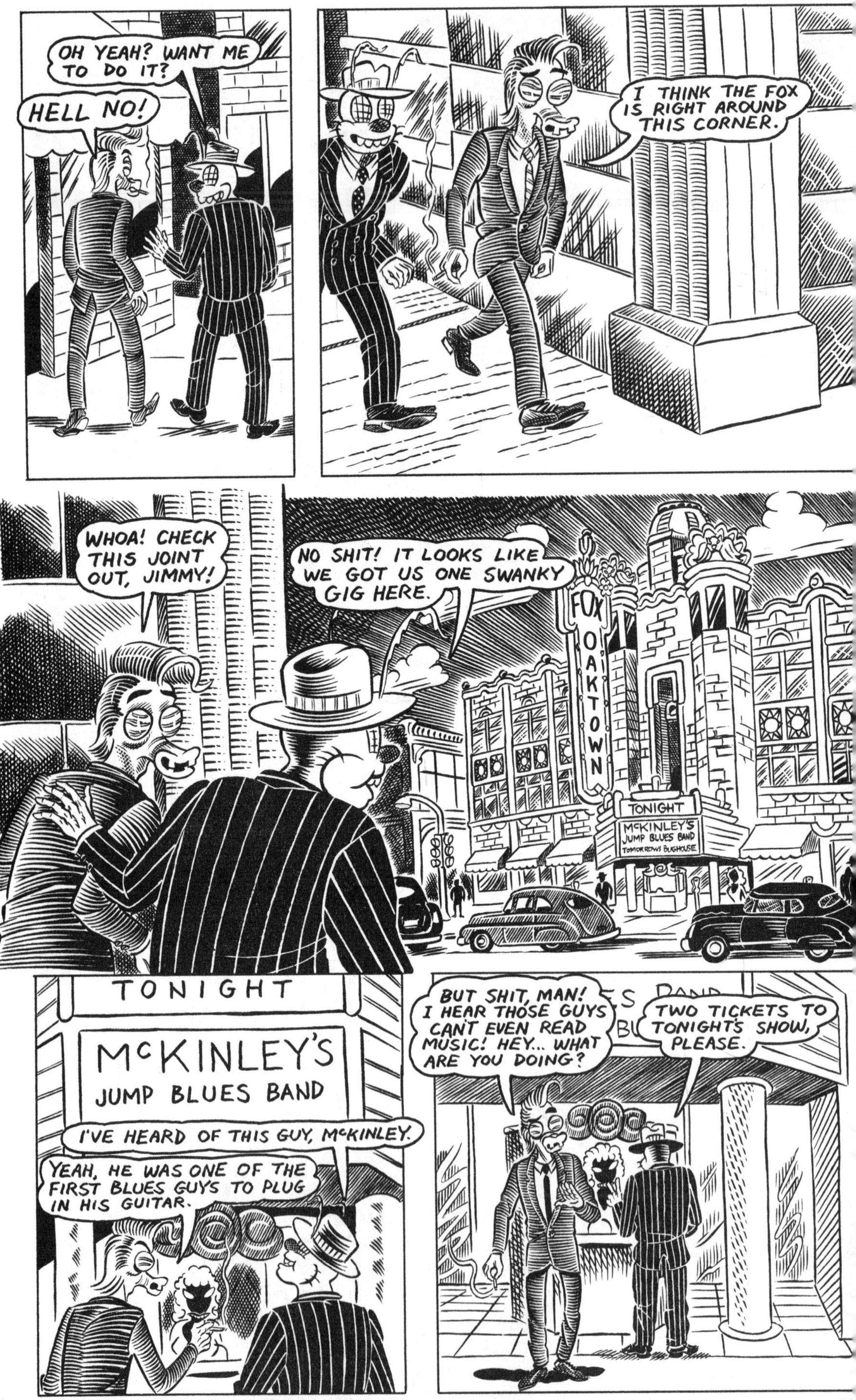
OH YEAH? WANT ME TO DO IT?
HELL NO!
I THINK THE FOX IS RIGHT AROUND THIS CORNER.
WHOA! CHECK THIS JOINT OUT, JIMMY!
NO SHIT! IT LOOKS LIKE WE GOT US ONE SWANKY GIG HERE.
FOX
OAKTOWN
TONIGHT
McKINLEY'S
JUMP BLUES BAND
TOMORROWS BUGHOUSE
TONIGHT
McKINLEY'S
JUMP BLUES BAND
I'VE HEARD OF THIS GUY, McKINLEY.
YEAH, HE WAS ONE OF THE FIRST BLUES GUYS TO PLUG IN HIS GUITAR.
BUT SHIT, MAN! I HEAR THOSE GUYS CAN'T EVEN READ MUSIC! HEY... WHAT ARE YOU DOING?
TWO TICKETS TO TONIGHT'S SHOW, PLEASE.

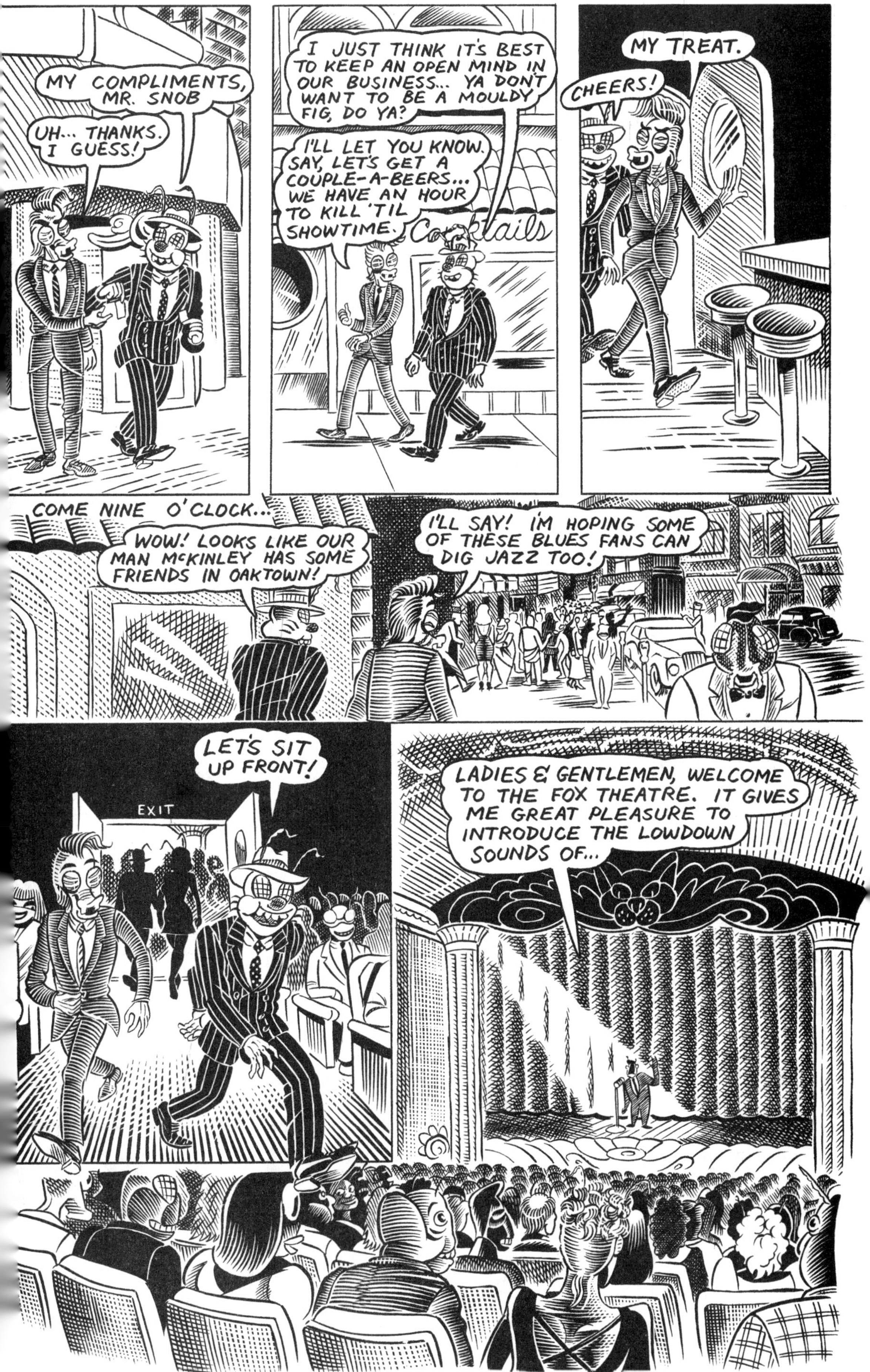
MY COMPLIMENTS, MR. SNOB
UH... THANKS. I GUESS!
I JUST THINK IT'S BEST TO KEEP AN OPEN MIND IN OUR BUSINESS... YA DON'T WANT TO BE A MOULDY FIG, DO YA?
I'LL LET YOU KNOW. SAY, LET'S GET A COUPLE-A-BEERS... WE HAVE AN HOUR TO KILL 'TIL SHOWTIME.
Cocktails
CHEERS!
MY TREAT.
COME NINE O'CLOCK...
WOW! LOOKS LIKE OUR MAN McKINLEY HAS SOME FRIENDS IN OAKTOWN!
I'LL SAY! I'M HOPING SOME OF THESE BLUES FANS CAN DIG JAZZ TOO!
LET'S SIT UP FRONT!
EXIT
LADIES & GENTLEMEN, WELCOME TO THE FOX THEATRE. IT GIVES ME GREAT PLEASURE TO INTRODUCE THE LOWDOWN SOUNDS OF...

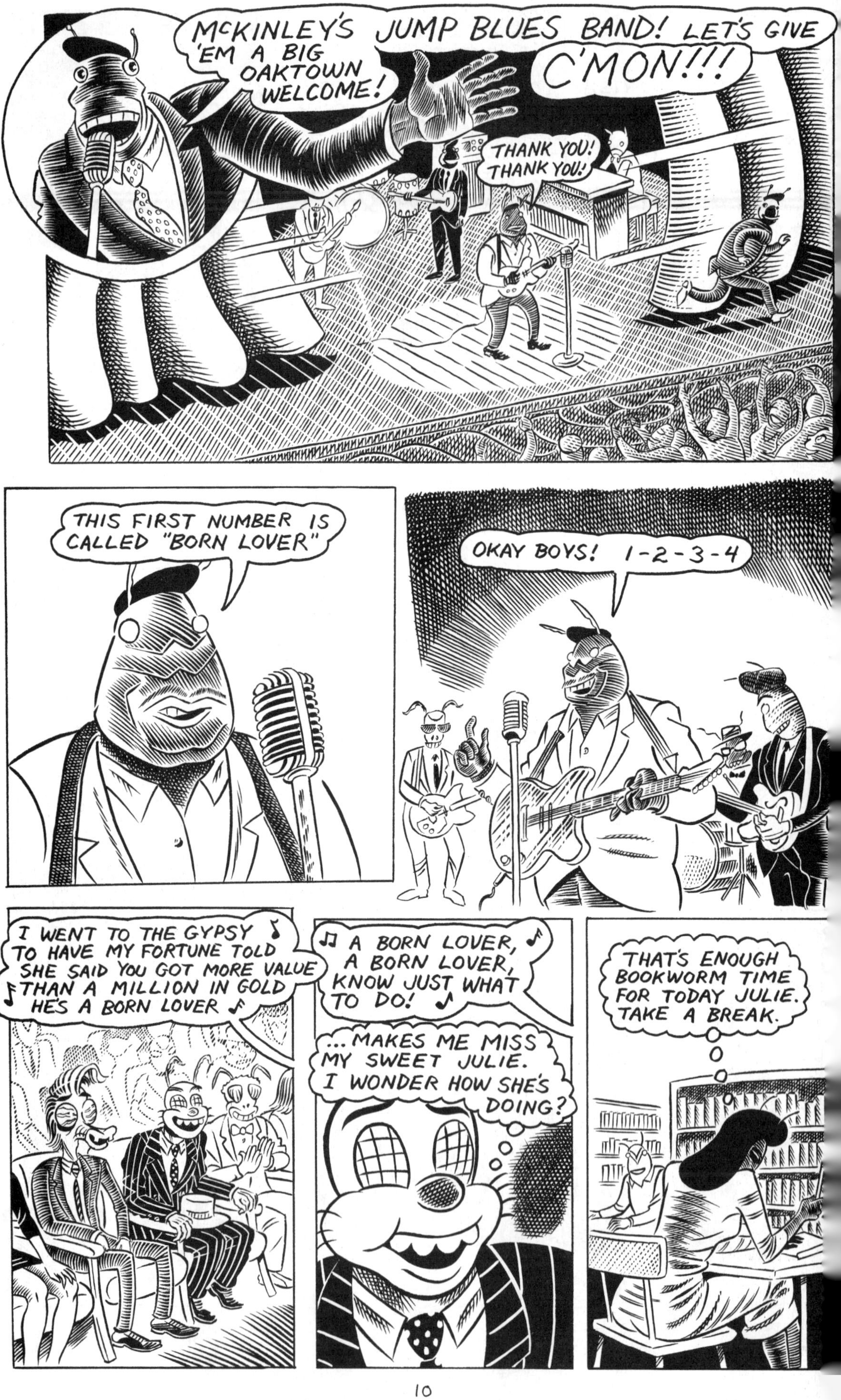
McKINLEY'S JUMP BLUES BAND! LET'S GIVE 'EM A BIG OAKTOWN WELCOME!
C'MON!!!
THANK YOU! THANK YOU!
THIS FIRST NUMBER IS CALLED "BORN LOVER"
OKAY BOYS! 1-2-3-4
I WENT TO THE GYPSY TO HAVE MY FORTUNE TOLD SHE SAID YOU GOT MORE VALUE THAN A MILLION IN GOLD HE'S A BORN LOVER
A BORN LOVER, A BORN LOVER, KNOW JUST WHAT TO DO!
...MAKES ME MISS MY SWEET JULIE. I WONDER HOW SHE'S DOING?
THAT'S ENOUGH BOOKWORM TIME FOR TODAY JULIE. TAKE A BREAK.

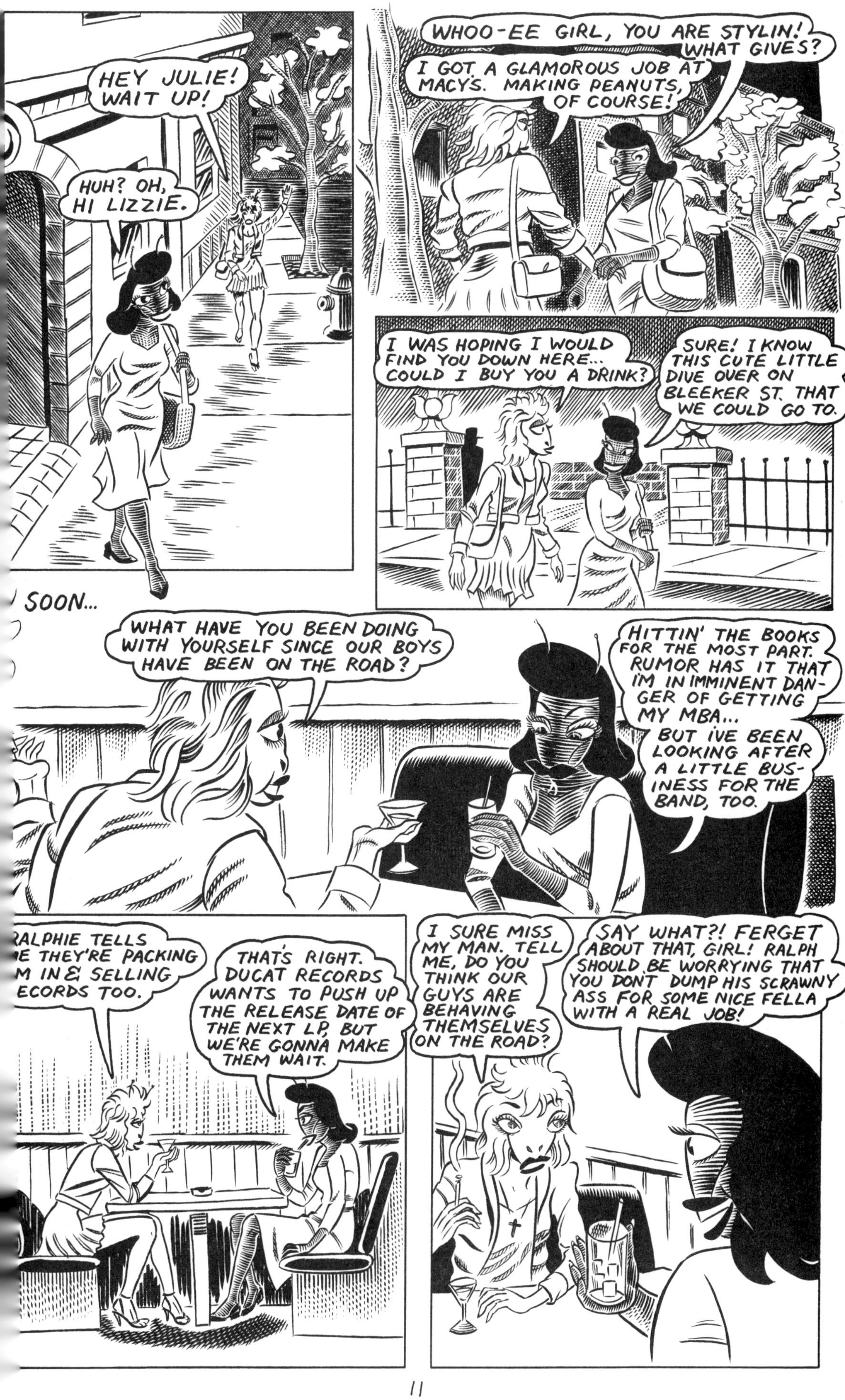

HEY JULIE! WAIT UP!
HUH? OH, HI LIZZIE.
WHOO-EE GIRL, YOU ARE STYLIN! WHAT GIVES?
I GOT A GLAMOROUS JOB AT MACY'S. MAKING PEANUTS, OF COURSE!
I WAS HOPING I WOULD FIND YOU DOWN HERE... COULD I BUY YOU A DRINK?
SURE! I KNOW THIS CUTE LITTLE DIVE OVER ON BLEEKER ST. THAT WE COULD GO TO.
SOON...
WHAT HAVE YOU BEEN DOING WITH YOURSELF SINCE OUR BOYS HAVE BEEN ON THE ROAD?
HITTIN' THE BOOKS FOR THE MOST PART. RUMOR HAS IT THAT I'M IN IMMINENT DANGER OF GETTING MY MBA...
BUT I'VE BEEN LOOKING AFTER A LITTLE BUSINESS FOR THE BAND, TOO.
RALPHIE TELLS E THEY'RE PACKING M IN & SELLING ECORDS TOO.
THAT'S RIGHT. DUCAT RECORDS WANTS TO PUSH UP THE RELEASE DATE OF THE NEXT LP, BUT WE'RE GONNA MAKE THEM WAIT.
I SURE MISS MY MAN. TELL ME, DO YOU THINK OUR GUYS ARE BEHAVING THEMSELVES ON THE ROAD?
SAY WHAT?! FERGET ABOUT THAT, GIRL! RALPH SHOULD BE WORRYING THAT YOU DON'T DUMP HIS SCRAWNY ASS FOR SOME NICE FELLA WITH A REAL JOB!

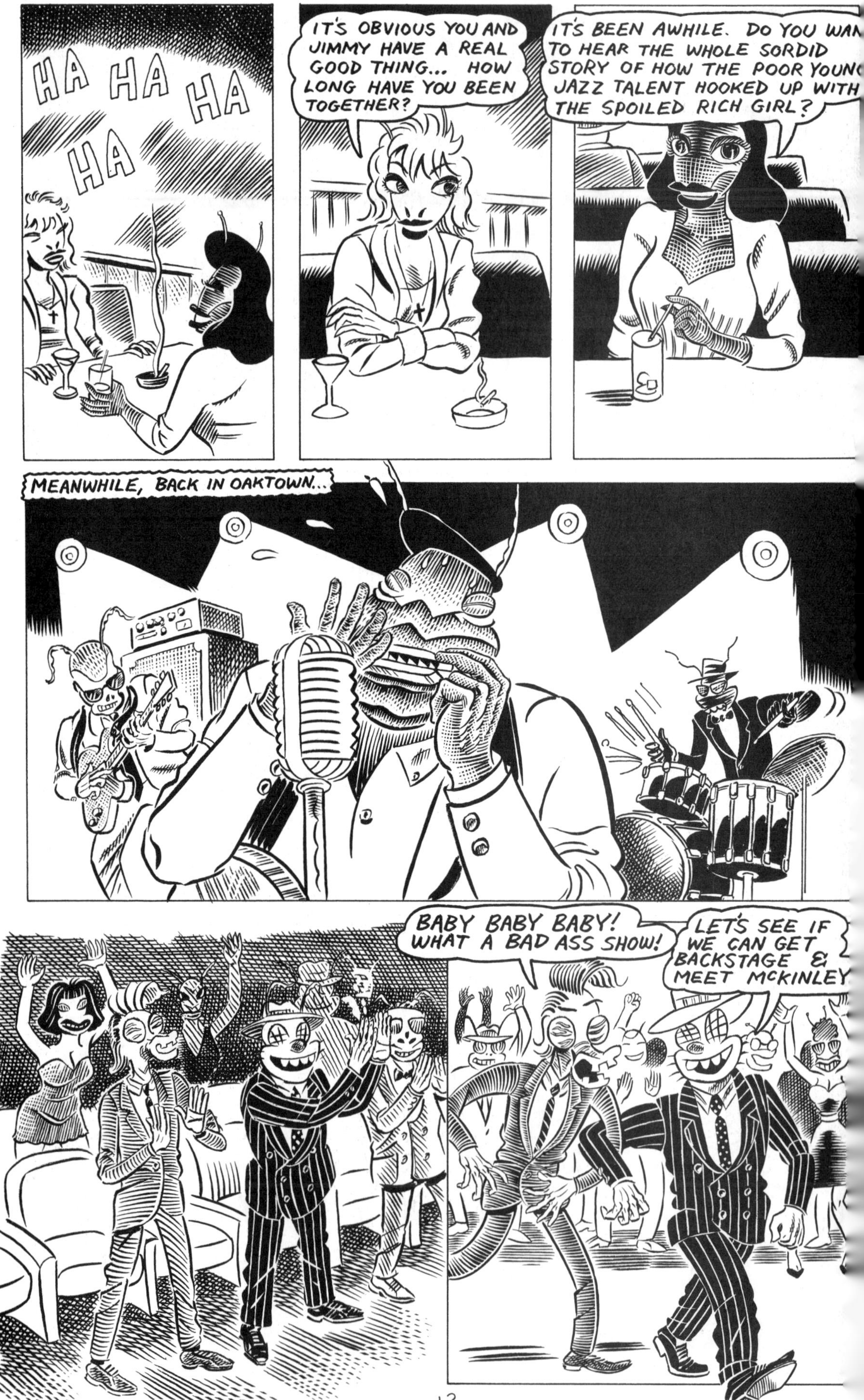
HA HA HA HA
IT'S OBVIOUS YOU AND JIMMY HAVE A REAL GOOD THING... HOW LONG HAVE YOU BEEN TOGETHER?
IT'S BEEN AWHILE. DO YOU WAN TO HEAR THE WHOLE SORDID STORY OF HOW THE POOR YOUN JAZZ TALENT HOOKED UP WITH THE SPOILED RICH GIRL?
MEANWHILE, BACK IN OAKTOWN...
BABY BABY BABY! WHAT A BAD ASS SHOW!
LET'S SEE IF WE CAN GET BACKSTAGE & MEET MCKINLEY

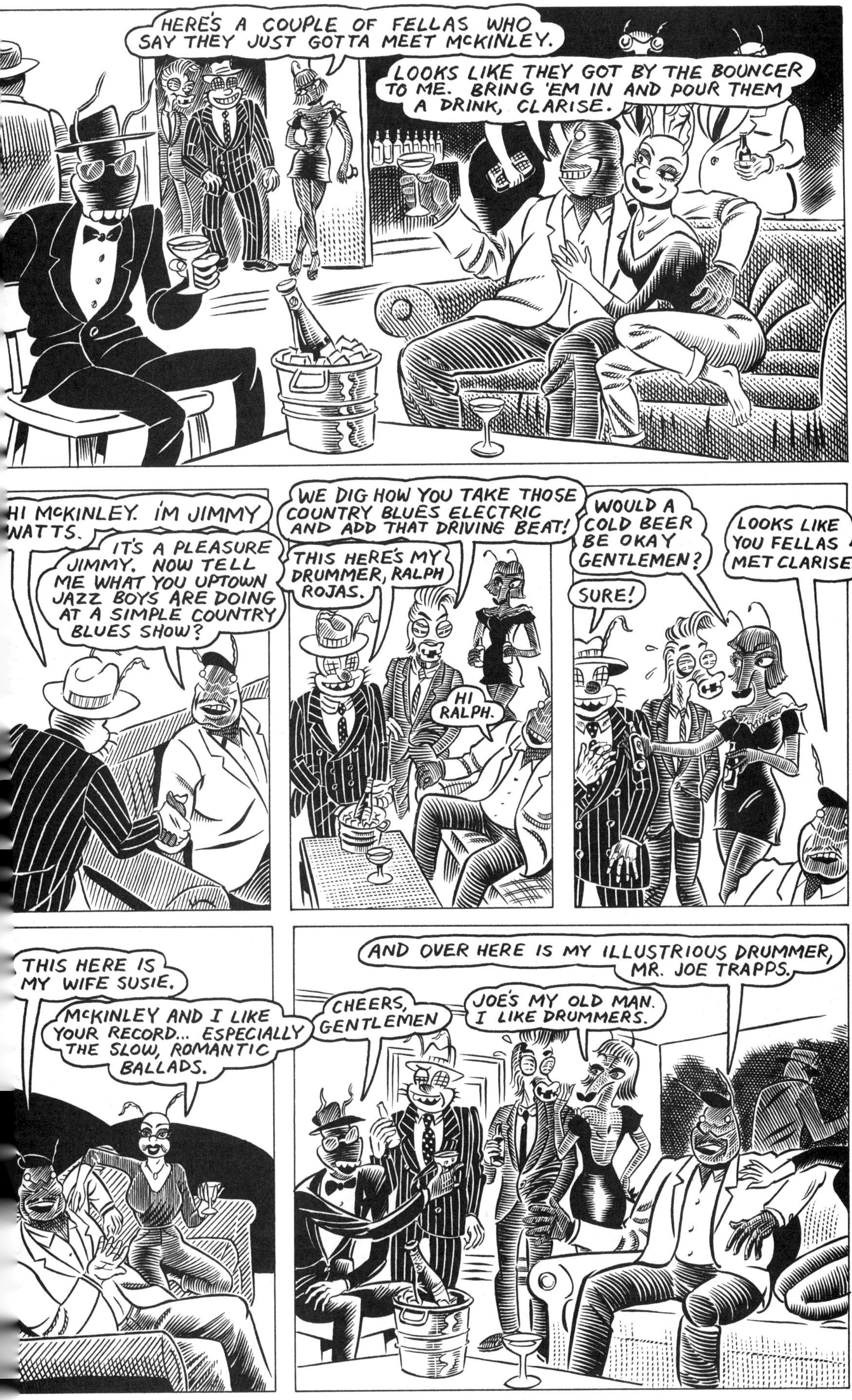
HERE'S A COUPLE OF FELLAS WHO SAY THEY JUST GOTTA MEET McKINLEY.
LOOKS LIKE THEY GOT BY THE BOUNCER TO ME. BRING 'EM IN AND POUR THEM A DRINK, CLARISE.
HI McKINLEY. I'M JIMMY WATTS.
IT'S A PLEASURE JIMMY. NOW TELL ME WHAT YOU UPTOWN JAZZ BOYS ARE DOING AT A SIMPLE COUNTRY BLUES SHOW?
WE DIG HOW YOU TAKE THOSE COUNTRY BLUES ELECTRIC AND ADD THAT DRIVING BEAT!
THIS HERE'S MY DRUMMER, RALPH ROJAS.
HI RALPH.
WOULD A COLD BEER BE OKAY GENTLEMEN?
SURE!
LOOKS LIKE YOU FELLAS MET CLARISE...
THIS HERE IS MY WIFE SUSIE.
McKINLEY AND I LIKE YOUR RECORD... ESPECIALLY THE SLOW, ROMANTIC BALLADS.
AND OVER HERE IS MY ILLUSTRIOUS DRUMMER, MR. JOE TRAPPS.
CHEERS, GENTLEMEN
JOE'S MY OLD MAN. I LIKE DRUMMERS.

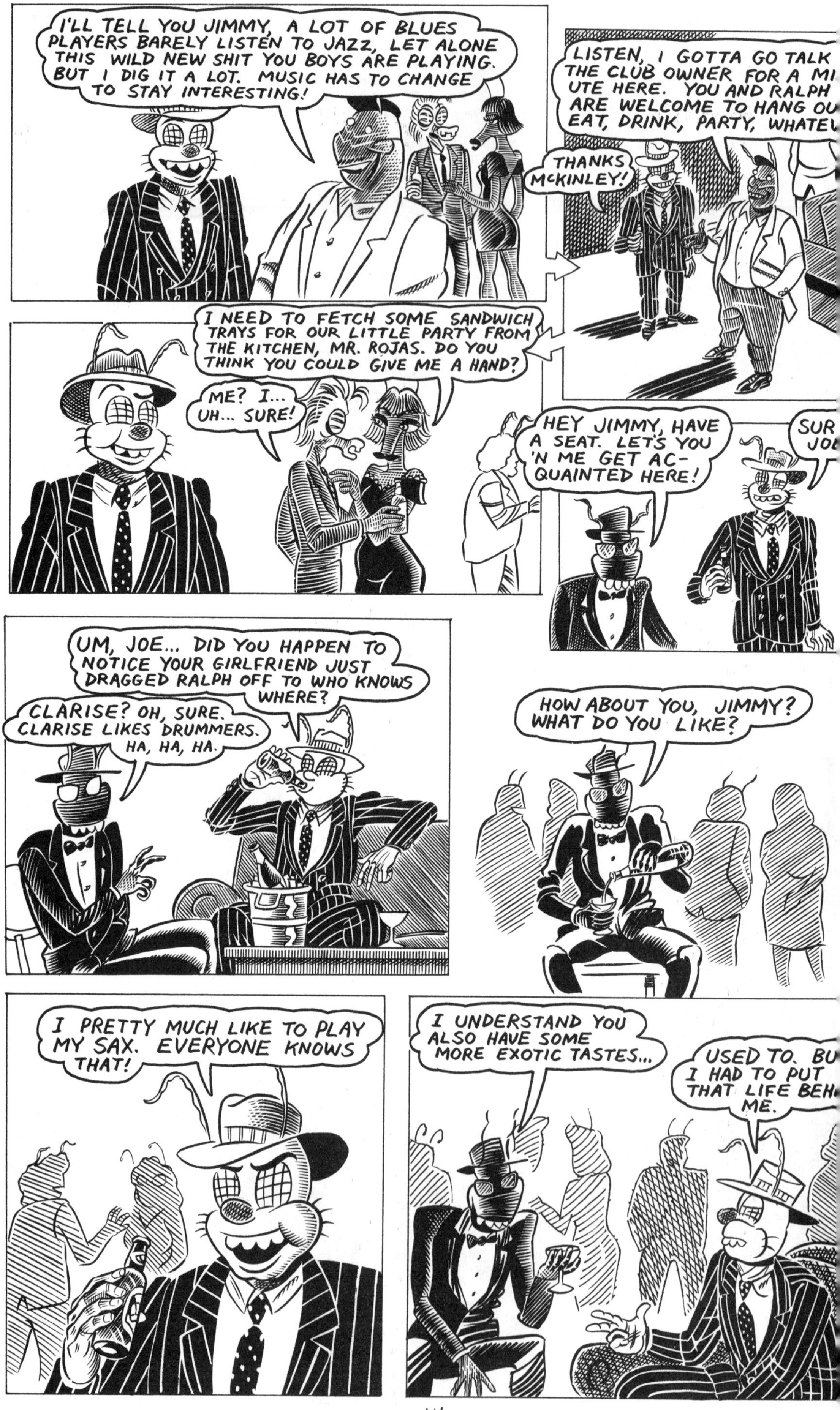
I'LL TELL YOU JIMMY, A LOT OF BLUES PLAYERS BARELY LISTEN TO JAZZ, LET ALONE THIS WILD NEW SHIT YOU BOYS ARE PLAYING. BUT I DIG IT A LOT. MUSIC HAS TO CHANGE TO STAY INTERESTING!
LISTEN, I GOTTA GO TALK THE CLUB OWNER FOR A MI UTE HERE. YOU AND RALPH ARE WELCOME TO HANG OU EAT, DRINK, PARTY, WHATEV
THANKS McKINLEY!
I NEED TO FETCH SOME SANDWICH TRAYS FOR OUR LITTLE PARTY FROM THE KITCHEN, MR. ROJAS. DO YOU THINK YOU COULD GIVE ME A HAND?
ME? I... UH... SURE!
HEY JIMMY, HAVE A SEAT. LET'S YOU 'N ME GET AC-QUAINTED HERE!
SUR JO
UM, JOE... DID YOU HAPPEN TO NOTICE YOUR GIRLFRIEND JUST DRAGGED RALPH OFF TO WHO KNOWS WHERE?
CLARISE? OH, SURE. CLARISE LIKES DRUMMERS. HA, HA, HA.
HOW ABOUT YOU, JIMMY? WHAT DO YOU LIKE?
I PRETTY MUCH LIKE TO PLAY MY SAX. EVERYONE KNOWS THAT!
I UNDERSTAND YOU ALSO HAVE SOME MORE EXOTIC TASTES...
USED TO. BU I HAD TO PUT THAT LIFE BEH ME.

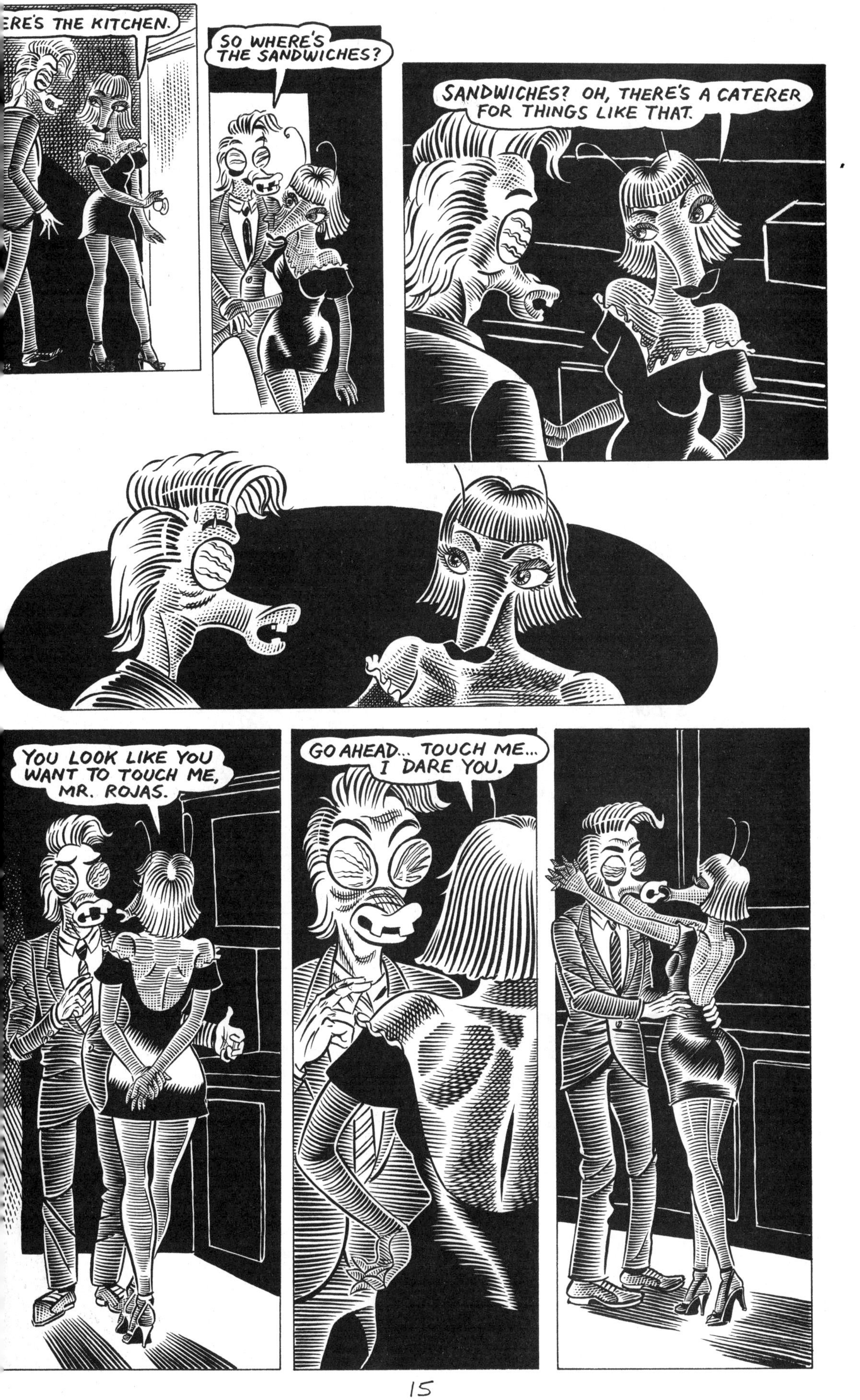
ERE'S THE KITCHEN.
SO WHERE'S THE SANDWICHES?
SANDWICHES? OH, THERE'S A CATERER FOR THINGS LIKE THAT.
YOU LOOK LIKE YOU WANT TO TOUCH ME, MR. ROJAS.
GO AHEAD... TOUCH ME... I DARE YOU.

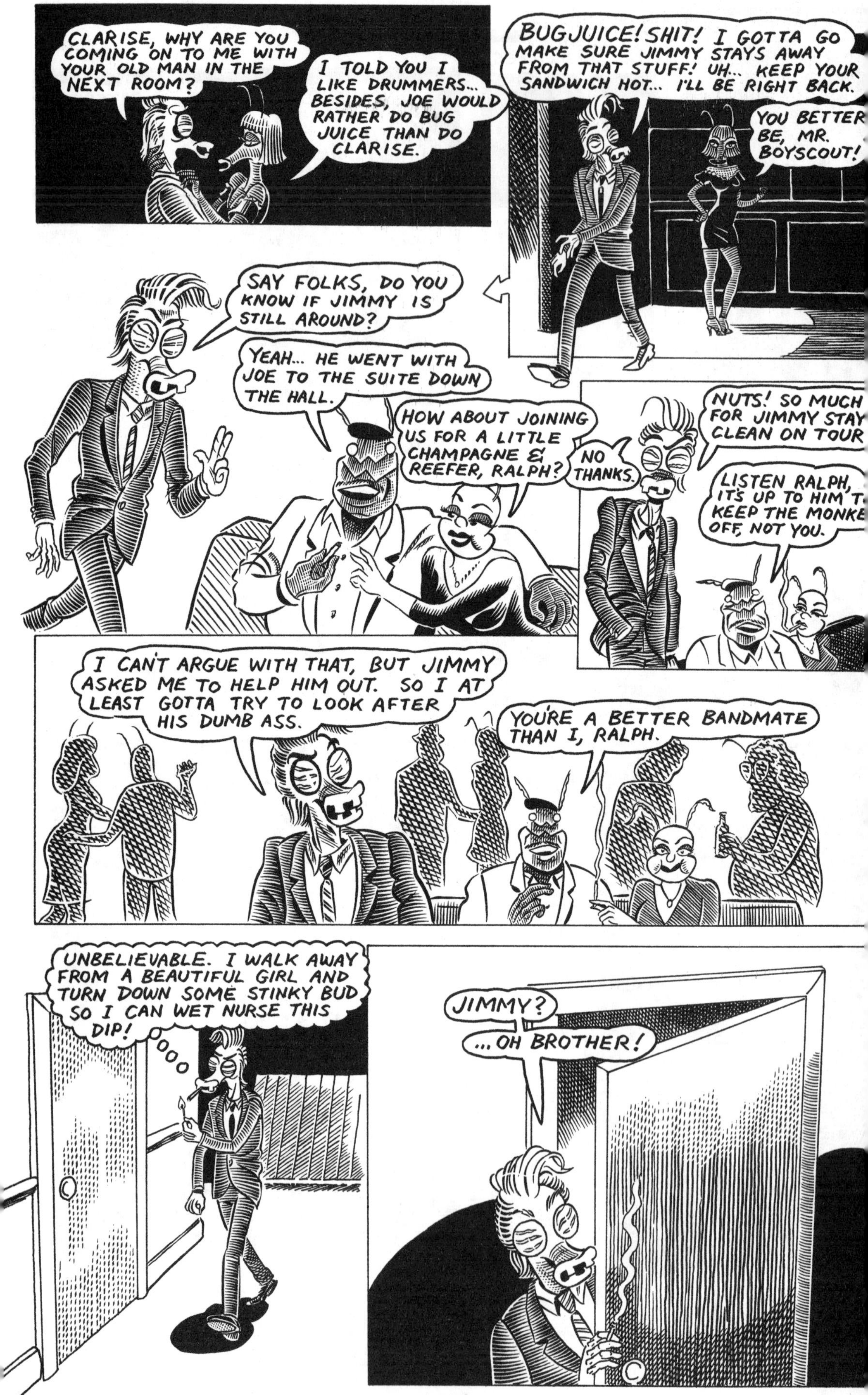
CLARISE, WHY ARE YOU COMING ON TO ME WITH YOUR OLD MAN IN THE NEXT ROOM?
I TOLD YOU I LIKE DRUMMERS... BESIDES, JOE WOULD RATHER DO BUG JUICE THAN DO CLARISE.
BUGJUICE! SHIT! I GOTTA GO MAKE SURE JIMMY STAYS AWAY FROM THAT STUFF! UH... KEEP YOUR SANDWICH HOT... I'LL BE RIGHT BACK.
YOU BETTER BE, MR. BOYSCOUT!
SAY FOLKS, DO YOU KNOW IF JIMMY IS STILL AROUND?
YEAH... HE WENT WITH JOE TO THE SUITE DOWN THE HALL.
HOW ABOUT JOINING US FOR A LITTLE CHAMPAGNE & REEFER, RALPH?
NO THANKS.
NUTS! SO MUCH FOR JIMMY STAY CLEAN ON TOUR
LISTEN RALPH, IT'S UP TO HIM T KEEP THE MONKE OFF, NOT YOU.
I CAN'T ARGUE WITH THAT, BUT JIMMY ASKED ME TO HELP HIM OUT. SO I AT LEAST GOTTA TRY TO LOOK AFTER HIS DUMB ASS.
YOU'RE A BETTER BANDMATE THAN I, RALPH.
UNBELIEVABLE. I WALK AWAY FROM A BEAUTIFUL GIRL AND TURN DOWN SOME STINKY BUD SO I CAN WET NURSE THIS DIP!
JIMMY?
...OH BROTHER!

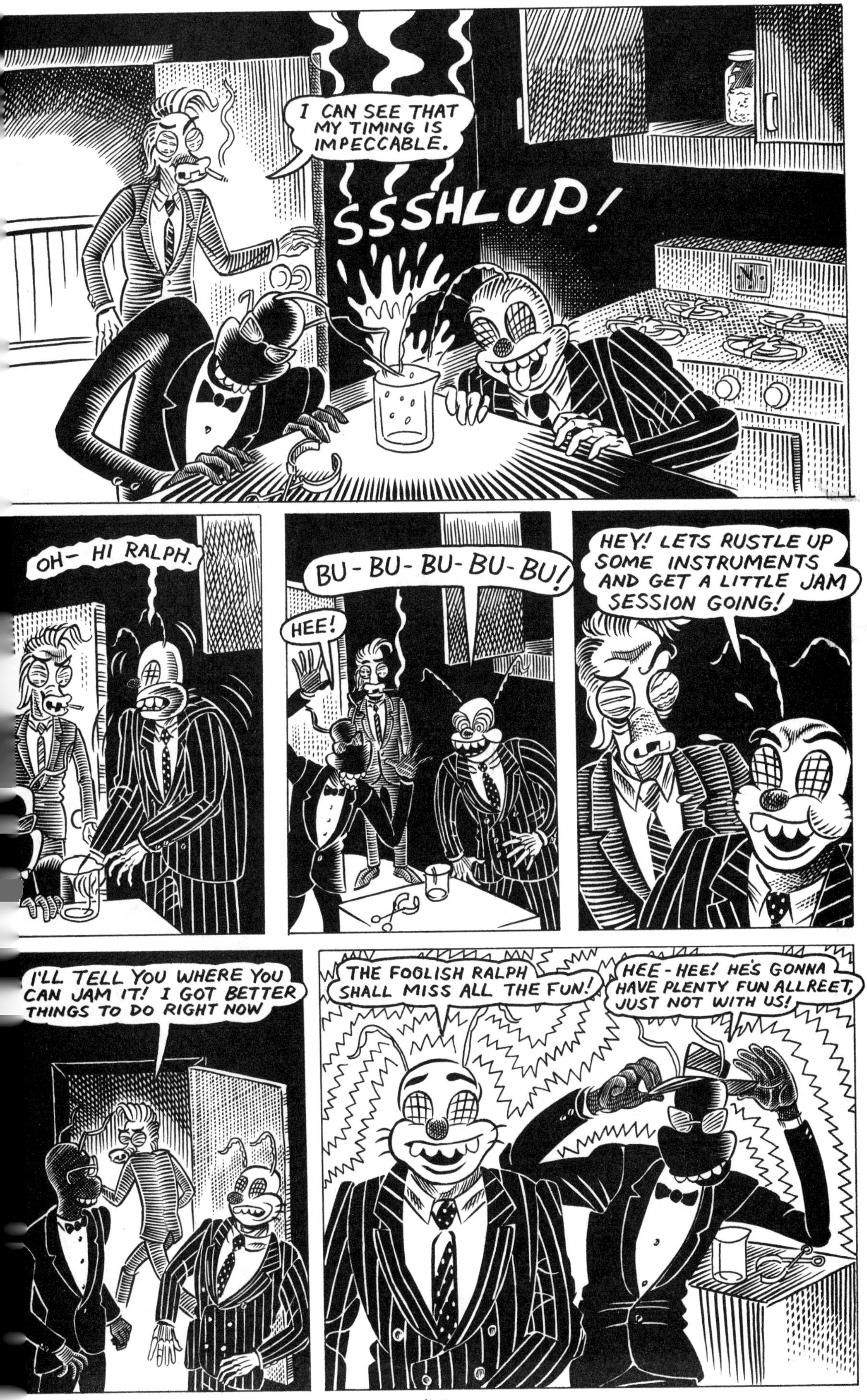
I CAN SEE THAT MY TIMING IS IMPECCABLE.
SSSHLUP!
OH- HI RALPH.
BU-BU-BU-BU-BU!
HEE!
HEY! LETS RUSTLE UP SOME INSTRUMENTS AND GET A LITTLE JAM SESSION GOING!
I'LL TELL YOU WHERE YOU CAN JAM IT! I GOT BETTER THINGS TO DO RIGHT NOW
THE FOOLISH RALPH SHALL MISS ALL THE FUN!
HEE-HEE! HE'S GONNA HAVE PLENTY FUN ALLREET, JUST NOT WITH US!

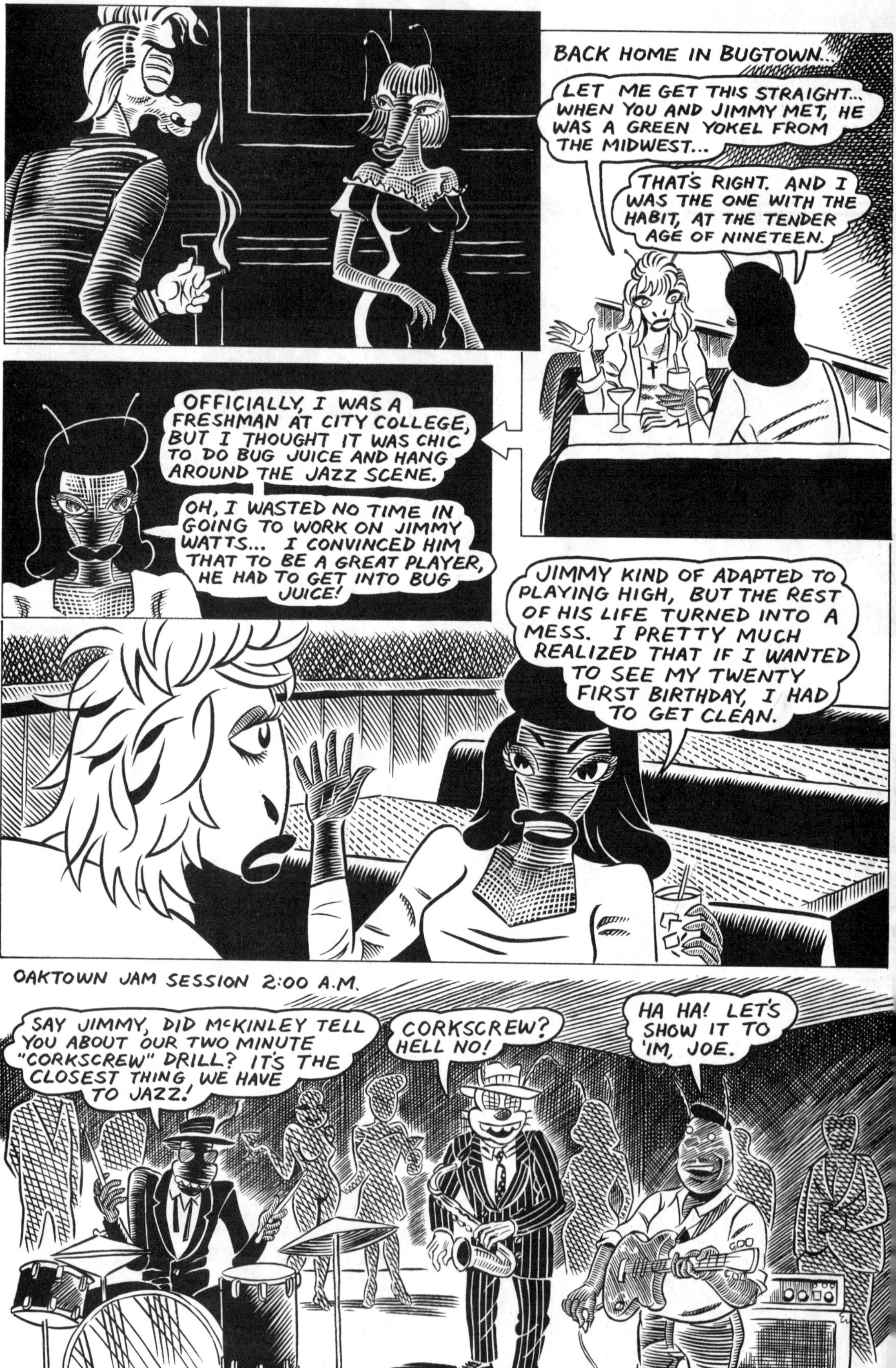
BACK HOME IN BUGTOWN...
LET ME GET THIS STRAIGHT... WHEN YOU AND JIMMY MET, HE WAS A GREEN YOKEL FROM THE MIDWEST...
THAT'S RIGHT. AND I WAS THE ONE WITH THE HABIT, AT THE TENDER AGE OF NINETEEN.
OFFICIALLY, I WAS A FRESHMAN AT CITY COLLEGE, BUT I THOUGHT IT WAS CHIC TO DO BUG JUICE AND HANG AROUND THE JAZZ SCENE.
OH, I WASTED NO TIME IN GOING TO WORK ON JIMMY WATTS... I CONVINCED HIM THAT TO BE A GREAT PLAYER, HE HAD TO GET INTO BUG JUICE!
JIMMY KIND OF ADAPTED TO PLAYING HIGH, BUT THE REST OF HIS LIFE TURNED INTO A MESS. I PRETTY MUCH REALIZED THAT IF I WANTED TO SEE MY TWENTY FIRST BIRTHDAY, I HAD TO GET CLEAN.
OAKTOWN JAM SESSION 2:00 A.M.
SAY JIMMY, DID McKINLEY TELL YOU ABOUT OUR TWO MINUTE "CORKSCREW" DRILL? IT'S THE CLOSEST THING WE HAVE TO JAZZ!
CORKSCREW? HELL NO!
HA HA! LET'S SHOW IT TO 'IM, JOE.

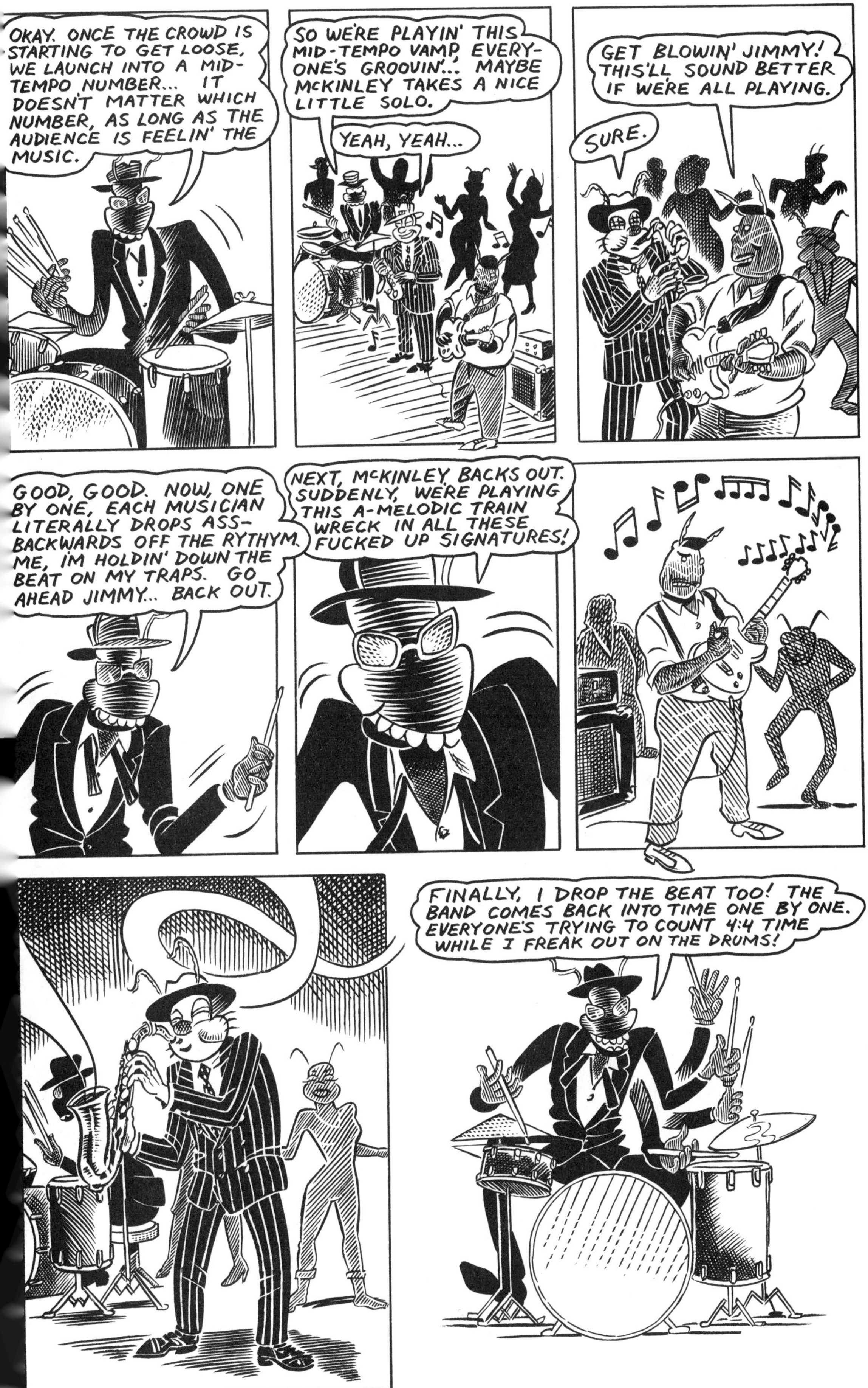
OKAY. ONCE THE CROWD IS STARTING TO GET LOOSE, WE LAUNCH INTO A MID-TEMPO NUMBER... IT DOESN'T MATTER WHICH NUMBER, AS LONG AS THE AUDIENCE IS FEELIN' THE MUSIC.
SO WE'RE PLAYIN' THIS MID-TEMPO VAMP, EVERYONE'S GROOVIN'... MAYBE MCKINLEY TAKES A NICE LITTLE SOLO.
YEAH, YEAH...
GET BLOWIN' JIMMY! THIS'LL SOUND BETTER IF WE'RE ALL PLAYING.
SURE.
GOOD, GOOD. NOW, ONE BY ONE, EACH MUSICIAN LITERALLY DROPS ASS-BACKWARDS OFF THE RYTHYM. ME, I'M HOLDIN' DOWN THE BEAT ON MY TRAPS. GO AHEAD JIMMY... BACK OUT.
NEXT, MCKINLEY BACKS OUT. SUDDENLY, WE'RE PLAYING THIS A-MELODIC TRAIN WRECK IN ALL THESE FUCKED UP SIGNATURES!
FINALLY, I DROP THE BEAT TOO! THE BAND COMES BACK INTO TIME ONE BY ONE. EVERYONE'S TRYING TO COUNT 4:4 TIME WHILE I FREAK OUT ON THE DRUMS!

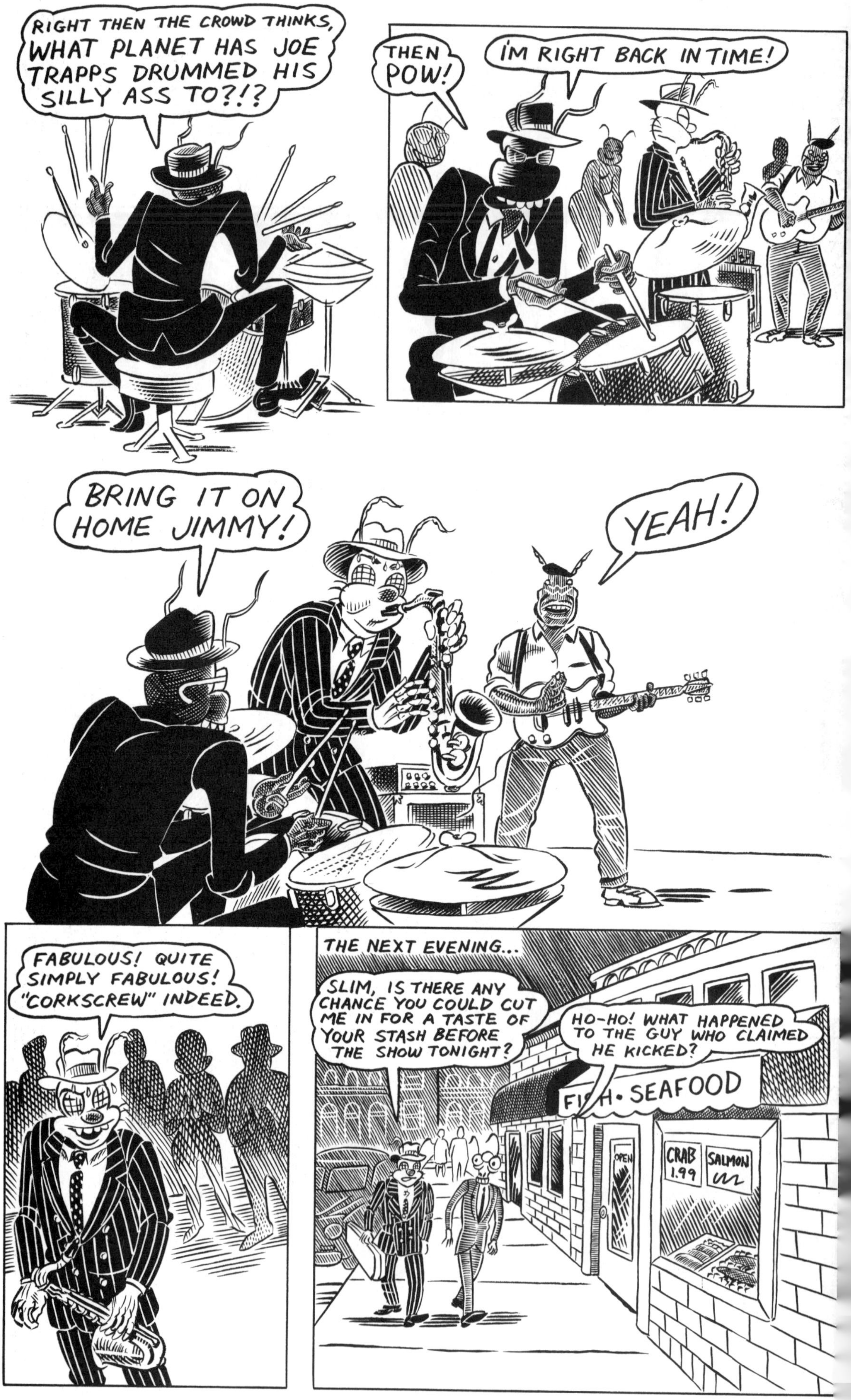
RIGHT THEN THE CROWD THINKS, WHAT PLANET HAS JOE TRAPPS DRUMMED HIS SILLY ASS TO?!?
THEN POW!
I'M RIGHT BACK IN TIME!
BRING IT ON HOME JIMMY!
YEAH!
FABULOUS! QUITE SIMPLY FABULOUS! "CORKSCREW" INDEED.
THE NEXT EVENING...
SLIM, IS THERE ANY CHANCE YOU COULD CUT ME IN FOR A TASTE OF YOUR STASH BEFORE THE SHOW TONIGHT?
HO-HO! WHAT HAPPENED TO THE GUY WHO CLAIMED HE KICKED?
FISH • SEAFOOD
OPEN
CRAB 1.99
SALMON

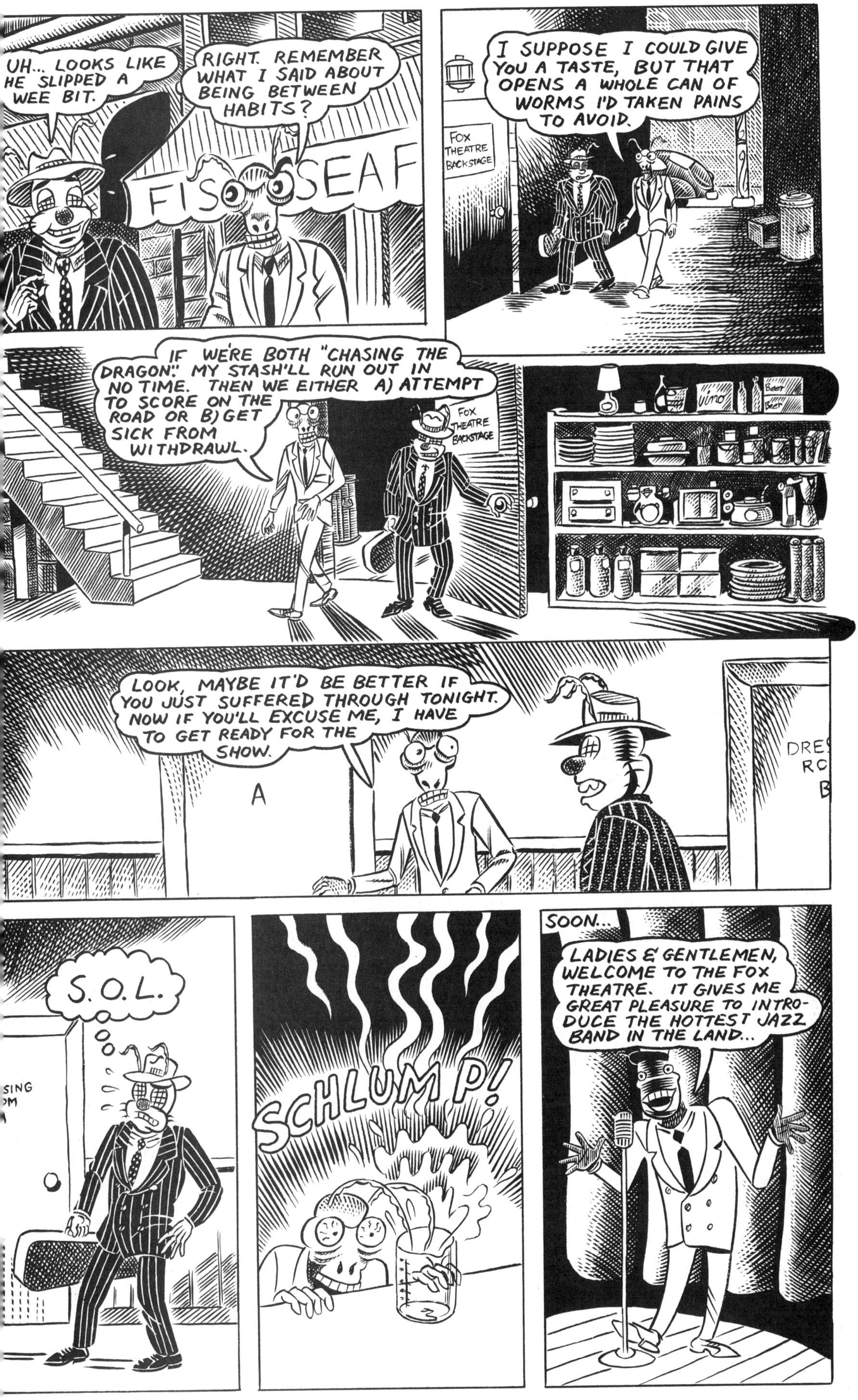
UH... LOOKS LIKE HE SLIPPED A WEE BIT.
RIGHT. REMEMBER WHAT I SAID ABOUT BEING BETWEEN HABITS?
FIS SEAF
I SUPPOSE I COULD GIVE YOU A TASTE, BUT THAT OPENS A WHOLE CAN OF WORMS I'D TAKEN PAINS TO AVOID.
FOX THEATRE BACKSTAGE
IF WE'RE BOTH "CHASING THE DRAGON" MY STASH'LL RUN OUT IN NO TIME. THEN WE EITHER A) ATTEMPT TO SCORE ON THE ROAD OR B) GET SICK FROM WITHDRAWL.
FOX THEATRE BACKSTAGE
VINO
BEER
BEER
LOOK, MAYBE IT'D BE BETTER IF YOU JUST SUFFERED THROUGH TONIGHT. NOW IF YOU'LL EXCUSE ME, I HAVE TO GET READY FOR THE SHOW.
A
DRES
RO
B
S.O.L.
SING
SCHLUMP!
SOON...
LADIES & GENTLEMEN, WELCOME TO THE FOX THEATRE. IT GIVES ME GREAT PLEASURE TO INTRODUCE THE HOTTEST JAZZ BAND IN THE LAND...

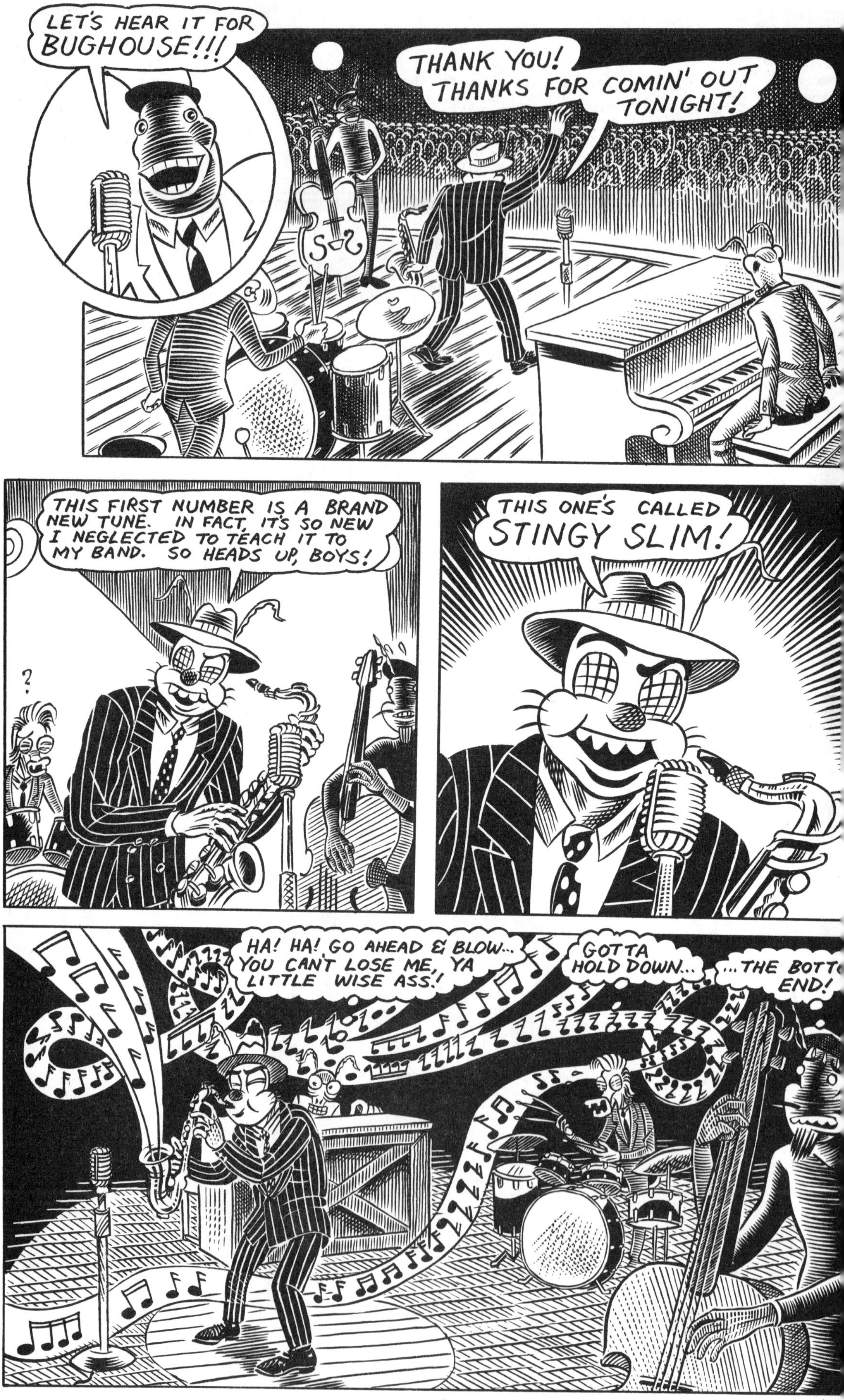
LET'S HEAR IT FOR BUGHOUSE!!!
THANK YOU! THANKS FOR COMIN' OUT TONIGHT!
THIS FIRST NUMBER IS A BRAND NEW TUNE. IN FACT, IT'S SO NEW I NEGLECTED TO TEACH IT TO MY BAND. SO HEADS UP, BOYS!
?
THIS ONE'S CALLED STINGY SLIM!
HA! HA! GO AHEAD & BLOW... YOU CAN'T LOSE ME, YA LITTLE WISE ASS!
GOTTA HOLD DOWN...
...THE BOTT END!

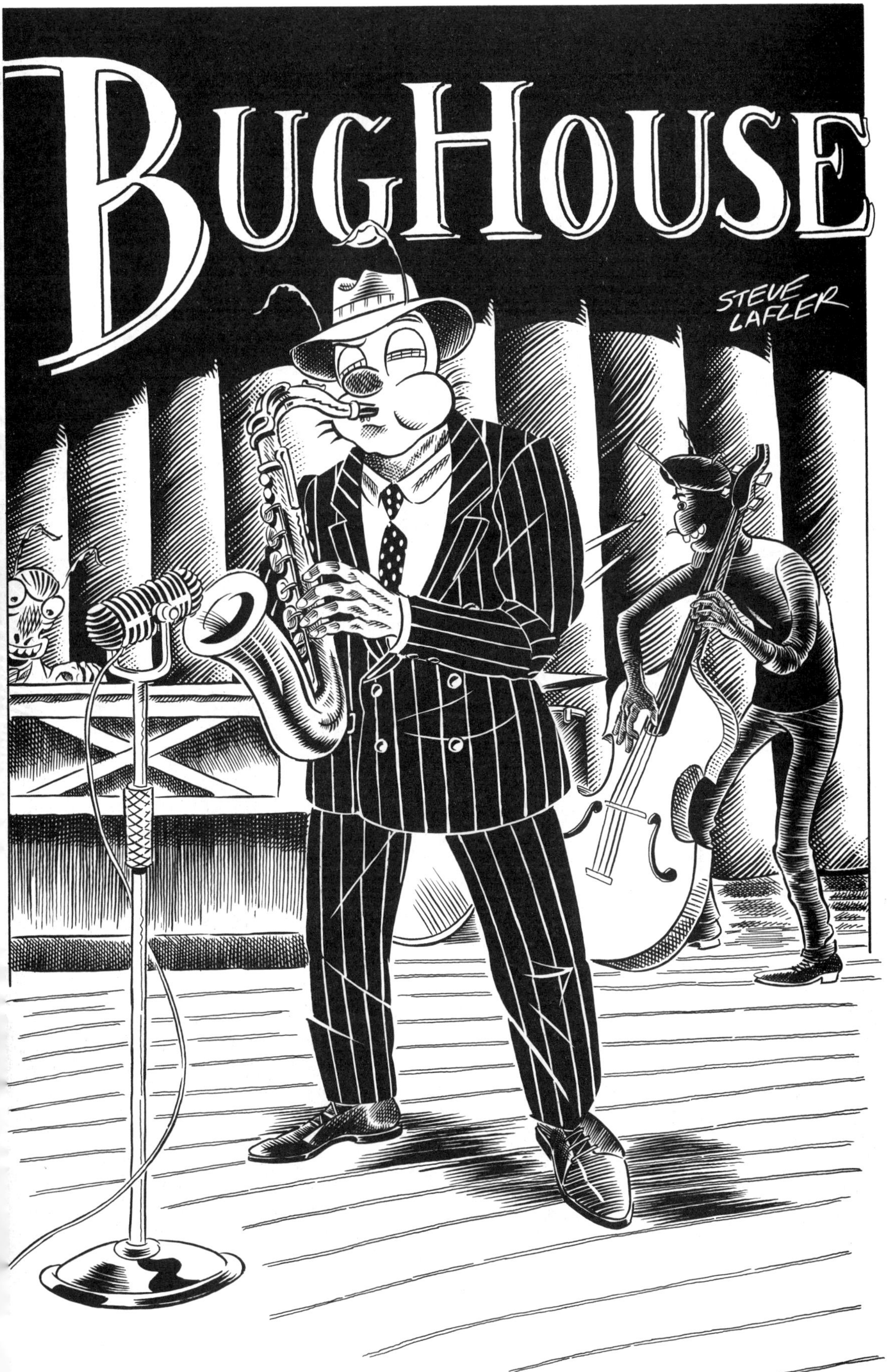
BUGHOUSE
STEVE LAFLER

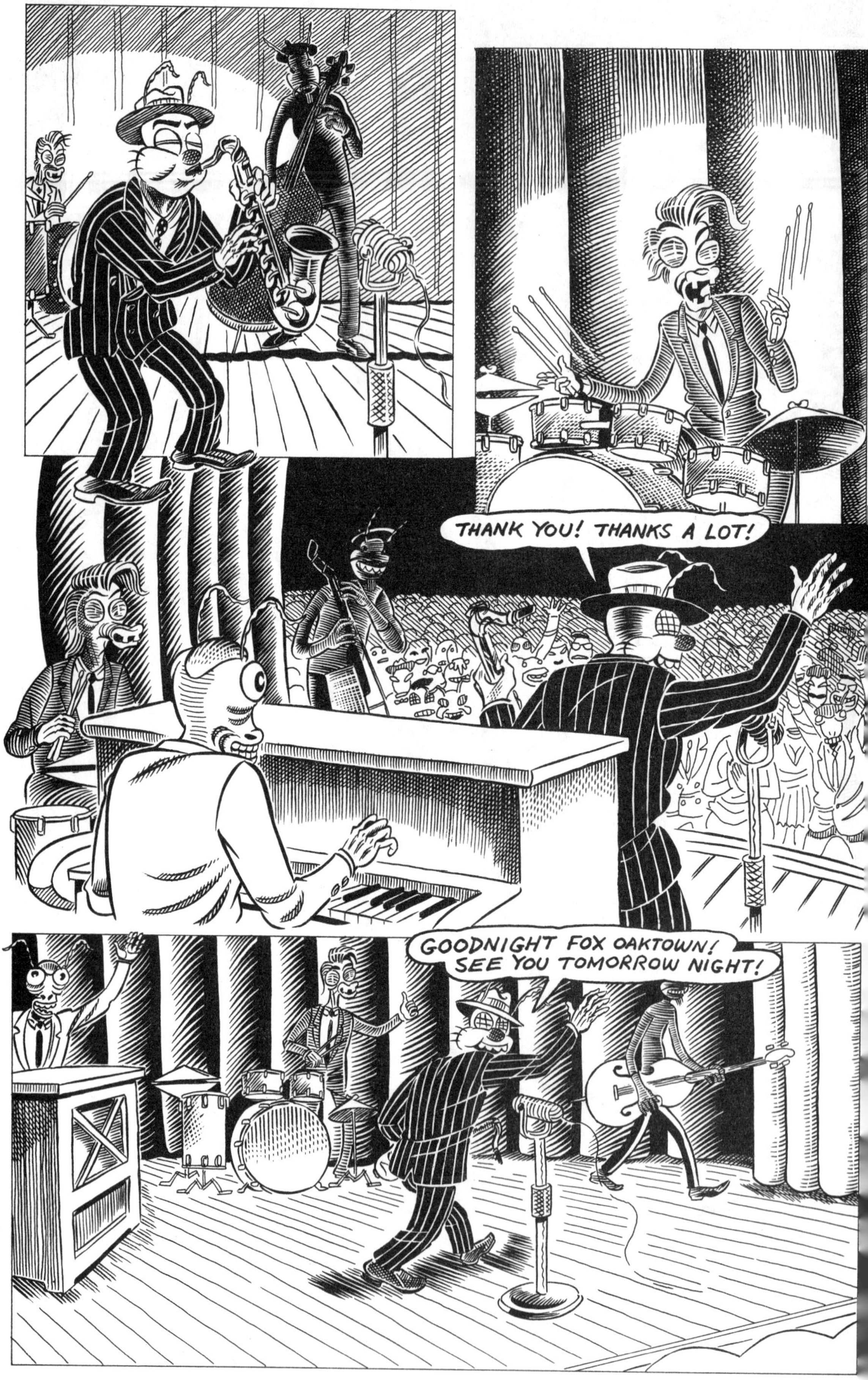
THANK YOU! THANKS A LOT!
GOODNIGHT FOX OAKTOWN! SEE YOU TOMORROW NIGHT!

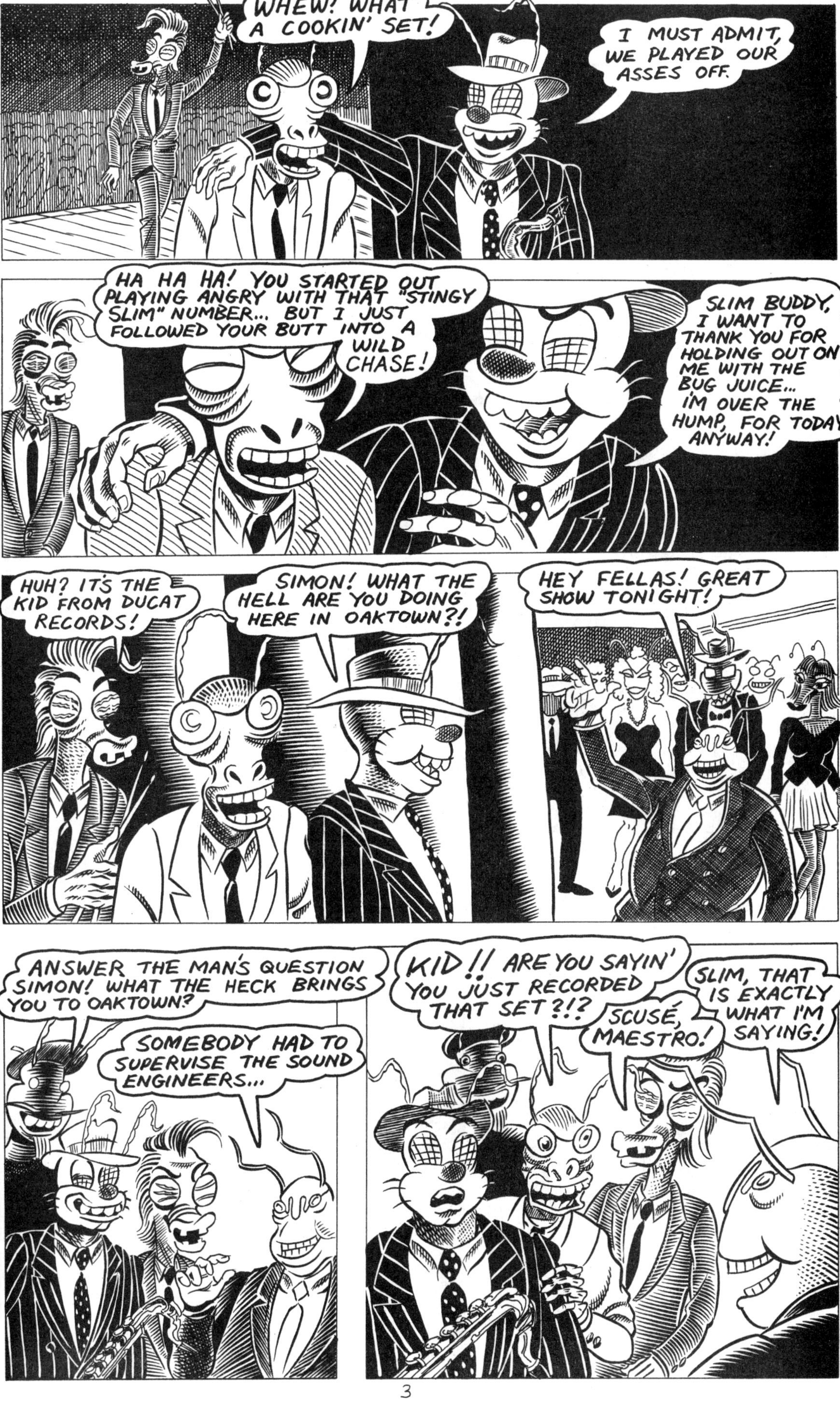
WHEW! WHAT A COOKIN' SET!
I MUST ADMIT, WE PLAYED OUR ASSES OFF.
HA HA HA! YOU STARTED OUT PLAYING ANGRY WITH THAT "STINGY SLIM" NUMBER... BUT I JUST FOLLOWED YOUR BUTT INTO A WILD CHASE!
SLIM BUDDY, I WANT TO THANK YOU FOR HOLDING OUT ON ME WITH THE BUG JUICE... I'M OVER THE HUMP, FOR TODAY ANYWAY!
HUH? IT'S THE KID FROM DUCAT RECORDS!
SIMON! WHAT THE HELL ARE YOU DOING HERE IN OAKTOWN?!
HEY FELLAS! GREAT SHOW TONIGHT!
ANSWER THE MAN'S QUESTION SIMON! WHAT THE HECK BRINGS YOU TO OAKTOWN?
SOMEBODY HAD TO SUPERVISE THE SOUND ENGINEERS...
KID!! ARE YOU SAYIN' YOU JUST RECORDED THAT SET?!?
SCUSÉ, MAESTRO!
SLIM, THAT IS EXACTLY WHAT I'M SAYING!

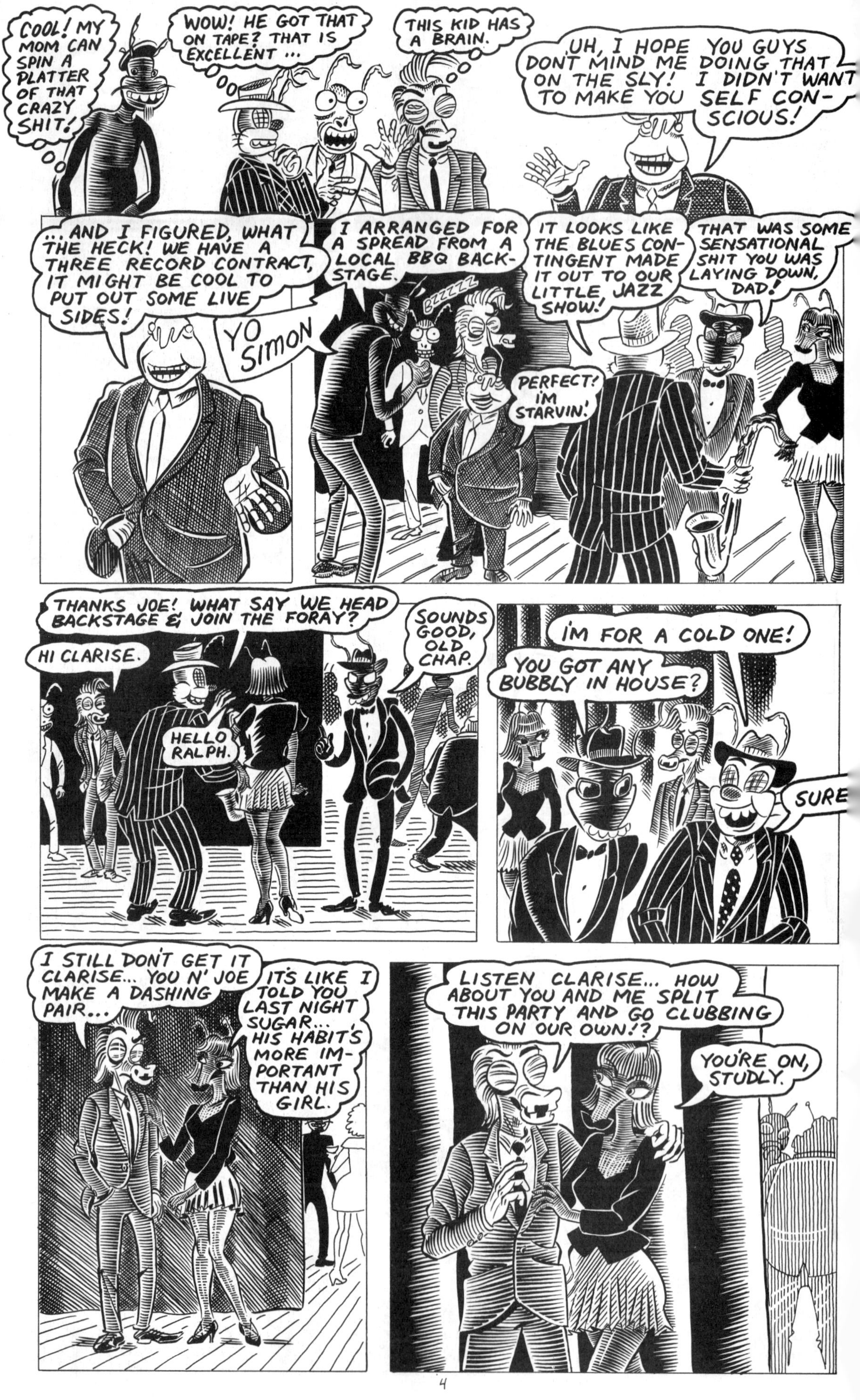
COOL! MY MOM CAN SPIN A PLATTER OF THAT CRAZY SHIT!
WOW! HE GOT THAT ON TAPE? THAT IS EXCELLENT ...
THIS KID HAS A BRAIN.
UH, I HOPE YOU GUYS DON'T MIND ME DOING THAT ON THE SLY! I DIDN'T WANT TO MAKE YOU SELF CON-SCIOUS!
... AND I FIGURED, WHAT THE HECK! WE HAVE A THREE RECORD CONTRACT, IT MIGHT BE COOL TO PUT OUT SOME LIVE SIDES!
YO SIMON
I ARRANGED FOR A SPREAD FROM A LOCAL BBQ BACK-STAGE.
BZZZZZ
IT LOOKS LIKE THE BLUES CON-TINGENT MADE IT OUT TO OUR LITTLE, JAZZ SHOW!
PERFECT! I'M STARVIN'.
THAT WAS SOME SENSATIONAL SHIT YOU WAS LAYING DOWN, DAD!
THANKS JOE! WHAT SAY WE HEAD BACKSTAGE & JOIN THE FORAY?
HI CLARISE.
HELLO RALPH.
SOUNDS GOOD, OLD CHAP.
I'M FOR A COLD ONE!
YOU GOT ANY BUBBLY IN HOUSE?
SURE
I STILL DON'T GET IT CLARISE... YOU N' JOE MAKE A DASHING PAIR...
IT'S LIKE I TOLD YOU LAST NIGHT SUGAR... HIS HABIT'S MORE IM-PORTANT THAN HIS GIRL.
LISTEN CLARISE... HOW ABOUT YOU AND ME SPLIT THIS PARTY AND GO CLUBBING ON OUR OWN!?
YOU'RE ON, STUDLY.

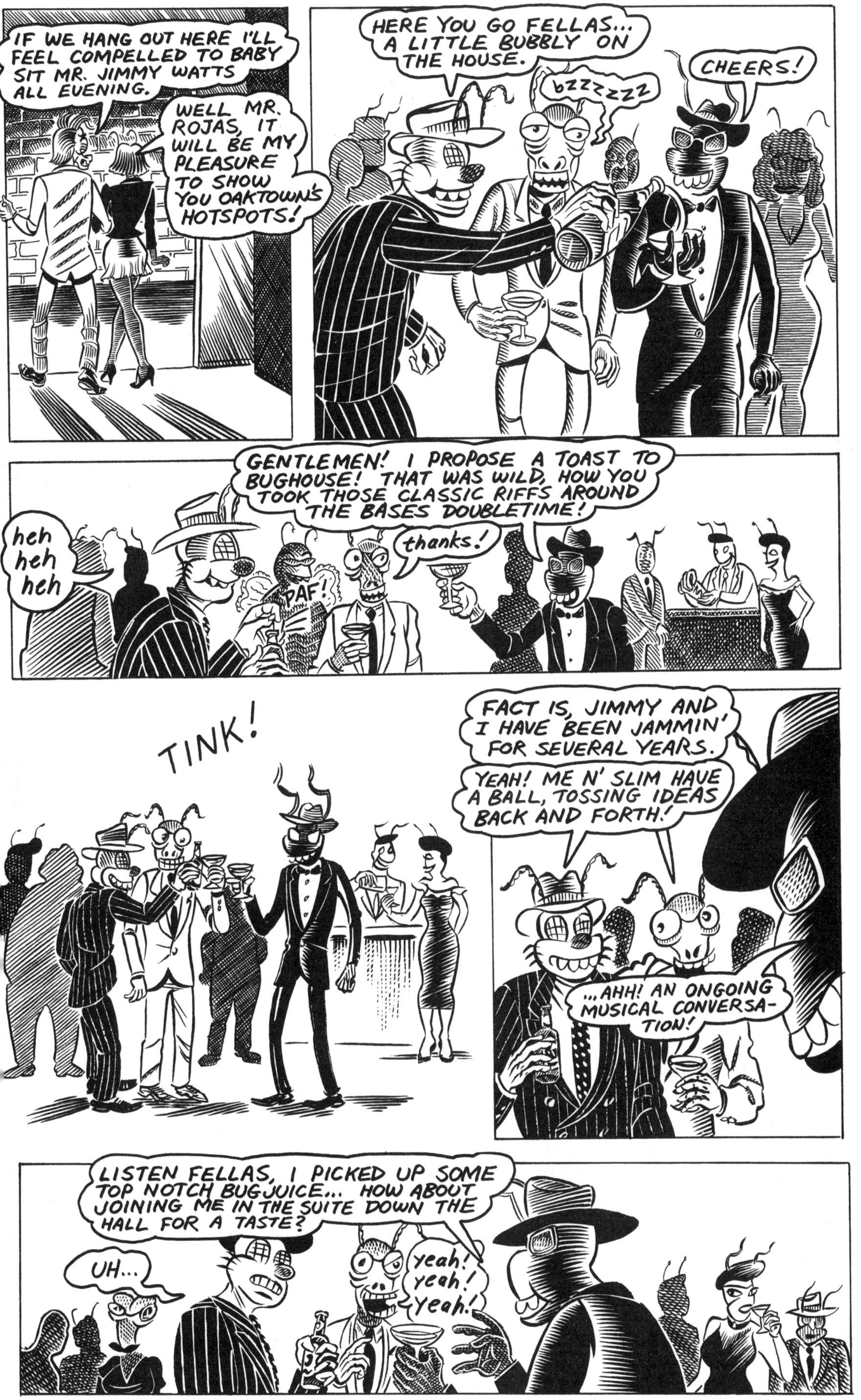

IF WE HANG OUT HERE I'LL FEEL COMPELLED TO BABY SIT MR. JIMMY WATTS ALL EVENING.
WELL MR. ROJAS, IT WILL BE MY PLEASURE TO SHOW YOU OAKTOWN'S HOTSPOTS!
HERE YOU GO FELLAS... A LITTLE BUBBLY ON THE HOUSE.
bzzzzzzz
CHEERS!
GENTLEMEN! I PROPOSE A TOAST TO BUGHOUSE! THAT WAS WILD, HOW YOU TOOK THOSE CLASSIC RIFFS AROUND THE BASES DOUBLETIME!
heh heh heh
PAF!
thanks!
TINK!
FACT IS, JIMMY AND I HAVE BEEN JAMMIN' FOR SEVERAL YEARS.
YEAH! ME N' SLIM HAVE A BALL, TOSSING IDEAS BACK AND FORTH!
...AHH! AN ONGOING MUSICAL CONVERSA-TION!
LISTEN FELLAS, I PICKED UP SOME TOP NOTCH BUGJUICE... HOW ABOUT JOINING ME IN THE SUITE DOWN THE HALL FOR A TASTE?
UH...
yeah! yeah! yeah!

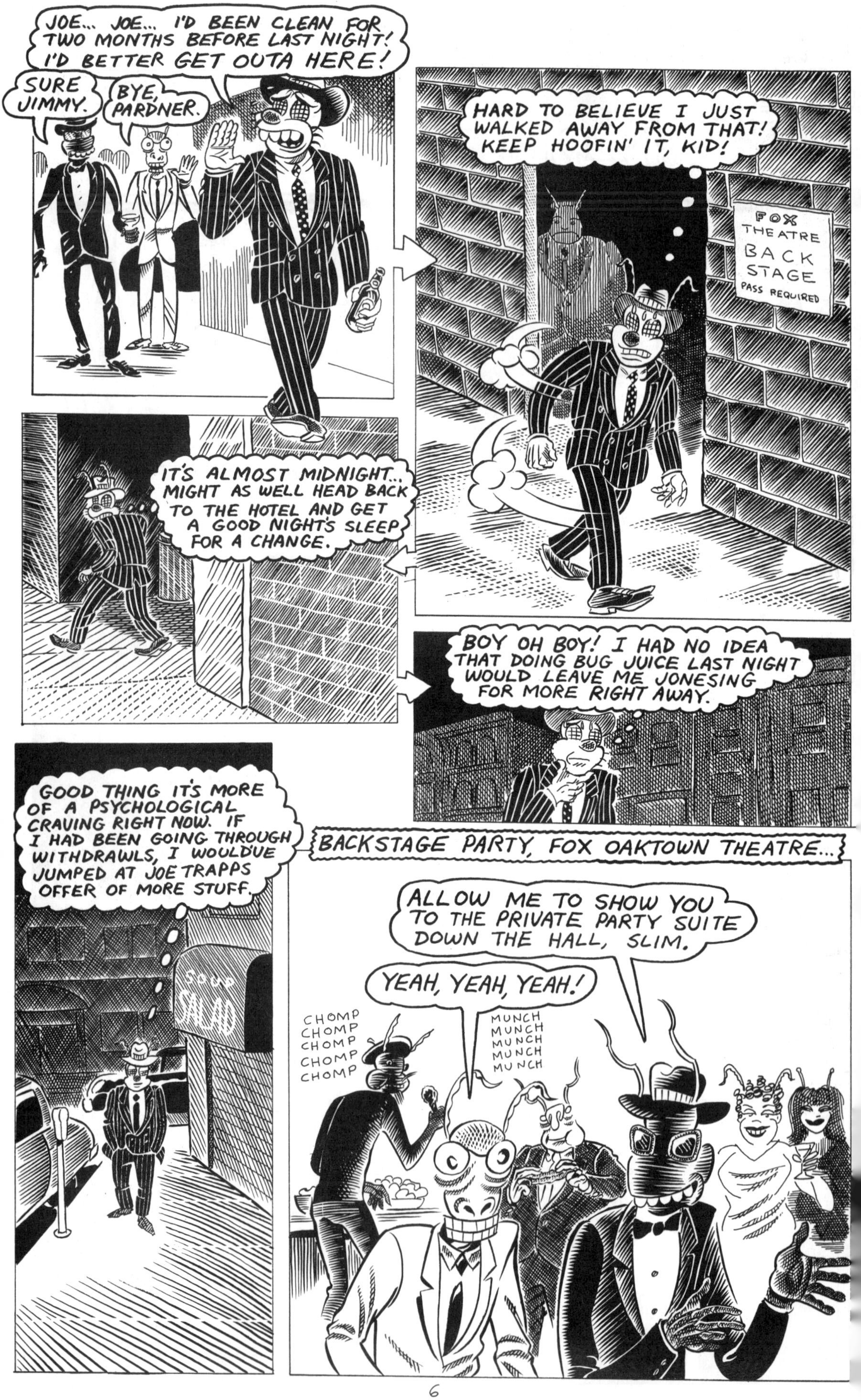
JOE... JOE... I'D BEEN CLEAN FOR TWO MONTHS BEFORE LAST NIGHT! I'D BETTER GET OUTA HERE!
SURE JIMMY.
BYE, PARDNER.
HARD TO BELIEVE I JUST WALKED AWAY FROM THAT! KEEP HOOFIN' IT, KID!
FOX THEATRE BACK STAGE PASS REQUIRED
IT'S ALMOST MIDNIGHT... MIGHT AS WELL HEAD BACK TO THE HOTEL AND GET A GOOD NIGHT'S SLEEP FOR A CHANGE.
BOY OH BOY! I HAD NO IDEA THAT DOING BUG JUICE LAST NIGHT WOULD LEAVE ME JONESING FOR MORE RIGHT AWAY.
GOOD THING IT'S MORE OF A PSYCHOLOGICAL CRAVING RIGHT NOW. IF I HAD BEEN GOING THROUGH WITHDRAWLS, I WOULD'VE JUMPED AT JOE TRAPPS OFFER OF MORE STUFF.
SOUP SALAD
BACKSTAGE PARTY, FOX OAKTOWN THEATRE...
ALLOW ME TO SHOW YOU TO THE PRIVATE PARTY SUITE DOWN THE HALL, SLIM.
YEAH, YEAH, YEAH!
CHOMP CHOMP CHOMP CHOMP CHOMP
MUNCH MUNCH MUNCH MUNCH MUNCH

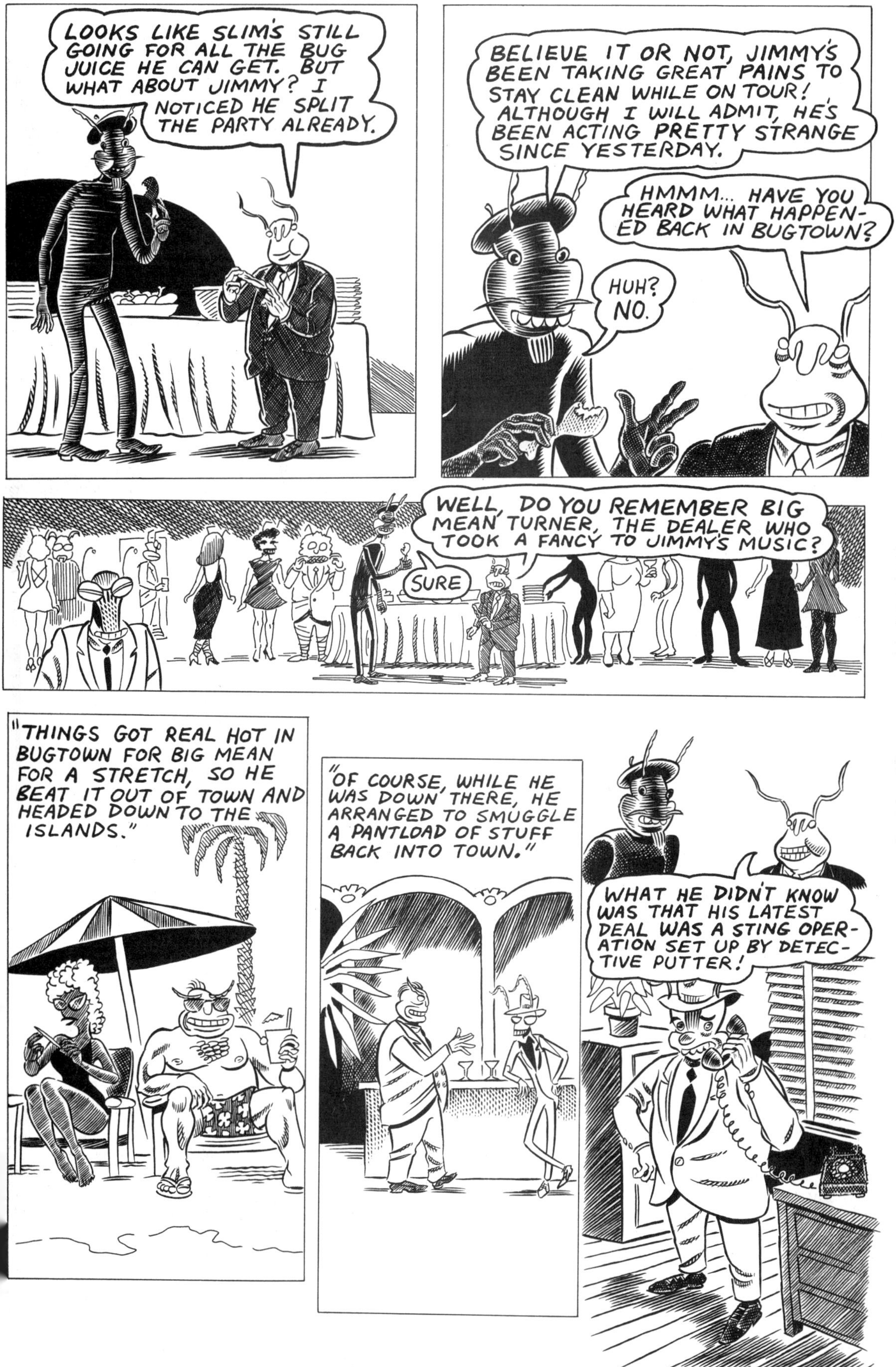
LOOKS LIKE SLIM'S STILL GOING FOR ALL THE BUG JUICE HE CAN GET. BUT WHAT ABOUT JIMMY? I NOTICED HE SPLIT THE PARTY ALREADY.
BELIEVE IT OR NOT, JIMMY'S BEEN TAKING GREAT PAINS TO STAY CLEAN WHILE ON TOUR! ALTHOUGH I WILL ADMIT, HE'S BEEN ACTING PRETTY STRANGE SINCE YESTERDAY.
HMMM... HAVE YOU HEARD WHAT HAPPENED BACK IN BUGTOWN?
HUH? NO.
WELL, DO YOU REMEMBER BIG MEAN TURNER, THE DEALER WHO TOOK A FANCY TO JIMMY'S MUSIC?
SURE
"THINGS GOT REAL HOT IN BUGTOWN FOR BIG MEAN FOR A STRETCH, SO HE BEAT IT OUT OF TOWN AND HEADED DOWN TO THE ISLANDS."
"OF COURSE, WHILE HE WAS DOWN THERE, HE ARRANGED TO SMUGGLE A PANTLOAD OF STUFF BACK INTO TOWN."
WHAT HE DIDN'T KNOW WAS THAT HIS LATEST DEAL WAS A STING OPERATION SET UP BY DETECTIVE PUTTER!

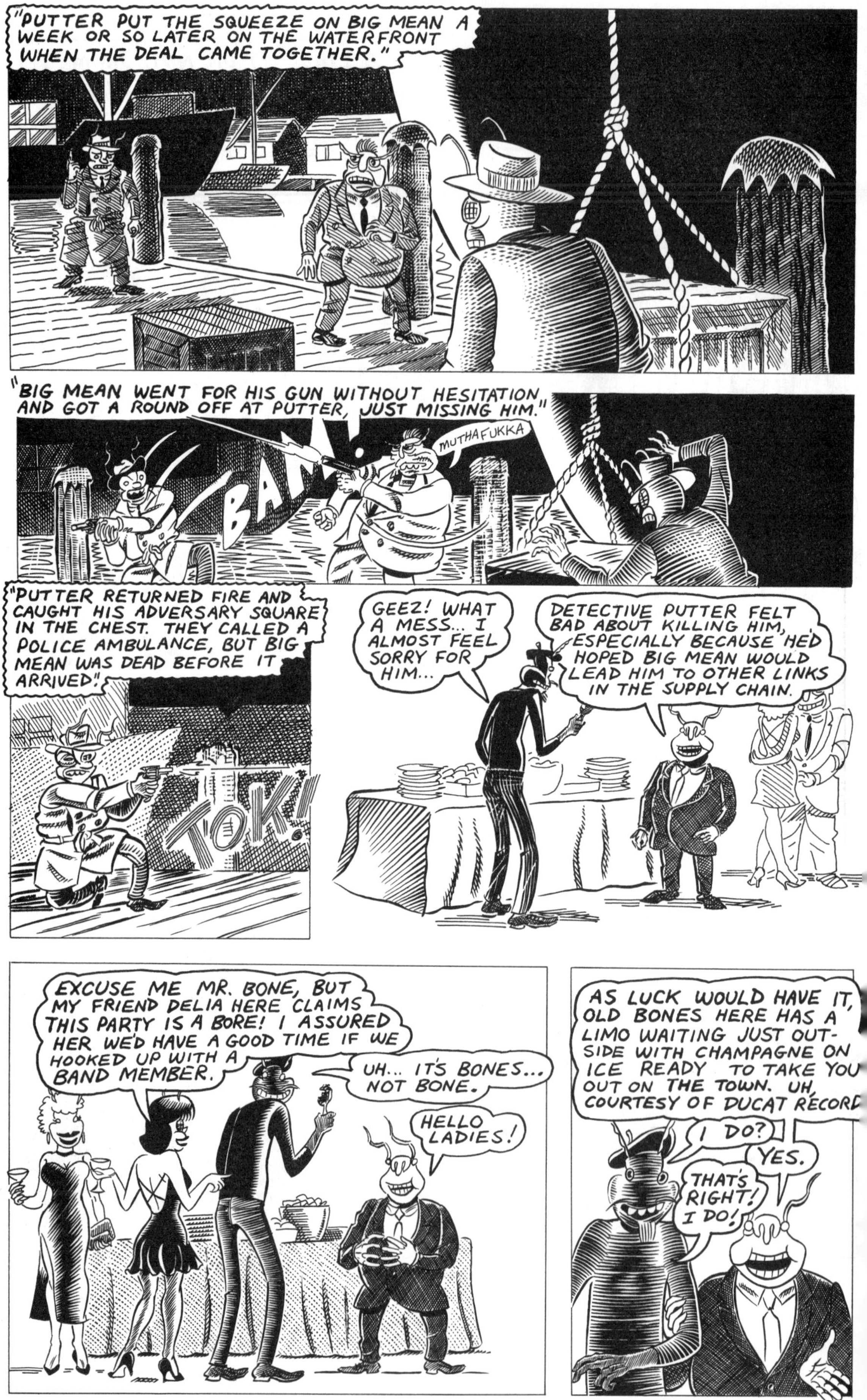
"PUTTER PUT THE SQUEEZE ON BIG MEAN A WEEK OR SO LATER ON THE WATERFRONT WHEN THE DEAL CAME TOGETHER."
"BIG MEAN WENT FOR HIS GUN WITHOUT HESITATION AND GOT A ROUND OFF AT PUTTER, JUST MISSING HIM."
BAM
MUTHAFUKKA
"PUTTER RETURNED FIRE AND CAUGHT HIS ADVERSARY SQUARE IN THE CHEST. THEY CALLED A POLICE AMBULANCE, BUT BIG MEAN WAS DEAD BEFORE IT ARRIVED."
TOK!
GEEZ! WHAT A MESS... I ALMOST FEEL SORRY FOR HIM...
DETECTIVE PUTTER FELT BAD ABOUT KILLING HIM, ESPECIALLY BECAUSE HE'D HOPED BIG MEAN WOULD LEAD HIM TO OTHER LINKS IN THE SUPPLY CHAIN.
EXCUSE ME MR. BONE, BUT MY FRIEND DELIA HERE CLAIMS THIS PARTY IS A BORE! I ASSURED HER WE'D HAVE A GOOD TIME IF WE HOOKED UP WITH A BAND MEMBER.
UH... IT'S BONES... NOT BONE.
HELLO LADIES!
AS LUCK WOULD HAVE IT, OLD BONES HERE HAS A LIMO WAITING JUST OUT-SIDE WITH CHAMPAGNE ON ICE READY TO TAKE YOU OUT ON THE TOWN. UH, COURTESY OF DUCAT RECORD
I DO?
YES.
THAT'S RIGHT! I DO!

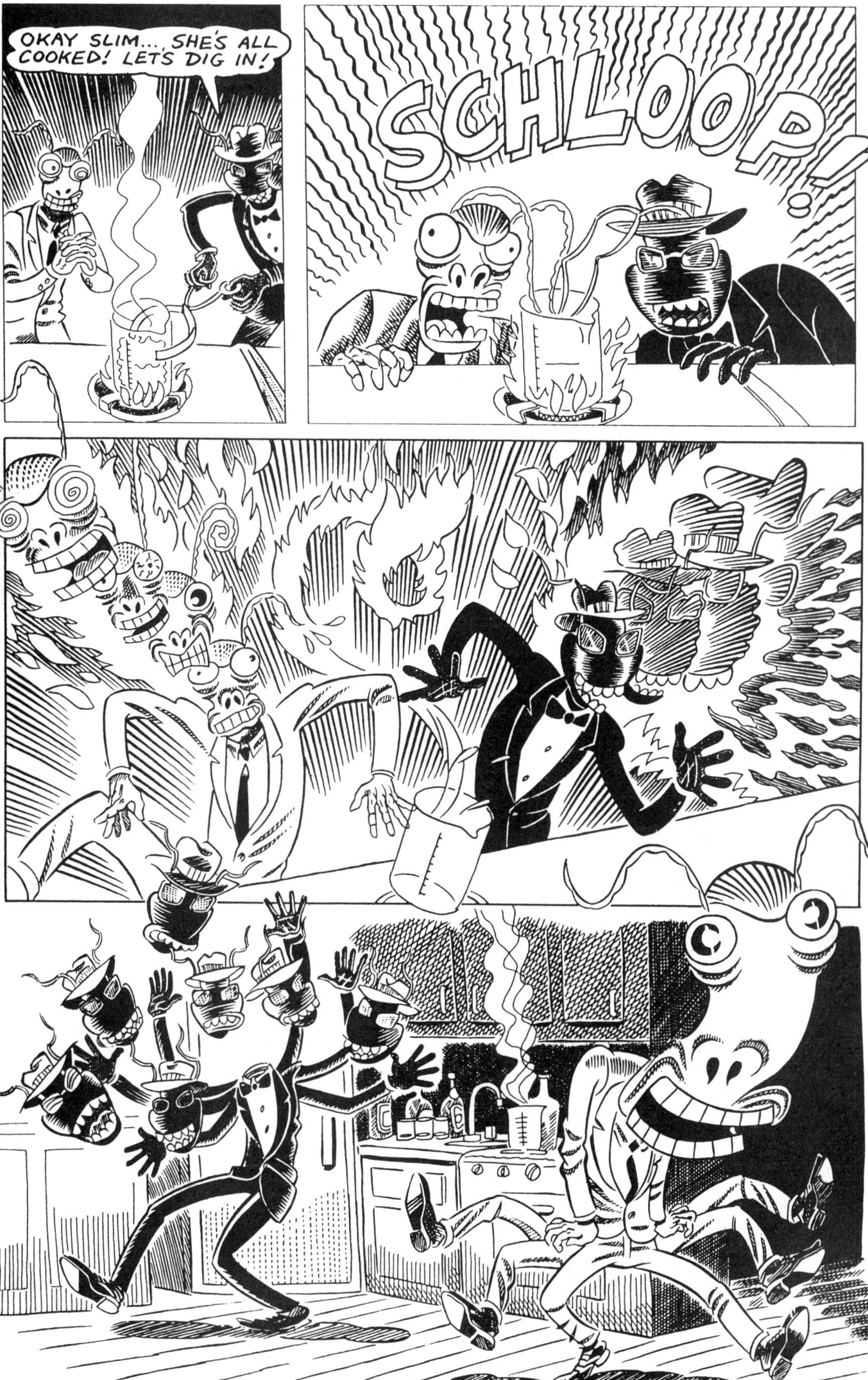
OKAY SLIM... SHE'S ALL COOKED! LET'S DIG IN!
SCHLOOP!

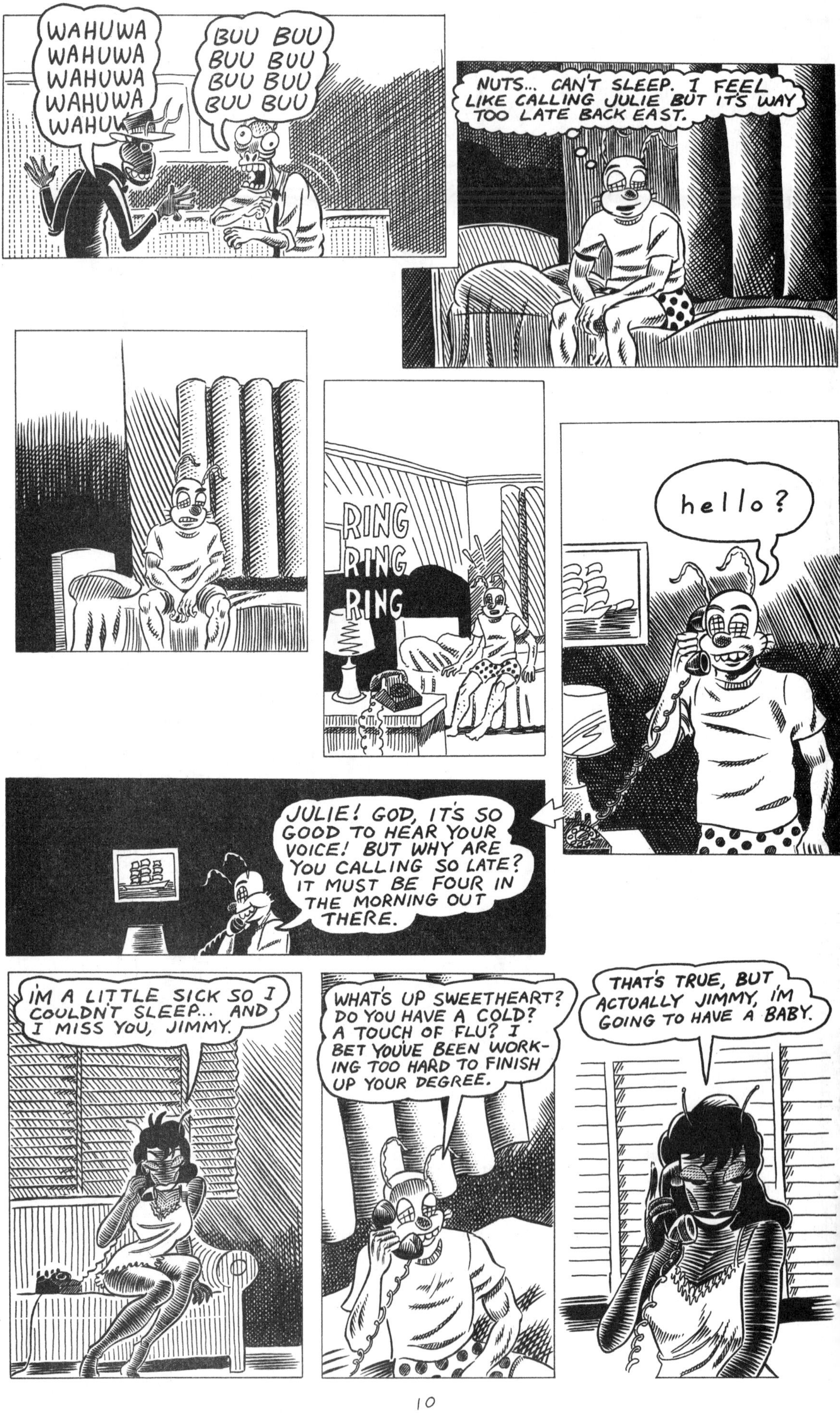
WAHUWA WAHUWA WAHUWA WAHUWA WAHUW
BUU BUU BUU BUU BUU BUU BUU BUU
NUTS... CAN'T SLEEP. I FEEL LIKE CALLING JULIE BUT ITS WAY TOO LATE BACK EAST.
RING RING RING
hello?
JULIE! GOD, IT'S SO GOOD TO HEAR YOUR VOICE! BUT WHY ARE YOU CALLING SO LATE? IT MUST BE FOUR IN THE MORNING OUT THERE.
I'M A LITTLE SICK SO I COULDN'T SLEEP... AND I MISS YOU, JIMMY.
WHAT'S UP SWEETHEART? DO YOU HAVE A COLD? A TOUCH OF FLU? I BET YOU'VE BEEN WORKING TOO HARD TO FINISH UP YOUR DEGREE.
THAT'S TRUE, BUT ACTUALLY JIMMY, I'M GOING TO HAVE A BABY.

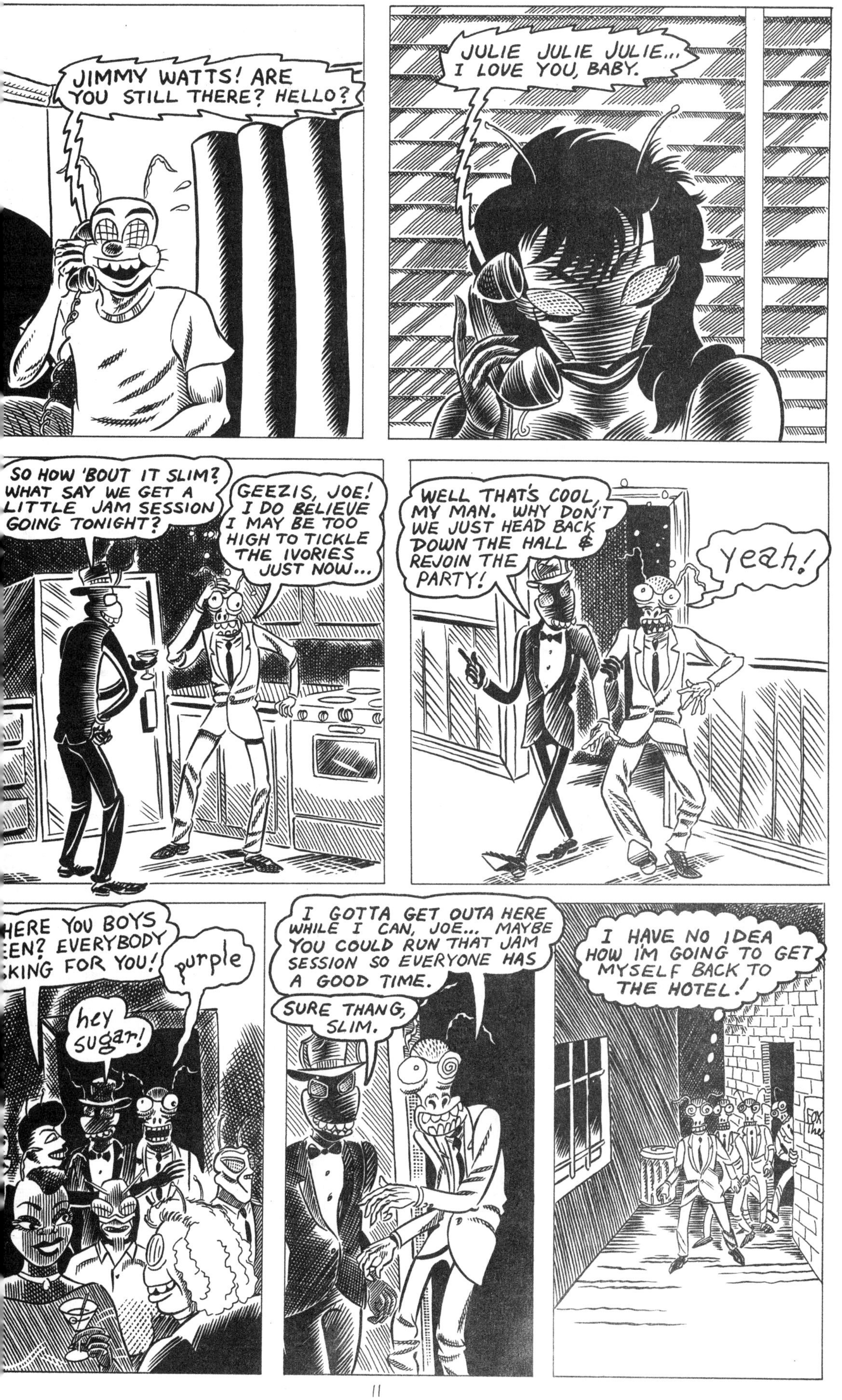

JIMMY WATTS! ARE YOU STILL THERE? HELLO?
JULIE JULIE JULIE... I LOVE YOU, BABY.
SO HOW 'BOUT IT SLIM? WHAT SAY WE GET A LITTLE JAM SESSION GOING TONIGHT?
GEEZIS, JOE! I DO BELIEVE I MAY BE TOO HIGH TO TICKLE THE IVORIES JUST NOW...
WELL THAT'S COOL, MY MAN. WHY DON'T WE JUST HEAD BACK DOWN THE HALL & REJOIN THE PARTY!
yeah!
HERE YOU BOYS
EEN? EVERYBODY
KING FOR YOU!
purple
hey sugar!
I GOTTA GET OUTA HERE WHILE I CAN, JOE... MAYBE YOU COULD RUN THAT JAM SESSION SO EVERYONE HAS A GOOD TIME.
SURE THANG, SLIM.
I HAVE NO IDEA HOW I'M GOING TO GET MYSELF BACK TO THE HOTEL!

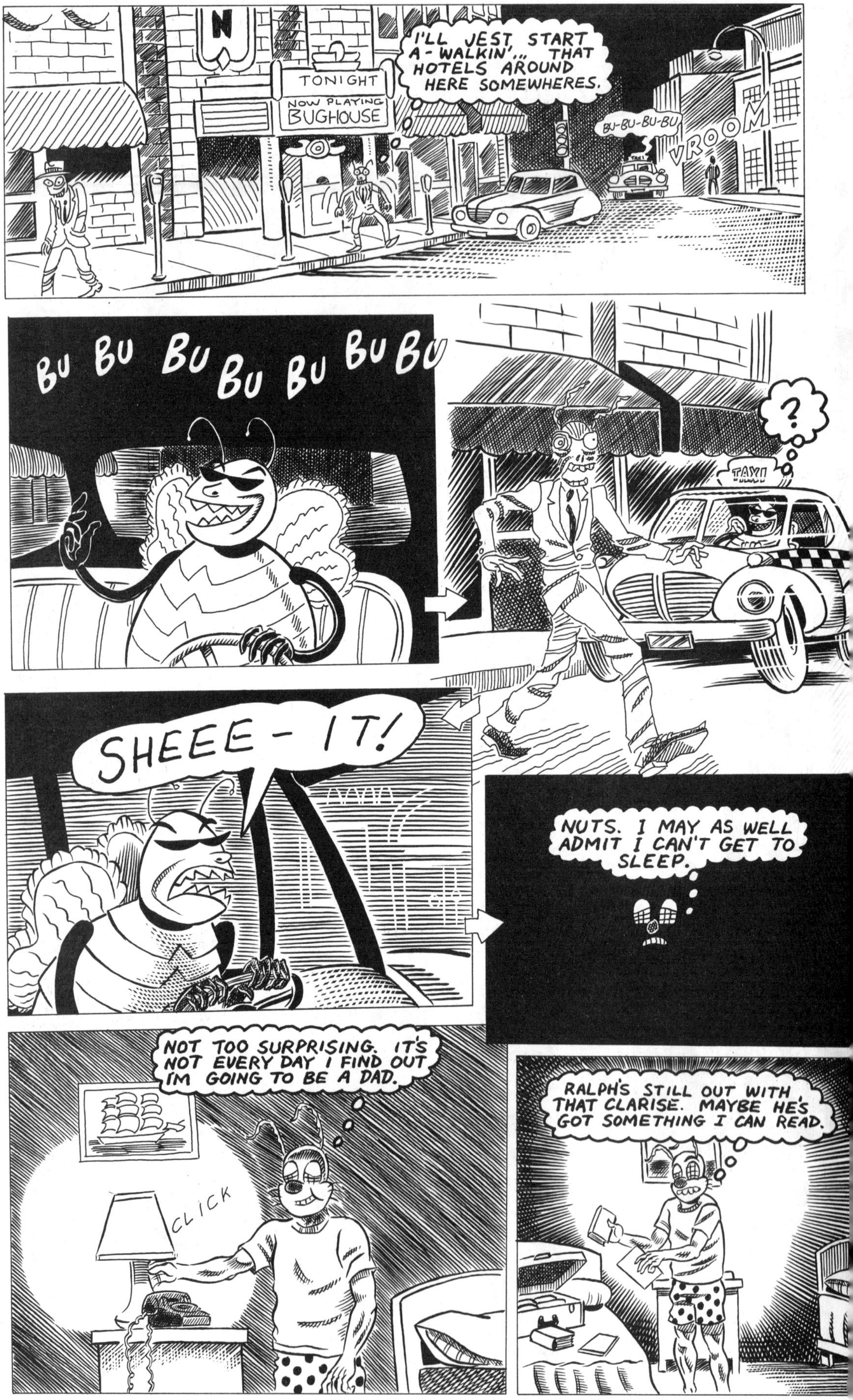

TONIGHT
NOW PLAYING BUGHOUSE
I'LL JEST START A-WALKIN'... THAT HOTELS AROUND HERE SOMEWHERES.
BU-BU-BU-BU
VROOM
TAXI
BU BU BU BU BU BU BU BU
?
TAXI
SHEEE-IT!
NUTS. I MAY AS WELL ADMIT I CAN'T GET TO SLEEP.
NOT TOO SURPRISING. IT'S NOT EVERY DAY I FIND OUT IM GOING TO BE A DAD.
CLICK
RALPH'S STILL OUT WITH THAT CLARISE. MAYBE HE'S GOT SOMETHING I CAN READ.

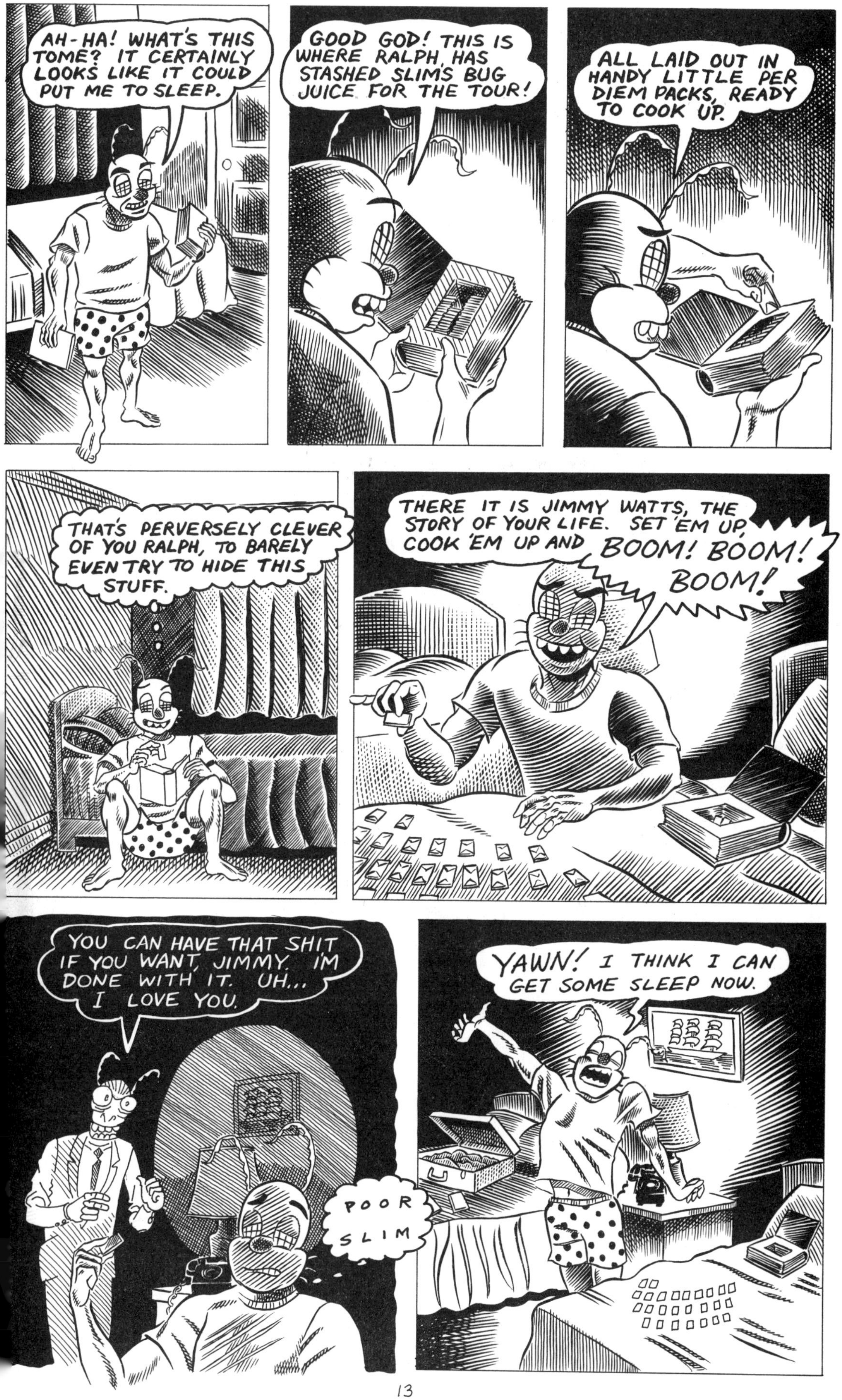
AH-HA! WHAT'S THIS TOME? IT CERTAINLY LOOKS LIKE IT COULD PUT ME TO SLEEP.
GOOD GOD! THIS IS WHERE RALPH HAS STASHED SLIM'S BUG JUICE FOR THE TOUR!
ALL LAID OUT IN HANDY LITTLE PER DIEM PACKS, READY TO COOK UP.
THAT'S PERVERSELY CLEVER OF YOU RALPH, TO BARELY EVEN TRY TO HIDE THIS STUFF.
THERE IT IS JIMMY WATTS, THE STORY OF YOUR LIFE. SET 'EM UP, COOK 'EM UP AND
BOOM! BOOM! BOOM!
YOU CAN HAVE THAT SHIT IF YOU WANT, JIMMY. I'M DONE WITH IT. UH... I LOVE YOU.
POOR SLIM
YAWN! I THINK I CAN GET SOME SLEEP NOW.

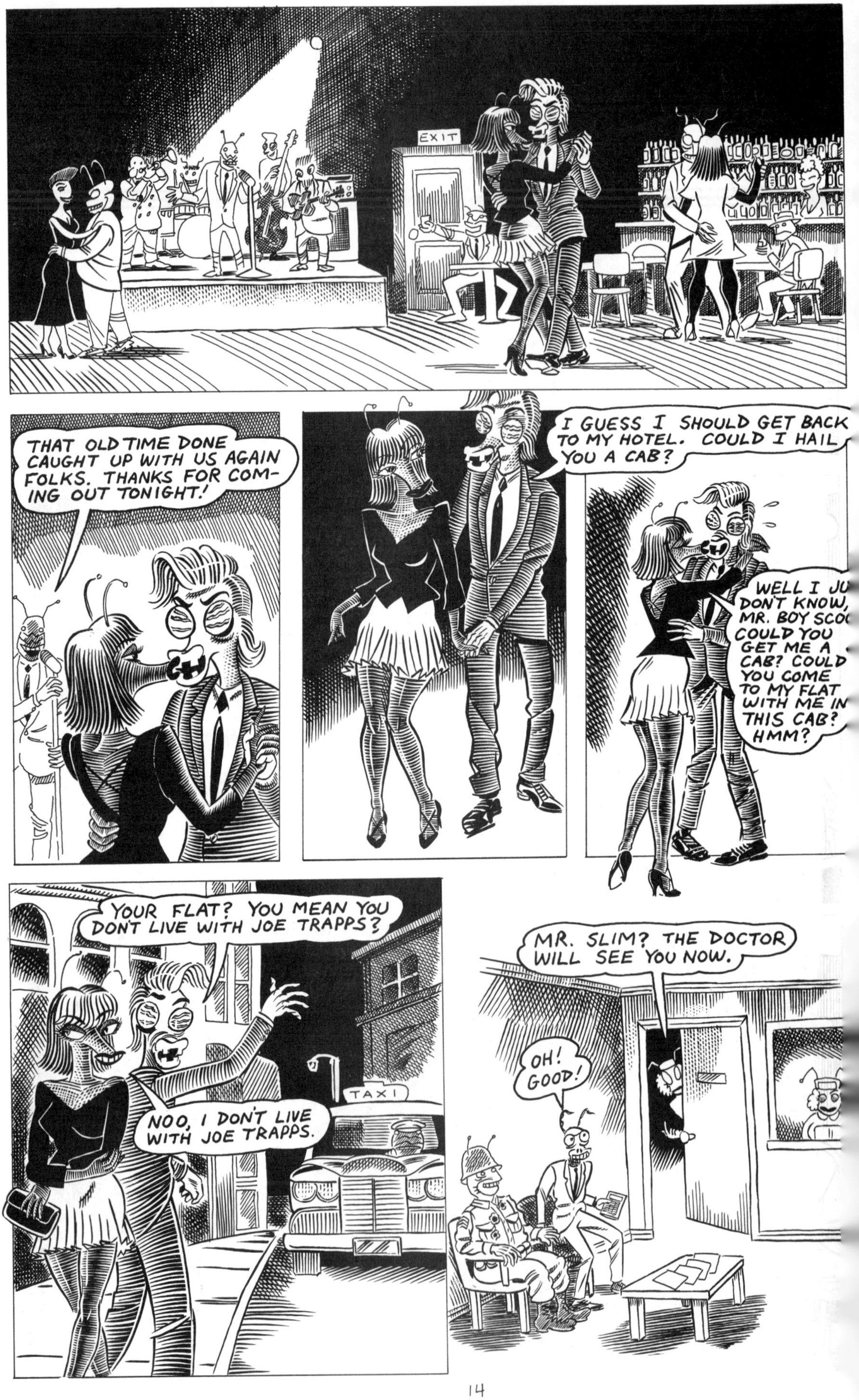
EXIT
THAT OLD TIME DONE CAUGHT UP WITH US AGAIN FOLKS. THANKS FOR COMING OUT TONIGHT!
I GUESS I SHOULD GET BACK TO MY HOTEL. COULD I HAIL YOU A CAB?
WELL I JU DON'T KNOW, MR. BOY SCO COULD YOU GET ME A CAB? COULD YOU COME TO MY FLAT WITH ME IN THIS CAB? HMM?
YOUR FLAT? YOU MEAN YOU DON'T LIVE WITH JOE TRAPPS?
TAXI
NOO, I DON'T LIVE WITH JOE TRAPPS.
MR. SLIM? THE DOCTOR WILL SEE YOU NOW.
OH! GOOD!

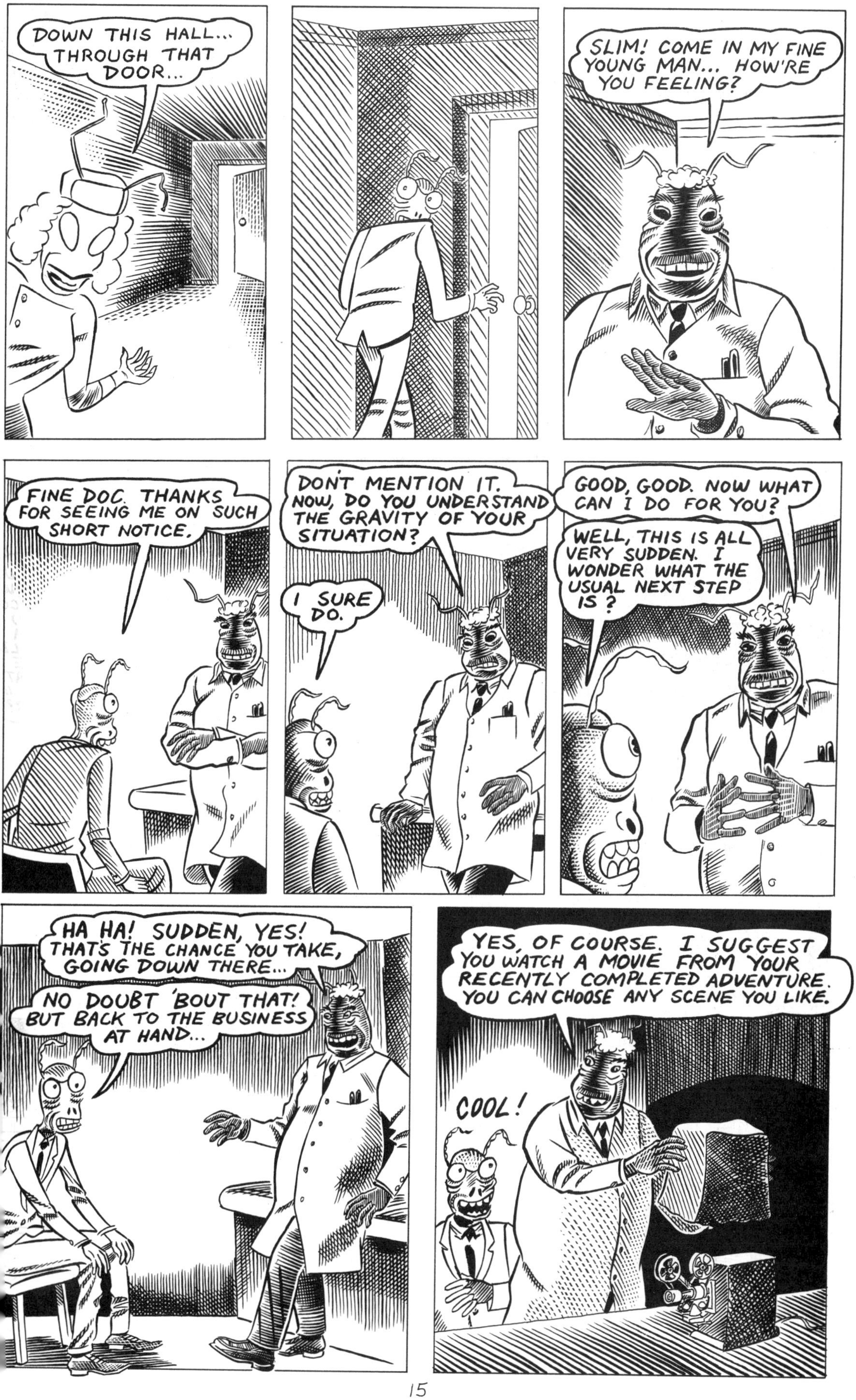
DOWN THIS HALL... THROUGH THAT DOOR...
SLIM! COME IN MY FINE YOUNG MAN... HOW'RE YOU FEELING?
FINE DOC. THANKS FOR SEEING ME ON SUCH SHORT NOTICE.
DON'T MENTION IT. NOW, DO YOU UNDERSTAND THE GRAVITY OF YOUR SITUATION?
I SURE DO.
GOOD, GOOD. NOW WHAT CAN I DO FOR YOU?
WELL, THIS IS ALL VERY SUDDEN. I WONDER WHAT THE USUAL NEXT STEP IS?
HA HA! SUDDEN, YES! THAT'S THE CHANCE YOU TAKE, GOING DOWN THERE...
NO DOUBT 'BOUT THAT! BUT BACK TO THE BUSINESS AT HAND...
YES, OF COURSE. I SUGGEST YOU WATCH A MOVIE FROM YOUR RECENTLY COMPLETED ADVENTURE. YOU CAN CHOOSE ANY SCENE YOU LIKE.
COOL!

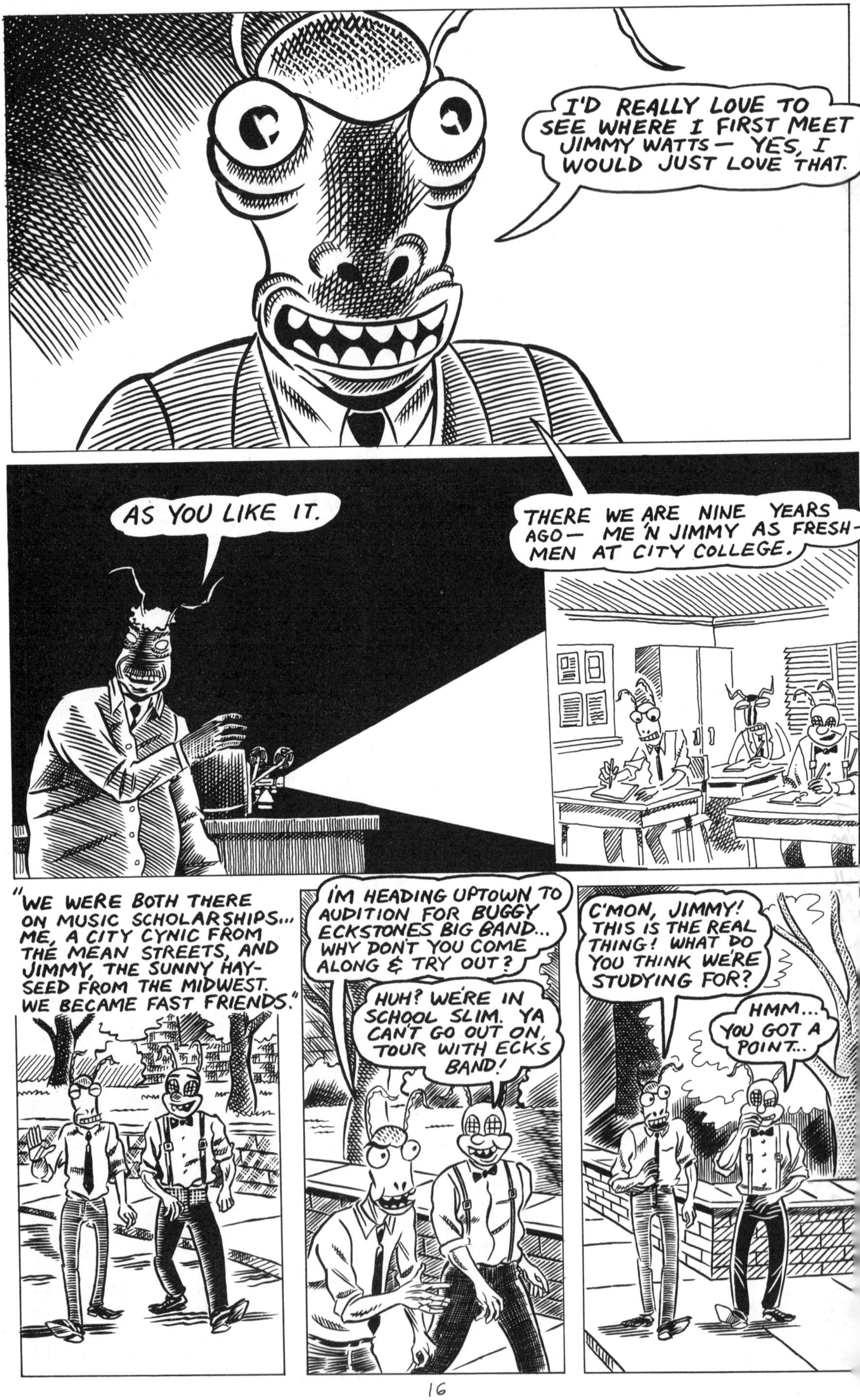

I'D REALLY LOVE TO SEE WHERE I FIRST MEET JIMMY WATTS— YES, I WOULD JUST LOVE THAT.
AS YOU LIKE IT.
THERE WE ARE NINE YEARS AGO— ME 'N JIMMY AS FRESH-MEN AT CITY COLLEGE.
"WE WERE BOTH THERE ON MUSIC SCHOLARSHIPS... ME, A CITY CYNIC FROM THE MEAN STREETS, AND JIMMY, THE SUNNY HAY-SEED FROM THE MIDWEST. WE BECAME FAST FRIENDS."
I'M HEADING UPTOWN TO AUDITION FOR BUGGY ECKSTONES BIG BAND... WHY DON'T YOU COME ALONG & TRY OUT?
HUH? WE'RE IN SCHOOL SLIM. YA CAN'T GO OUT ON, TOUR WITH ECK'S BAND!
C'MON, JIMMY! THIS IS THE REAL THING! WHAT DO YOU THINK WE'RE STUDYING FOR?
HMM... YOU GOT A POINT...